**Praise for *New York Times* bestselling author
Carla Cassidy**

"The first page of this Wild West Bodyguards
book pulls the reader in just for the opportunity
to learn more about Charlie. An interesting
mystery with surprising twists...will keep the pages
turning."
—*RT Book Reviews* on *The Rancher Bodyguard*

"Small towns, dangerous secrets and painful pasts
are expertly conveyed in Cassidy's clever hands,
speeding readers toward surprising revelations."
—*RT Book Reviews* on *Scene of the Crime: Widow Creek*

"Cassidy crafts sympathetic characters...along
with a strong, well-developed plot. A charmingly
sweet and ruggedly strong hero is the icing on the
cake..."
—*RT Book Reviews* on *Cowboy with a Cause*

"With flawed but heartwarming characters, and a
flair for storytelling, Carla Cassidy shines."
—*RT Book Reviews* on *To Wed and Protect*

CARLA CASSIDY

is a *New York Times* bestselling and award-winning author who has written more than one hundred books for Harlequin. Before settling into her true love—writing— she was a professional cheerleader, an actress and a singer/dancer in a show band.

Carla believes the only thing better than curling up with a good book to read is sitting down at the computer to write her next story. She's looking forward to writing many more books and bringing hours of pleasure to readers. Visit her website at carlacassidy.com.

Books by Carla Cassidy

Harlequin Romantic Suspense

Cowboys of Holiday Ranch Series

A Real Cowboy
Cowboy of Interest

Men of Wolf Creek Series

Cold Case, Hot Accomplice
Lethal Lawman
Lone Wolf Standing

Cowboy Café Series

Her Cowboy Distraction
The Cowboy's Claim
Cowboy with a Cause
Confessing to the Cowboy

The Coltons Series

The Colton Bride
Her Colton Lawman

Visit the Author Profile page at Harlequin.com for more titles.

Carla Cassidy

HOME ON THE RANCH: OKLAHOMA

HARLEQUIN® THE COWBOY COLLECTION

Recycling programs
for this product may
not exist in your area.

ISBN-13: 978-0-373-60133-2

Home on the Ranch: Oklahoma

Copyright © 2015 by Harlequin Books S.A.

The publisher acknowledges the copyright holder
of the individual works as follows:

Defending the Rancher's Daughter
Copyright © 2005 by Carla Bracale
The Rancher Bodyguard
Copyright © 2009 by Carla Bracale

Printed in U.S.A.

CONTENTS

DEFENDING THE
RANCHER'S DAUGHTER

Chapter 1

Kate Sampson pulled the pickup out into the center of the wide expanse of pasture. In the distance storm clouds gathered, hanging low and black and occasionally rumbling thunder.

The weather forecast was for the potential of severe storms and as she walked from the truck to check a stock water tank, the oppressive unsettled atmosphere pressed thick against her chest.

Or was it grief she felt? It had only been two weeks since her father's death. Two weeks of the worst kind of sorrow she'd ever felt and two weeks of insidious suspicions.

She shoved thoughts of her father aside, needing to get finished and to get inside the house before the storm vented its fury.

Beneath the clouds not too far away the large herd

of cattle lowed and stomped hooves with unsettled restlessness as if sensing the approaching storm.

She had three more stock tanks she hoped to check before the storm hit. It was merely a routine maintenance task she could have asked one of the ranch hands to do, but she'd wanted to do it herself.

She'd needed something to pass the long hours of the late afternoon, something to keep her mind away from the grief and the questions that ripped at her heart in those quiet moments of solitude and inactivity.

A flash of lightning ripped through the black clouds, followed by a roar of thunder. She decided checking the other stock tanks would have to wait. She didn't want to be out in an open pasture with an electrical storm overhead.

She checked the tank, saw the windmill spinning and that the water level was where it was supposed to be, then turned to head back to where she'd parked her pickup a distance away.

At that moment a loud noise seemed to come from the back side of the pasture near the cattle. Kate froze, trying to identify the odd, sharp noise. Not thunder, then what?

Within seconds the ground began to tremble beneath her feet and a dust cloud formed over the bawling cattle.

As she stared in horror, she saw the herd break into a run, frightened cows bumping shoulders, slamming hooves against the ground in a stampede of beasts. And they were running directly at her.

She shot a frantic glance at her pickup, which suddenly seemed too far away. Still, she took off running toward it, knowing it was the only thing that would keep her from being crushed beneath the onslaught of frightened animals.

The ground seemed to have stolen the thunder from the sky as Kate ran. Her heart crashed into her ribs as the herd came closer…closer.

She was just about to the truck when the first animal careened into her with a force that sent her airborne. She crashed down on one foot then crumbled as her ankle screamed in pain.

Panic clawed up her throat as she saw the rest of the livestock bearing down on her, close enough that she could see the frantic roll of their eyes.

She tried to scramble to her feet, but her ankle couldn't hold her and she fell to the ground once again. Dust choked her and she smelled the sweat of the cattle, heard the snorts of distress as they approached like a locomotion at full steam.

Trampled. Within seconds she was going to be trampled to death. Frantically she looked at the truck and realized her only hope.

As fast as she could, she rolled across the ground. She'd just slid beneath the truck as the first of the herd thundered by.

The hooves against the dry earth kicked up a dust storm and Kate squeezed her eyes tightly closed as she heard bodies crash into the sides of the vehicle, heard the bawling of calves being trampled.

As the last of the livestock went by, she could hear the sounds of fence breaking and the frantic cries of cowboys trying to corral the crazed herd.

She remained beneath the truck, coughing dust and trying to ignore the painful throb of her ankle as the sounds faded in the distance. Her heart pounded almost painfully as she realized how close she had come to a terrible death.

Hooves approached and as the horse was reined in next to the truck, a pair of faded boots hit the ground. She recognized the snakeskin as belonging to Sonny Williams, the ranch manager.

He leaned down and peered beneath the truck. "Ms. Sampson, are you all right?" his deep, familiar voice asked urgently.

She took a deep breath and released it slowly, the panicked fear ebbing away. "Yes, I'm okay." She scooted out from beneath the truck and pulled herself up to a sitting position.

The wooden fencing at the far end of the property was gone, as was most of the herd. A calf lay dead and nearby another calf limped slowly, bawling like a frightened baby.

Kate wanted to bawl, as well. If she'd been alone, she'd curl up and cry, but instead she swallowed against her tears, unwilling to show any sign of weakness in front of Sonny.

She'd had enough problems with the ranch hands since her father's death. The last thing she wanted them to see was any sign of weakness on her part.

"I got the men out rounding up the herd and once we get them all back, we'll get the fence mended," he said, then held out a hand to help her up.

She reached out to grab the middle-aged man's hand and pull herself up, but instantly nearly crumbled as she tried to put weight on her left foot.

"You need to go have that looked at," Sonny said, his gaze on the ankle that had already swollen up to twice its normal size. "I'll drive you in to the hospital."

"No, it's okay. I can drive myself," she replied, leaning heavily against the driver's door. At least it was her left foot and the truck was an automatic. "I need you here to take care of this mess." Her sentence was punctuated by a loud clap of thunder.

He looked toward the fence and shook his head. "Guess it was the storm that spooked them?"

"Who knows?"

"Are you sure you're okay to drive yourself to the emergency room?" His weathered features worked into a deep frown.

"I'll be fine. Just take care of things here. When I get home you can give me a full damage report." She slid into the truck.

"I'll open the gate for you," he said.

She nodded and started the engine as Sonny remounted his horse. She followed him to the gate and, when he opened it, she drove through.

The pain in her ankle worried her. She couldn't afford to be down, didn't have time for a broken bone. Not only did she have questions about her father's riding accident two weeks ago, and suddenly finding herself running the ranch, but now she had some disturbing questions about what had just happened to her.

For the past two weeks she'd entertained dark thoughts, suspicions that had kept sleep at bay and a gun next to her bed.

She'd told herself she was overreacting, that grief did terrible things to people and she was just desperately trying to make sense of her father's untimely death.

She'd tried to convince herself that the overwhelming job of suddenly running the ranch was skewing her thinking. But such rational thoughts did nothing to dispel the darkness that had claimed her soul.

Maybe it was time to speak her suspicions out loud to somebody. But who? Sheriff Jim Ramsey was good at arresting drunk and disorderly cowboys on a Saturday night, but she wasn't sure she trusted his investigative skills in working a murder case.

Besides, she'd tried to talk to him soon after her dad's death and he'd dismissed her concerns with a pat on her head and a sympathetic sigh.

Funny, when she thought about who she trusted most to talk to, it was also the man she detested more than anyone else in the world.

Zack West.

Her fingers tightened on the steering wheel as she thought of the cowboy who had been the source of her first passionate fantasies and for years the bane of her very existence.

Zack worked for his family business, Wild West Protective Services. Zack's father had begun the business years ago and it now was a multimillion dollar enterprise offering bodyguard services to people all around the world. Zack, along with his four brothers and sister, worked the business.

It had been years since she'd seen him; he spent most of his time away from Cotter Creek and on location. She'd heard through the grapevine that he was back in town. As soon as she got to the hospital, she'd give him a call. As much as she hated it, she needed him.

The throb of her ankle brought back the memory of the strange sound she'd heard just before the cattle had stampeded.

The loud noise had had nothing to do with natural

phenomena. Now that she had a moment to consider it, she thought the sound had been like that of a bull horn.

Yes, it was time to talk to Zack.

She needed to tell him that she suspected her father's deadly fall from a horse hadn't been an accident. She believed somebody had murdered Gray Sampson.

She also needed to tell him that somebody had started a stampede that could have killed her. She gripped the steering wheel with suddenly sweaty hands as she thought of that mass of frightened cattle racing toward her.

If she hadn't been so quick on her feet, if she'd paused another single second before racing for the truck, she wouldn't be driving herself to the hospital right now. She'd be dead.

It was at that very moment that she realized somebody had just tried to kill her.

Zack West heard her before he saw her.

"If it's not broken then tell Dr. Greenspan to get in here and wrap it so I can get out of here." Her familiar voice, filled with agitation, drifted out the open door of Exam Room Four. "I've got lost cattle wandering around the countryside and broken fencing. I don't have time to waste hours in here."

Zack hesitated just outside the door, summoning the strength to face the spoiled, willful girl who had never hidden her dislike of him.

Why had she called him? The only way he'd know what she wanted was to go into the exam room and to speak to her. He met a nurse hurrying out, a harried expression on her face.

He entered the room and hoped his face didn't radiate his shock at the sight of her. When he'd gotten the call from her stating that she was in the emergency room and needed to talk to him, it had been sheer curiosity that had prompted him to respond. He'd been curious to see her and interested to find out why she was at the hospital.

She was staring out the window, unaware of his presence. He took that moment to reconcile the woman he saw to the wild teenager of nearly five years before.

The last time he'd seen her she'd been a gangly seventeen-year-old with a bad haircut and mascara-smeared eyes.

There was nothing gangly about the woman in front of him. Her feminine curves were evident despite the blue flowered hospital gown she wore. The hair he remembered as an uneven burnt-copper mess now hung below her shoulders.

One of his hands unconsciously rose to his cheek, where the last time they'd been together she'd ripped sharp fingernails down his skin at the same time she'd kicked him in the shin so hard he'd thought he'd be crippled for the rest of his life.

"Katie."

Her head whirled around and he saw that her eyes were still the same intense blue that he remembered, minus the raccoon rings of mascara.

There was a long moment of awkward silence and he wondered if she, too, was remembering the debacle of their last meeting.

Her gaze swept him from head to toe, reminding him that he hadn't shaved this morning and was about a month overdue for a haircut. The fact that he even thought about his own physical appearance irritated him.

"I'm here, so what do you want?" he asked brusquely.

"Zack. Please close the door." Her voice gave nothing away of her emotions.

He shut the door, then turned back to face her, a heavy tension in the air between them.

"Please, have a seat." She gestured to the chair next to the examining table where she sat.

"I'm fine." He jammed his hands into his pockets. He didn't want to sit. He didn't intend to stay. "What happened?" He pointed to her ankle, which was swollen and turning ten shades of purple.

"Somebody tried to kill me."

He raised a dark eyebrow. It was the kind of dramatic statement she'd often made as a girl. "How? By squeezing your ankle to death?"

The baleful look she leveled at him would have sent lesser men running for the hills. Zack merely stood his ground, waiting for her to explain.

She broke the gaze first, looking down at her hands clenched tightly in her lap. "I was out in the pasture checking a stock tank and somebody caused my herd to stampede. If I hadn't managed to roll underneath my truck, I would have been killed."

Despite the fact that he didn't want anything to do with her, she'd certainly grabbed his attention. He swept his cowboy hat from his head and sat in the chair. "What do you mean, somebody caused your herd to stampede?"

As he listened to her explain what had happened, he tried to figure out why she had called him. She'd certainly made it clear years ago that she didn't like him, had resented his relationship with her father.

She'd been a brat, trying to undermine him, competing with him for her father's attention and generally making his life miserable when they'd been younger. So why on earth had she called him?

"Are you sure it wasn't the storm that spooked the cattle?" he asked. "There was a lot of thunder and lightning, enough to spook a herd."

"The storm had them restless, I'll admit to that." She shoved a strand of her long, shiny hair behind her ear. "But I heard something like an air horn blow and that's what spooked them into the stampede. Somebody did this on purpose and the only reason for them to have done this was in hopes that I'd be trampled to death."

At that moment the door opened and the doctor entered. "X-rays are back. No break, just sprained. We'll get that ankle wrapped up and get you out of here."

Zack headed for the door, but paused as she called his name. "Would you wait for me? I still need to talk to you."

He hesitated.

"Zack…please."

It was the first time he'd ever heard that word from her lips and it seemed to be pulled from someplace deep inside her. "I'll be in the waiting room," he said grudgingly, and left the exam room.

For the past month Zack had felt as if the world had gone mad. A woman he'd come to respect and love had been murdered, his eldest brother, Tanner, had gotten married, Gray Sampson had died and now Katie had said please.

He threw himself into one of the cheap orange plastic chairs in the waiting room, unsurprised to find himself alone. The Cotter Creek Memorial Hospital was small and most folk knew that if an injury was serious, the best place to go was to one of the bigger hospitals in Oklahoma City, a two-hour drive away.

He twisted the rim of his hat between his fingers, his thoughts on the woman he'd just left. Katie Sampson, all grown up. She had turned twenty-three years old a month ago and was as pretty as any woman he'd ever seen—not that he cared.

He was just surprised that the wild-haired, skinned-knee brat had become a lovely young woman. Lovely to look at, he reminded himself, but still Katie Sampson.

As he waited, he thought about what little information Katie had given him. He dismissed the idea that somebody had intentionally spooked the herd in an effort to kill her. She'd always been given to melodrama and although unusual, it wouldn't be out of the realm of reality for a storm to cause a herd to stampede.

A loud boom of thunder crashed overhead, but still no rain peppered the glass. Looking toward the windows, he wondered why he'd agreed to wait around, what else she could possibly want to tell him.

She entered the waiting room on crutches, her ankle cloaked in a bright purple wrap. Once again he was struck by the physical changes that had occurred since last time he'd seen her.

Her scrawny neck was now a graceful, slender column. Her grass-stained jeans clung to curvy hips and long, lean legs. That palpable tension again filled the air and he watched as she walked over to the window and stared out.

For a long moment she said nothing and he merely watched her, waiting for her to explain what she wanted, why she needed to talk to him.

"You didn't even come to his funeral." Her voice

was low, but vibrated with a rich bitterness. She turned to face him, her pretty features twisted into an angry mask. "He loved you like a son, but you couldn't even show up to pay your last respects."

Grief ripped through him as he thought of her father. Gray Sampson had been far more than a neighbor to Zack. The older man had been like a second father to him. During Zack's turbulent teenage years, Gray had been the voice of wisdom and unconditional love.

But he wasn't about to explain himself to her. "You call me down here to talk about what I should or shouldn't have done in the last two weeks or is there something else on your mind?"

Some of the anger left her face and for just a moment a raw vulnerability shone from her eyes and her shoulders sagged as if she carried the weight of the world on them. Zack preferred her anger, it was familiar.

"I want to hire you. Whether you believe it or not, somebody tried to get me killed this afternoon."

He frowned. "Haven't you heard? I'm not working for the family business anymore. I'm not for hire. Call Dalton, he's in charge of the business while Tanner is on his honeymoon. He'll assign somebody to you if that's what you want."

Zack's father had semiretired a year before and Zack's eldest brother, Tanner, had taken over the reins of running the company. However, Tanner had gotten married a week before and was now on his honeymoon, leaving Dalton, Zack's second eldest brother in charge of the business.

Zack had worked as a bodyguard for the past ten years, since his twenty-first birthday, but a month ago he'd quit the family business when his last assignment had gone bad.

"I don't want anyone else. I want you." Whatever touch of vulnerability he'd thought he'd seen earlier in her was gone. Her eyes were steely, reminding him of when she'd been a young girl and had wanted her own way.

"I just told you, I'm not for hire anymore."

To his surprise, she leaned toward him and placed a hand on his arm. "You're the only person I really trust in this town and it's not just about what happened to me this afternoon."

Her blue eyes suddenly radiated an emotion he'd never seen in them before. Fear. Her fingers tightened on his arm. "Zack, I think somebody murdered my father."

Chapter 2

She'd forgotten the raw masculinity that radiated from him. It was there in the simmering depths of his moss-green eyes, in the shadow of whiskers that darkened his jaw and the broad shoulders that strained at the confines of his navy T-shirt.

She dropped her hand from his arm, all too aware of the heat of his skin and her nearness to him. His scent surrounded her, the smell of the wind and the approaching storm and the underlying hint of maleness that might have stirred her if she'd allow it.

Taking a deep breath, she took a step backward as he stared at her in disbelief.

"What are you talking about?" His deep voice radiated skepticism. "From what I heard, Gray fell off his horse and hit his head. A senseless tragedy but hardly murder."

"Dad was a championship bronco rider. There wasn't a horse alive that could throw him. And he wasn't riding some spirited mount that morning, he was riding Diamond, the same horse he'd been riding for the past seven years."

The words bubbled from her like smoke from a boiling cauldron. All the fears she'd fought for the past two weeks suddenly seemed too close to the surface.

She needed somebody to listen to her. She needed somebody to really hear her. Another rumble of thunder boomed overhead.

"Katie, accidents happen, even to the most skilled riders. You should know that. All it takes is a moment of inattention, a snake on the path, anything can make a horse rear and throw a rider." He raked a hand through his shaggy dark hair and she knew she was losing him.

"But we aren't talking about some greenhorn, Zack. We're talking about my father." She turned around to stare out the window at the dark, angry clouds, despair eating at her.

"Something bad is happening at my ranch, Zack," she continued. "And it started before my father's death."

"What do you mean?"

She turned back to face him and again felt the jolt of his physical presence. Damn, she'd hoped that four years of college and an additional year of wisdom and growth and life experiences would somehow kill the intense physical attraction she'd always felt for him.

If she lived to be a hundred, she'd never understand the contradiction of disliking him and being physically attracted to him. Even when she'd been young, the eight-years-older Zack West had excited her in ways she hadn't understood.

When she'd heard he was back in town a month before, she'd steeled herself for a visit, but he hadn't come around. She'd been relieved and yet oddly disappointed by his absence.

Then, at her father's funeral, she'd looked for him, appalled by the fact that he hadn't been there. But she tamped down the simmering resentment about that and instead focused on what she needed to tell him.

"A month ago Dad was going up to the hayloft in the barn and he fell through one of the rungs of the ladder. If he hadn't managed to grab on to the step above, he would have fallen to the floor. We discovered that it looked like the rung had been partially sawed through."

Zack frowned, the gesture pulling together his thick dark eyebrows. "Have you talked to Jim Ramsey about these things?"

Kate sighed as she thought of the sheriff of Cotter Creek. "I spoke to him a week after dad's death. He seemed to think I was making mountains out of molehills, that I needed to go home and grieve and stop looking for boogey men at the ranch."

At the look on Zack's face, she wanted to cry. She saw his disbelief and knew that he was probably thinking the same thing as Sheriff Ramsey had, that her grief was making her somehow delusional.

"Look, Katie..."

"It's Kate," she corrected, and saw his jaw clench. "I outgrew Katie when I stopped wearing pigtails."

"Kate, just answer me one question." He gazed at her intently. "Why on earth would anyone want to kill your father? Everyone liked Gray. He didn't have any enemies in the world."

"If I knew why somebody wanted him dead, then

maybe I'd know who is doing these things." She moved over to one of the orange chairs and lowered herself into it. She noticed he hadn't asked why anyone would want to kill her.

He probably thought she deserved whatever came her way. Certainly he'd never hidden his dislike for her. "Look, I know we haven't exactly had a stellar relationship in the past, but I need you to come work at the ranch and to find out what's going on. Don't do this for me. Do it for Dad. He loved you like a son."

Funny, after all this time the thought of Gray's love and adoration for Zack still had the capacity to wrankle her heart just a little bit. But she didn't have time to examine old baggage and resentments. As much as she hated it, she needed Zack.

"Katie—Kate," he corrected himself. "I already explained to you, I don't work for Wild West Protective Services anymore. I quit a month ago." He set his hat back on his head and she couldn't believe he was going to walk out on her.

She struggled to her feet, cursing the ankle that forced her move across the floor on crutches as he started for the door. "I guess my father was one poor judge of character," she said to Zack's back.

He slowly turned to face her, his eyes flat and emotionless. "And just what is that supposed to mean?"

As the events of the afternoon replayed in her mind, it wasn't just anger that built inside her, but also fear. "Dad believed you hung the moon and stars. He thought you were a man of honor and he'd turn over in his grave if he knew you were turning your back on him."

He stood frozen, his features utterly devoid of emotion. In the long pause of silence, her anger outweighed her fear. "Get out," she exclaimed, overwhelmed by so many emotions she thought she might explode. "I must have been out of my mind to call you in the first place. Just get out, get out of my sight."

He didn't wait for her to tell him again. He turned on his heels and left the waiting room. Kate walked back to the window and looked out with regret.

If only she could call back the last three minutes of their conversation. Whenever she was stressed or feeling powerless, she had a tendency to respond with anger. It was a curse and a habit she'd worked hard to change, but ten minutes with Zack and she'd reverted to old form.

She watched until he pulled out of the lot and out of her sight. It was only then that an unexpected sob rose up in her throat. She swallowed hard against it.

Other than tears spent upon her father's death, it had been years since she'd cried. In fact, the last time she remembered crying had also been the last time she'd seen Zack. Of course, she'd been a headstrong almost-eighteen-year-old at the time and he'd been the very bane of her existence.

She had promised herself a long time ago that she would never again cry over Zack West. She angrily wiped at her eyes as she limped out of the hospital and toward her truck.

The storm was passing, without a drop of rain having fallen. Early June and already they were suffering a drought. But the weather conditions were the last thing on her mind as she left the hospital behind and headed back toward the ranch.

Instead she focused on the stampede, worrying about the damage that had been wrought by the out-of-control herd. New fencing cost money, dead cattle were a loss and, for a moment, she felt overwhelmed by the choice she'd made to take over the reins of the ranch after her father's death.

They were supposed to have been partners, she and her father. After college, when she'd decided to return to the ranch, she'd hoped that the two of them would work side by side on the land they both loved. She'd hoped to have the time to make her father proud of her. But time had been stolen from them.

He'd been murdered.

Nothing and nobody would ever be able to convince her otherwise. And nothing and nobody would be able to make her believe that the stampede that had nearly taken her life hours before had been an accident.

Something bad was happening at her ranch and the one man she'd believed might be able to help her had walked away, leaving her alone to face whatever evil had come to stay at Bent Tree Ranch.

It was just after seven the next morning when Zack drove toward the Sampson place. Nightmares had driven him out of bed at a few minutes before five and for the last two hours he'd been sitting at his kitchen table, drinking coffee and thinking about Gray and his daughter.

The nightmares had been a part of his life for the past month, but the thoughts of Gray and Katie were new and confusing. He didn't believe that Gray had been murdered, nor did he believe that somebody had tried to kill Katie by stampeding her herd the day before.

As a girl, Katie'd had a penchant for finding drama and creating trouble. Zack certainly knew what grief could do to somebody, how it could work in the brain and create all kinds of crazy scenarios. He'd learned that the hard way over the past month.

But the fear he'd seen in Katie's eyes had been very real and his love and respect for Gray weighed heavy in his heart.

Gray had been his sanity through the insanity of adolescence. Gray had been his family when he'd felt isolated, invisible in his own. As one of six kids, Zack had gotten lost amid his siblings and if not for Gray's love and counsel, Zack had no idea how he might have survived those years of seeming isolation.

He'd decided to give Katie a couple of days, to sniff around the ranch to see if anything nefarious was going on. He wasn't doing it for her. He'd do it in the memory of the man he'd loved like a father.

Dammit. He'd do it even though he didn't want to be anywhere around her, have anything to do with her. Besides, in the past month he'd grown tired of his own company, tired of not knowing what direction his life would take.

He turned into the entrance of the Sampson place and saw the tree that had given the ranch its name. Bent Tree Ranch. The tree was an old oak bent at the waist like an old woman with a short cane. Many times as a teenager he'd arrive at the ranch to see Katie sitting in the limbs, a mutinous glare on her face.

This morning there was no sign of Katie in the tree, but Zack did see the signs of trouble in the overgrown lawn and the fact that he didn't see a single ranch hand working anywhere on the property.

He pulled up in front of the house and before he

could cut the engine, the door opened and she stepped out into the early-morning sunshine.

Her hair caught the fire of the sun and glistened as her pretty features radiated surprise at his appearance. Clad in a pair of worn, tight jeans and a light blue T-shirt that only enhanced her attractiveness, she stood motionless.

Zack shut off his truck, already regretting the impulse that had brought him here.

"What do you want?" No hint of friendliness or relief in those blue eyes of hers. There was also no sign of the crutches.

"I didn't think this was about what I wanted, but rather what you wanted," he replied. "You said you needed my help. I'm here."

She hesitated, and for a moment he wondered if she would send him away again. Fine by him. He was here under duress, haunted by the memories of her father, tormented by the trauma he'd suffered on his last assignment.

"Come in," she finally said, and opened the screen door to allow him entry. He nodded and walked past the two redwood rockers on the front porch, trying not to remember the hundreds of nights he and Gray had sat on the porch and solved world problems.

Although it had been almost a year since Zack had been inside the house, he felt embraced by the familiarity as he walked through the door and into the living room.

Gray's wife had died when Katie had been a year old and the absence of a feminine touch had always been present in the house. The furniture was sturdy, in neutral earth colors.

The focal point of the room was a large television. On either side of the television were shelves that held trophies and ribbons, ornate buckles and photos of Gray's years as a professional bronc rider.

The room smelled of furniture polish and an underlying remnant of cherry pipe tobacco. The familiar scent shot a wave of sorrow through him. He should have visited Gray when he'd arrived home from his last assignment.

He should have taken the time to come talk to the old man. But he'd been so wrapped up in rage, in despair, he hadn't wanted to visit anyone, and now Gray was gone.

"Come on into the kitchen," she said.

He swept his hat from his head and followed behind her, trying not to notice the slight sway of her hips in her tight jeans. Maybe the sway was because she was limping slightly.

He touched his cheek, in the place where a faint scar had remained, to remind himself of their history. Kate. Not Katie, he reminded himself.

Papers strewed the round oak kitchen table and she quickly gathered them up as she gestured him into one of the chairs. "I was just going over some figures, trying to see what the stampede is going to cost me."

"Damage bad?" he asked, and eased into the chair.

"Bad enough." She walked over to the counter where a coffeepot was half full. "Want a cup?"

"All right," he agreed. This all felt far too civil and every muscle in his body tensed as if in anticipation of some kind of explosion.

She set a cup of coffee in front of him, then carried her own to the chair next to his and sat. "I lost three cows, six calves and half a fence line."

"I also heard you've lost a number of your ranch hands in the last couple of weeks."

She raised an eyebrow. "Where did you hear that?"

"Smokey mentioned it to me." Smokey Johnson wasn't just the cook and housekeeper for the West clan. When Zack's mother had been murdered years ago, Smokey had been working as the ranch manager. He'd moved into the house to help Zack's father with the six motherless children, all under the age of ten.

She shook her head. A faint smile curved her lips, there only a moment, then gone. "That man seems to know everything about everyone in this town. And yes, about half the men walked off in the week following my dad's death. I'm not sure whether it was because they didn't want to work for a woman or they assumed I'd be selling the ranch. They ran like cockroaches in the light of day. But I've got some good men left." A frown lowered her perfectly arched eyebrows. "At least, I think they're good men."

"Are you thinking about selling out?"

"Not a chance." Her eyes flashed with a touch of anger. "That vulture, Sheila Wadsworth, came to see me the day after my dad's funeral to see if I was interested in selling. I told her to get off my property and stay off."

"Sheila's just doing her job." Sheila Wadsworth owned one of the two real-estate agencies in the town.

"She acts like the Donald Trump of Cotter Creek, wheeling and dealing, and she has the sensitivity of a brick." She bit her lower lip, a lip he didn't remember being so full.

"What happened to your crutches? Aren't you supposed to be using them?" He needed to focus on something other than the shape and fullness of her lips.

"Those things are aggravating. I can't move fast enough with them. Besides, I can bear weight on the ankle this morning."

"When you called me yesterday, what did you want me to do? What did you have in mind?" He took a sip of the coffee and found it bitter. It seemed somehow appropriate, a reflection of their past relationship.

"I want you to investigate my father's death. I'd like for you to stay here at the ranch, in the bunkhouse, to see if you can find out who might have been responsible for his death and also who spooked my herd yesterday."

Zack believed it was a goose chase and apparently his feelings showed on his face. She sighed impatiently. "If you don't believe what I've told you, then why are you here?"

Why was he here? What had prompted him to leave the self-imposed isolation he'd been in for the past month? To momentarily surface from the darkness that had threatened to destroy him?

"I'm here because I loved your father." It was the simplest of explanations. He wouldn't tell her that the fear he'd seen in her eyes had haunted him, that despite the fact that he thought her spoiled and pushy and obnoxious, he'd seen her fear and couldn't help but respond.

His answer seemed to satisfy her, for she nodded and stood. "Then the first thing we should do is get you settled into the bunkhouse."

"No, the first thing I'd like to do is see where Gray fell off his horse." He knew Katie well enough to know that if this was going to work at all he had to establish control from the very beginning.

Her eyes narrowed, as if she was aware that a power

struggle had begun. In those calculating blue depths he saw the moment she decided to acquiesce. She averted her gaze from him. "Fine. We'll need to saddle up some horses. He was on a trail about a mile from here."

They had just stepped off the porch when a handsome blond male approached them. At the sight of her, he swept his dusty brown Stetson off his head and smiled. "Kate, you doing okay this morning? Are you supposed to be off your crutches so soon?"

"I'm fine, Jake." She flashed the cowboy a warm smile that Zack felt down to his toes.

"I'm heading into town to order the lumber for the fence. Do you need anything?"

Zack took a step toward the man and held out his hand. "Zack West," he said.

"Jake Merridan." He shook Zack's hand. "Nice to meet you."

"Zack is coming to work for me," Katie said. "We were just going to saddle up and take a little tour of the place."

"Nice to have you aboard," Jake replied.

"Jake is fast becoming one of my most valuable ranch hands," Katie said, once again offering the blond a full smile. "He's been with us for the last couple of months but has already made himself invaluable."

Zack saw the look in Jake's eyes as he gazed at Katie, a look that told Zack the man would be happy being something much more than a valuable ranch hand. More power to him, Zack thought.

Within minutes Jake was on his way and Zack and Katie were in the stables saddling up a couple of mounts. "Where did you find Mr. Wonderful?" he asked as he tightened a saddle strap.

"Who? Oh, you mean Jake? He came to work for Dad when the Wainfield ranch sold." Despite the obvious tenderness of her ankle, she swung up into the saddle with the grace he remembered from her as a young girl.

Kate had always been a horsewoman. Like her father, she loved the big creatures and could have been a successful barrel racer, but she'd lacked the discipline and had been too wild, too reckless.

He mounted, as well, and they left the stables heading west across the hard, dusty earth. The horses walked side by side and Zack found his attention drawn to her over and over again.

If he didn't know her at all, if he hadn't just gone through a terrible lesson about love and loss, he might have found himself attracted to her.

Her facial features were bold yet feminine and spoke of inner strength. Physically she was the kind of woman who always caught his eye…long-legged and with a little meat on her bones. He frowned, irritated by his observations, and focused his gaze straight ahead.

They rode toward a wooded area and in the distance he saw several other men on horseback and assumed they were some of her men.

"I heard you graduated from college," he said to break the silence.

She cast him a sideways gaze. "Don't sound so surprised," she said dryly. "I might have once been a bit of a handful, but that doesn't mean I was stupid."

"I didn't mean to imply that you were stupid. I was just kind of surprised to hear that you'd come back here to work with Gray on the ranch."

"Why would that surprise you? This is my home."

"I don't know, Gray just mentioned to me several

times that you seemed to be enjoying college life in Tulsa." Actually, Gray had worried about her, afraid that her rebellious and impulsive nature would get her into some kind of trouble.

"So, why did you quit Wild West Protective Services?"

He had the distinct impression she was changing the subject on purpose. "I just decided it was time for something different." He wasn't about to share with her the personal trauma that had led him to make that particular painful decision.

"So, what are your plans?"

"I don't have any plans other than to give you a couple of days."

She stopped her horse in its tracks and stared at him in disbelief. "A couple of days? Zack, I need more than a couple of days of your time. This isn't just about my father. I think it's about something bigger, something evil."

With the bright sun heralding a beautiful day, her words sounded just shy of silly. It was impossible to imagine evil in this place of sweet smelling grass and lingering morning dew. It was impossible to imagine evil anywhere in the small, picturesque town of Cotter Creek, Oklahoma.

But Zack had learned the hard way that evil existed where you least expected it. He'd learned that sometimes no matter how hard you tried, no matter what lengths you went to, evil had its day.

"Show me where your father fell."

"It's just ahead."

They rode a few minutes longer, then she stopped and dismounted. He did the same. "Every morning for as long as I can remember, Dad rode this path along the tree line."

Her eyes darkened slightly. "He enjoyed his solitude. Anyway, two weeks ago he took off for his ride like he usually did, but an hour later Diamond returned to the stable without him.

"Jake and Sonny and I took off looking for him and we found him there." She pointed to an area nearby. "There's a rock there, and it appeared that he'd fallen or been thrown off the horse and hit his head on the rock in the fall."

For the first time he saw a flicker of emotion other than irritation or anger in her eyes and he realized how difficult it had been for her to bring him to this place of her father's death.

Despite the fact that he hadn't particularly liked her as a girl and had no idea what kind of woman she'd become, he couldn't help the empathy that rippled through him.

He reached out and lightly touched her on the shoulder, standing so close to her he could smell the scent of her, a clean, sweet scent. "Stay here. I'll just be a minute or two."

He left her with the horses and went to the area she'd indicated that Gray had ridden his last ride. The ground was packed hard and cracked from lack of rain, making it impossible for him to discern any pattern of horse hooves that might have existed.

As he crouched to look at the ground around the rock where Gray had apparently hit his head and died, a wave of grief overtook him. There had been too much death in his life lately.

Dammit, he shouldn't even be here, immersing himself in Katie's latest drama. Accidents happened. People died. There wasn't a boogey man behind every curtain and there was no way he intended to get sucked into Kate Sampson's life.

He winced as he saw the blood splattered on the top of the rock. Ugly, but keeping with the aspect of a fall and a bang of the head against an unforgiving element.

He glanced over to Katie, who stood next to her horse, her arm wrapped around the gelding's neck. For just a moment as their gazes met, their crazy, explosive past was gone and only the present shined from her eyes—fear and regret and a million other emotions he couldn't begin to understand.

What he suddenly wanted to do was to put her fears to rest. He wanted to tell her that rungs to lofts rotted, that storms spooked cattle and a good man had been thrown to his death from his horse.

He wanted to tell her that she was overreacting, falling into her pattern of histrionics, that she needed to deal with her grief and to get on with her life.

He broke the gaze and instead focused on the rock once again. He picked it up and turned in over and in that instant everything changed.

Chapter 3

The moment she saw the expression on his face, she knew. He dropped the rock to the ground and stepped backward, as if the rock was a rattlesnake, and as his gaze caught hers, she knew.

"What?" she asked, her voice nothing more than a mere whisper. She had no idea what he'd found, what he thought, but she knew it was bad.

He walked to where she stood by the horses. "We need to call the sheriff. He needs to get out here."

"What did you find?" Thick emotion pressed tightly against her ribs, making it hard for her to take a deep, full breath.

His eyes, normally so distant, were now filled with emotions that frightened her. There was a softness there she'd never seen.

The grief she'd been fighting off since the morning

they'd found her father's lifeless body swelled up inside her and unwanted tears sprang to her eyes.

"Gray didn't just fall and hit his head on that rock." His voice was steady, but soft. "If I was to guess, that rock was used to beat your father in the head."

Every ounce of oxygen seemed to expel from her body. "I knew it." She managed to gasp as she stumbled away from the horse and turned her back on Zack. Tears tumbled down her cheeks as painful sobs racked her.

Murdered. She'd known it in her heart. The moment she'd found her father lying motionless on the ground, she'd known deep inside that something wasn't right.

Her father had been murdered, and along with this knowledge came the complete and painful acceptance of his death.

"Katie."

She sensed Zack right behind her and she turned blindly into his arms. As she buried her head in the sunshine freshness of his T-shirt, it didn't matter that she'd disliked him for as long as she could remember. It didn't matter that she believed him responsible for most of the unhappiness in the early years of her life.

All that did matter was that she needed somebody to hold her tight and his strong arms enfolded her and pulled her against his solid body.

She leaned into him, tear after tear escaped.

She'd never see her father again. She'd never again spend evenings on the porch, rocking and listening to him reminisce with stories of her mother who had died when Kate was a baby. She'd never have the opportunity to prove to him that she was as good as any son might have been.

Grief slowly gave way to anger. Her father hadn't

died a natural death, nor had he been taken in a tragic accident. Somebody had stolen his life, stolen him from her.

As the sorrow ebbed away, she became conscious of where she was and whose arms held her. Zack's chest was solid muscle and his arms radiated strength even as he awkwardly patted her on the back.

She had once promised herself that Zack West would never see her cry again and within twenty-four hours of seeing him again, she was in his arms weeping.

She jumped back, mortified by her momentary lapse of control. "I'm sorry," she said as she wiped her cheeks.

"No apology necessary." He stuck his hands into his pockets, his features devoid of all emotion.

She looked away from him, needing a moment to gain control of herself. She took several deep, cleansing breaths, then looked at him once again.

"I need you, Zack. I need you to find out who did this to my father. If it takes two days, then I need you for two days. If it takes a year, I need you for a year. But I won't rest until I know who is responsible for this."

He held up his hands and backed away from her, as if what she asked was too much. "Whoa, let's take it one day at a time. The first thing we need to do is get back to the house and call Sheriff Ramsey."

"But you'll see this through?" She wasn't sure why, but it seemed imperative that she get a definite commitment from him. "I need to know that you won't quit until my father's murderer is behind bars." She needed to know that the outrage that burned in her was just as white hot in him.

"One day at a time, Katie. That's all I'm willing to

commit to right now." His eyes held a distance she didn't understand, a remoteness that confused her.

"What is your problem, cowboy?" She stepped closer to him. The anger that coursed through her needed a target and he was the most convenient around. "My father loved you like a son, and he thought you loved him, as well, but obviously he was mistaken about your feelings for him."

She started to spin away from him but gasped as he reached out and grabbed her by the wrist. He pulled her closer, so close she could see the tiny flecks of gold in the depths of his green eyes, smell the faint scent of coffee on his breath.

Her heart seemed to stop beating as his gaze held hers intently. For a moment she felt the crackle of electricity in the air and with it the knowledge that she'd pushed him too hard.

"Don't ever doubt the fact that I loved Gray. I told you, we'll take this one day at a time. If that's not agreeable to you, then get somebody else. My feelings for your father are mine alone and the way I deal with his murder isn't any of your business." He released her wrist. "Now let's get back to the house."

He mounted his horse and she did the same, her skin still burning from contact with him and her heart pounding just a bit unsteadily.

"That boy's nothing but raw emotion," Gray used to say about Zack. "He just hasn't figured out how to control it yet."

Of course, at the time her father had spoken of Zack, she'd had the feeling he was really trying to tell her something about herself.

Apparently, Zack had learned control. Or maybe he'd

lost his ability to have any emotions. She wasn't sure which, but as they rode back toward the house, once again his features gave nothing away of his internal thoughts or feelings.

"If you tell any of my men I lost it and cried, I'll personally take my shotgun and shoot you in your cold, mean heart."

He gave her a wry, tight smile. "Now that's the Katie Sampson I know and remember, always using vinegar when sugar might work as well."

She bit back a retort and for a few moments they rode in silence. Once again she found herself wondering what on earth had possessed her to call him of all people? He'd never pretended to like her, had always shown her nothing but disdain.

Her father had not only loved Zack, but had admired him, had believed him to be an honorable man. That's why she'd called him, because she knew no matter what he thought of her, he'd do what was right. He'd find Gray's killer.

"You're sure of what you saw on that rock?" she asked, breaking the silence that had grown distinctly uncomfortable.

"There's blood on both sides, and on the underneath there's some matted hair. That's not consistent with a fall." He grimaced. "I wish I'd had on gloves when I picked it up."

"Do you think Jim might be able to get fingerprints off it?"

"Anything is possible. But, even if he does manage to get fingerprints off the rock, they won't mean anything unless the perpetrator has a record with prints on file."

Kate frowned as they rode into the stable. At the moment everything seemed so complicated, so overwhelming. She wanted to fix the damage from the stampede, to catch her father's killer and whoever had spooked the herd the day before, then get on with her life.

They dismounted and she gestured to a tough-looking man who was in the process of mucking out a stable. "Brett, would you unsaddle our horses and brush them down?"

Brett Cook tossed the shovel aside, a surly expression on his deeply tanned, scarred face. Kate tried to ignore the expression. Brett could be difficult and she should let him go, but at the moment she couldn't afford to lose another ranch hand, even a bad one.

As he approached them, Kate made the introductions. "Brett, this is Zack West. He'll be working for me. Zack, Brett Cook."

The man thrust out a beefy hand and Zack shook it.

"Nice to meet you," Zack said.

"Likewise." Brett dropped his hand and began to unsaddle one of the horses.

"That's a man who looks like he's been on the wrong side of trouble more than once," Zack said as they left the stable. "That scar down the side of his face looks like an old knife wound."

"It is. He got it a year ago in a bar fight at Crazy Joe's."

"He also smells like he slept in a brewery."

"I know. Dad fired him twice in the past year, then rehired him. He's a quick-tempered alcoholic and I should fire him, but he's good with the horses and I can't afford to lose any more men right now."

"Why did Gray hire him back?"

"You know Dad, he was always a sucker for a sob

story. Brett apologized and told Dad he'd do better, that he needed the job to make child support payments."

Zack nodded. "I'll need a list of those men who work for you now and those who left after your father's death," he said. "It also would help if you could give me the names of men who left Gray's employment in the past year or so. I also think it would be better if we'd go see Jim Ramsey in person rather than talk to him on the phone."

"All right." They reached the front porch. "Just let me get my purse and lock up so we can go see Sheriff Ramsey. Then we'll come back here and get you settled in the bunkhouse."

Within minutes they were in Zack's truck and headed into town.

Cotter Creek held a charm she'd thought she'd never find anywhere else in the world. As Zack drove down Main Street toward the sheriff's office, that charm was evident. People meandered down the sidewalks, as if they had all the time in the world to explore the various shops.

There had been a time before her graduation from college that Kate had considered remaining in Tulsa and not returning to the small town of Cotter Creek. In the midst of college partying and new friends, Kate had thought this place provincial and dull, but as maturity had set in and she'd faced the rest of her life, she'd known this was where she belonged, this was where she wanted to live and raise a family.

Of course, she'd barely gotten settled back into town and ranch life when she'd suddenly found herself in charge of running the ranch by herself.

She slid a glance at Zack. "You ever think of leaving here and living someplace else?"

Despite the morning sunshine, his hat cast shadows across his face, making it impossible for her to read his expression.

"When I was younger I couldn't wait to leave Cotter Creek. I wanted to move someplace where I wasn't 'one of those West boys.' But for the past couple of years I've been doing a lot of traveling and I've realized this is where my roots are, where I want to be for the rest of my life. What about you?"

"While I was in my first couple of years in college I got it into my head that I'd never go back to the ranch, that I'd stay in Tulsa and build a life there."

"So what happened to change your mind?"

She leaned back in the seat and thought about her answer. "There was no real defining moment. As time went on I missed the ranch. I missed Cotter Creek and most of all I realized that I wanted the opportunity to get closer to my father."

Emotion once again pressed hard against her chest. She swallowed and continued. "Besides, I'd done all the city things, clubbed and danced and drank myself half silly. I'd shopped and eaten in fancy restaurants and done everything Tulsa had to offer. But I realized when the time came for me to build my life, to get married and have a family, I wanted to do it here."

He pulled into an empty parking place in front of the sheriff's office, then turned to look at her. "Are you sure you're up to this? We need to be calm and rational so Jim takes what we have to say seriously."

"Don't worry about me," she said, half irritated by his words of caution. "All I want is for Jim to take this seriously and to do whatever he can to find out who killed my father."

"Good, then we have a common goal." He opened the truck door and got out. Kate hurriedly did the same.

Before they could get into the sheriff's office a familiar voice called Kate's name. Sheila Wadsworth hurried down the sidewalk toward them, the smile on her face rivaling the brightness of the rhinestones that decorated her tight denim dress.

"Zack West, I swear, honey, you get more handsome every time I see you," she exclaimed.

"Ah, Sheila, you're nothing but a sweet talker," he replied dryly.

She giggled, an affected girlish sound Kate found particularly annoying, especially since it came from a woman well over the age of fifty. She braced herself as Sheila turned her attention in her direction.

"Kate, darling. I just wanted to apologize for my behavior after your daddy's funeral," Sheila said. "I should have given you more time to mourn before approaching you." Her expression was properly contrite. "But now that you've had some time to think, are you still planning on keeping the ranch?"

"Sheila, read my lips. I'm not selling...ever."

"You have a buyer lined up?" Zack asked.

Sheila's plump shoulders moved up and down with a shrug. "Nobody in particular. I just know it would sell quickly and make Kate a wealthy woman. She could make enough money to live anywhere she wanted to."

"I want to live where I'm living right now," Kate replied evenly.

"Well, dear, if you change your mind you know

where I am." She wiggled two fingers, then turned and marched back up the sidewalk from where she'd come.

"That woman is quickly becoming the bane of my existence," Kate said.

"Forget her. She's always been a pushy opportunist. We've got more important things to take care of." Zack paused on the sidewalk just outside the office and turned to look at her once again. "Let's not complicate the issue by mentioning your suspicions about the stampede."

Her first impulse was to buck and kick. Dammit, somebody had spooked her herd on purpose yesterday and she'd nearly been killed.

But reluctantly she recognized the wisdom of Zack's words. She also suspected Zack didn't believe her about the intentional stampede, but she knew better than to push that particular issue with him at the moment.

There was no concrete evidence of what had happened in the pasture the day before. Right now the important thing was to get Jim Ramsey investigating her father's death. As much as she hated to admit it, Zack was right. There was no point in confusing things.

She nodded and together they entered the office. A woman seated at a desk manned the reception area. "Morning, Kate, Zack." Sarah Lutten smiled, the gesture pulling all her wrinkles upward.

"Good morning, Sarah. Sheriff in?" Zack asked.

"He's in. Let me just check to make sure he's available." She got up from the desk and disappeared through a door that Kate knew led back to the sheriff's personal office and the jail cells.

As they waited for Sarah to return, Kate thought of those moments when Zack had held her while she'd cried. His arms had been so strong around her and for a brief moment she wished she were back in those arms once again.

She straightened her spine. She had to get hold of herself. She needed Zack for his investigative skills, for the resources he and his family business could bring to the table. But the last thing she needed was to become emotionally dependent on him in any way.

"You can go on back," Sarah said as she reentered the room.

They entered the small inner office and Sheriff Jim Ramsey rose to greet them.

"Katie, Zack, what brings you two to see me on such a fine morning?" He gestured them to the two chairs in front of his desk then sank into his big leather chair.

"Murder." The word escaped from Kate before she could stop herself.

Zack shot her a look of warning and she sat back in the chair and bit her bottom lip to keep anything else from escaping her mouth.

It was probably just as well she sit back and let Zack handle things. Sheriff Ramsey had always been one of those men who listened to men better than he listened to "the little ladies" in town.

Jim frowned and absently plucked a piece of lint off his protruding belly. "Murder?" His gaze went from Kate to Zack. "You want to tell me what's going on?"

"That's what we'd like for you to find out," Zack said. "I rode out to the place where Gray had his accident. How much investigating did you do into his death?"

Jim's frown deepened. "It was an open and shut case. His head was on a rock, Kate and some of her men told me his mount had come back without him to the stables. It seemed pretty obvious what had happened. You should know these kinds of accidents happen occasionally out here in ranching territory."

There was an edge of defensiveness in his tone. "Dr. McCain pronounced Gray dead due to head trauma. It was ruled an accidental death and that was that."

And that was that. Those words resonated in Kate's heart with a hollow ache. That was that. Her father was dead and nothing in this world would bring him back. She would never again have the opportunity to make him proud. She would never be able to tell him just how much she'd loved him.

"Did you check out the rock where Gray fell?" Zack asked.

Jim shrugged. "No reason to. When it looks like a duck, it's a duck."

Zack leaned forward, his eyes narrowed slightly. "It didn't quack and it wasn't an accident."

"What are you talking about?"

As Zack explained what he'd found on the rock, Kate watched him. In the five years since she'd seen him, the lines radiating from his eyes were a little bit deeper, his mouth appeared more sensual than she remembered and his face held a strong maturity that hadn't been evident years ago. His shoulders appeared wider, but his stomach and hips were as lean as when he'd been a teenager.

He'd always affected her on some base, visceral level. His nearness to her had always charged the atmosphere with dangerous electricity. It still did.

She frowned and tore her gaze from him, realizing she was studying him in an effort to distance herself from the details of her father's murder. She became conscious of her ankle throbbing and told herself that when she got back to the ranch she needed to prop it up for a while.

"We'd like a full investigation into Gray's death," Zack said to Jim. "And of course we'll do whatever we can to assist you."

Jim leaned back in his chair and raked a hand through his salt-and-pepper hair. "If what you think is true and that rock was used to bludgeon Gray to death, it was kind of stupid for the murderer to leave it right there at the scene."

"On the contrary, it was very smart. If the rock hadn't been there then you would have instantly ruled Gray's death suspicious. As it was, the murderer counted on you chalking it up to a tragic accident," Zack replied.

"And that's just what I did," Jim said mournfully.

Kate wasn't sure whether the sheriff felt badly about not fully investigating the situation in the first place or the fact that he now had to do something about it.

Sheriff Jim Ramsey wasn't known for his energy and enthusiasm for his work. Most people in the town were hoping that retirement was just around the corner for him so they could vote in a new sheriff, somebody younger and more committed to the position.

"I'll get right on it," Jim said, and stood, as if to indicate to them that the meeting was over.

"We appreciate it, Sheriff." Zack stood, as well, and shook Jim's hand.

Kate got up, vaguely irritated that Jim had listened to Zack when he hadn't listened to her two weeks before. The good-old-boy network was apparently alive and well in Cotter Creek.

As she and Zack left the office and got into his truck, she tried to tamp down her irritation. "It's good that bad things don't happen too often in Cotter Creek because that man is barely competent."

"He's just lazy," Zack replied.

"He was certainly lazy in the way he handled Dad's death."

"He was the one who found my mother's body when she was murdered. Of course, he was just a deputy then."

His words shocked her. "I'd forgotten about your mother's murder."

He shrugged. "It was a long time ago. I was only six when she was murdered."

There was nothing in his voice to evoke her sympathy, but sorrow swept through her as she realized she wasn't the only one who had lost a parent to senseless murder.

"They never found the person who killed your mother, did they?"

"No. She left one night to get groceries in town and several hours later was found strangled along the side of the road." He turned his head and gave her a quick look. "But don't worry. We'll find the bastard that killed Gray."

She should have found comfort in his words, but she didn't. Although she desperately wanted to know who had killed her father and why, she knew discovering those answers wouldn't heal the hole left in her heart.

"How did you get through it? When you lost your mother? How did you get through the pain?"

"I was young. The only thing I really remember about that time was that it upset me because my father cried a lot." He glanced at her again and this time the green of his eyes appeared darker, slightly haunted. "I think loss is more difficult to handle when you're older and less resilient." His fingers tightened on the steering wheel, turning his knuckles white as he directed his attention back out the truck's front window.

They didn't speak again until they reached the ranch. "I'll take you to the bunkhouse and get you settled in," she said as he parked the truck and they got out.

"Almost everyone in town knows I'm no longer working for Wild West Protective Services, so as far as anyone is concerned, I've just signed on here temporarily to help you out with the ranch work until you can hire new help."

"That's fine with me," she agreed.

He reached behind the seats and grabbed a large duffel bag, then they began the long walk toward the bunkhouse in the distance.

As they walked she thought again of that look she'd seen for a brief moment in his eyes. She had the feeling that he knew intimately about loss as an adult and that made her curious.

It had been years since she and Zack had interacted in any way. She certainly liked to think she'd changed in that interval of time and wondered how he might have changed. What might have happened that had caused the darkness she'd seen in his eyes?

She knew that for several years he had dated Jaime Coffer, a gorgeous blonde who had one day simply up and left Cotter Creek. Somehow she didn't think that had caused the dark shadows. He'd seemed fine after Jaime had left and had never lacked for female companionship.

"Did you enjoy all the traveling you did for the business?" she asked.

"It was all right."

"I'll bet you've met a lot of interesting people."

"Interesting enough."

"Are you always so chatty?" she asked dryly.

He stopped walking and turned to face her, his features once again partially shadowed by the brim of his hat. "I'm not here to socialize. I'm here to catch a killer."

She felt the blush that warmed her cheeks. Nothing had changed. In the blink of an eye, in the tone of his voice, he'd managed to make her feel like the nuisance she'd been as a child.

Once again she was aware of the throb of her ankle. She was eager to get back to the house, prop up her foot and get away from him.

He continued to walk and she followed behind, remembering all the times as a young girl he'd made her feel like an interloper in her own life.

She reminded herself once again that she didn't have to like him to need his expertise. She didn't have to enjoy his company to use his investigative skills. But, perversely, she couldn't help the fact that she wouldn't have minded his arms around her one more time.

Chapter 4

Zack was relieved when Katie left him alone in the bunkhouse. He'd felt off balance since that moment out in the pasture when she'd turned into his arms and wept for her father.

Even though he'd known Katie since she'd been a child, it was only the second time he'd ever seen her cry. The first time had been tears of rage and embarrassment when he'd picked her up and carried her away from a party she should have never attended. This time her tears had been ones of sorrow, of grief.

But it hadn't been her tears that had disconcerted him. It had been the warmth of her body against his, the press of her full breasts against his chest, the sweet, feminine scent of her that had so rattled him.

At that moment his body had reacted powerfully, like a man's to a woman's, and it had stunned him. The last thing he'd expected was to feel any kind of physical desire for Katie. Hell, he hadn't liked her as a kid and the verdict was still out on whether he would find her tolerable as an adult.

He shoved thoughts of her away as he placed his personal items in the footlocker at the end of the single bed that would be his sleep arrangement for as long as he was here.

The bunkhouse had at one time been an integral part of every ranch, but in recent years had become less important as ranch hands had transportation and often lived off the ranch where they worked.

Just before Katie had left, she'd told him that he'd be sharing the space with four other men. His bunk mates would be Brett Cook and Jake Merridan, whom he'd already met, and Mike Wilton and George Cochran, whom he had yet to meet. Katie had also told him that ranch manager, Sonny Williams, lived in a small cottage near the main house. The rest of the ranch hands lived off the ranch.

Besides the beds, the large open building boasted a small kitchen area, complete with refrigerator, microwave and a two-burner stovetop, and table and chairs.

A sofa and a couple of chairs formed a living room, the central piece, a midsize television. Gray had always believed in a bit of comfort for his men. "Happy men make happy workers," he'd often say.

The bathroom was built for more than one man and had two shower stalls.

Zack finished storing his items in the trunk, then eyed the other trunks that sat at the end of each bed. He was alone. It would be easy to take a moment to sneak a peak into the personal items of the others, but a glance at his watch made him put that particular action on hold.

It was nearly noon and at any moment the men would be coming in for lunch. The last thing he wanted was to be caught snooping. Besides, at this moment he wasn't sure what he'd be looking for.

He walked to the door and stepped outside, looking over the land, and for a moment he felt as if Gray stood beside him.

Gray had always considered this land his little piece of heaven on earth. Bent Tree Ranch had pastures of sweet green grass, groves of thick trees that provided shelter to herds and all the outbuildings a ranch needed to help it be successful.

A little piece of heaven, but what Gray hadn't known was that there was a serpent loose in the garden. Zack was determined to find out just who that serpent was and why he'd wanted Gray dead.

Lunch with the men was interesting. Mike Wilton and George Cochran seemed friendly but reserved. Brett Cook was sullen but tolerable and Jake exuded a friendly enthusiasm that Zack didn't trust.

Zack had always relied on his instincts when it came to people, but the lunch was too brief for him to form any real impressions.

He knew the best way to learn about a man was to work beside him and so after lunch he went with Brett and Jake to work on the fence that had been destroyed by the stampede the day before.

"Katie told me you worked on the Wainfield ranch before coming here," Zack said to Jake as the two worked to unload the lumber he'd bought in town.

"Yeah. I was there for two years. Then Joe had that tractor accident and his kids sold off the place." Jake shook his head. "Damned shame. He was a good man." He slid Zack a curious glance. "So, are you and Kate old friends?"

"Something like that," Zack replied, knowing he was being vague. It was easier than trying to explain the crazy relationship between himself and Katie.

"This place is awfully big for a woman to run alone." It sounded like an idle observation but Zack knew Jake was subtly staking a claim. "I've gotten real close to Kate since I've been working here." Staking a claim and perhaps warning off any competition.

Zack leaned against one of the fence posts, pulled a handkerchief out of his back pocket and wiped it across his forehead. "As far as I'm concerned, getting close to Katie is kind of like getting too close to a wildcat. She can appear nice and calm, but you never know where she's going to claw your skin off."

Jake laughed, obviously pleased by Zack's reply. "I've always liked a bit of a wildcat in my women. There's nothing finer than gentling a wildcat."

At that moment the sound of an approaching horse caught their attention. Sonny Williams rode toward them. As he reined in and dismounted, he nodded to Zack. "How you doing? Ms. Sampson told me you'd hired on."

"Doing good, Sonny." Sonny had worked for Gray for years, so he was no stranger to Zack.

"What the hell are you doing here? I thought you worked for that fancy business with your dad and your brothers and sister."

"I quit that a month ago. I've been kicking around for

the last couple of weeks trying to decide what I want to do with my life. Smokey mentioned to me that Katie had lost some men after Gray's death, so I figured I'd sign on and do some honest work here until she can hire on more men and I can decide exactly what I want to do."

"Right now we can use all the help we can get." A frown tugged at Sonny's weathered features. "Things have been tough around here. I still can't believe Gray is gone."

The frown lifted and he looked around. "Well, it looks like you men are on top of this job. I'll just leave you to get back to work. Don't forget tomorrow Doc Edwards is going to be here to tag all the new calves. I'll need all hands to help with the process."

With a nod to all three men, Sonny remounted and headed in the opposite direction from where he'd come, and Zack and the others got back to work.

The men worked on the fencing until the sun began to set, then knocked off for the day. Zack and George let Jake, Mike and Brett use the facilities first as they intended to head into town. It was Friday night and payday and Sonny had distributed the checks an hour before.

George and Zack showered after the other two had left, then ate a quiet meal. After cleaning up, George settled in one of the chairs in front of the television and promptly fell asleep and began to snore.

Zack eased down into one of the other chairs, his mind sorting through his impressions of the men he had met so far. It didn't take him long to become bored with his thoughts and slightly irritated by the blare of the television.

He got up and drifted outside. Dusk had fallen and

night shadows crept across the ground. He leaned against the building and looked toward the main house. The porch light was on and he thought he saw a figure seated in one of the two chairs on the front porch.

Katie. He wondered how many nights in the past year she and Gray had sat side by side, just like he and Gray had years ago. It somehow didn't seem right for her to be sitting there all alone.

As he walked toward the house he told himself he was only going to ask her about the list of employees he'd requested from her. It had nothing to do with the fact that she looked so lonesome in the encroaching darkness.

She stood as he approached and once again he was struck by her physical presence. She was a good four or five inches shorter than his own six feet, but she gave the impression of being taller.

She'd obviously showered and changed since he'd seen her earlier in the day. She was clad in a blue sundress that bared her tanned arms and did amazing things to her eyes in the illumination from the porch light overhead. The scooped neckline revealed just a hit of cleavage and a new tension settled into Zack's gut.

"Evening, Zack." She sank onto the chair.

"Katie." He swept his hat from his head. "I was wondering if you'd had a chance to get together that list of employees for me."

"I've got it inside." She seemed disinclined to get up again. "Why don't you sit for just a few minutes?"

He hesitated. He'd told himself he'd walked up here to get the list, then go back to the bunkhouse, but there was a wistfulness in her voice, a softness he'd never heard before. It intrigued him. He sank into the chair next to hers, once again feeling unbalanced by her.

The anger she'd displayed at the hospital when she'd told him to get out of her sight had been pure Katie, so familiar it was almost comfortable.

This softer, almost vulnerable Katie disconcerted him. He wasn't at all sure he trusted it. "Friday night and you don't have a hot date?" he asked.

"I haven't had a hot date since I left college behind," she replied. "What about you? No town hottie waiting for your company?"

He grinned. "I've been gone for so long I don't think I know any of the town hotties anymore." Zack would never admit to her just how long it had been since he'd been out with a woman. For the past year work had consumed him, leaving no time for personal relationships of any kind.

For a few minutes they were silent. It wasn't a restful, peaceful kind of silence. Zack had learned long ago that there was little restful or peaceful about Katie Sampson.

"This is the time of the evening I miss him most," she said, her voice soft and low. "In the hours just after supper and right before bedtime. I never knew a house could be so quiet."

He set his hat on the porch next to his chair. "As I recall, you never seemed particularly fond of silence," he said dryly. He tensed, knowing she might see his words as bait.

He saw the flash of her white teeth as she smiled at him. He'd noticed that smile earlier in the day when it had been directed at Jake. It was a beautiful smile and completely unexpected.

"I suppose that's your way of telling me I was always

making noise when I was younger." She leaned deeper into the chair. "I suppose I'm willing to admit that I was a bit of a handful when I was younger if you're willing to admit that you were an arrogant, egotistical, over-bearing pain in the neck."

He bristled at her characterization of him. "I'll admit half of that is true."

"Gee, let me guess which half you'll admit to," she replied. She released an audible sigh, one that spoke of weariness.

For a long moment neither of them spoke. Zack was normally quite comfortable with silence, but this one felt thick and charged with an energy he couldn't define.

"Did you find out anything this afternoon?" She broke the silence.

He leaned back and directed his gaze toward the bunkhouse in the distance. "Not really. George and Mike seem like decent men. Brett doesn't seem like a decent man and Jake seems to be developing a major crush on you." He turned to catch her surprised expression.

She laughed, a deep, sexy sound that shocked him. He realized it was the very first time he'd heard her laugh. Odd, that in all the years he'd hung out here, he'd never heard her laughter before. And never would he have expected it to be such a pleasant sound.

"Now you're going to have me questioning your investigative skills," she said. "Jake has certainly been a godsend since Dad's death. He helped me take care of the arrangements for the funeral and has been a comfort, but there's certainly no romance there. He's just a good employee."

Maybe she didn't see any romance on her end, but

Zack knew with a man's instinct that Jake's interest in Katie had nothing to do with him being her employee.

"What are you going to do with the list of names I'm giving you?" she asked.

"I'll give them to Dalton. He'll do a complete background check on each of them." He relaxed as the conversation turned to his work, the reason he was here. "Within a couple of days, a week at the most, I should know everything there is to know about the men on your list."

"But you won't know which one of them killed my father. You won't know which one of them stampeded my herd."

"Probably not," he agreed. "At least not from looking at their backgrounds, although that information might give me a clue as to who is capable of such a crime."

"You really don't believe me about the stampede, do you?"

Zack felt the dangerous ground beneath him. So far she'd shown him a calm, rational nature that he'd never seen before. But he suspected she was on her best behavior because she needed him.

There seemed to be a tenuous peace between them, but he was certain it was a peace easily shattered. Still, he wasn't going to lie. "I don't know what I believe," he finally replied.

"I'll go get the list for you." She stood abruptly and he got a whiff of her fragrance. The pleasant scent did nothing to diffuse the sudden tension that crackled in the air.

"Katie, if you wanted a yes man to help you out with this, then you've hired the wrong man. I wasn't there in the pasture yesterday. I didn't see what happened, so I can't make a judgment call."

"By not believing what I've told you happened, you've made a judgment call about me," she replied. Without waiting for an answer she went into the house, allowing the screen door to slam shut behind her.

Kate didn't know why it was so important to her that he believe her, but it was, and the fact that she knew he didn't frustrated her. And if she were to look deep inside she'd know what she'd find there was fear.

Somebody had killed her father. That was a fact. Somebody had intentionally spooked her herd and nearly caused her to be trampled to death.

If her death had been the intent, then the attempt had been unsuccessful, which meant there might be another attempt. She didn't want her death to be what made a believer out of Zack.

Still, her desire for him to believe her went beyond the fear for her personal safety. She frowned, not wanting to take the time to examine her feelings where Zack West was concerned.

As it was, she was aware of the fact that she was far too conscious of him as a strong, good-looking man rather than an intelligent, trained investigator.

She hadn't liked the way her heart had jagged just a bit in her chest when she'd seen him heading toward the house. The night shadows had clung to him, making him look tall and strong as he'd strode toward her.

She told herself she'd just been grateful for the company, for anyone's company in the quiet hours of the evening.

She grabbed the manila folder that held the list she'd

prepared for him that afternoon then returned to the porch, where he now stood next to the railing. "I wasn't sure how far back you wanted me to go on former employees. You mentioned a year, so that's what I did."

"At least this gives us a place to start." He took the folder from her then leaned back against the porch railing.

"Sonny mentioned this afternoon something about Doc Edwards coming out tomorrow to tag new calves. What's that about?" he asked.

"We're not branding anymore. One of the things I implemented when I got back from college was electronic tags for the cattle. That way if they're stolen, we can track them by computer to find out where they are."

"What made you decide to do that?" he asked. "Branding has always been good enough for most people around here. Besides, I thought cattle rustling went out with disco."

"Haven't you heard? Cattle rustling is back in fashion. With the new fad of low carb diets, rustlers have discovered that beef is big business again. I talked Dad into tagging last spring when he lost twenty head of cattle to rustlers."

She saw one of his dark brows raise slightly. "I guess I've been out of touch with the ranching world since working for Wild West Protective Services." He gazed at her thoughtfully. "It's been several months since I last saw your dad. I asked you before, but maybe you've thought of somebody he'd had problems with? I don't just mean here around the ranch."

She sighed and stared out at the brilliant blanket of stars strewing the night sky. "I've thought about it for the past two weeks and I can't think of anyone Dad had problems with or exchanged a harsh word with. Brett has been an ongoing problem, but when he came to Dad with a sob story Dad rehired him, so surely he wouldn't have any grudge to hold."

She looked at him once again. "You of all people should know how easygoing Dad was. He didn't have a temper. He didn't go looking for problems. I just can't imagine anyone having a reason to hurt him. You know he was on the town city council. I have gone to most of the meetings and there's always arguing about issues, but never does it feel mean-spirited."

"Maybe I need to check out the local politics, go to the next council meeting."

"The next meeting is a week from tomorrow. Every second Saturday evening of the month. I just can't imagine any city business that would result in somebody wanting to kill Dad."

He stared off into the night. "If we can figure out a motive, then it will be easier to solve the crime. Unfortunately it's possible there is no motive, that it was a crime of rage, a crime of passion." He returned his gaze to her and his eyes glittered in the artificial porch light.

"What do you mean?"

"I mean maybe out there on the trail Gray encountered somebody and they had a fight that ended tragically."

"There was no fight," she countered. "At least, not a fair one. Dad was a big man and quite capable of taking care of himself. I saw him, Zack. I saw him on the ground. I held one of his hands in mine." Her voice cracked and she took a deep breath to steady herself. "There wasn't a mark on his face, a scratch or bruise on his hands. He never got a chance to defend himself."

Without conscious thought she stepped forward and curled her hand around Zack's strong forearm. "It was an ambush, Zack. That's what happened on the trail that morning. Somebody ambushed my father and killed him."

He covered her hand with his own, his eyes holding not a haunted but a dangerous glint. "I told you we'll get him, Katie, and we will."

His hand was hot on hers and for a moment her breath caught. She licked her dry lips. "Kate," she said, her voice a mere whisper. "It's Kate. I'm not a little girl anymore, Zack."

"Yeah. I noticed." His voice sounded deeper than usual and in that moment Kate remembered how many times in her youth she had dreamed of Zack's hand holding hers, his mouth touching hers and his body possessing hers.

She wondered what his mouth tasted like, if it would taste as dangerous, as sensual as it looked.

There was something in his eyes that filled her with a crazy, sweet longing and, with a rush of anticipation, she leaned forward.

Chapter 5

Zack's senses swam with her. All memories of the negative way he'd once felt about her, what he'd once thought about her, disappeared as she leaned closer, close enough that if he wanted he could capture her full, sensual lips with his.

For just a brief, charged moment he saw only the fact that she was a beautiful woman with eyes that beckoned and a scent that half dizzied him.

Would kissing her somehow ease the ache that had been in his heart for the last month? Would pulling her body tight against his somehow diminish the anger that had festered in him for too many days, too many nights?

The desire to find out might have tempted him if he didn't remember all too clearly the last time she'd looked at him with her eyelids half open and her lips parted as if expecting a kiss.

He stepped backward, breaking their physical contact as he pulled away from her. "Last time I stood that close to you, you scratched half the flesh off my cheek," he said.

Her eyes widened, then narrowed. "If you expect me to apologize, you'll be waiting a long time. You were where you didn't belong and it really wasn't any of your business."

"You were where you didn't belong, as well," he reminded her.

Her cheeks deepened in color. "That was a long time ago. What's important isn't the past, what's important is the here and now."

"Easy for you to say. I bear the scars of the temper tantrum you threw in the past." He reached up and touched his cheek where the small scar had ensured that he'd never completely forget Katie Sampson.

"You're joking, right? I didn't really leave a scar, did I?" She stepped closer to him and once again he tensed as the scent of her surrounded him. Before he knew her intent, she reached up and traced a soft, warm finger across his cheek.

She gasped and jerked her hand away. "Oh, Zack. Tell me the truth? Did I do that or did you get it some other way and you're just trying to make me feel bad?"

What in the hell was he doing? As he looked at her face, her features taut with concern and maybe just a touch of remorse, he wondered why he'd even brought up that night so long ago.

"I'm just giving you a hard time," he finally said. "I got this scar in a bar fight several years ago, and you're right, what's important is the here and now." He stepped down from the porch. "I'd better get back to the bunkhouse before the other men come back from town."

"Of course. I'd like to go with you when you take the file to Dalton."

"That will be first thing in the morning. Dalton won't be in the office in town tomorrow, but he has everything he needs at the ranch to start working the background checks. Don't you need to be here for the cattle tagging?"

He didn't want her with him. He'd been less than twenty-four hours in her employment and she was already bothering him in a way that confused and irritated him.

"No. Doc Edwards and the men know how to handle it." She leaned against one of the porch railings once again, her features obscured by the night shadows. "Zack, I have no intention of you running this investigation without me. I want to be beside you every step of the way. Partners, so to speak."

"I don't work with partners," he said.

"Well, you've just changed your work habits," she replied. "I'll be ready first thing in the morning to go with you to speak to Dalton."

Before he could protest again, she turned and disappeared into the house. Zack stared at the closed door, his cheek still burning from her touch.

He placed the manila folder in his truck parked at the side of Katie's house, then headed back to the bunkhouse with the moonlight overhead guiding his way.

When he'd decided to give Katie a couple of days, he figured the worst he'd have to put up with from her was her explosive temper tantrums and impertinence.

He never would have guessed that the scent of her

would twist his guts into knots, that her simple touch to his face would generate enough electricity to start a storm. He never would have guessed that her mouth would tempt him to forget the fact that he had no intention of ever getting deeply involved with a woman again.

It had been one hell of a day. First, the realization that Gray's accident hadn't been an accident after all and now the knowledge that Katie Sampson had the power to stir him on a level where he hadn't been stirred in a very long time.

George's snores greeted him as he entered the bunkhouse. The middle-aged man had moved from in front of the television to his bed.

With the aid of a night-light that gleamed from the kitchen area, Zack made his way to his own bunk. He shucked off his jeans, pulled his T-shirt over his head, then crawled beneath the crisp white sheets on the bed, but sleep remained elusive.

He would have liked an opportunity to read through the file before going to bed to see if any names leaped out at him. Although Zack was aware of the American romance with cowboys, he also knew that in reality many of the workers who drifted from ranch to ranch were misfits, ex-cons and bad apples. Every rancher probably had a horror story about one of his ranch hands, but not every rancher was killed by one of his own.

Katie had to be right about one thing. If Gray had suffered no defensive wounds, then somebody had ambushed him on the trail. Gray had been a big man, no slouch when it came to physical strength and agility.

Zack had to guess that the first blow had come from behind, that Gray had been blindsided.

That meant he probably hadn't been on his horse when he'd been attacked. He'd dismounted to meet somebody? To speak with somebody he'd met on the trail? It had to have been somebody he knew. A man usually didn't dismount a horse for a stranger.

She'd been so warm in his arms. The stray thought sliced through his head as he remembered holding Katie as she'd wept. He thought of that moment on the porch when she'd leaned toward him and he'd had the crazy impulse to kiss her.

Partners, indeed. The last thing he needed in his life was a woman. He'd emotionally invested as a teenager and early twenty-year-old in the wrong woman and most recently been involved with a client who had ended up dead.

As far as he was concerned, emotional investment in anything or anyone was vastly overrated. The Katie he had always known was nothing more than a big vacuum of emotion and he wasn't about to get sucked into her by unexpected physical desire or the fact that they both mourned the same man.

He was still awake around midnight when the men came in from town. He feigned sleep and listened to them stumbling around, talking in half-drunk whispers as they fell into bed. Within minutes the room was once again silent.

Was one of these men a murderer? Had one of them met Gray on the trail that early sunny morning and killed him? At the moment Zack had no clue, not even the faintest inclination as to who might be responsible.

* * *

He awoke suddenly, his heart pounding, and for a moment disoriented as to where he was. He sat up and full consciousness gripped him.

He had no idea if he'd been asleep for five minutes or fifty. The nightmare. That's what had awakened him. The nightmare about Melissa's death.

Certainly it wasn't an unusual occurrence. In the past month, nightmares about his client's death had haunted him regularly.

Knowing from experience that sleep wouldn't come easily again, he slid out of bed and pulled on his jeans and boots. He moved quietly, not wanting to awaken any of the other men, and slipped out of the bunkhouse door and into the darkness of the night.

He leaned against the bunkhouse and for a moment wished he had a cigarette. Even though he'd quit smoking more than a year before there were still times, especially lately, that he thought about a calming lungful of smoke. Fortunately, the impulse never lasted long.

Melissa. He hadn't been in love with her, but he'd loved her. He'd been hired to keep her safe from an abusive, soon-to-be ex-husband and in the couple of months he'd spent with her he'd come to respect and admire her strength and indomitable spirit.

When she'd told him she didn't need his services anymore, when she'd released him from her employment, his instincts had told him the danger still existed. But he'd ignored his instincts and now she was dead.

The nightmare that haunted him was always the same. Even though when Melissa had been killed by her ex-husband Zack had been a hundred miles away, he dreamed of that moment of her death.

In his dream, she stepped out of her car and waved to him, her face radiating the warm smile of a close friend. Clad in a white sundress, she looked cool and confident, stronger than he'd ever seen her in the time they'd shared together.

As she started walking toward him, a shot rang in the air and the front of her white dress blossomed with scarlet as she crumpled to the ground. That was always when Zack awakened.

He should have followed his instincts. He should have insisted that he remain as her employee for another day, another week, another month.

His instincts were silent now, as if killed by the tragedy of Melissa's senseless death. When he'd first heard about Gray's death he should have known something wasn't quite right, but the instincts he'd relied on so much in his line of work were quiet.

Maybe what had awakened him hadn't been nightmares at all, but rather dreams of Katie. Nothing had surprised him more than his physical response to her. It was more than the fact that he hadn't been with a woman for nearly a year.

Perhaps the biggest surprise of all was that he wasn't the only one who felt the magnetic pull of physical attraction. Katie felt it, as well. He'd seen it in her eyes as they'd stood so close together on the porch. He'd felt it simmering between them every moment they spent in each other's company.

Hell of a thing. The world had gone half mad. He turned to go back inside to bed, but hesitated as something caught his attention.

A flicker of light that didn't belong on the side of the dark house. It was there only a moment, then gone.

He continued to stare, a surge of adrenaline filling his veins. There…again a flicker. As he stood trying to discern what it was, a lick of flame shot upward and he knew.

Fire!

His brain screamed it before his mouth could form the word. He remained frozen for only a millisecond, then threw open the door to the bunkhouse.

"Fire," he said. "The main house is on fire."

He didn't wait to see how fast the men would respond. With his heart pounding frantically, he turned and ran for the house, knowing that the area where he'd seen the flames was where Katie's bedroom was located.

Hot. She was hot and she knew it was all Zack West's fault. If his eyes weren't such a beautiful green, if his mouth wasn't so sensual, then she wouldn't be hot and bothered by him at all.

The heat he generated in her wasn't just a mental thing, but a physical thing, as well. Her body was slick with perspiration. Her hair clung to her neck in damp tendrils as she moved her hands down his sweaty, muscled chest.

Hot.

Too hot.

What had begun as sensual pleasure had become something uncomfortable, almost painful. She twisted away from him, needing some air, needing to cool off before she internally combusted. In that instant she surfaced from the dream to find herself alone in her bed.

Although she left her dreams behind, it took several moments for her brain to completely clear. She remained still, eyes closed, and wondered if perhaps she'd somehow nudged the thermostat into a heat mode instead of cool.

As full consciousness struck, she smelled smoke in the air, heard a strange, faint crackling that snapped her eyes open.

Instantly she squeezed her eyes tightly closed as acrid smoke made them water. Smoke? Why was the bedroom filled with smoke?

Smoke. Heat. Fire!

She sat up, her frantic gaze instantly captured by the deadly flames dancing across the pane of her bedroom window. Before she could move, the window shattered and flames shot inside. With a scream she leaped out of bed. Her thoughts scrambled, heart hammering in terror as she raced toward the bedroom door.

What was happening? How had the house started on fire?

She hesitated only the duration of a heartbeat before touching the bedroom door, hoping, praying, that the fire was only on the outside of the house and not racing throughout. The wood was warm, but not hot.

She gasped in relief as she touched the doorknob and found it cool to her fingers. Apparently the fire wasn't in the main section of the house but rather confined to the outer wall of her bedroom area.

With a whoosh, the curtains in the bedroom went up in flames and with another scream Kate grabbed the knob and pulled on the door. It didn't budge.

The heat had become unbearable and in the light provided by the fire she could see the smoke that billowed in the room, stinging her eyes and stealing her breath.

Out. She had to get out! Why wouldn't the door

open? She grabbed the knob with both hands and pulled as hard as she could, but the door refused to open.

Frantic voices drifted in through the window above the roar of the flames. Zack. She heard his deep voice barking orders, and even though she should have been comforted by the fact that her men had abandoned their beds to fight the flames, she knew she'd die in this room before they got the fire extinguished.

"Zack!" She moved as close to the window as possible and yelled his name over and over again. A spasm of coughing momentarily overwhelmed her and she fell to her knees.

"Katie!"

Zack's voice penetrated her smoke-filled head and she saw his face outside the busted window. "Get out!" he cried. "Get out of there."

"I can't," she replied. Her voice sounded no louder than a whisper as once again a fit of coughing gripped her. "The door is jammed or something." Tears streamed down her face and she felt as if she were being boiled alive.

She was going to die. While her men sprayed water on the house to fight the fire, she was going to die in here from the smoke. Low. She needed to get low. She dropped to her knees. The smoke wouldn't be as thick near the floor.

How had this happened? Had she fallen asleep without blowing out one of the candles she loved to burn in the evenings? But that didn't make sense. The fire was on the outside coming in, not on the inside burning out.

What difference did it make now? She couldn't breathe…there was nothing but smoke…nothing but darkness.

Her bedroom door exploded inward and with a grateful sob she saw Zack. His face was grim as he swept her up into his arms and carried her out of the room.

She wound her arms around his neck and buried her face against his hot, bare chest. Tears streamed down her cheeks, tears from the smoke along with ones of relief.

When he left the house and stepped out onto the porch, she lifted her head and dragged in deep cleansing breaths of the cool night air. He laid her on the cool grass.

"Are you all right?" he asked. She nodded, once again coughing as her lungs cleared of the noxious smoke. "I want you to get in my truck and lock the doors."

She frowned, wondering if the smoke had somehow addled her brain. Why would he tell her to lock herself in his truck?

"Katie, don't ask questions. I'll explain later." He grabbed her by the hand and pulled her up to her feet. "Go. Lock the doors and don't open them for anyone except me."

Too weak to protest, too confused to even try to make sense of anything, she obeyed. He watched until she was in the passenger seat of his truck and locked inside, then he disappeared around the corner of the house where the fire still burned.

Kate leaned her head back against the seat and closed her stinging, watering eyes. What had just happened? She couldn't make sense of it. She felt as if she were still asleep and all of this was just a horrible dream.

Why hadn't she been able to get out of her room?

She opened her eyes and saw Jake approaching the truck. He, too, was covered with soot, his handsome features tight with concern. With Zack's words ringing in her ears, she cracked the window down only an inch.

"Are you all right?" he asked. "God, Kate. I've never been so frightened for you."

"I'm fine, just shaken." It felt ridiculous to be speaking to him through the small crack in the window and again she wondered what had prompted Zack to tell her to lock herself into his truck. "Can you tell what happened?"

Jake shrugged. "All I know is that it looks like you lost part of your bedroom." He pointed toward the side of the house. "I'd better get back to help. I just wanted to make sure you were all right."

She nodded and he hurried away, disappearing into the darkness that now hung over the landscape. She wanted to see the damage. She wanted to know what was going on. Her impulse was to get out of the truck. This was her ranch and she should know what was happening.

What stopped her was the grim glint that had darkened Zack's eyes as he'd ordered her into the truck. Once again she leaned her head back and closed her eyes as the cool night air caressed her from the slightly open window.

She suddenly remembered what she'd been dreaming before she'd awakened. Her dreams had been filled with Zack. She'd dreamed of his arms around her, his lips taking full and utter possession of hers. She'd imagined running her hands over his hot, smoothly muscled chest and wanting him to make love to her.

She jumped as a knock fell on the driver window. She leaned over and unlocked the door for Zack. He slid into the seat, bringing with him the smell of wildness, of the remnants of an inferno.

For a moment, neither of them spoke. She felt his exhaustion and something deeper, darker, that she wasn't at all sure she wanted to explore.

"We got it out," he finally said. "The outer wall of your bedroom will need to be replaced. I don't know how much smoke damage is inside the house. I would guess your room is pretty well trashed between the smoke and water."

She fought a weary sigh. "I've never heard anyone say that ranch life isn't filled with challenges." He stared at her for a long moment, as if she'd somehow surprised him. "What were you expecting? Tears and feet-stomping?"

"It wouldn't be completely out of character," he observed.

She refused to rise to his bait. "So, could you tell what happened? How the fire started?"

He pulled a set of keys from his pocket. "I'm taking you to my place for the night."

She sat straighter in the seat. "I can't leave," she protested.

"You can't stay, at least not for the rest of the night." He placed the key in the ignition and started the engine. "I already told Sonny I'd make arrangements for you for tonight and he's posting a guard so nobody will go into the house through the damaged area."

"Zack, I can't leave my home."

"You can for tonight." His voice held a firmness that brooked no argument. He put the truck in gear and pulled away.

Kate frowned, a flutter of worry coursing through her. "You want to tell me what's going on?"

"I'll tell you this, I believe you about the stampede."

Of all the things she'd expected him to say, this hadn't been one of them. "How did we get from here to there?" she asked as they drove through the Bent Tree Ranch gates.

"I believe that it's possible somebody intentionally spooked your herd in an effort to hurt you because of what I found when I broke down your front door to get you out of that burning bedroom."

"What did you find?" Her heart began to hammer an unnatural rhythm.

"Somebody had tied a rope from your doorknob to the bathroom doorknob, making certain you wouldn't be able to get out of that room." He cast her a quick glance, his eyes glittering in the light from the dashboard. "Somebody tried to kill you tonight, Katie."

Chapter 6

Zack tightened his fingers on the steering wheel as he thought of the rope he'd found, the rope that had made it impossible for Katie to escape the inferno of her bedroom. It had been a devious mechanism for death.

He felt her gaze on him, stunned and with more than a touch of fear. He glanced at her, noting her widened electric-blue eyes, the paleness of her skin beneath the thick layer of soot.

"The way I see it, the plan was that you would probably be overcome by smoke, the fire would overwhelm the house and that rope would have eventually burned away, leaving no trace of its existence."

"Who spotted the fire?" she asked. Her voice held the slightest tremble.

"I did. I couldn't sleep so I stepped outside the bunkhouse and just happened to glance toward the main house. That's when I saw the flames and sounded the alarm."

"So, if you'd gotten a good night's sleep you probably would have found me dead in the morning."

His hands once again tightened on the steering wheel. "It would seem that was the intent."

She leaned back against the seat and released a weary sigh. "Any suspicions on who might have set the fire?"

He turned down the narrow road that led to the West property, wishing he had a different answer for her than the one he had. "None. When I woke up I just assumed all the men in the bunkhouse were sleeping, but appearances can be deceiving."

"So it might or might not have been one of the men in the bunkhouse." Her voice was as weary as he'd ever heard it.

"Katie, we're not going to figure this out tonight. I'll call Ramsey, but it's too dark for anything to be done tonight. Let's just get to my place, shower off the soot and smoke and get a few hours of sleep." He felt her gaze on him and turned to meet it. "What?"

"I don't even know where your place is. Do you live with your father and Smokey?"

"No, I live in a two-bedroom house that was originally built for the ranch manager. It's small, nothing fancy, but it's my space and gives me my privacy."

They didn't speak again as he pulled through the gates of the West ranch and he drove past the large, sprawling ranch house. "What's that?" she asked as his headlights fell on a smaller house that was in the building process.

"That's Tanner's place. It burned down several weeks

ago. While he's on his honeymoon, he's got a crew of men working to rebuild it."

"Yes I heard about that. Are fires a normal occurrence in the lives of the West men?" she asked dryly.

He offered her a tight grin. "I'd say it's less about the West men and more about the women they choose to hang out with."

He wondered how long she could maintain her calm, her seemingly nonchalant attitude in the face of her own attempted murder. He had a feeling she was suffering some sort of shock.

No lights shone from the small, two-bedroom cabin Zack called home. As he pulled up front he recognized that over the past couple of hours his mind had gone from unwilling investigator to determined bodyguard.

His head clicked and whirled with suppositions and possibilities as he parked and shut off the engine. "I want you to wait here while I check things out inside," he said.

By moonlight he once again saw her eyes widen. "Surely you can't believe somebody might be inside waiting for us."

"If I'm to believe what you told me about the stampede and with what happened tonight at your place, I'd be a fool not to consider any and all possibilities. I'll check things out, then we'll get settled inside."

Armed with a heavy-duty flashlight that he pulled from beneath his seat, he left her locked in the truck. As he approached his front door he cursed the fact that he didn't have his gun by his side, but rather had left it in the storage trunk at the foot of his bed in Katie's bunkhouse.

When he'd seen the flames of the fire, his gun had

been the last thing on his mind. All he'd thought about was getting to the house and getting her out of danger.

He had another gun inside and vowed that from now on he would go nowhere without a weapon. Using the powerful beam from the flashlight, he checked around the front door, making sure nothing appeared out of place or that the lock didn't appear tampered with.

He recognized that he was being overly cautious. Nobody could have known that he'd spirit Katie away to his place for the night, but he'd rather err on the side of caution just to be safe.

He unlocked the door and carefully eased it open, all senses on alert. He flipped on the light switch that illuminated the living room. Before going further into the house he went to the small desk, opened the bottom drawer and withdrew the 9 mm.

Armed with the gun, he set aside the flashlight and systematically checked the remainder of the two-bedroom cabin. It took only minutes for him to clear the cabin and to feel secure that nobody had been inside since he'd last been here.

He returned to the truck and opened the driver's door. "It's okay. You can come on in."

She got out of the truck and he followed her across the short expanse of grass and through the front door. It was at that moment he realized what she wore.

The silky, short, pink nightgown was smoke-blackened, but clung to her curves and exposed nearly the full length of her long, shapely legs.

For just a brief moment as he walked behind her and took in the figure beneath the skimpy gown, he felt as if he'd plunged back into the flames that had engulfed the side of the house.

The minute they were inside he closed and locked the door. She wrapped her arms around her shoulders and stood in the center of the room as if shell-shocked.

"Why don't I get you some clean clothes and you can get into the shower? Then you can catch a couple hours of sleep before you have to deal with anything else." He needed her to get out of that gown and into something, anything, less revealing. He had a feeling that if she stood just right in the light he'd be able to see right through the gauzy material.

She nodded and he went into his bedroom and found her a black T-shirt and a pair of boxers. From the hall linen closet he grabbed a clean towel and washcloth, then returned to the living room to find that she hadn't moved.

Accepting the things he handed her, her eyes flickered with a whisper of anger. "If I wasn't so exhausted, I'd be pissed off about all this."

He smiled, oddly relieved to hear those words. He'd rather her show a little spirit than be beaten into the ground. "Go take your shower. There will be plenty of time tomorrow to be pissed off."

As she disappeared into the bathroom, he breathed a sigh of relief and forced a mental image of her out of his mind. He had more important things to think about.

He went into the spare room to make sure it was ready for her. There wasn't much to get ready. He hadn't lied when he'd told her there was nothing fancy here.

While he'd been working for the family business, he'd spent little time here. The house was functional, but Spartan. The spare room held only a chest of drawers and a single-size bed. He knew the sheets on the bed were clean and was more interested in checking to make sure the window was locked and secure.

He left the room and went to the linen closet to grab a towel. He'd shower later, when she was asleep, but he wanted to wash off the worst of the soot and grime.

As he stood at the kitchen sink, using hot water and dish soap to scrub himself, his mind worked to make sense of what had happened.

Somebody had tied Katie into her bedroom then had set a fire outside her bedroom window. He replayed in his brain those moments when he'd first awakened from his nightmare and had stumbled toward the door to get out of the bunkhouse.

He'd told her that when he'd left the bunkhouse he'd assumed the men were sleeping, but the truth was, he wasn't sure of that at all.

He hadn't paid any attention to the other men in their beds. For all he knew those beds could have been empty. It had been dark and he'd been half asleep. He couldn't swear that all the men had been where they were supposed to be…in bed.

Not only did he have those men to worry about, he also needed to find out who else worked for Katie who lived in town. It would have been relatively easy for somebody to park their car some distance away and carry a can of gasoline and a length of rope for their mission of death.

How had the person gotten into the house? Had Katie neglected to lock the doors? Had an unlocked window been an open invitation? How many people had keys to the Sampson house? So many questions and no answers to speak of.

Good, that gave him time to call Ramsey. It took

him only minutes to speak with the sheriff, who assured him that the police would begin an investigation first thing in the morning.

He finished cleaning up, then went into the living room. The sounds of the shower let him know it would still be a few minutes before Katie came out of the bathroom.

He sat on the edge of the sofa. He would sleep here for the remainder of the night, where he could hear if anyone tried to come in through the front door or the back door in the kitchen.

Leaning back, he raked a hand through his hair and released a long, deep sigh. He'd vowed to himself he'd never do this again, that he'd never put himself into a position to be responsible for the safety of another human being. And now he found himself in the very position he'd vowed never to be in again.

But he couldn't walk away now. Even though there had been countless times in the past he'd personally wanted to throttle Katie Sampson, there was no way he could walk away from her and leave her alone and vulnerable for a killer.

Kate dried off and pulled the clean T-shirt on over her head, her mind curiously numb. The shirt hit her midthigh and swallowed up the shorts Zack had given her, making it appear she was clad only in the shirt. She wadded the ruined nightgown into a ball and threw it into the trash can next to the sink.

She found a comb in one of the vanity drawers and pulled it through her shoulder-length hair and it was only then that she realized how badly her hands trembled.

She set the comb aside and sat on the edge of the

tub, her stomach rolling with nausea as the enormity of what had just happened struck her.

The stampede had scared her, but if she were perfectly honest with herself she had to admit that she'd entertained just a tiny bit of doubt about what, exactly, had spooked the herd.

She'd believed she'd heard an air horn or something like that just before the stampede, but there had been a little part of her that had acknowledged that it might have been nothing more than a strange clap of thunder.

There was no way she could make what just had happened a strange quirk of nature. Somebody had tried to kill her. Just as somebody had already killed her father. A chill raked up her spine, a chill she worried would never go away.

The idea that somebody had tied her into a burning bedroom terrified her. Who would do such a thing? Who could hate her enough to want her dead?

She rose to her feet. The cold grip of fear certainly wasn't going to go away sitting here alone in Zack's bathroom.

As she entered the living room and he stood from the sofa, it was obvious he'd done some cleaning up of his own. His face and torso were clean and his hair damp.

"You can sleep in my spare room and I'll bunk here on the sofa for the night," he said. His eyes slid down the length of her and a muscle ticked in his jaw. "The sooner you get some sleep, the better we can deal with all this in the morning."

"I don't even know where to start dealing with all this," she replied. "But I'll tell you one thing, nobody is going to force me to stay away from the ranch. I'm here tonight because it's the smart thing to do, but tomorrow morning I intend to be back home where I belong."

"We need to take things one at a time. First thing in the morning we'll deal with the problem of making your place secure. Until that's done, you aren't staying there."

There was a note of finality in his voice that made her want to kick and protest. She felt as if she controlled nothing at the moment and the feeling was frustrating.

"I'd like to tell you that I intend to stay at my place whether it's secure or not. Emotionally I don't like that I feel as if you're making that decision for me, but intellectually, I know you're right. I can't stay there unless the damage to the wall in my room is repaired so nobody can just waltz into the house from outside."

"Thank you for seeing things my way."

She offered him a small smile. "I'm only seeing things your way because at the moment it's the right way."

"Let's get some sleep," he said. She followed him into a small bedroom and once again the icy hand of fear seemed to curl and squeeze around her heart. "I know it doesn't look like much, but the bed is good and firm and you'll be safe for the night."

He started out of the room but stopped as she called his name. For just a moment she didn't know what to say to him. She refused to tell him just how frightened she really was, didn't want him to know the depth of the despair that gripped her at the moment.

"I know we've butted heads in the past, but I'm glad you're here. I'm glad I'm not facing this all alone," she finally said.

"Sleep with the door open," he said, then turned and left the room.

Sleep with the door open? She'd like to sleep in his arms! Not because he was Zack, but rather because she felt so unsafe, so utterly alone.

Foolish woman, she thought as she pulled down the navy cord bedspread, then shut off the light in the room. Tomorrow when she got back to her place she'd get out her dad's gun and strap it to her side. She didn't need a man's arms around her, especially Zack's. All she needed was the comfort of a Smith & Wesson.

She'd expected to have problems falling asleep, but she awoke with the first stir of dawn lighting the sky. For a long moment she remained unmoving, playing and replaying the last two weeks of her life in her mind.

She'd thought the bottom had dropped out when her father had died. She'd believed nothing could get worse. She'd been wrong.

The night replayed in all its horror…the smoke, the flames and the moment when she'd felt sure death was a heartbeat away. If Zack hadn't noticed the fire and hadn't been able to break down her door, she wouldn't be here now.

The scent of freshly brewed coffee filtered in through the open door of her room, letting her know that Zack was already up and around.

She got out of bed, finger-combed her hair and pulled on the shorts she'd kicked off before climbing beneath the sheets the night before. It took her only a moment to make the bed, then she left the room.

Zack sat at the small kitchen table, facing the direction of the living room. He raised a hand at the sight of her. She returned the gesture and beelined into the bathroom. She wished she had a toothbrush, a hairbrush, her own clothes. But she used her finger to brush her teeth, Zack's comb to untangle her sleep-tousled hair, then left the bathroom in search of a cup of the coffee.

"Morning," she said to Zack as she entered his small kitchen area and spied the coffeemaker on the countertop. She poured herself a cup, then joined him at the table.

Clad in a clean white T-shirt and a pair of jeans, he smelled of minty soap and shaving cream. He might look rested, but he still had a grim expression on his face.

"Did you get some sleep?" she asked.

"Some…enough," he replied. "It's going to be a long day."

"I have a feeling it's going to be the first of many long days," she replied.

They sipped their coffee in silence, as if each mentally prepared themselves for what lie ahead. Kate's thoughts were purely practical ones as she wondered how much work it would entail to fix the damage from the fire so she could stay at her house tonight.

First the dead cattle and broken fencing and now this, additional expenses she hadn't planned. If these kinds of things continued, how long could she survive? She wasn't made of money. She shoved these disturbing thoughts aside.

She refused to be displaced from her father's home, from her own home. Her father would never want her to turn tail and run away from any conflict or danger. But he'd also want her to be smart.

"As soon as you're finished with your coffee, we'll head up to the main house and give that file to Dalton," he said, breaking the silence. "I'll call Jim Ramsey from there to check in. My sister should have a pair of shoes you can borrow until we get back to your place."

She downed the last of her coffee and stood. "I'm ready when you are. I'm eager to get back to the ranch and get things going on fixing up the damage."

He stood, as well. "Before we go anywhere I need to get you something else to wear." The muscle that had ticked in his jaw the night before was back.

"What's wrong with what I've got on?" Shorts and a T-shirt were not uncommon attire for her.

The muscle ticked faster. "The shorts are too short. It looks like you don't have anything but legs beneath that shirt." Before she could reply, he disappeared into his bedroom and returned with a pair of sweatpants. "Put these on, then we'll go."

Kate returned to the bedroom where she'd slept and took off the shorts and pulled on the sweatpants, her heart hammering rapidly, not in the rhythm of fear, but rather in the beat of something entirely different.

There had been just a moment as he'd handed her the pants that she'd seen something burning in his eyes, something she'd never expected to see from Zack West.

Desire.

She'd thought she'd seen it in the depths of his eyes last night just before he'd left her porch, but she'd dismissed it.

She'd assumed the crackling electricity between them had something to do with the negativity of their past relationship, but now she recognized what she'd been feeling for him was desire. And apparently he felt it, too.

She had little time to digest this novel idea. She had a sheriff to talk to, a house to rebuild and a killer to catch.

Zack was obviously ready to get the day under way for he stood at the front door, jingling the keys in his hand.

They drove toward the main house. The West residence was a huge, rambling ranch that made Kate's house look quaint. Of course, it had only been Kate and her father living at Bent Tree Ranch, while the West place had been home to Zack, his father, Smokey, Zack's four brothers and his sister.

A stab of ancient resentment stirred inside her and she consciously tamped it down, knowing the worst thing she could do was allow it to take hold.

They pulled up and immediately the front door opened and Smokey Johnson and Red West stepped out onto the front porch. Red was a big man, with the same broad shoulders as his sons and an easy warmth that made people immediately trust him.

Smokey was shorter, with gray hair and bushy eyebrows pulled together in a perpetual frown. Kate wasn't put off by the frown. She knew Smokey possessed a heart of gold beneath his gruff exterior.

Red embraced Kate in a quick hug, then looked at his son with open curiosity. "Awful early for a visit. Let's head inside and you can tell me what's going on."

Minutes later they were seated at the kitchen table being served coffee by Smokey. Kate knew that years ago Smokey had worked as ranch manager for Red, but a fall from a horse had left him with a limp and a new job helping to raise Red's kids.

Zack had just begun to fill them in on what was going on when Dalton entered the kitchen. Two years older than Zack's thirty-one years, Dalton shared the West green eyes and dark hair, but his features were softer, less sculptured than Zack's.

Dalton took the file folder Zack had carried in with him and agreed to get to work right away on the background checks, then Zack excused himself to go into the office to make a call to Sheriff Ramsey and get Katie a pair of shoes.

"Hell of a thing," Red said when Zack had left the room. "We're losing the good men and women of Cotter Creek right and left, first Joe Wainfield in that terrible tractor accident, then your father and now this… somebody trying to hurt you."

"If anyone can figure out who's behind this, it's Zack," Smokey said, his affection for Zack apparent in his gruff voice. "He's got a good head on his shoulders."

"Anything you need, Kate, anything we can do, you just let us know," Red added. "We're always here for Zack and we're here for you, too."

Her heart filled with a combination of gratitude tempered by a renewed flare of old resentment. The love and support Zack received from his family was evident on their faces, in their words, in the very air of the room.

So why hadn't that been enough for him? Why had he felt the need to steal her father's love and respect from her?

Chapter 7

By the time Katie and Zack returned to her ranch the sheriff and the fire chief were waiting for them.

"We've already questioned the ranch hands who are here," Sheriff Ramsey said. "Unfortunately nobody saw or heard anything. It's also going to be tough to check alibis. Most of the men will tell me they were in bed at the time the fire began."

"There's no question arson was involved," Chief Buddy Norval said. "From the fire pattern it's easy to see that the fire was set directly beneath the bedroom window." He looked at Kate. "You were lucky, little lady, that your men saw the fire and came to the rescue."

"There will be a full investigation," Jim promised as he got into his patrol car. He pulled away from the ranch, the fire chief following behind him.

"Golly, that was a lot of help," Katie said dryly.

Zack grimaced, knowing that the odds of them discovering the guilty party were negligible. Somebody had almost gotten away with murder the night before. It had only been a stroke of luck that had kept Katie alive.

In the early morning light the full extent of the damage was visible, although not as devastating as Zack had feared. The exterior plywood had burned away to reveal the 2x4s beneath, but at least they and the roof had been saved.

"Half a day's work and we'll have the plywood replaced," Zack said as they stood side by side surveying the damage. "We'll just board up the window for the time being. Let's go inside and take a look at the bedroom."

He followed behind her as they entered the house. She'd been unusually quiet since they'd left his place and he wondered what thoughts whirled around in her head.

She continued to surprise him with her composure, her calm in the midst of a storm. She had to be frightened, but she'd displayed little of that emotion.

He found himself wondering what life experiences in the past five years had transformed her from the out-of-control wild child into a reasonable, rational woman facing apparent danger with a calm, steely resolve.

"Looks like I won't be sleeping in here anytime soon," she said as they stepped into her bedroom. The walls were smoke-damaged and the floor and furnishings were wet from the fire-extinguishing water that had been sprayed through the broken window.

He watched as she walked to her closet and opened the door. The clothing inside appeared fine, but he knew each article would retain the smoky scent of the fire.

"Everything will have to be washed," she said, as if she'd tapped into his thoughts. She grabbed several pairs of jeans from a shelf, a handful of shirts and two pairs of shoes.

"Need some help?" he asked.

"No, thanks, I'll just take what I need for the next couple of days and get a load of laundry started." Although her voice remained calm, her features radiated the first cracks in her facade. She appeared pale, a small wrinkle danced across her brow and her lips were compressed in a taut line.

He followed her from her bedroom into the laundry room just off the kitchen. He watched as she put the first load into the washer and started the machine, then she turned to him, her frown deepening.

"Are you going to follow me around like a shadow all day long?"

"Depends on where you go and what you intend to do," he replied. "In case you've forgotten, somebody tried to kill you last night."

Her lips thinned as she clenched her jaw for a moment. "I'm not likely to forget anytime soon." She leaned back against the washing machine, her eyes holding a whisper of haunting.

Before he could reply, Jake's voice called from the front door. "Kate?"

Zack stepped aside so she could leave the laundry room, then followed her to the front door. He stood back and watched as Jake took Kate's hands in his.

"Are you all right? I was worried sick about you all night." The handsome blond cowboy cast a quick glance at Zack, the brief eye contact managing to radiate a wealth of resentment.

"I'm fine," she assured him, and didn't seem in a hurry to reclaim her hands from his.

"The sheriff and Chief Norval said the fire was intentionally set. What's going on?" Jake asked.

"I wish I knew," Katie replied, and finally withdrew her hands from his.

Jake stepped closer to her and Zack felt every muscle in his body tense. He told himself that it was a protective response, that he wanted to make sure Jake did nothing to harm Katie.

"What can I do to help, Kate?" he asked. "I'm not talking about feeding cattle and cleaning horse stalls. I'm talking about you personally, what can I do to help you get through this?"

Zack wanted to tell him to step back from her and give her a chance to breathe. For crying out loud, the man stood so close to her he had to be stealing all the oxygen in her immediate area.

"What I need most from you and the other men is to keep the ranch running smoothly and help get the side of the house repaired before nightfall," she said.

Zack could tell Jake didn't like her words, would have preferred something more personal from her. Maybe he wanted to rub her feet or stroke her brow, he thought irritably.

"Of course." He finally stepped back from her and Zack relaxed a bit.

"And tell Sonny I need to speak with him," she added.

He nodded. "I'll go find him right away."

"Thanks, Jake."

He flashed her a big grin, shot Zack another quick glance filled with simmering resentment, then left.

"That boy has got it bad for you," Zack observed as she closed the front door.

She sighed and worried a hand through her long, shining hair. "Too bad romance is the very last thing on my mind. In fact, I haven't had time for romance since I left college and came back here."

"What about before then? In college?" He had no idea why he'd asked the questions. It had nothing to do with his job in finding her father's murderer and keeping her alive. It fell under the heading of useless information he didn't need to know.

"In college I had time for romance," she answered succinctly, and offered no more details. "So, what's the plan for the day?"

"If you're going to stay inside and do laundry, then I'll go outside and help the men with the house. But the rules are that nobody comes inside unless I'm in here, too. No exceptions."

"That's not a problem. I'm not in the mood for company this morning. In fact, if I thought about it real hard, I could probably work up a case of crankiness."

"Maybe you need a nap," he offered, although he was feeling a bit cranky himself. "Neither one of us got a good night's sleep."

A knock on the front door interrupted the conversation.

She opened it to Sonny, whose features showed the same worry Jake's had worn. "I'm ashamed to say I slept through the excitement last night," he said, a hangdog expression on his face.

Kate placed a hand on his shoulder. "Don't worry about it, Sonny. All's well that ends well. The men from the bunkhouse rose to the alarm and thankfully managed to put out the fire before I got cooked."

"Hell of a thing," Sonny said, and shook his head. "The sheriff and Chief Norval spoke to all the men about the fire," he said. "I just want you to know that I can't imagine one of my men being responsible for something like that."

"I know. I don't want to think that one of our men could be responsible," Katie replied.

As the two spoke about what needed to be done for the day, Zack watched the old man carefully, knowing that from this moment on every single person in Katie's life was a potential suspect.

Still, it was difficult to think of Sonny as a viable suspect. The man had worked for Gray for years, had been a trusted right-hand man to Katie's father. That didn't let him off the hook entirely, but as far as Zack was concerned, there were others of more interest.

He thought about Jake. It was obvious the man desperately wanted a relationship with Katie. Was it possible the handsome face hid a devious mind?

Was it possible he'd killed Gray to get closer to Katie? Then had set the fire and planned to be the hero? As Zack remembered the night's events, Jake had been only a step behind him in getting through the front door and into Katie's bedroom.

Was it possible Brett Cook, who had been fired and rehired by Gray more than once, harbored such a hatred for his boss that killing him hadn't been enough? His hatred demanded more…the death of Gray's daughter?

Zack had nothing but speculation and even he recognized that this kind of speculation was wild and that he was reaching for answers. The truth of the matter was, he didn't have enough information on which to base any speculation.

When Sonny and Katie had concluded their conversation, Sonny left and Zack was once again alone with her. "I want you to lock the front door and don't let anyone inside. I'll work on the house and keep an eye on the men. Later this afternoon we'll figure out where we go from here."

He left her inside and went out to join the men. Besides the cowboys who had been his bunk mates for part of the night, there were others, as well.

Sonny introduced him to the five men who lived in town but worked the ranch each day. As Zack took stock of each of them he thought how much easier life would be if the homicidal tendencies in some men's hearts shone visibly from their eyes. Unfortunately, killers rarely wore their mask of evil on the outside.

The work on the house went on through the morning. Zack worked beside the others, not talking but listening to the conversations swirling around him. Later he would make notes of his impressions of each of the men who worked for Katie.

Zack had worked as a professional bodyguard for the family business since the time he was twenty-one years old. He knew through experience that much of the personal protection business wasn't just about muscle and guns, but rather crawling into the mind of a suspect and keeping logs and notes about those who might be potential suspects.

He welcomed the physical labor that made it difficult to think about Katie in that skimpy nightgown, Katie in his T-shirt, Katie in his arms. His sleep the night before had been almost nonexistent as he lay on the sofa with thoughts of Katie filling his head.

At noon Doc Edward's lumbering van pulled up. The middle-aged veterinarian greeted all the men like old friends.

"Zack, I heard through the grapevine that you'd taken up ranch work," he said.

Zack nodded. "Got tired of the family business and all the traveling I was having to do for that job." He was aware of Jake standing nearby, eavesdropping on the conversation. "I got a hankering for the smell of hay and the feel of a few calluses on my palms."

Mark Edwards smiled. "Nothing like a little physical labor and ranch life to set a man's world right." He looked at the new plywood on the side of the house. "What's all this?"

"Had a little trouble last night. Seems we've got a firebug in the area."

Edwards frowned. "Kate okay?"

"She's fine," he replied.

A small smile curved the vet's lips. "I'll bet she's madder than a wet hen. Kate's never been one to let somebody step on her toes without stepping back. I know that from the town council meetings."

Anything else he might have said was cut short by Sonny, who motioned toward him. "Well, I'd better get to work. It will take most of the afternoon to tag the cattle."

As Zack got back to work with the rest of the men, Mark's words played and replayed in his head. Obviously the temper he remembered Katie possessing was still there, she just hadn't displayed it to him yet. But apparently she'd displayed it to others.

Now all he had to figure out was if Gray had died because he had made somebody mad at him or if perhaps he'd died because Katie had made somebody mad as hell at her.

Kate sat at the kitchen table, listening to the washing machine agitate, her thoughts doing the same thing. She wanted to be outside, watching the cattle being tagged, overseeing the day's activities and interacting with the men.

But she knew she'd be too stupid to live if she just arbitrarily decided to go about her business as usual knowing that somebody had tried to kill her the night before.

So she had to be content following Zack's rules, remaining in the house alone while life went on as usual around her.

She spent the morning doing loads of laundry. While the washing machine washed and the dryer dried, she sat at the kitchen table making a list of things she wanted to do when life returned to normal.

Mostly it was a list of chores, things that had needed to be done for the past several years but had never been accomplished. The spare bedroom needed to be repainted, the root cellar on the side of the house needed to be cleaned out and she needed to pack up her father's clothing and donate it to one of the charities in town.

Her heart ached as she thought of this particular task. It would be the final goodbye to the father she had never really felt had given her the respect she'd hungered for, the unconditional love she'd sought from him all her life.

By noon she had changed out of the clothes she'd

borrowed from Zack and into one of the newly washed sundresses that had been hanging in her closet.

As she sipped a glass of iced tea she thought about what Zack had said about Jake. Even though she had feigned ignorance of Jake's obvious interest in her, she'd been aware of the cowboy's subtle overtures of romance.

Jake was handsome and nice and most any girl would probably be pleased to catch his eye, but Kate wasn't any girl. There was no electricity when Jake gazed at her, no tingles of pleasure or excitement when he touched her. There was no breathless anticipation when he came near.

She was still thinking about her lack of interest in Jake when Zack came inside at noon. He was shirtless, his T-shirt slung carelessly over one shoulder. His muscled chest glistened with sweat from his labor outside. Instantly, Kate's stomach muscles tightened at the compelling physical picture of utter masculinity he presented.

"We finished up the side of the house and Doc Edwards is here tagging your calves." He went to the cabinet next to the sink and withdrew a glass.

As he filled it with water Kate tried not to notice the breadth of his tanned back and the snug fit of his jeans over his buttocks.

She stared down at the paper where she'd been listing chores that she hoped to take care of when things got back to normal, but his half-naked image was burned into her brain.

Why, with everything that was happening in her life, did her hormones choose this moment to kick into high gear? And why, oh, why, did every hint of desire she'd ever felt always center around Zack West, a man she wasn't at all sure she even liked?

"Katie?"

The impatience in his tone made her realize he must have said something before her name. She looked up with a frown. "What?"

"I said we need to talk." He set his glass in the sink, then sprawled into the chair across from her at the table.

"Didn't your father and Smokey teach you any manners? It's not proper to sit at a table without a shirt." She couldn't concentrate with his beautiful bare chest staring her in the face.

"Gosh, a lecture on proper from Katie Sampson, what a concept," he said dryly, but to her relief he pulled on his shirt, covering the object of distraction.

He leaned back in the chair and studied her for a long moment. Her cheeks warmed beneath his scrutiny. "What?" she asked. Once again she felt not in control and that feeling provoked a touch of irritation inside her.

"We've been focused the past twenty-four hours on who might have wanted your father dead, on who he might have made angry. I think maybe it's time we look at you and who you've ticked off lately."

She sat back in her chair in surprise. "You think this is about me? That somebody killed Dad because they hate me?" Her heart clenched. The thought was positively horrifying.

"I think we need to consider all possibilities," he replied. "Doc Edwards led me to believe you might have gone a round or two with somebody at a town council meeting."

She frowned. "The town meetings are always a touch contentious and I certainly speak my mind when it comes to issues that affect our town, but I can't imagine that anything I've said to anyone there led somebody on a murderous rage."

"Having been on the receiving end several times when you decided to speak your mind in the past, I can tell you that you might not be aware of how you affect people," he said, one of his dark eyebrows lifting wryly.

The irritation that had flittered around inside her all morning flared stronger. His words both offended and frightened her. "Zack, I know I don't often mince words, but I get the feeling you keep making judgments about me from my childhood, not from who I am now."

His dark green eyes remained somber. "I don't know who you are now," he said with an edge to his voice.

"Then take the time to find out," she retorted sharply. He wasn't being fair to her and she didn't like it.

He pulled a hand through his dark, thick hair and released a sigh. "All I know is that somebody apparently wanted your father dead and now somebody wants you dead. We need to figure out why if we're going to figure out who." He leaned forward. "If you pissed somebody off at a town meeting, then I need to know about it."

She frowned thoughtfully. In the year she'd been back to the ranch she'd usually accompanied her father to the monthly town meetings. "I had words with Bill Garrett last month," she said.

"Bill Garrett? Isn't he the pesticide salesman?"

She nodded. "Dad and I had agreed that we no longer wanted to use his pesticide on the crops. I'd been encouraging Dad to look for alternatives to the strong chemicals that had been used for years."

"And Garrett took offense?"

"I think he was afraid our decision would become

everyone's decision and he'd be out of a job. He got loud and belligerent with me and told my father he was a wimp for letting his silly daughter make business decisions. I told Garrett he'd been breathing his own pesticides for too many years and had obviously suffered extensive brain damage."

One corner of Zack's lip slid upward, then fell. "So, Garrett's name goes on our list of potential suspects."

"I can't imagine Bill having anything to do with any of this. He's a creep, but he's a worm without backbone."

"You never know what a person is capable of," Zack replied. "Anyone else you've had words with?"

She frowned, her thoughts working through the many town meetings she'd attended. "The mayor, but everyone has words with him."

"About what?"

"About everything." She stood, finding Zack's nearness disconcerting.

"Can you be a little more specific?"

She began to pace the small area in front of the table. "Mayor Sharp has delusions of grandeur for Cotter Creek. He'd like to see the town transformed into a thriving tourist trap. He's always proposing changes that everyone votes down because we like Cotter Creek just the way it is."

"What kind of changes?"

She shrugged. "He wanted a Cotter Creek exit off the freeway. He wants to fill the downtown area with gift shops and stage mock gunfights on the weekends. He has ridiculous ideas, but I can't imagine him as a killer." She threw herself back in the chair. "I can't imagine anyone I know being a killer."

Her heart constricted and for a moment she was suffused with a guilt, a grief almost too difficult to bear. She swallowed hard. "If we find out that something I said or did to somebody is the reason Dad was murdered, I don't know how I'll live with it."

Zack's eyes darkened as he held her gaze. "You'd be amazed with what you can learn to live with." He shoved back from the table and stood. "So, here's the plan. I'll spend the day working around the house while you're locked inside. Then tonight I'll move my things from the bunkhouse into here."

She looked at him in surprise and stood, as well. "You really think that's necessary? I have Dad's gun here. I won't be taken by surprise again."

"I'm not willing to gamble with your life. Last night somebody got in through one of the windows, tied a rope from your bedroom door to the bathroom door, then left the house the way they had entered and you didn't hear a sound. You hired me on to find your father's killer, but whether you like it or not, you no longer have an additional ranch hand, you now have yourself a personal bodyguard."

Chapter 8

For the third time that evening Zack checked the doors and windows to make sure they were all locked up tight. He tried to ignore Katie, who sat on the sofa in the bright pink sundress that should have clashed with her red hair.

Instead the pink material made her eyes appear bluer, her skin look creamy and soft as the feminine and flowery scent of her filled every corner of the room.

He'd spent the afternoon working outside with the men, never venturing far from the house where she was locked inside. It hadn't been until sunset that he'd retrieved his personal items from the bunkhouse and made the move. That had been two long hours ago.

"Surely nothing will happen tonight," she said to him as he came from the bedrooms after checking the locked windows. "Whoever set the fire last night has to know we're on to him and won't try anything else anytime soon."

He pulled his 9 mm from his waistband and set it on the end table, then sat in the chair opposite her and frowned thoughtfully. "The problem is we just don't know what might happen and when." He frowned in frustration. "I can't get a handle on any of this. I don't have enough information to crawl into the head of the perp."

"Is that what you do? Crawl into the head of bad people?"

"That's what I try to do when I'm working a job."

Her gaze lingered on him. "I would think that's a tough way to make a living, constantly seeing the bad in people."

"It was tough," he conceded, "but the good part was, I kept a lot of nice people safe over the years. It was tough, but rewarding work." Until the end, he thought. Until Melissa's death.

"Then why did you quit?"

"I was ready for a change, needed a break." He didn't want to share with her the trauma that had led to his burnout with the family business. The depth of that pain he'd been unable to share with anyone.

"And I've sucked you right back in with the mess going on in my life," she replied softly. "I'd tell you I'm sorry I got you involved in all this, but I'm not. If I hadn't gotten you involved, I probably would have died last night in the fire."

He frowned. "It's interesting that so far all the incidents that have taken place have been to make everything look like an accident. Your father's death was dismissed as an accident initially. If the stampede had been successful in killing you then everyone would have talked about it as if it were an accident. Same with the fire last night. I noticed there were several candles in your bedroom. If the fire had burned successfully, then everyone would have figured it was because you were burning candles in your room."

"So, whoever wants me dead doesn't want to make it look like a murder."

"True, but somebody wants you dead, that's for sure." His voice was low, his tone grim. "And now all bets are off as to whether it needs to look like an accident or not."

It was her turn to frown. "It's a scary thing…to know that somebody wants you dead." She curled her legs up beneath her. "Anyone ever want you dead?" She flashed him a quicksilver smile that seemed to light her from the inside out. "I mean, besides me?"

Despite the tension that had taken possession of him the moment he'd set his duffel bag inside her front door, he couldn't help but return her smile. "You made it very clear you wanted me dead the night I carried you out of that party at the motel."

"I was so mad when you showed up," she replied. "I couldn't believe it when you walked in the door."

"You had no business being in that motel room with Jeb Walker and his friends." Jeb Walker had been bad news in Cotter Creek. At the time Katie had gone to the party, he'd been a thirty-year-old bully who liked young girls and drugs and she'd been a vulnerable, unworldly seventeen-year-old.

"I knew that," she replied easily. He looked at her in surprise and she continued. "I knew that bunch of people were too old for me, too wicked, and I had absolutely no business being there. But I wanted my father to come and drag me away, that's why I made sure he knew where I was going. Instead he sent you."

He heard the edge of an old wound not quite healed in her voice. "Katie, your father sent me after you because he thought it would be a lot less embarrassing if I showed up than if your daddy showed up to drag you back home where you belonged."

She laughed, a dry humorless sound. "Yeah, it was definitely less embarrassing for you to burst in, throw me over your shoulder and carry me out of there."

He grinned at her. "You survived the humiliation far better than I survived your temper fit. As I remember, besides practically clawing my face off, you also delivered a kick to my shins that I thought might leave me crippled for the rest of my life."

The grin that had curved her lips instantly fell. "I did make that scar on your face, didn't I?"

The regret that shone from her eyes bothered him. He didn't want anything soft and welcoming coming from her.

He stood, the tension back, tightening muscles he didn't know he possessed. "It was a long time ago. We were both hotheaded kids. What we need to do is focus on the here and now." He wiped a hand down his jaw, trying to center his thoughts away from how pretty she looked and toward who might want her dead.

"Have you gone through your dad's papers? His personal items and day planner to see if there might be a clue there?"

She uncurled her legs from beneath her, the delicate frown once again dancing in the center of her brow. "I went through the bills to see what was pending, but I haven't gone through his files or anything like that."

"What about his will? Were there any surprises there?"

She hesitated a moment and he thought he saw a flicker of resentment in her gaze. She looked away and shook her head. "No, there were no surprises. He left everything to me."

"Maybe it's time we go through Gray's files, see if we find any surprises there." He needed something to do, something besides sitting around and looking at her, talking to her.

He'd told her he didn't know who she was as an adult and she'd told him to take the time to get to know her. He didn't want to know her. He just wanted to find out who wished her harm, neutralize the threat, then return to his own cottage and his own solitary life.

"Dad's file cabinet is in his bedroom." She stood from the sofa and he followed her down the hallway to the master bedroom.

He knew she'd moved her things into the spare bedroom rather than into the room that had been her father's. She'd told him he could stay in here, but he'd insisted that he intended to sleep on the sofa in the living room.

Gray's bedroom was neat and tidy and looked as if it awaited his return. A pair of his reading glasses sat on the nightstand beside a paperback book. The closet door was open, displaying a collection of shirts and jeans hanging neatly in a row.

Katie walked over to the closet and closed the door, as if the sight of his clothes bothered her. "Earlier this morning I made a list of things that I wanted or needed to do when my life gets back to normal. Packing up Dad's things is on my list." She pointed to the wooden file cabinet in one corner of the room, then sat on the edge of the double-size bed.

"What else was on your list?" he asked, more to make conversation than from any burning need to know. He opened the first drawer of the file cabinet and gazed at the neatly tagged manila folders.

"Clean out the root cellar, paint the spare bedroom, weed out the flower gardens in the front yard."

Zack pulled out two thick files as she continued to tick off a list of chores. He carried the files to the bed and sat next to her. "You want to help me go through these or would you rather I do it myself?"

Her eyes darkened as she stared at the files in his hands. "If we both do it, we'll get through them twice as fast." She took one of the files from him. "What are we looking for?"

"I wish I could tell you," he said, and opened the file next to where he sat on the bed. "Often the key to a murder lies in the victim's life. I'm hoping in these files we'll find a reason why your dad was murdered, but I have no idea exactly what that might be."

"And if we can't find anything in Dad's life to point to the murderer, then we have to examine my life?"

"You have secrets to hide?"

Some of the tension left her features and she smiled. "You know me, Zack. I've never been able to hang on to a secret. Everything I do or say or think is right out there for anyone to know."

You know me, Zack. The problem was, he didn't know her and he had no idea what she might have done, said or thought to pique the rage of a killer.

He watched through narrowed eyes as she sprawled on her stomach on the bed, the file open in front of her. Her feet were by his side and if he looked in that direction he knew he'd get an eyeful of long, tanned leg.

His gaze slid sideways, up the tanned length of leg. No scabs on the knees, no cuts or scrapes to mar the perfection. He jerked his gaze back to the file next to him.

"Maybe we should take these into the kitchen. It would be easier to go through them at the table," he said.

There was no way he'd be able to concentrate with her long, shapely legs inches from where he sat. There was no way he could focus with the two of them on the bed, with her scent eddying in the room.

He stood and grabbed the file he intended to look at, grateful when she did the same. Together they went into the kitchen and sat side by side at the table.

"Why don't I make a pot of coffee before we get started?" she offered.

"Sounds good." He had a feeling that for the near future he'd be functioning on a combination of caffeine and adrenaline. Sleep would be light and in snatches as night was a vulnerable time and killers loved the cover of darkness.

The fragrance of the freshly brewed coffee covered the scent of her, but didn't ease his hyperawareness of her. He told himself it was because she was in danger, that he always became acutely aware of the clients he had to protect. But he had a feeling it was something more than that.

If he went back in time to when he'd pulled her out of that motel room party, he had to admit to himself that on that night he'd felt his first stir of physical desire for her.

She'd been wearing a pink dress and as he'd thrown her over his shoulder he'd been intensely aware of slender curves and the bewitching hint of full maturity.

He now watched as she poured them each a cup of coffee. Those curves were fuller now, much more inviting than they'd been years ago.

She set a cup in front of him then returned to her seat at the table. "Thanks," he murmured, then opened the file folder and gazed at the contents.

For the next few minutes they focused on the files in front of them. Zack's file held financial ledgers for the ranch for the last two years and it was a relief to focus on the numbers in the ledger.

He went through them with meticulous care, seeing nothing that would cause a raised eyebrow. No strange income, no strange expenses, just the usual ranch-related financial reports.

"I've got nothing here." He closed the file. "What about you?"

She shook her head, her hair gleaming in the overhead light. Years ago he'd always thought of her hair as just plain red, but there was nothing plain about the gold and copper strands.

"Nothing here, either. Just tax returns and everything looks okay." She stood. "I'll go get some more of the files." She held out her hand to take the file from him and as she did their fingers brushed.

An electric current tingled through him and he wondered how long he'd be able to share her space, spend time with her and not act on the intense desire for her that had filled him since the moment he'd walked into the hospital emergency room.

Kate was grateful to escape the kitchen. She'd thought her dad's bedroom too small for the both of them, but in the last few minutes she'd felt as if the walls of the kitchen had closed in, making the room feel half as large as it was.

As she returned to the bedroom to retrieve more files, she tried to put her feelings for Zack in proper perspective. She'd always been aware of a fierce physical attraction to him and it was just as strong now as it had been years ago. But she couldn't forget that he'd stolen her father from her.

She had to remember that he was the man who had been responsible for much of the sadness, the utter loneliness of her life. He'd had a family of his own, but had stolen the only family she'd had away from her.

She had a feeling that much of the desire she felt for Zack at the moment had to do with the new vulnerability she felt. Without her dad in her life, she was completely alone. She'd made few friends since returning to town after college.

She'd been so bent on showing her father she was a responsible, competent partner that she hadn't taken the time to forge friendships or to begin relationships with any of the single women or men in town.

Now she found herself wishing she had a girlfriend, somebody she could talk to about her confusing emotions where Zack was concerned, about the fear that now ruled her every movement, about how overwhelmed she felt about everything in her life at the moment.

Grabbing a handful of files, she shoved those

thoughts away. She'd never had much time for needy, weak people and she certainly didn't intend to become one herself. She'd get through this.

She returned to the kitchen to find Zack pouring himself another cup of coffee. "This is probably a waste of time." She placed the files in the center of the table.

"Maybe." He carried his coffee cup back to his chair and sat. "But it's been my experience that it's the little things that sometimes matter the most. I'd rather waste time than overlook a clue."

She sat back in her chair with a frown. "It should be Jim Ramsey doing all this investigation work. As sheriff, that's his job."

"True," he agreed easily. "But would you be comfortable leaving the investigation in his hands?"

She grinned ruefully. "I wouldn't be comfortable leaving a donut in his hands."

He returned her grin as he reached for one of the files. She grabbed a file, too, trying not to think about how handsome he looked when he smiled.

Again they focused on the material contained in the files. No matter how hard she tried to concentrate on the information, Zack kept intruding into her thoughts.

"How did you meet my father?" she asked, realizing she'd never known what had brought the teenage Zack and her father together in the first place.

He leaned back in his chair and although only a hint of a smile curved the corner of his lips, his eyes warmed as if the memory was a pleasant one.

"I was sixteen-years-old and having a bad night. I wound up sitting on the bench in front of Crazy Joe's bar looking for somebody of legal age who'd go inside and buy me a bottle of booze."

She looked at him in surprise and this time his smile involved his entire face. "Don't look so shocked. I'd guess most every teenager suffers at one time or another with a dose of healthy teenage rebellion."

"Ha, you didn't act that way the night you dragged me out of that motel room," she countered. "That night you were full of self-righteousness and judgmental and acted like you'd never seen anyone indulging in a little rebellion."

"By that time I was older and wiser and I couldn't believe you had been so foolish." His eyes darkened just a bit. "You could have been drugged or raped that night."

She felt the flush that warmed her cheeks. "Let's get back to the part of the story where you were young and rebellious and probably foolish, as well."

He grinned. "Okay, anyway, there I was sitting on the bench trying to get somebody, anybody, to buy me some booze and along comes Gray. He sits next to me on the bench and asks me which of the West boys I am. I told him who I was and we just struck up a conversation."

His smile faded but the light in his eyes remained warm, almost soft. "I can't tell you what we talked about that evening. I just remember we sat on that bench for hours and at the end of it all Gray told me that if I ever felt like talking or just needed to sit a spell that his porch was a much better place to sit than in front of Crazy Joe's. That was the beginning."

The beginning of the end as far as Kate was concerned. She'd been ten years old when Zack had first started coming around in the evenings. Her reaction to him had been one of irritation and resentment. She'd hated the handsome young man who seemed so easily to capture her father's time and attention.

She'd always believed deep in her heart that her father had wished she were a boy, that his life would have been much easier if Kate's mother had died and left him with a son rather than a daughter. As far as Kate was concerned, Zack was the son her father had always wanted.

"Why didn't you come to his funeral?" she asked as a burst of that ancient resentment fluttered through her.

He hesitated a long moment, then replied. "I did. I was out at the cemetery, but I stood up on the hill and watched the proceedings from there."

Shock filled her. "Why didn't you come down and join the rest of us?"

The light of his eyes was warm, so soft, then hardened before he looked away from her and took a deep sigh. "I'd just come off a bad assignment and didn't feel like socializing. I said my private goodbye to your dad and that's all that was important to me."

He cleared his throat and leaned forward. "And now we'd better get through these files. It's getting late and I'd like to get through these before we call it a night."

As he focused back on the paperwork, she did the same but her thoughts were on the information he'd just given her. So, he had been at the funeral.

She hadn't realized until this moment how much she'd resented him for not being there. But he had, saying his own private goodbyes.

He'd said he'd come off a bad assignment and she wondered what he meant. Was the bad assignment what had made him quit the family business? She shot him a quick glance. His expression looked closed off and forbade her to ask any questions about what he'd experienced before he'd returned to Cotter Creek.

Besides, she reminded herself, it was none of her business. She had no desire to know Zack West in any capacity other than his work as her investigator and bodyguard.

It was nearly ten when they grabbed the last two files from the center of the table. Kate opened hers at the same time she stifled a yawn. Exhaustion had set in about a half an hour ago. She'd had little sleep the night before and the bed in the spare room was calling her name louder and louder with each passing moment.

The file folder in front of her was filled with what appeared to be receipts for farm equipment, some un-framed awards from her dad's bronco riding days and miscellaneous other papers too important to throw away but not falling under any particular category.

Occasionally she found a slip of paper holding her father's handwriting and the sight squeezed her heart with pangs of grief. Her father hadn't been an old man. He'd only been fifty-five years old, far too young to die.

She still couldn't believe that he wouldn't be around to walk her down the aisle when she eventually married, wouldn't be here to spoil and love the grandchildren she might have given him. She was only twenty-three, too young to be all alone in the world.

Thick emotion pressed against her chest and she knew it was probably overtiredness that made her feel vulnerable to the grief she'd tried desperately to keep at bay.

"Nothing here," Zack said with a weariness in his voice.

"I just have a few more papers to go through."

"You want any more coffee? If you don't, I'll go ahead and shut it off."

"No more for me," she replied. "I can't wait to finish this up and get some sleep." She returned her attention to the papers in front of her.

All trace of sleepiness disappeared as she picked up the next-to-last piece of paper in the file. She stared at it for a long moment, knowing what it was and yet not understanding its very presence.

"Katie?"

She looked up at him as her heart plunged into the pit of her stomach.

Chapter 9

Katie had one of the most expressive faces Zack had ever seen. There had never been an emotion that she could hide and the expression on her face now indicated to him that she'd found something...something not necessarily pleasant.

"What is it?" he asked. He returned to the table as she held up two sheets of paper.

"It's an appraisal."

"An appraisal? Of what?"

"The ranch...this house, the land." She held the papers out to him and he saw the slight tremble of her hands.

He took the papers from her and looked at them, noting that apparently the appraisal had been done six months ago. It was a straightforward form, detailing the condition of the house and the outbuildings, a legal description of the property and the appraisal price of value.

He looked at Katie once again and noted the paleness of her skin, the hollowness in her eyes, and knew she was upset, but he didn't understand why.

"I don't see how this could have anything to do with your dad's murder," he said. He set the papers down on the table. "What's wrong, Katie?"

She stood and without saying a word left the kitchen. He stared after her in surprise, wondering what was going through her head.

He waited a moment to see if she'd return. When she didn't, he got up from the table and went into the living room, but she wasn't there. Frowning, he went down the hallway, past the empty bathroom and the master bedroom to the spare room. The door was closed but he could hear that she was inside and she was crying.

For a long moment he stood in front of the door wondering what he should do, if he should do anything. What was wrong with her? Was it simply grief that had sent her away from the table and into the bedroom?

He knocked on the door. "Katie?"

"Go away," her muffled voice replied.

He told himself there was nothing he'd love to do more than go away and leave her alone. He had no desire to entangle himself in her grief, her drama, but he couldn't go away. Not now, not knowing if the reason she was crying had anything to do with a potential motive for her father's murder.

He twisted the doorknob and opened the door. She sat at the foot of the double bed and scowled at him, her cheeks wet with tears. "How can you possibly mistake 'go away' for 'come in'?"

He ignored the scowl and her words and sat next to her. "You want to tell me what has you so upset?"

She bit her bottom lip as if to stem another flow of tears. Her hands clenched tightly in her lap and the sight of her whitened knuckles let him know how hard she fought for control.

"Katie, talk to me," he said softly as silent tears once again trekked down her cheeks. There was something heart-wrenching about a woman weeping without sound, without any discernible sobs.

She took a deep breath and unclasped her hands, then moved them up to wipe at her cheeks. "That appraisal was done six months after I came back here from college, six months after I told Dad that I wanted to work the ranch, be his partner."

She stood and walked over to the window, her back to him. "He never believed in me. That's what the appraisal was all about. He never believed I would be able to run this place and so he was going to sell out."

Zack got up and walked to the window. With one hand he pulled the cord to drop the miniblind and with the other hand he took her arm to steer her away from the window.

Even though she was caught up in an emotional tailspin, he was aware that she'd be a perfect target standing in front of a lit window at night.

She allowed him to guide her back to the bed, where they once again sat side by side. "Katie, you can't know the reasons your dad had an appraisal done. It's possible it had absolutely nothing to do with any sale of the ranch."

"Why else would he have one done?" she asked, her voice filled with the yearning of a woman wanting answers that made sense, answers that would still the misery coursing through her.

"There are lots of reasons people have appraisals done. Maybe he intended to remortgage the ranch or get some kind of equity loan. Maybe he was just curious as to what this place was worth in today's market."

Her blue eyes held his gaze and he saw how desperate she was to believe him. "Katie, the appraisal was done six months ago. If your father intended to sell the ranch, don't you think he would have taken the next step? Told you his plans? Prepared you for losing your home?"

Some of the hollowness in her eyes disappeared. "Surely he would have done that," she agreed slowly. She reached out and covered one of his hands with one of her own. "Thank you, Zack." She laughed uneasily. "I guess I just got a little carried away."

"Look, we're both tired. It's been a long day and what we both need is a good night's sleep." He stood, the action pulling his hand from hers. "Go to bed, Katie, with the knowledge that Gray would have never sold this place without telling you. He would never have put you out of your home. He loved you, Katie. He loved you more than anyone else on this earth."

For a moment her eyes shimmered with new tears. "Good night, Zack," she said softly.

"Sleep with the door open, okay? And I'll see you in the morning." He left the bedroom and breathed a sigh of relief. In the few hours he'd been inside her house he'd learned that bedrooms were much too small for the both of them.

Over the years there had been occasions when Zack had bunked on Gray's sofa. He knew the linens he needed would be in the closet in the hallway. He grabbed a sheet and a spare pillow from the closet then returned to the living room.

It took him only minutes to prepare the sofa for sleeping. He shut off the kitchen light, then the one in the living room. He pulled off his T-shirt, then eased down into the familiar contours of the sofa, his 9mm on the coffee table within easy reach.

As he lay there in the dark he could hear the sounds of Katie preparing for bed. A vision of her in that pink filmy nightgown flashed in his head. Did she have another one of those sexy little nightgowns? Was that what she was putting on right now?

As always when he was on an assignment, all his senses were more finely attuned. He heard the chirp of crickets coming from someplace outside the living room window, the hum of the refrigerator from the kitchen. The light went out in the spare room and he heard the groan of the mattress beneath Katie's weight as she settled in for the night.

He tried to keep his mind away from the mental vision of Katie in bed, wearing something skimpy and smelling like a field of wildflowers. He needed to stay focused on business.

He heard nothing amiss, nothing to indicate any danger lurking nearby. If it were physically possible, he would have gone without sleep until the threat to Katie had passed, but human limitations made that impossible.

The best thing he could do was sleep lightly and keep in mind that danger could occur at any time. With this thought in mind he closed his eyes and willed himself to relax.

* * *

It was a beautiful day. The sun shone brightly as he stood on the courthouse steps, waiting for Melissa to arrive. Summer rode the air with its sweet, flowery fragrance and he felt the pride of a job well done.

He'd managed to keep her safe from her abusive ex-husband. She would have a bright and wonderful future and after all the abuse and misery she'd experienced, she now deserved all the happiness that life could bring her.

That was his wish for her...a life of happiness and love. He straightened as he saw her car pull into the parking lot. She stepped out of the car, wearing a pristine-white sundress. He raised a hand in greeting and at that moment a shot rent the air and the front of her dress exploded in a blossom of red.

Zack shot up, his heart pumping like a piston. It took only seconds for him to orient himself and to realize that the woman in his dream had not been Melissa, but rather had been Katie.

He wiped a hand down his face as his eyes adjusted to the semidarkness of the room broken only by the shafts of moonlight that filtered through the windows.

Katie.

How had she made it into the nightmare that had haunted him for the past month?

A sound from the kitchen froze his blood. He stared toward the kitchen doorway at the same time his hand reached out and he grabbed his gun.

Somebody was in the house...in the dark of the kitchen. Without making a sound, scarcely breathing, he eased up to a sitting position, his mind whirling with suppositions.

Had the windows in the kitchen not been locked? He'd checked them twice. Had he missed something? He slid off the sofa and stood, the gun steady and reassuring in his hand.

He approached the kitchen doorway, nerves calm, blood cold. As he moved closer to the door he spied a shape that didn't belong standing just to the side of the refrigerator.

"Freeze!" he said, and jumped into the room.

"Don't shoot! It's me."

Zack muttered a curse, lowered his gun hand and hit the light switch to see Katie standing next to the refrigerator eating out of a carton of ice cream. "Jeez, Katie. I could have killed you."

"Sorry. Want some?" She held out a spoonful of black-speckled green ice cream. "It's chocolate mint."

"What in the hell are you doing in here?" He was angry, but not at her. He was angry because she'd managed to sneak right past him and into the kitchen. He'd been sleeping too damned soundly. Mistakes like that got clients killed.

She put the lid back on the ice cream carton and placed the carton back in the freezer. "I couldn't sleep. I sometimes get up in the middle of the night and eat ice cream. It soothes my nerves."

"Yeah, well, it could have gotten you shot," he retorted. He set the gun on a nearby countertop, hoping the surge of adrenaline would slowly filter out of him.

She put her spoon in the sink then leaned back against the counter, her gaze holding his intently. He was grateful she wasn't wearing one of those silky, see-through nightgowns but instead was clad in an over-size T-shirt.

"Are you ready to go back to bed?" he asked.

"Not just yet." Her eyes held a strange light as she continued to gaze at him. "You were moaning."

"Excuse me?" He returned her gaze blankly.

She pushed off the counter and advanced toward him, and every muscle in his body tensed once again. "When I came through the living room and passed the sofa, you were moaning in your sleep."

He stared at her, horrified by the very idea. "You must have been mistaken."

"No. I'm not mistaken." She moved to within mere inches of him, so close he could feel the heat of her body radiating toward him.

Had he moaned her name? Had the nightmare of her death so troubled him that he'd whispered her name in his sleep?

"Go to bed, Katie." His voice was deep, gruff, as he recognized his tenuous grasp on control.

She stood too close, he'd been fantasizing about her too much and he knew if he didn't get control right now something might happen that would forever change the relationship between them.

"Zack, I'm feeling very alone right now and I don't want to go back to bed. I want you to hold me."

Before he had a chance to step away, she moved closer, so close her breasts touched his chest, so close she leaned her head forward on his shoulder.

The sweet scent of her hair filled his nose as the warmth of her curves filled his arms. He held himself stiff, not yielding to his desire until she curled her arms around his neck and raised her head to look at him.

Her lips were parted, as if in open invitation, and despite all his firm resolve to do otherwise, he leaned his head forward and captured her lips with his own.

She tasted of minty ice cream and forbidden pleasure and as she returned his kiss he knew he was about to make a mistake, but was helpless to stop himself.

When she'd gotten up to eat ice cream she'd had no intention of disturbing Zack, although she could have sworn as she walked by his sleeping form he'd moaned her name.

But when he'd burst into the kitchen, gun drawn, with his bare chest gleaming and the jeans slung low over his lean hips, she'd been electrified.

Now, with his lips scorching hers, she knew she wouldn't be satisfied until he possessed her completely, entirely. She wouldn't be satisfied until she was weak with exhaustion, sated by his lovemaking.

His kiss was just as she'd always imagined it would be, hot and demanding, filled with barely leashed passion and a simmering of underlying danger.

His hands tangled in her hair as his tongue danced with hers. She moved her hands from the nape of his neck down his smooth, muscled back and her knees weakened at the sensual feel of his skin beneath her fingertips.

As she leaned closer to him she felt his arousal, knew with certainty that the electricity she'd felt every time he was near wasn't one-sided. He wanted her, too, and the knowledge of that drove her half insane.

"Katie," he whispered as he tore his mouth from hers. She couldn't imagine him calling her anything else, knew that she'd never ask him to call her Kate again.

He placed his hands on her shoulders and pushed, putting an inch of separation between them. "We need to stop this now. We're about to make a big mistake."

If he'd released her entirely, she might have come to her senses, but he didn't. His fingers lingered on her shoulders, caressing with a heat she felt through the thin material of her T-shirt.

"Most of the mistakes I've made in my life have been unintentional," she said, her voice husky with the desire that coursed through her. "If this is a mistake, then it's one I'm making intentionally."

She took one of his hands and he grabbed his gun from the countertop as she led him from the kitchen. Neither of them spoke a word as they went through the living room and down the hallway to the door of her spare bedroom.

It was only then that he stopped in his tracks, his features evident in the moonlight illuminating her bedroom.

"Katie, if I go in there with you it won't be just to hold you." There was not just a warning in his voice but a promise, as well.

"I don't want you just to hold me. I want you to make love to me, Zack." She saw the flare of his eyes at the same time she reached out and stroked her hand down his bare chest.

He caught her hand with his and held it tight. "It won't change anything, it won't mean anything."

"I don't want to wear your ring or be your girl. I just want you to make love to me tonight." She pulled her hand from his and stepped back from him.

She felt as if this moment had been predestined from the time she was an adolescent girl trying to understand the feelings that Zack evoked in her. She'd wanted him before she understood what want meant.

She reached down, grabbed the bottom of her T-shirt and with one graceful movement pulled it off over her head, leaving her clad only in a pair of wispy silk panties. She dropped the T-shirt to the floor, then turned to enter the room. "Are you joining me?"

She gasped as he grabbed her by the hand and whirled her back around to face him. He grabbed her to him with a force that stole her breath away. He crashed his lips to hers, plundering her mouth with fiery intent.

Together, with mouths still locked, they moved toward the bed. She was vaguely aware of him placing his gun on the nightstand before he tumbled her backward onto the mattress.

Heart pounding, she watched in the moonlight as he unzipped his jeans and took them off, leaving him clad in a pair of briefs that couldn't hide his arousal.

He joined her on the bed, gathering her into his arms as his mouth once again sought hers. She felt just as she had the night before when she'd been dreaming and in her dream Zack had been kissing her, caressing her, and she'd been hot...so hot.

His hands moved between them to cup her breasts and as his thumbs razed across her nipples she gasped with pleasure. His scent worked like an aphrodisiac on her. The combination of his woodsy cologne and the underlying male musk exhilarated her, stimulated her to a height of sensation and pleasure she'd never known before.

His strong legs pressed against hers, his arousal hard against her center, the only barrier their underwear. He raised his head and looked at her, his eyes glittering like something feral and wild.

"I've wanted to do this since I walked into the ER and saw you sitting there." His voice was nothing more than a low rumble of suppressed emotion.

"I've wanted this since I was sixteen years old and my stomach tied in knots every time you were around," she replied breathlessly.

The hunger between them was palpable in the charged air. "You know this is crazy," he said.

"Doing crazy things has always been a part of my existence." She moved her hips against his, saw his eyes darken just before he dipped his head and captured one of her nipples with his mouth.

A rush of sweet heat flowed from his mouth through every vein in her body as his lips and tongue teased her. It was so easy to forget any resentment she might feel toward him, to let go of any other emotion the last couple of days had wrought and just give herself to the pleasure and excitement of him.

His hands left her breasts and blazed a trail down her rib cage, across the flat of her abdomen and she gasped again as he rubbed his hand across the front of her panties.

All the nerve endings in her body seemed to be concentrated beneath his hand and she trembled with his touch. Wanting to be an active participant in their lovemaking, she reached down and traced the length of his hardness outside his briefs.

He moaned, a sound that seemed to come from someplace deep inside him. The wordless expression of pleasure did more for her than anything he might have said. Emboldened, she plucked at his briefs, wanting them off, wanting to feel him without the barrier that stood between them.

He pushed her hand aside, as if her touch irritated him, but she knew it wasn't irritation that drove him to slide her panties down her thighs and off her legs. It wasn't irritation that sent him off the bed to remove his briefs.

Before he returned to the bed she heard him fumbling with his jeans. After a moment he was back on the bed, this time pulling her naked length firmly against his as their mouths met in hunger.

A condom, she thought with relief as she realized what he'd done in the minute that he'd been out of bed. He'd apparently had a condom with him and had put it on, assuring both her safety and his own.

She moved her hips against him, rubbing against his turgid length with a fervor she'd never known before. His hands gripped her buttocks, aiding her as she moved against him in a frenzy. Gasps and moans of pleasure escaped her lips as the tension in her body increased and she felt herself shattering into a million pieces.

Before she could recover from the mind-blowing intensity of her release, he entered her. She sighed at the feel of him so deep, so full, inside her. She started to move her hips, but he gripped them and held her tight, unmoving.

His eyes glittered down at her. "Wait," he whispered, the muscles in his face taut with tension. "Give me a minute or this is going to be over before it begins."

He stroked her hair away from her face and kissed her, his mouth soft and gentle against hers. She'd expected his passion, she'd anticipated the lust, but she hadn't expected tenderness.

As his lips softly plied hers, she felt a warmth invade her heart, a warmth unwelcome and just a little bit frightening.

Before she could assess her own emotional reaction, he moved his hips, stroking into her and driving all other thoughts out of her mind.

The passion that had momentarily ebbed peaked to a new height as they moved together in unison. They began slow, almost languid, kissing with gasps and moans of pleasure at the same time he stroked long and deep inside her.

It didn't take long before slow became more frenzied as need exploded. Once again tension coiled inside her, a sweet evocative tension that begged for release.

His mouth nipped at her neck as he possessed her and she felt herself climbing up...up...spiraling completely out of control. Her climax came at the same time he tensed against her and cried out her name.

Once their breathing had begun to resemble a rhythm more normal, he eased from the bed and disappeared out into the hall.

She rolled over onto her side and wondered if he'd come back to the bed or if he'd go directly to the sofa and spend the remainder of the night without saying another word to her.

She hoped he came back. If he didn't, it would somehow diminish what had taken place between them and it had been wonderful.

The relief that coursed through her as he came back into the bedroom and slid next to her beneath the sheets surprised her. "I thought maybe you'd go right back to the sofa when you left," she said.

He raised one arm beneath his head and with the

other pulled her closer against his side. "I got up and checked out the house, made sure everything was still secure. Besides, it breaks one of Smokey's rules of engagement to get up in the middle of the night and leave a woman you've just had sex with."

She lay her head on his chest, enjoying the pound of his heartbeat beneath her ear. "Smokey has rules for sexual encounters?" she asked in surprise. "What about your dad?"

"Dad gave all us boys the general birds-and-bees talk, but it was Smokey who got down to the nitty-gritty."

"Like what?" It wasn't so much that she was burning with the need to know what Smokey had passed on to the West boys, but she loved the sound of his deep voice in the darkness of the room, the slight rumble of his chest beneath her face as he spoke.

"Never leave the house without a condom in your wallet. Never kiss and tell no matter how much you want to brag about a conquest, and always make sure your partner is pleased before you please yourself."

He'd certainly done that, she thought. For a moment they were silent. Although his heartbeat was slow and regular, she felt the tension in his muscles.

"Zack, I know you'd rather be anywhere but here," she murmured sleepily. "You don't have to worry about this changing anything between us. I know I'm not your idea of Cinderella and you certainly aren't my idea of Prince Charming. I'm just glad you're here now. I've been so lonely since Dad's death."

"Go to sleep, Katie," he said softly.

She closed her eyes and told herself that it wouldn't have mattered whose warm body was next to her, she just felt better not being alone in the darkness of the night.

She was almost asleep when a thought struck her. "It's weird—isn't it?—that what happened to Dad and what almost happened to me was made to look like an accident and poor Joe Wainfield really did die in an accident."

Chapter 10

Zack sat at the kitchen table sipping coffee, grateful that Katie was still asleep in the bedroom. He wasn't ready to face her, needed some time to think about the huge mistake he'd made the night before.

Making love with Katie was right up there among the worst mistakes of his life. And like all the other big mistakes of his life, it was an experience that couldn't be easily dismissed or forgotten.

She'd been softer than he'd expected, far more giving as an intimate partner. She'd seduced him from the moment he'd burst into the kitchen.

She'd seduced him with the enticing light in her eyes, the breathless length of her sexy legs and the words he needed to hear to allow himself to be seduced.

Who was he fooling? She might have seduced him, but he had been ripe and ready for her. The desire he'd felt for her since he'd walked into the emergency room had simmered and burned in his gut every moment they'd been together. It had taken very little to nudge him into acting on it.

Zack shoved away from the table and walked to the window, where dawn's light illuminated the eastern skies. The problem was that somewhere in the back of his mind he'd thought that by acting on his desire where Katie was concerned, he'd destroy it and never be bothered with it again.

But when he'd opened his eyes this morning to find her warm body curled up next to his, her beautiful copper hair splayed against the pillow and the scent of her surrounding him, his desire for her had kicked him in the gut once again.

He'd wanted nothing more than to awaken her by kissing the soft, sleep-warmed skin of her throat, by caressing her full breasts, by burying himself in her moist heat once again.

Instead he'd slid out of bed, angry with her and even angrier with himself. She'd said all the right words to put his worries to rest. She'd assured him that he wasn't her idea of a Prince Charming, but that didn't make their lovemaking any less a mistake.

The last thing he could afford was to become emotionally attached to Katie. She was the daughter of a beloved friend, nothing more. She was a job, nothing more. That's the way it had to be for his own peace of mind.

He frowned as he saw several men leaving the stables on horseback. Jake and Brett rode out to begin the morning chores. Jake directed a glance toward the house and Zack could almost feel the man's animus radiating across the yard and through the windowpane.

By staying in the house with Katie, Zack knew he had garnered Jake's hostility. What he didn't know was what the man might be capable of, what role he might have played in Gray's murder.

Until Zack had more information about all the men working the ranch, he knew he'd do well to watch his back as well as Katie's. He returned to the table and once again picked up his cup of coffee.

Joe Wainfield. The name that Katie had muttered the night before just before falling asleep filled his head. Joe had been killed in what had been ruled a tragic farm accident when he'd somehow fallen off his tractor and the vehicle had run over him.

Katie's sleepy comment hadn't made much impact on him the night before when his head had still been filled with the overwhelming pleasure of their lovemaking. But now he found himself considering her words.

It was interesting that everything that had happened here at Bent Tree Ranch had been made to look like an accident and on the ranch next door to Katie's an accidental death had occurred.

It could be nothing more than an intriguing coincidence. What made it even more interesting was that Jake Merridan had worked for Joe before Joe's death and now he worked on this ranch, where accidents were happening on a far too regular basis.

Coincidence or something more sinister? He simply didn't have enough information to have an informed opinion. He got up and poured himself another cup of coffee, finding his thoughts about the case far more comfortable than thinking about Katie.

Why did she think he wasn't Prince Charming material? The question popped into his head out of nowhere and he shoved it away, irritated that he'd spent even a second thinking about what she'd said.

He'd just finished his second cup of coffee when he heard the sound of gravel crunching beneath car tires. He left the kitchen and went through the living room to look out the front window and saw his brother Dalton getting out of his car.

He opened the front door and stepped out onto the porch.

"I know it's early, but I figured you'd be up," Dalton said in greeting.

"I'm up, but Katie isn't."

"Want to talk out here?" Dalton reached the porch and Zack saw the thick folder of paperwork he carried with him.

"Nah, come on in. As long as we keep our voices down, we shouldn't disturb her." He opened the screen door to allow his older brother to enter ahead of him.

As Dalton got settled at the table with a cup of coffee, Zack went down the hallway and checked on Katie, who appeared to be sleeping soundly. Good. She'd needed to sleep. She'd gotten precious little since the night of the fire.

He lingered for a moment in the doorway and stared at her. In sleep her strong features were soft and vulnerable. He knew beneath the sheets she was naked and the impulse to forget Dalton and crawl back into bed with her was strong. He muttered a soft expletive and turned away from the door.

He returned to the kitchen and refilled his own coffee cup, then joined his brother at the table.

"Got some preliminary information for you and thought you'd want it sooner rather than later," Dalton said.

"Definitely," Zack agreed. "So, what have you got?"

"Some surprises."

"Really? Like what?" Zack leaned forward with interest, glad to focus on business instead of the woman sleeping naked in the other room.

"The men who worked for Gray don't all have pristine records," Dalton replied. "I doubt if it's a surprise to you that Brett Cook has seen the inside of the Cotter Creek jail probably as regularly as he changes his underwear. Mostly drunk and disorderly charges, a couple of assault charges that were eventually dropped."

"No real surprise there," Zack agreed. "So, surprise me."

"Know a man named George Cochran?"

Zack nodded and thought of the man who had snored in front of the television the one night Zack had bunked in the bunkhouse. "Older guy, real quiet."

"Also was a guest of the Oklahoma Corrections Institute for fifteen years on the charge of second degree murder."

Zack raised an eyebrow in surprise. "Really? Who'd he kill?" The information reminded him that it was impossible to judge a book by its cover. The last man he would have guessed capable of committing a crime of violence would have been George.

"From what I've been able to learn, he killed a girlfriend in some kind of domestic dispute."

"Who killed his girlfriend?" Katie's voice came from the doorway.

Instantly, tension stiffened Zack's shoulders as he

saw her. She was clad in a long, lightweight robe that covered her adequately, but her hair was sexy and tousled and he found himself wishing she were a woman who awakened with sleep-creased skin and swollen eyes, with tangled hair and a drool-stained chin.

Zack was grateful Dalton was there so that he and Katie wouldn't sit across from each other at the table, sipping coffee and rehashing the events of the night. He didn't even want to think about the night before, let alone talk about it.

"Good morning, Dalton. You're an early bird this morning," she said as she moved gracefully across the kitchen floor to the counter holding the coffeemaker. "So, who killed his girlfriend?"

"George Cochran," Zack replied.

"That's old news," she said, then turned her back on the men to pour herself a cup of coffee.

"So, your dad knew about George's murder conviction?" Zack asked.

"Yes." She joined them at the table.

"Nothing worse than domestic abuse," Zack said harshly, then drew a deep, audible breath. "Okay, so you knew about George's criminal record. What about Mike Wilton?"

"What about him?" she asked with interest. She raked a hand through her hair, the strands rippling with burnished color in the morning sunshine.

"He's not a stranger to the legal system," Dalton said, his attention still focused on the papers. "He's been in and out of prison for a multitude of charges, mostly fraud."

"I don't think Dad knew about that," she said.

"What did you find out about Jake Merridan?" Zack asked.

Dalton flipped through his papers and withdrew a sheet from the stack. "Jake Merridan. Nothing. Not even a speeding ticket in his past." Dalton took a drink of his coffee and shoved the papers toward Zack. "Pretty much all I've got here are the criminal background checks on the men. I'm planning to start on work history later today."

"Thanks, Dalton. I really appreciate this," Zack said.

Katie placed a hand on Dalton's arm. "Yes, I can't thank you enough. I truly believe that whoever killed my father was not a stranger, but rather somebody he knew and trusted." A dainty frown creased her forehead. "I hate to admit it but my gut instinct tells me it's got to be somebody who works here, or worked here in the recent past."

"If he's on the list you gave me of employees, then we'll find him," Dalton said. "We'll do whatever we can to help. We all thought a lot of your father." He stood and looked at Zack. "Anything else you need from me?"

"Actually, there is something else I'd like for you to do." Zack stood, as well. "I'd like you to cross-check the names of Katie's employees with anyone who was working the Wainfield ranch before Joe passed away." He felt both Katie's and Dalton's intrigue at his suggestion.

He shrugged. "It may be nothing, but I'd just like to know besides Jake Merridan if anybody else worked for Joe before coming here to work."

"I'll do what I can to find out for you," Dalton agreed, then checked his watch. "Anything else?"

Zack frowned thoughtfully. "Yeah, check out our

local pesticide salesman, Bill Garrett. He and Katie exchanged some heated words at a town council meeting."

"The man is a worm," Katie exclaimed.

Dalton flashed her a smile. "Then I'll check out the worm. I've got to get moving. Katie, don't get up, I can see myself out."

"Thanks again, Dalton," Katie said, her attention on the papers he had left behind.

"I'll walk with you," Zack replied.

Together the two brothers left the kitchen, walked through the living room and out onto the front porch.

"You doing okay?" Dalton asked the minute the two men were alone.

Zack knew his brother wasn't asking about his well-being on this particular case, but rather about his emotional health overall.

When Zack had come back from his last assignment he'd been a mess. Melissa's death had nearly destroyed him. For nearly a month he'd isolated himself from his family and spent his days and nights drinking too much, brooding too much.

"I'm fine. Even though I swore I wouldn't work for Wild West Protective Services again I have to admit it feels good to be doing something constructive. Have you heard from Tanner?"

Dalton nodded. "He called to check in last night. He and Anna are somewhere in Europe and plan on returning here sometime next week. He sounded happy. Marriage apparently agrees with him."

Zack shook his head as he thought of his eldest brother. "I still can't believe he's married."

"Yeah, me, either." Dalton looked out over the land,

then looked at Zack. "You have any idea what's going on here?"

"None." Zack frowned. "I still haven't figured out a motive for Gray's murder or why somebody would want Katie dead."

"You know you need anything, we'll use all the resources we have at Wild West to help you."

"I know. I just don't know where to go from here." Zack swallowed a sigh of frustration.

"What's the deal on the Wainfield ranch?"

Zack shrugged. "Just a desperate grasp. Joe died in an accident and accidents seem to be a regular occurrence around here." He looked at his older brother. "Actually, there's one more thing I'd like you to do. I know Joe's son and daughter-in law live in Oklahoma City. Could you get me their addresses and phone numbers? I'd like as soon as possible. I think maybe Katie and I are due for a road trip."

"I'll call you with the information." He stepped off the porch, then turned back to Zack. "You think it's a good idea for you to go back to Oklahoma City?"

Zack's stomach knotted at thought of returning to the city where Melissa had been murdered, but once again he shrugged. "It's just a city. I'll be fine."

The two brothers said their goodbyes and Zack watched as Dalton returned to his little sports car. Zack stood on the porch until the car had disappeared from sight.

He wasn't sure which would prove more difficult, returning to the city where he'd lost a cherished friend to murder or returning to the kitchen and facing the aftermath of the mistake he'd made the night before.

* * *

Kate couldn't remember a time in her life when she'd felt nervous. She'd experienced anger, frustration, happiness and all the other myriad human emotions, but nervousness wasn't one she usually indulged.

As she waited for Zack to return to the kitchen, nerves fluttered like butterflies in her stomach and uncomfortable frenetic energy raced through her veins.

She had no idea what to expect from him after the night they had shared. Was he now regretting their lovemaking? She certainly wasn't. Even though she still harbored years of resentment toward him, despite the fact that she often found him utterly maddening, she couldn't regret her night in his arms.

She also had no idea if she would have made love to him if she hadn't found that damned appraisal. The thought that her father had intended to sell the ranch had stunned her, had nearly devastated her.

In her heart, she'd always worried that her father hadn't thought her smart enough, committed enough to work the land he'd loved. She'd always believed he'd have preferred a son...a son just like Zack.

She looked up as he entered the kitchen, but he didn't meet her gaze. He grabbed his cup from the table and went to the counter to refill it.

"Dalton was an early bird this morning," she said when he returned to the table. She wanted to break the silence, test the waters. He'd certainly been pleasant enough to his brother, but he had yet to direct a comment to her.

"He's been an early bird all his life. Even as a kid he was always the first one up no matter how late we'd been up the night before."

"You and he were close growing up?" she asked.

"Not really." His gaze met hers, distant and with a hint of coolness. "Tanner and Dalton as the two oldest were close. Clay and Joshua as the youngest were close. Now, enough about my family history, I need to look over this information."

"Okay," she replied slowly. So, it was going to be like that. It was obvious from his curt tone of voice and the remoteness in his eyes that he not only regretted making love with her the night before, but he also intended to subtly punish her for it.

Fine with her. She could take whatever Zack West dished out to her. She'd spent a good portion of her life dealing with his disdain.

"While you're reading over the paperwork would you like me to make you some breakfast?" Just because he intended to be unpleasant didn't mean she intended to be.

"Don't go to any trouble on my account," he replied, not looking up from the papers.

"No trouble. Scrambled eggs and toast all right?"

He nodded and she got to work making the meal. As she beat a bowl of eggs, she tried not to get worked up about his attitude.

She really shouldn't have expected anything different from him. He was a jerk. He'd always been a jerk, albeit a sexy, handsome one. But, he hadn't made love like a jerk. He'd been exciting and giving as a lover.

Although he appeared to be absorbed in the reading material several times while she worked, she felt his gaze on her, but when she'd meet that gaze he'd frown and quickly return his attention back to the work in front of him.

She'd just placed breakfast on the table when the telephone rang. "I'll get it," Zack said as he jumped up from the table. "I'm expecting a call from Dalton."

As he grabbed the phone, Kate sat at the table, fighting a surge of irritation. She certainly hadn't expected morning kisses and hearts and flowers.

So, what did you expect? a little voice whispered in her head.

It disturbed her that no answer was forthcoming. She'd led with her heart and with a healthy surge of hormones last night and hadn't taken a moment to consider the consequences of her actions.

As she nibbled on a piece of toast, her gaze went to Zack, who was making a note on a piece of paper. Although he had apparently showered before she'd gotten out of bed, her skin still wore his scent. If she focused on it long enough she had a feeling it would evoke a renewed simmer of desire for him in her.

He hung up the phone and returned to the table. "After you eat breakfast you might want to shower and get dressed. We're going to take a road trip."

She looked at him in surprise. "Where are we going?"

"To Oklahoma City." He picked up his fork and tackled his eggs with single-minded focus.

"What's in Oklahoma City?"

"Jimmy Wainfield. I want to talk to him about his father's accident."

A sense of disquiet swept through her as she digested his words. "So, you think this is bigger than just my father and me?" The very thought made her appetite wane.

"I don't know what I think," he said, dark frustration

evident in his voice. "I just want to appease my own curiosity where Joe's accident is concerned and the best way to do that is talk to his family."

"Couldn't you accomplish what you want by just calling Jimmy?"

The scowl on his face deepened. "I have no desire to be cooped up inside the house all day long waiting for something to happen."

She had a feeling he didn't want to be cooped up *with her* all day long. Fine, she wasn't particularly looking forward to being his prisoner for the day anyway. "What time do you want to leave?"

He looked at his watch. "Around nine. That will get us into the city by noon."

"Then I'll be ready by nine."

They ate their breakfast in silence. Zack remained focused on the papers and she remained focused on Zack.

Making love with him hadn't stilled the resentment that she'd felt for him as a young girl. When Zack entered the picture, her worst fears that her father wanted a son had been realized. Zack had garnered Gray's attention like Kate had never been able to do.

"Daddy, look at me!" had become her battle cry as she'd done every crazy thing in her power to steal Gray's attention away from the handsome young cowboy.

She'd ridden her horse at breakneck speed across the front yard, she'd jumped from one of the highest branches of a tree near the front porch. She'd climbed the porch columns to the roof and a variety of other things to prove to her father that she was worthy of his love...far more worthy than Zack West.

The hollow ache in her chest was back, produced by

thoughts of her dad. She finished eating then carried her plate to the sink and rinsed it.

The hollow ache wasn't the only thing she felt at the moment. Her thoughts had brought back all her resentment toward Zack. His treatment of her this morning had intensified her feelings.

She left the kitchen without saying anything to him. Two could play at the cool, silent treatment. Besides, she was eager to shower and wash away the scent of him.

Last night had been a mistake she certainly had no intention of repeating.

Chapter 11

By nine o'clock they were under way. Zack kept his attention focused on the road, refusing to be distracted by how pretty Katie looked.

Dressed in a sleeveless white blouse and a pair of navy shorts, with her hair pulled back in a ponytail that exposed the slender, graceful column of her neck, she looked fresh and beautiful.

Since the moment Dalton had left the house the tension between Zack and Katie had grown. He knew he was responsible for most of it, but that didn't make it any easier to handle.

Still, he had to distance himself from her, needed to protect himself from any sort of emotional attachment. It was the only way he could do his job effectively. It was the only way he could survive the assignment.

He knew this trip was probably a wild-goose chase,

but he hadn't wanted to spend the day in the house with her, had felt oddly vulnerable to his own desire where she was concerned.

As they passed the Wainfield ranch, Zack noticed the place looked deserted with the grass nearly knee-high and weeds starting to take over everything. It had been more than a month since Joe's death. Where were the new owners of the property?

"Do you know who bought the Wainfield place?" he asked, breaking the silence that had grown to mammoth proportions.

"I don't have a clue," she replied, then turned her head to look out the passenger window, apparently unwilling to contribute any more to the conversation.

Zack made a mental note to check with Sheila to find out who had bought the place. It was odd that in the month since Joe's death nobody had moved in.

He checked his rearview mirror to make sure they weren't being followed by anyone. He didn't want any surprises on the road.

It was much easier to keep Katie safe by keeping her imprisoned in her house. By taking her out, the risk was greater. He was reassured by the fact that nobody appeared to be following them.

"I can't imagine what Joe's accident would have to do with what happened to my dad or with the attempted stampede and threat on my life," she said after they'd driven in silence for fifteen minutes or so.

"Truthfully, I can't imagine, either," he replied. "But when you mentioned Joe's accident last night it got me wondering what exactly happened to him and if there were any signs of foul play."

"Surely, if there had been signs of foul play, Jim Ramsey would be investigating it."

He gave her a wry half smile. "Yeah, just like he investigated your father's accident."

"Point taken," she replied. She stared out the side window at the passing landscape. "I probably should have just stayed at the ranch today and let you make this road trip alone."

"There was no way I would have allowed that to happen." He sensed her stiffening in the seat at his words. "Katie, I'm not trying to pull some macho male crap on you, but you hired me because somebody killed your father and somebody has attempted to kill you. It would be irresponsible for me to take off and leave you alone at the ranch."

She was silent for a long moment. "Your home should be the one place on earth where you feel safe and secure."

The wistfulness of her voice hit a note inside him. When his last assignment had left him devastated, all he'd wanted was the safety and familiarity of his own home. He'd wanted to crawl inside and lock the doors, keeping the world and its pain outside.

He fought the impulse to reach over and touch her hand in reassurance. Besides, he couldn't reassure her that her house was a safe haven. The fire the other night had proved that wrong.

"I still think whoever is responsible for this is working the ranch," she continued. "Dad's death felt personal."

"Every death feels personal to the loved ones left behind," he replied.

Once again she turned her attention out the window and he felt himself begin to relax a bit. The brief conversation had at least broken the ice that had lingered between them.

"Do you remember your mother?"

The question caught him off guard and for a moment his head filled with distant memories of a beautiful woman who had loved to sing and had filled the West house with laughter.

"A little bit," he answered. "I remember her laugh and how she always found time to make each and every one of us feel special. Why do you ask?"

"I don't know, I've just always wondered if it's worse to have memories or worse to have none. I was just a baby when my mom died so I have no memories of her whatsoever."

"Gray didn't talk about her with you?"

"Not much. Not often. I think it hurt too much for him to talk about her. I asked him once why he'd never remarried. He said that he'd gotten it so right the first time he was reluctant to take a chance on getting it wrong the second time."

"I think my dad felt the same way, although it probably would have been difficult for him to find a woman willing to take on six kids all under the age of eleven."

"Have you ever been in love?"

Once again her question surprised him and the tension that had begun to ebb surged inside him again. He hoped what had happened between them last night hadn't put romance and love in her head.

"Nope," he answered. "Never been in love, never expect to be. What about you?" Damn, he'd had no intention of asking that, but his brain had momentarily taken leave of his mouth.

"I thought I was in love in college for a brief period

of time," she replied. "His name was Dan and he was a year older than me." She sighed. "We dated for about a year, then we just sort of drifted apart and broke up. That's when I realized it wasn't really love after all, because I was relieved rather than heartbroken when we parted ways."

He didn't reply. He didn't know what to say in response, but more, he didn't want to indulge this particular topic of conversation with the woman he'd slept with the night before, the woman he had no intention of ever sleeping with again.

He'd be glad when they got to Jimmy Wainfield's place and his mind focused on something other than Katie Sampson. He needed to figure out what was going on, to solve the problem, then let Katie get on with her life…without him.

Silence reigned for the rest of the trip. By the time they reached the outskirts of Oklahoma City, Zack's shoulders were stiff with tension.

The last time he'd driven to Oklahoma City it had been to meet with Melissa Cannon. Over the three months he'd worked for her, he'd gotten too close to his client, had become emotionally involved, and the end result had nearly destroyed him.

He couldn't allow this assignment to last too long. At the moment he couldn't imagine spending another week with Katie. It was important that he get to the bottom of things then get on with his preferred loner lifestyle.

"Are Jimmy and his wife expecting us?" Katie asked as they exited the interstate.

"Yeah, I called them this morning while you were in the shower. They're expecting us around one. I figured we'd get some lunch before heading to their condo."

Within fifteen minutes he'd found a restaurant and they were seated across from each other in a booth. As he studied the menu, he felt her gaze on him. He looked up to meet her eyes.

"Are we just not going to talk about it? Pretend that it never happened?" she asked.

He closed the menu with a sigh. He should have known she wouldn't be able to leave it alone. "That was certainly my intention."

Her gaze was cool as it lingered on him. "Is that one of the rules of engagement that Smokey taught you? That the morning after you treat the woman like a speck of dirt?"

He saw the hint of anger in her eyes. "I'm not treating you like dirt," he said seriously. "I just don't see the point in talking about something that shouldn't have happened."

Her eyes narrowed slightly and she picked up her knife and toyed with it, making him wonder if she were mentally stabbing him in the heart or castrating him.

"You're right," she finally replied, "it shouldn't have happened and no amount of wishing will take it back. But I will tell you this, I wouldn't want to take it back."

He sat back against the seat, surprised by her words. "You wouldn't?"

She shook her head and laid the knife down. "For years I wondered what it would be like to make love with you. I'd always imagined it would be wonderful and now I know for sure."

"Know what? That it was wonderful or that it wasn't?" He couldn't help himself, he had to know. But why did he care?

She smiled, a smile that warmed the blue of her eyes

and made his stomach twist into an impossible knot. "It was better than I'd imagined, far better than wonderful."

Thankfully at that moment the waitress appeared at their table, making it unnecessary for him to reply. As much as he believed making love to her had been a mistake, as much as he wished he could take it back, he was ridiculously pleased that she'd found the experience as mind-blowing as he had.

"When we get back to the ranch, we're going to have to make some definite plans concerning your safety," he said the moment the waitress left their table, eager to change the previous topic to one more comfortable.

"Like what?" She eyed him with a touch of humor, as if she knew exactly why he had changed the subject.

"If you really believe that one of your men is responsible both for your father's death and for the threats against you, then I need to be out among your men to see if I can figure out who it might be."

She nodded. "That makes sense."

"But that means I can't be inside the house protecting you." He leaned forward. "Maybe we need to bring Dalton into this, have him stay in the house with you while I'm out in the field."

"No. I don't want to do that. I'm not comfortable with Dalton like I am with you. Besides, all I have to do is agree to stay in the house with the doors and windows locked and I'll be fine. I've got Dad's gun and I know how to use it."

"Then at least let me arrange for a security system to be put in the house."

She frowned thoughtfully. "How much is this going to cost me?"

"Possibly your life if you don't do it."

She uttered a small laugh, one devoid of humor. "Gee, don't mince words just for my benefit." She sighed and leaned back against the seat. "All of this wasn't exactly in the ranch budget."

"Is the ranch in financial trouble?"

"Not really. You saw the records. We're holding our own, but there certainly isn't a large surplus to spend frivolously."

"I don't consider your safety a frivolous matter," he replied.

She smiled, this time a genuine smile that shot warmth through his stomach. "And I thank you for that, at least."

The waitress arrived with their meals and they fell silent, focusing their attention on the food. As they ate they made small-talk. She told him a little bit about her years in college and they ventured into a good-natured argument about local politics.

When they were finished eating they got back into his truck and headed for Jimmy Wainfield's condo.

He found the complex with little trouble and pulled into a parking space out front. Across the street a city park beckoned with huge shady trees, winding walks and wooden benches.

"I don't know why, but I'm nervous," Katie said as they got out of the truck.

"Do you know Jimmy?" he asked.

"I'd know him on sight, but he was so much older than me, I didn't know him personally," she replied. "What about you? Do you know him?"

"No, he was Tanner's age and we didn't hang out with the same crowd." Together he and Katie went into the high-rise building and to the bank of elevators. "They live on the tenth floor and his wife's name is Jane."

Zack was surprised to find that he, too, felt a bit anxious about the interview he was about to conduct. It would be terrific to get something definitive, to learn something that would help him get to the bottom of what was happening at Bent Tree Ranch. But, as terrific as it would be, he had no illusions about easy answers.

They were just about to step off the elevator when Katie grabbed his arm. "Zack, if we don't get any answers here, you aren't going to quit on me, are you?" Her blue eyes pleaded with him.

He'd been reluctant to give her a firm commitment before. Now he didn't know if it was because he'd spent the previous night making love with her, but he knew with certainty he wasn't about to walk away from her until he knew her safety was assured.

"I'm in this for the long haul, Katie," he said.

She squeezed his arm, her relief evident in her eyes. "Then let's get this done."

Jimmy Wainfield answered Zack's knock, his pleasant features radiating warmth and curiosity. "Zack, Kate, please come in." He ushered them into an attractive living room decorated in Southwestern decor. A pretty, dark-haired woman stood from the chair where she'd been seated as they entered the room.

"This is my wife, Jane," Jimmy said, and completed the introductions.

"Can I get you anything? A cup of coffee or something cold to drink?" she asked.

"No, thanks. We're fine," Katie said.

"Please, have a seat." Jimmy gestured them toward the sofa, where they sat side by side. "We were very surprised to get your call. I understand you want to talk about my father's accident." He looked at his wife, then back at Zack. "I'm not sure how much we'll be able to help you. We were here when it happened."

"Sheriff Ramsey called us to tell us," Jane said. "He said Joe had fallen off the tractor and somehow gotten run over."

"According to the sheriff it appeared that Dad had fallen from the tractor and hit his head hard enough to render him unconscious, then somehow the tractor went awry and ran over him."

Zack frowned. He hadn't realized until now that Joe had been unconscious when the tractor had run over him. A fall that had rendered him unconscious or a blow to the head as Gray had suffered? "Did your father have a medical condition, something that might have caused his fall?"

"Dad was in good health for a man his age. No heart problems, no blood pressure issues, nothing that would make him dizzy or disoriented. His cholesterol was a bit high, but that was it. We just assumed it was some kind of a freak accident." He looked at Katie, then back at Zack. "Were we wrong?"

"I don't know. Did you hear about Katie's father's accident?"

Jimmy nodded. "We still have friends in Cotter Creek. They keep us informed about what's going on in the community." He looked at Katie, his brown eyes filled with sympathy. "I'm sorry for your loss. Believe me, I know exactly how you feel."

"We think Gray's death wasn't an accident. It was murder," Zack said. He explained to them what they'd discovered about Gray's death and the events that had occurred to Katie since. It was obvious Jimmy and his wife were stunned by his words.

"I'm not sure I understand. Are you saying you think it's possible my father's death wasn't an accident at all?" Jimmy asked.

"We just thought it was too coincidental that your father died in an accident and mine died in what appeared to be an accident but wasn't," Katie explained.

"You were close to your father? Spoke to him often?" Zack asked.

"We talked together on the phone almost every night." Jimmy's eyes held a whisper of grief. "He and my mother divorced several years ago. She moved to Florida and he was all alone out there. We tried to talk him into selling and moving in here with us, but Dad loved that ranch."

"Did he mention having problems with any of his men? Anyone else in town?" Zack asked.

Jimmy frowned thoughtfully. "Nothing specific. He occasionally complained about somebody not doing a job right or being lazy, but nothing more serious than that."

Jane got up from her seat and went to stand behind her husband's chair, her hand on his shoulder in obvious support. "Joe was a kind, good man. I can't imagine him having an enemy in the world," she said.

Just as he and Katie couldn't imagine Gray having an enemy in the world, Zack thought. "So, after your dad's death, you had no desire to take over the ranch?"

Jimmy smiled, a smile that didn't quite reach the sadness in his eyes. "Dad knew I wasn't a rancher, had never developed any real affinity with the land or the lifestyle. He was happy that Jane and I had built such a good life here. He was my biggest supporter when I went into computer programming. I'm sure deep in his heart he harbored some hope that I'd eventually come to my senses and return to the ranch, but he also knew the odds of that happening were minimal."

"He left you the ranch?" Zack asked.

"I was his only heir and he left everything to me. Right after the funeral, Sheila Wadsworth approached me and asked if she could list the property and within two days she had a buyer."

"Who bought the place?" Zack asked.

"Somebody named Adam Crosswell. Sheila said he was a successful businessman from someplace back east who was eager to move his family to the Midwest."

Eager, but after a month hadn't yet made the move, Zack thought. Still, not exactly the smoking gun he'd been looking for. But worth looking into, he told himself. He couldn't leave any detail, no matter how small, unchecked.

A wave of disappointment swept through him. He didn't know what he'd expected to learn, but hadn't learned anything to help him discern a guilty party where Katie and Gray were concerned.

"We really appreciate you talking with us. We've taken up enough of your time," he said, and rose from the sofa.

They all stood and Katie gave Jane an impromptu hug. "Yes, thank you for your time," she said, then hugged Jimmy, as well.

Jimmy patted her on the back. "We know your pain, Kate, and I hope you get the person responsible for your father's death. I'll ride down with you."

They said their goodbyes to Jane, then the three of them left the condo and walked to the elevator. "It isn't necessary for you to ride down with us," Zack said.

"I don't mind," Jimmy replied.

Zack had the instinct Jimmy wasn't finished talking yet, but didn't want to talk in front of his wife. When they entered the elevator, his instinct proved correct. "There isn't anything you aren't telling us, is there?" he asked, his wide brow creased with worry.

"No. We've told you everything we know, which unfortunately isn't much," Zack replied.

The elevator hit the bottom floor and the three of them got out. As they stepped out of the building, Zack handed Kate the car keys. "I'll be right there," he said, unsure if Jimmy was looking for a moment alone with him.

She grabbed the keys and headed down the stairs and Zack turned to Jimmy. "Your father's accident was probably just that, a tragic accident. We don't know what happened to Gray, but it probably has nothing to do with your father's death."

Jimmy nodded. "If there's anything else Jane and I can do to help, please don't hesitate to call us. I would appreciate it if you'd let us know what you find out about Gray's murder."

"Thanks, will do." The two men shook hands, then Jimmy disappeared back into the building.

Zack turned to see Katie at the passenger door waiting for him. He'd just taken his first step when a sharp crack split the air.

Adrenaline surged. A shot. Katie raised her hand to wave at him as the front of her pristine blouse blossomed in scarlet. Melissa. Katie. For a horrifying moment Zack plunged into his nightmare.

"No!" he yelled. "Melissa!"

Chapter 12

The backfire of the passing car was followed by Zack's cry. The woman's name seemed to be ripped from his throat. Kate looked at him in stunned surprise. He stared at her with hollow eyes, his face bloodless.

"Zack?"

He appeared to be a man in shock as he ran down the stairs, past the car where she stood and across the street into the park.

Kate slammed the truck door and hurried after him, her heart pounding with anxiety. What was going on? And who was Melissa?

She found him on a bench beneath a shady oak tree, his face buried in his hands. She sank next to him. "Who is she?" she asked softly.

He uncovered his pale face and tipped his head back, staring at the leaves overhead. "She was my last client. She's dead now. She was killed by her estranged husband."

"Oh, Zack. I'm so sorry." She'd never seen him so vulnerable. Now she understood his strong reaction when he'd heard about George's crime. He'd always been so strong, so emotionally together, and this glimpse of him in pain drew her to him. She couldn't help but wonder exactly what this Melissa had meant to him.

He raked a hand through his hair and took a deep sigh. "I heard that car backfire and saw you standing at the truck with your white blouse and suddenly I was in the depths of my nightmare."

"Tell me about your nightmare."

He looked at her, his green eyes dark and tortured. "You don't need to hear about all this," he protested.

"Maybe not," she agreed, "but maybe you need to talk about it."

He averted his gaze from her and instead stared down at the ground at his feet. "I was with her for three months. When she filed for divorce, her husband threatened to kill her, and since he was a violent man who'd regularly abused her in the past, she took his threat quite seriously."

"And so you were assigned to protect her."

He nodded. "Tanner sent me out on the job. Melissa did everything she could to get the divorce finalized. She felt that once the divorce was a done deal, he'd move on and leave her alone."

He stretched his legs out in front of him and once again tipped his head back, staring overhead. "Despite everything that she'd been through, she was one of the strongest, most optimistic people I'd ever met. She was full of plans for the rest of her life. She was going to open up an antique business and get a dog. She was going to do all the things she'd been unable to do while under the thumb of her husband."

He stood abruptly, as if finding it impossible to sit. He walked to the side of the tree and leaned with his back against the broad trunk, his face dappled in shadow.

"Two days before the divorce would have been finalized, she heard from her husband's friends and relatives that he'd taken off, left town. His best friend told her that he'd packed up everything he owned and had left for Arkansas, where he had an old girlfriend."

Katie wanted to say something, anything, to alleviate the tortured depths in his voice, but she didn't know what to say, knew that nothing she said could fix this or make it better, easier for him.

"Anyway, the bottom line is that she told me to go home and that she didn't need protection anymore. She believed what everyone told her, that the danger was gone."

His voice was positively wretched now. Kate stood, finding it impossible to remain seated while he relived what must have been one of the worst experiences of his life.

She wanted to take him in her arms, but his tense body forbade her touch. Whatever demons he fought, he appeared determined to fight them alone.

She stood in front of him, his gaze holding hers intently. In his eyes she saw the ghost of the woman he'd tried to save and enough pain to fill up a wide prairie.

"Reluctantly, even though my instincts told me otherwise, I left her. I was almost back to Cotter Creek when a police officer I'd become friendly with called me to tell me she'd been gunned down by her husband." He closed his eyes and took another deep breath.

She had to touch him. She couldn't stand seeing him this way. His pain resonated inside her, forcing her to lean into him and to wrap her arms around his neck, to pull his head down to her shoulder.

They stood that way for long minutes, neither of them speaking. His heart thundered against hers and after a bit of time she felt some of the tension start to ebb from his body.

She now understood why he'd quit the family business, why he'd been reluctant to get involved with protecting her. The fact that he had, despite his heartbreak, in spite of his pain, filled her heart with guilt almost too great to bear.

He finally moved out of her embrace and once again sat on the bench. She joined him there and waited for him to speak again.

"The nightmares started a week after her death." His voice was low but steady and without the intense emotional stress that had been in it moments before. "Even though I wasn't there when she was killed, I see it in my dream. I see her get out of her car and she's wearing a white dress. A shot rings out and the front of her dress turns bloody as she falls to the ground."

Kate ran a hand down the front of her white blouse. So this explained his reaction to the car backfire. A shot, a woman in white and deadly results.

"Were you in love with her?" she asked.

He didn't answer for a long moment. "No. I loved her, but I wasn't in love with her, not in a romantic sense. I just feel so responsible."

"Responsible? How could you be responsible? She'd sent you away."

"But I shouldn't have left," he said, the torment back in his voice, back in his eyes. "I should have listened to my instincts."

She placed a hand on his arm, felt the taut muscles beneath her fingertips and searched deep inside herself, finding the place that had haunted her since her father's death.

"The morning that Dad went for his last ride, he asked me to join him. But I was still half asleep. I didn't feel like going and so I told him no." Her heart constricted painfully as she remembered that morning and the fateful decision she'd made.

"After he was found, I kept thinking that if I'd gone with him, then he wouldn't be dead. Of course, that's not true. Somebody wanted my father dead and if it hadn't happened that particular morning it would have happened on some other morning.

"Zack, you can't blame yourself for Melissa's death. You had no choice but to leave. Unless you were willing to spend the rest of your life guarding her, you probably couldn't have stopped what happened. If it hadn't happened on that particular day at that particular time, it would have happened sooner or later."

He stood abruptly. "There's been too damned much death lately." He hit the tree trunk with the palm of his hand. "Come on, let's get the hell out of here and get back home."

Together they left the park and got into his truck. It was a silent ride back to the ranch, although not the same kind of tense silence they had shared driving to the city.

There had always been a part of her that had questioned whether Zack was capable of any kind of emotional attachment. When he hadn't visited her father in the month that he'd returned to town, she'd suspected that his feelings for Gray hadn't been as strong as her father's had been for him.

Even years ago when Jaime Coffer, the girl Zack had dated, had left town, he hadn't seemed affected by the loss. He'd never shown any real attachment to his own family members, except maybe Smokey, who he obviously admired.

But any question she'd had about Zack's capacity to care about another human being had been answered by what he'd shared with her.

"Tell me what your brothers and sister are up to," she said when they had driven about halfway home. She had the feeling he would welcome small talk.

"You know Tanner and Anna are in Europe on their honeymoon and are supposed to be back sometime next week."

"Is Joshua still in New York?" Joshua, the youngest of the West clan, was two years older than Kate.

"Yeah, he's knocking them dead on Wall Street as a stockbroker." A faint smile curved his lips, a welcome sight after the trauma of his memory. "We have bets on how long it will be before he leaves the city behind and returns to his roots."

"And Meredith?"

"She was on an assignment in Texas for a couple of weeks and now I think she's in South Dakota somewhere."

"Does she still have a bad haircut?"

Zack laughed. "There's that Katie trait of always speaking your mind."

She welcomed his laughter. "What? You've never noticed that your sister's hair always looks like its been cut by a chain saw?"

He laughed again and cast her a warm glance. "As a matter of fact, you used to remind me a little bit of Meredith. As the only girl in our family, she was spoiled and temperamental, hotheaded and dramatic." He shot her another look of amusement. "And I remember a night when you used a pair of pinking shears to cut your hair."

She laughed at the memory and pulled the ponytail holder from her hair, allowing the thick strands to fall around her shoulders. She'd been about ten at the time and had decided if she looked like a boy maybe her dad would love her more. "When I got finished and saw myself in the mirror, I cried for a week. I couldn't believe what I'd done to myself."

"At least you didn't color it purple or pink," he replied.

"What about Clay? Where is he?" she asked, getting back to his siblings.

"Last I heard he was in New Orleans on an assignment."

"Are you all ever home at the same time?"

"Holidays we try to be home together, but it doesn't always work out that way."

They fell silent once again. Kate tried to imagine what Christmas must be like in the West household. It must be wonderful with the entire family together, wonderful and maybe a little bit crazy.

She didn't want to think about what her next Christmas would be like. Christmas was for family and she'd be all alone.

They had just turned into the entrance to home when Zack looked at her again. "Thanks, Katie," he said softly.

"For what?"

"For everything you said earlier." He pulled up in front of the house, parked and shut off the engine. He turned to face her. "I didn't realize until you said it how badly I needed to hear somebody say that it wasn't my fault, that I probably couldn't have stopped the murder no matter how hard I tried."

"I didn't say that just to make you feel better. I said it because it's the truth." She touched his arm lightly. "Come on, let's get inside and I'll rustle us up some dinner."

"When we get inside the front door I want you to stay there while I check the rest of the house." In Zack's simple statement the reality of her situation came back to haunt her.

Somebody wanted her dead. And if they didn't figure out who and why, she'd probably end up like Melissa and Gray.

"I've arranged for a security system to be put in tomorrow morning," Zack said an hour later as they sat at the table eating the burgers Katie had fixed for dinner. "Once the system is up and running, then during the days I'll go back to working outside with the men knowing you're safe inside the house."

"You don't have to tell me to make sure the security is on all the time and to not allow anyone inside the house when you aren't here."

"Good, then I won't tell you that." He reached for another handful of potato chips. It was amazing to him that he felt lighter, more clear-headed than he had since Melissa's death.

The trauma of her death had festered in him like a boil and by talking about it with Katie the boil had been lanced and the patient was going to live.

"Isn't the town council meeting this week?"

"Saturday night," she replied.

"I think we should go. I've been much too absent from the town business in the past."

"Okay. The meetings always start promptly at seven and usually end around ten." Anything else she might have said was interrupted by a knock on the door. She got up, but Zack stopped her with a hand on her shoulder.

"I'll get it," he said. As he left the kitchen he grabbed his gun from the counter where he'd placed it.

He peered out the window and saw Sonny standing on the porch. He opened the door and greeted the older man.

"I need to check in with Kate," Sonny said. "There's some ranch business we need to discuss."

"Sure, come on in. We were just finishing up supper." Zack escorted the man into the kitchen, where Katie had begun to clear the table.

"Oh, good," she said at the sight of her manager. "I was hoping you'd come by." She gestured him into a chair at the table, then sat across from him.

Zack leaned against the refrigerator and listened as the two discussed the delegation of chores, the health and well-being of both animals and crops.

Zack was struck by Katie's decisiveness, her business

acumen, as he listened to the conversation. A grudging admiration filled him. She'd grown so much in the past five years. It was difficult to compare the strong, rational woman she'd become to the headstrong, tempestuous girl she had been.

Her compassion when he'd shared with her the details of Melissa's death had been heartfelt and welcomed. Somebody would be lucky to have a woman like Katie as a life partner, sharing both the good times and the bad.

He frowned, disturbed by these kinds of thoughts. Funny, he had been worried about how she might react to their love-making and he was the one who was finding it difficult to forget. He was the one who was suddenly thinking things about Katie Sampson he shouldn't be contemplating.

They had been brought together due to strange circumstances. She didn't need him in her life as a lover. She needed him to keep her alive and he'd do well to remember that was the only reason he was back in her life.

"Even though I know we're short-handed right now, sooner or later something is going to have to be done about Brett," Sonny said, bringing Zack back to the conversation.

"What's going on with Brett?" Zack asked, for the first time inserting himself into the discussion.

"He was so hung over this morning I couldn't get much of any work out of him until afternoon. And when he's drunk or hung over, he's surly as hell."

Katie frowned thoughtfully. "I'll talk to him."

"Maybe you should put him on some sort of probation for a couple of weeks," Sonny suggested. "I hate to do without him altogether, but since your dad's death he's gotten worse than ever."

"Maybe I should talk to him," Zack offered.

Katie shook her head. "No, it's my job. I'll handle it." She looked at Sonny. "I think we're done here for tonight. At least for the time being, I won't be out around the ranch, so I'd like a report from you every evening."

Again Zack felt a tinge of admiration for her. It would have been easy for her to allow him to take care of the difficult task of talking to Brett, but she wouldn't shirk her duty. Gray would have been proud of her.

Sonny got up from the table. "Is there anything else I can do?" He looked at Katie, then toward Zack. "I'm assuming you aren't just working as a ranch hand around the place, that you're working as a member of your family business because of the fire that happened the other night."

"I'm here with Katie because I'm her friend," Zack replied.

"Good enough," Sonny said, and turned to leave the kitchen. Zack followed him to the door and after saying goodbye, locked up behind him.

He returned to the kitchen to find Katie washing the few dishes they had used for supper. He picked up a dish towel and began to dry.

"Thanks," she said. "Not only do I have a friend, but he actually dries dishes."

"It was easier to tell Sonny I was here as a friend rather than try to explain the complicated relationship we've shared."

She rinsed a plate and handed it to him. "It has been complicated, hasn't it?"

"More so in the past than now."

She eyed him curiously. "And how do you see our relationship now?"

Not for the first time he felt shaky ground beneath his feet where she was concerned. "Still under construction," he finally replied.

She nodded, as if she found his assessment agreeable, then handed him the last plate to dry. "What time will somebody be here in the morning to put in the security system?"

"Early." He dried the plate, put it into the cabinet, then folded his dish towel and set it on the counter.

She drained the dishwater, then dried her hands. "I think maybe I'll go take a bath." She raised her shoulders, then dropped them, as if easing tension. "It's been a long day."

"Sounds like a good idea. While you're doing that, I'll check the place, make sure everything is locked up tight for the night."

They left the kitchen and parted ways in the hallway. She disappeared into the bathroom and a moment later he heard the water running in the tub.

He tried to keep visions of Katie in a tubful of bubbles out of his mind as he went from room to room, checking windows to make certain the house was secure.

It was just after eight and he wondered how long it would be before she went to bed. Soon, he hoped. The last thing he wanted to do was to sit in the living room with her.

Under construction. He supposed that described his relationship with Katie as well as anything. He'd come into this expecting her to be the same demanding, spoiled girl she'd been. She'd proved herself to be anything but that.

After checking all the doors and windows, he got his linens from the hall closet to make up his bed on the sofa. The water shut off in the bathroom and once again his head filled with a vision of Katie.

He sat on the sofa and instead tried to focus on what little they'd learned from Jimmy Wainfield. The fact that Joe had fallen and somehow been knocked unconscious might be nothing more than a coincidence.

Knowing how Gray had died, it was easy to imagine somebody fighting with Joe, knocking him out, then running over him with the tractor.

But Zack couldn't make the leap to see what on earth Joe and Gray had in common. Who might have wanted to kill both men? And what had been the motive?

He leaned back and rubbed the center of his forehead, grappling to make sense where none was forthcoming. It was difficult to believe that what had happened to Joe had anything to do with what had happened to Gray. Still, he made a mental note to check to see what other ranching accidents had taken place in the last couple of months.

He didn't know how long he'd been sitting there when he heard the door to the bathroom open and close and realized Katie had gone into the spare bedroom.

A moment later, she appeared in the doorway of the living room and the expression on her face drove all thoughts of sex out of his head.

"What's wrong?" he asked, aware that something was wrong by the paleness of her face and the wide expression of her eyes.

"Somebody was in the house while we were gone today."

He stood and grabbed his gun. "How do you know?"

"Dad's gun. It was in the nightstand in the spare room and now it's gone."

Chapter 13

"What do you mean, it's gone?" Zack stared at her as if she were an apparition from another world.

She fought back a burst of half-hysterical laughter. "What part of 'gone' don't you understand?"

"Are you sure it was in the nightstand?"

"Positive. I put it in there after the fire and I saw it there this morning before we left." The thought that somebody had been in the house and stolen the gun sent an icy chill through her.

"Is anything else missing?"

"Not that I can tell." She looked around the living room, her chill intensifying, invading the very marrow of her bones.

Zack gave her a grim look and disappeared down the hall toward the spare bedroom. She followed behind him and watched as he checked the windows, then opened the nightstand drawer and rummaged around, as if the gun might be hidden beneath a box of tissues or the bible.

"It was right there," she said. "Both the gun and a box of bullets."

He slammed the drawer, a deadly expression on his face. "And you don't see anything else missing?"

She shook her head and followed him out of the bedroom and back into the living room, where he motioned her to the sofa.

She sank onto the cushion and he sat next to her. "I checked all the other windows a few minutes ago and they're all locked up tight. There's no sign of forced entry anywhere. Who has a key to the house?"

She frowned thoughtfully. "I know Sonny has a key and maybe Mike. He used to come in and do odd jobs for Dad. To be honest with you, I don't know who all might have keys. There could be any number floating around. You know Dad, he trusted everyone. Any of the men might have one. The locks on the house are the same they've been since I was a kid."

It was obvious her answer didn't please Zack. It didn't particularly please her, either. A scowl cut across his forehead. "Tomorrow the security system will be installed and we'll have all the locks changed at the same time. Nobody will be getting inside after that without us knowing about it."

"And in the meantime somebody has Dad's gun and somebody wants me dead." The chill worked up into a shiver and she wrapped her arms around herself, wondering if she'd ever be warm again. "I don't know why, but this scares me more than anything that's happened so far." She wondered if her father's gun would be the means of her death.

She gazed at Zack, the fear bubbling up inside her. "I don't want you to see me as weak or silly, but I'm scared, Zack. I've never been so frightened in my entire life."

To her utter relief he placed an arm around her shoulder and pulled her tight against his side. She lay her head on his shoulder, welcoming his body warmth to ward off the cold that had invaded her soul.

"I don't think you're weak or silly," he replied softly. "Unfortunately you'd be silly if you weren't afraid." With one hand he caressed the strands of her hair.

Had the gun been stolen so it could be used as a weapon against her? Had it been taken in the hope that she wouldn't realize it was gone and would therefore be unprotected? But she wasn't without protection. She had Zack.

"Talk to me, Zack. Talk to me about something, anything other than murders and accidents. Tell me about the other assignments you've worked."

As he told her about the places he'd been, the people he'd protected, she listened to his deep voice and began to relax. It didn't really matter what words he said, just that he talked in that low, soothing voice.

It was difficult to imagine anything bad happening to her while Zack's arms enfolded her.

She closed her eyes and listened as he talked about faraway places and the people who had come into and out of his life.

As he spoke she caressed his jeans-clad thigh, feeling the warmth, the taut muscles beneath the denim material. Strength. He radiated such a reassuring strength.

He calmed her, with his words, with his nearness. He chased away the overwhelming fear and transformed it into something manageable.

He made her feel safe despite the danger she knew existed, despite the fact that his last client had been lost. She knew no matter what, he would do everything in his power to keep her safe.

Whatever negative things she'd once thought about him had long disappeared, dissipated by his commitment to keeping her safe, his determination to find the person responsible for her father's death.

She didn't know how long they sat there when he said her name, his voice deeper, more strained than it had been. She raised her head and looked at him questioningly and saw the dark flame that lit the depths of his eyes.

"Maybe you should head on to bed," he said. "It's getting late."

"Maybe I should," she agreed, but didn't move from his arms. It was desire she saw in his gaze and the familiar electricity crackled in the air between them.

She moved her hand higher on his thigh and with a muttered oath he captured her hand with his and held it still. "Katie, I told you this morning that last night was a mistake," he said, his voice uneven.

Had it just been last night that he'd made sweet love to her? It felt like a lifetime ago. The desire that thrummed inside her at this moment felt as if it had been building for weeks, months…years.

She licked her lips, which were suddenly aching and dry. "Sometimes a mistake needs to be repeated several times before you really learn your lesson," she said half-breathlessly.

His eyes flashed. "Damn you, Katie Sampson," he said just before his mouth crashed down on hers.

She welcomed his kiss, reveled in it. It didn't matter to her that just that morning she had sworn she'd never make love with Zack again, it didn't matter to her if this was just another mistake in her life.

All that did matter was that it felt right and good to be in his arms, to have his mouth touching hers.

Even though he'd cursed her, there was no anger in his kiss, only tenderness and rich, raw desire. She returned the kiss with a desire of her own, her tongue dancing wildly with his.

Still kissing, he lowered her back so that she lay prone on the sofa, then he stretched out on top of her. For the first time Kate was grateful that the sofa was large and overstuffed.

His hands moved up beneath her T-shirt and she was glad that after her bath she hadn't bothered with a bra. She caressed his broad back beneath his shirt, his bare skin feeling almost feverish with heat.

He broke the kiss and stared down at her, his body taut against hers. "Katie, you're frightened and probably feeling all alone. I don't want to take advantage of you in your present state of mind."

She placed a hand on his jaw, felt the stubble of whiskers against her palm. "Maybe you haven't realized it yet, but I'm not the type of woman to allow a man to take advantage of me. I know what I want, Zack. I know what I need, and right now it's you."

Her words seemed to shatter any reservations he might entertain. With another muttered oath, he took possession of her mouth once again.

He cupped her breasts, his thumbs razing across her

taut nipples. He pulled his mouth from hers and trailed nipping kisses across her jaw and to the sensitive skin just beneath her ear.

She gasped with pleasure, feeling as if her entire body was nothing more than a mass of sensation. Wherever he touched, wherever he caressed, her nerves screamed with delight.

When he'd finished with the searing kisses, he undressed her, lavishing kisses on every inch of skin he bared. By the time he finished, she was moaning with need.

Once again he remembered protection, undressing and putting on a condom before rejoining her on the sofa. Although she was ready for him, moist and needy, he didn't take her, but rather used his mouth to lathe her breasts, used his fingers to bring her over and over again to the brink.

"Zack, please," she begged, needing him to take her all the way, to give her the release his every touch, his every kiss promised.

When he did finally enter her she nearly sobbed with the exquisite sensation. It wasn't just a physical union, but an emotional bond, as well.

The deep-seated feelings of inadequacy that had always been with her were silenced as Zack made love to her. Her fears were stilled, her heart and head unable to hold anything but him.

They moved together faster and faster, gasping and moaning with pleasure as they sought release. When it came, the intensity shuddered through her in wave after wave. At the same time she was aware of him crying out her name as he stiffened against her.

For long, silent moments they remained locked

together. As her breathing resumed a more normal rhythm, he finally raised his head and stared down at her.

"This is madness," he said.

"I know, but it's a wonderful kind of madness, isn't it?" she replied.

His eyes darkened with what looked like confusion and he got up and left her. He grabbed his jeans from the floor and disappeared into the bathroom.

She sat up and reached for her T-shirt, which had been tossed to the floor earlier. She pulled it on over her head and wondered if sex would always be wonderful with Zack.

If they made love a hundred times, a thousand times, would he still be able to steal her breath away with his kisses? Would the scent of him still stir her and twist her stomach into knots?

"Katie." He stood in the doorway, his expression somber. "We have to stop this before somebody gets hurt."

She wanted to protest, to tell him that making love with him was the only thing good in her life at the moment and she didn't want to stop. But deep in her heart she knew he was right.

Something had happened to her this time when they'd made love. She'd felt him not on a physical level, but in her heart, as well. He was right, if they continued, somebody was going to get hurt and she had a feeling that in the end it would be her who came out of this with a broken heart.

Zack rode Diamond, Gray's favorite mount, toward the house as the sun began to set. It had been one hell of a long week. The security system had been installed and the locks changed on Tuesday morning and for the past four days Zack had been working with the men while Katie was locked up in the house.

Unbeknownst to Katie, he'd hired one of the men who worked for the agency. Wild West Protective Services wasn't employed only by the West family, but also half a dozen additional men to stand guard on the house while he worked the ranch. Even though the security was top-notch, Zack wasn't taking any chances with her safety.

The days hadn't been too bad, but the evenings had been sheer torture. He and Katie were living a quasi-marriage that promoted an uncomfortable intimacy.

Each evening when he came in from outside she had dinner waiting for him. They ate, small talked, then shared the chore of clearing the table.

After dinner they played gin rummy at the table, watched movies on the television or indulged in some other benign activity to pass the time until bed.

The real torture came for Zack each night when she disappeared into the spare room and he settled in on the sofa. Thoughts of her passion made him toss and turn. Memories of her hot mouth, her yielding softness and warm caresses kept any real sleep at bay.

Not making love to her again was the most difficult thing he would ever do. Every moment they spent together his want grew, feeling not like mere desire, but almost painful need.

At least tonight they had the town meeting to attend, he thought as he reached the stable. Hopefully he'd glean some information there because he'd certainly learned nothing new while working with the men the past several days.

He unsaddled Diamond and worked out a healthy dose of frustration by brushing down the horse. He'd hoped that by being out among the men he'd hear a bit of gossip, sense an evil boiling inside somebody, but so far he'd heard nothing, seen nothing, that might lead to the guilty party.

He'd contacted Jim Ramsey about the missing gun and Jim had admitted to him that they had no leads where the fire was concerned. No leads. That was becoming the story of this assignment.

The stable was quiet. He assumed most of the other men had collected their paychecks and were preparing for a night on the town.

He'd like to get into the bunkhouse to check out what each man had in his trunk, to see if the personal belongings would yield the missing gun from Katie's drawer, but so far he hadn't chanced it. A man could get shot snooping where he didn't belong. Besides, the last thing he wanted to do was to alienate the men.

"Zack."

He whirled around to see Jake standing in the stall entry, a pitchfork in his hand. He tensed. He'd expected a confrontation from the man every day for the last week. It appeared the confrontation was about to occur. "Jake, what's up?"

"I think we need to talk."

Although the man didn't hold the pitchfork as a weapon, Zack had a healthy respect for the pronged tool. "I don't have much interest in talking to a man wielding a pitchfork," he observed.

Jake stuck the fork in a pile of straw, then gazed

at Zack through narrowed eyes. "I was just wondering if you could tell me what's going on between you and Kate."

Zack set the brush he'd been using aside, wanting both his hands free in case Jake made a move. "I think it would be best if you ask the lady that question."

"I'd love to ask the lady, but you've got her locked up tight in the house and she isn't talking to anyone except Sonny." Jake cracked his knuckles, as if itching for a fight.

Zack frowned. Although he wouldn't back down from any fight, he had no desire to go a round or two with Jake. He'd never fought over a woman and he wasn't about to start now, especially when that woman was Katie, a woman who was his client and nothing more, he told himself.

"If you want to speak to Katie, you're more than welcome to come with me to the house," he said.

Jake shook his head, the tension in his body visibly relaxing. "Sonny said you were hired on as protection for her."

"That's right," Zack agreed. "The fire frightened her, so she asked me to move inside and keep an eye on her."

Jake's eyes narrowed a bit. "I've seen the way you look at her. It's more than just an old friendship, isn't it?"

Zack didn't know how to reply. He hadn't taken the time to examine deeply his feelings where Katie was concerned. Didn't want to take the time. "Like I said, if you want to talk to Katie, you're welcome to come with me to the house," he said, deciding not to attempt to answer Jake's question.

Jake sighed audibly. "No point in me talking to her.

She's made it fairly clear that even though I'm interested in her, she isn't much interested in me."

Zack's mind whirled with supposition. Was Jake Merridan a victim of unrequited love, so sick with twisted emotion that if he couldn't have Katie he'd make sure nobody else did? Nothing Dalton had dug up in the man's past indicated that kind of illness, but that didn't necessarily mean anything.

"I just don't want to see her get hurt," Jake said, his eyes narrowed once again. "She's one hell of a woman and she deserves the best."

"I have no intention of hurting her," Zack replied. "My job is to make sure nobody hurts her."

"You know I'm not talking about her getting hurt physically. I'm talking about somebody taking advantage of her."

"Trust me, it would take a better man than me to take advantage of Katie Sampson," Zack replied dryly. He moved toward the stall entrance. Jake moved aside to let him by. "Are we done here?"

Jake stuck his hands into his pockets. "I suppose we are."

As Jake headed toward the bunkhouse, Zack walked toward the house, his mind a jumble of thoughts. Although he had no reason not to, he didn't trust Jake.

Hell, he didn't trust anyone working on the ranch. When he reached the porch he greeted Burt Randall, a trusted employee of Wild West Protective Services.

"Anything I need to know about?" he asked.

Burt shook his head. "It's been quiet. Nobody coming and nobody going. I think Kate caught sight of me this afternoon. I was doing a walk-around of the house and spied her staring out the window at me."

"No problem," Zack replied. "Same time tomorrow morning?"

Burt nodded. "See you then."

Zack watched him walk across the lawn toward the barn. Burt's truck was parked behind the building. Zack hadn't particularly wanted Katie to know that Burt was on duty. He hadn't wanted her to know that he didn't trust the integrity of the security system alone to keep her safe. She had enough to worry about.

Although he knew he should get inside, he remained on the porch, reluctant to enter and face Katie.

It bothered him that Jake believed he saw something in the way Zack looked at Katie. How in the hell did he look at her?

More than just an old friendship? He and Katie had never shared a friendship. She'd been a contentious little brat who had irritated him to no end. She'd been like a young puppy, yapping and nipping at his heels.

But over the past week they had become friends. To his surprise he'd discovered her to be a woman he enjoyed being around, an intelligent woman who could hold her own in any conversation, a compassionate woman who cared about the town and her neighbors.

He frowned, leaned against the porch railing and watched the sun dipping lower and lower on the horizon. He should get inside and get showered up for the town meeting, but for some reason he wasn't ready to go inside to Katie.

The talk with Jake had disturbed him more than he cared to admit. He didn't want to care about Katie on a personal basis. There had been far too much loss in his life and he'd sworn after Melissa that he'd never allow anyone to get close to him again.

It was so much easier to be alone, so less risky. The women in his life never hung around for long. His mother had died, Jaime had left him and Melissa had died. Too much pain in one lifetime. He never intended to put himself in the position to feel that kind of pain again.

He was aware that it was getting late and Katie would have the evening meal waiting for him. Conscious of the fact that he needed to get showered and changed for the council meeting, he knocked on the front door and waited for Katie to let him in.

What bothered him more than anything was that despite his desire to remain unconnected, in spite of his desire to stay emotionally absent from Katie Sampson, the last couple of nights when he'd entered the house he'd had the feeling of coming home.

Chapter 14

Kate felt as if she had earned parole from prison as she and Zack left the house for the town council meeting. She wasn't accustomed to being cooped up inside for so many hours and days. The past week had been difficult as she'd tried to run the ranch from her kitchen table.

She'd dressed for the evening in a blue dress with a flirty ruffle across the hem. Matching sandals adorned her feet and despite the fact that they were attending the meeting and coming right back home, she looked forward to the outing every bit as much as if they were attending a party.

The only fly in the ointment was that her "date" for the evening appeared to be in one of his foul moods. He'd been silent as a tomb as he'd eaten dinner, then had disappeared into the bathroom to shower and change.

She cast him a surreptitious glance as they got into

his truck. He might be in a foul mood, but he was devilishly handsome in a pair of jeans, a navy dress shirt and a lightweight jacket. She knew beneath the jacket he wore his shoulder holster and the thought that he was attending the council meeting armed reminded her of the danger that still surrounded her.

"It feels so good to be out of the house," she said as he started his truck and they pulled away.

"Even though you're dressed in your party clothes, this isn't exactly a social outing." His tone was curt.

He was in a mood, she thought. "What did you do? Come down wrong in the saddle while you were out riding today?"

A small smile curved one corner of his mouth although he didn't look at her. "No, I didn't come down wrong in the saddle." The smile disappeared. "I'm just frustrated. I'm no closer to figuring out who killed your dad than I was on the day you called me to come to the hospital."

"Surely sooner or later somebody will show their hand."

"I hope it's sooner than later," he replied.

She turned her attention out the passenger window, wondering why his words caused a tiny pain to resonate inside her.

Of course he wanted it to be sooner. He didn't want to spend the rest of his life guarding her, didn't want to spend any more time than necessary on this particular job. She didn't need him underfoot, didn't need the tension that simmered between them each and every night.

She'd spent every night since the last time they had made love tossing and turning, wishing he were next to her in the bed, wanting him with a desire that seemed to consume her. Surely things would be easier when he was out of her life. Surely then she could forget about what they had shared so briefly.

She turned to look at him again. "What are your plans after this? Will you go back to work for Wild West?"

"To be honest, I don't know. I haven't decided what I'll do. If Jim Ramsey would retire, I might throw my hat in the ring for sheriff."

"Really?"

He flashed her a quick glance. "Don't look so surprised. Surely I could do the job at least as well as he had."

"No...I mean, of course you'd make a terrific sheriff. I'm just surprised that you aren't going back to work for your family's business."

He frowned. "I'm tired of living life on the road, constantly being in different cities, responsible for different people. I'm ready to put down roots and I can't do that if I'm working for Wild West."

"Do you think Ramsey is going to retire?"

He shrugged. "Rumor has it he's been thinking about it." He flashed her a wry grin. "But you know about the rumor mill in this town. You can only believe about a fourth of what you hear."

"When Jaime Coffer left town the rumor was she was pregnant with your child." She'd always wondered about the pretty blonde who had chosen to leave town, leave Zack years ago.

He looked at her in surprise, then chuckled. "I hadn't heard that one."

"Was it true?" She knew it was none of her business and wouldn't be surprised if he told her so, but she had a hunger to know everything about him, all the forces that had shaped him into the man he'd become.

"Nothing could be further than the truth," he replied. "Jaime and I weren't even lovers." It was her turn to gaze at him in surprise. "Oh, I know everyone assumed we were," he continued. "Even though we dated for a long time, we both knew from the beginning there was no future there."

"Why not?"

"Jaime couldn't wait to get out of Cotter Creek. She wanted to travel. She was a big-city girl with big-city dreams. She'd spend hours poring over travel magazines, making lists of places she wanted to go, potential places she'd like to live."

"And even though you dated her all that time, you weren't in love with her?"

This time when he shot her a glance it was dark and filled with an unspoken warning. "I'm just not the loving kind, Katie."

His words sent a ripple of disappointment, of unexpected sadness through her. Oddly enough she wanted to argue the point with him. She'd never known a man with more potential for loving than Zack. He'd shown that potential with his respect and attention to her father. He'd shown it when he'd talked about Melissa and the trauma of her death.

"Hopefully tonight we can get a handle on who is behind your problems, then I'll worry about what I'm going to do with the rest of my life," he said as he turned into the community center parking lot.

Foolish woman, she berated herself as she got out of his pickup. She'd been the first one to tell Zack that their lovemaking meant nothing, that she had no expectations of any kind of relationship with him other than that of a working one.

But if she were to look deep inside herself, examine the feelings that lived in the very depth of her, she'd have to acknowledge that Zack had touched her in ways no other man had ever done in her life.

It went far beyond the fact that his lovemaking had been magnificent. In the evening hours when they played cards and talked, he'd shown himself to be a man firm in his convictions, committed to making a difference in the world and intensely loyal to his family.

As they started walking toward the one-story brick building, he placed a hand in the small of her back. "Stay close to me," he said softly. "I don't want you wandering away from me for any length of time."

In that instant she recognized her love for Zack West. She loved him. He was the man she wanted in her life, by her side forever. She wanted to laugh, she wanted to shout with joy and she wanted to weep. Not even three minutes before, the man she loved had told her that he wasn't the loving kind.

She had little time to indulge in wistful what-ifs or to berate herself for her own stupidity as they walked into the throng of people already in the community center.

Friends and neighbors greeted them as they made their way inside. Zack kept his hand firmly on her back as he steered her toward the back row of chairs set up for the meeting.

They were just about to sit when Smokey Johnson and Zack's father approached them. "How you doing, Kate?" Smokey asked as Red and Zack took a step away and conversed in soft undertones.

"I'm hanging in there, Smokey."

"Our boy treating you all right?" Smokey's grizzled gray eyebrows danced up with his question.

He's treating me so well I've fallen in love with him. He's treating me so well I can't imagine what my life will be like when he's gone. She swallowed the words before they could actually fall from her lips and instead merely nodded.

"He's a good man. Was hell on wheels when he was younger, but he managed to turn out okay."

Before she could reply, Zack and his father moved closer. Red smiled at her. "Good to see you here, Kate. We can always use a voice of reason at these meetings."

She slid a pointed look at Zack. "There are some people who think maybe I speak my mind a little too much."

"Nothing wrong with that," Smokey replied. Kate fought back a grin. Smokey had a reputation for being painfully outspoken and cantankerous to boot.

"We'd better find ourselves a couple of chairs," Red said. "It looks like Mayor Sharp is about to call the meeting to order."

As Kate and Zack took their seats, Red and Smokey went to a couple of empty chairs near the front. As she sat, she realized Bill Garrett was in the seat in front of her. She fought the impulse to punch him in the back of his head. She hadn't forgotten how disrespectful he'd been to her dad when they'd made the decision not to use his pesticides on their crops.

Bill Garrett wasn't the only person in the room who had the capacity to boil Kate's blood. Although Sheila Wadsworth sat across the room, her affected girlish laughter rang through the air.

Zack appeared to be relaxed but Kate noted the way

his alert gaze swept the floor, never lingering long on any one person. Kate followed his gaze, looking at first one person, then another.

Friends and neighbors, the room was filled with people she had known for most of her life. But she had to keep in mind that it was quite possible somebody in this room had wanted her father dead. Somebody nearby might want her dead.

Mayor Aaron Sharp was a man who loved the sound of his own voice. Zack didn't know the handsome middle-aged man well, having met him only on a couple of occasions. Aaron had struck Zack on those times as an ambitious go-getter, a political smooth-talker who enjoyed his position of power in the town. Aaron was certainly dressed for success in a charcoal suit that complemented his dark hair and blue eyes.

As the mayor droned on and on, Zack found his attention drifting. They'd arrived late enough that there had been little time to socialize before the meeting had begun. He expected that after the meeting people would mill about and visit with one another. Perhaps then he'd see something in somebody's eyes, hear something in a tone of voice that would indicate a murderous rage directed at Katie.

Twice Mayor Sharp called for discussion and he sensed Katie getting ready to speak. Each time he grabbed her hand and squeezed to keep her silent. If she spoke up and made somebody mad, it would only complicate things.

The last time he'd grabbed her hand he hadn't released it and her fingers now twined with his. She had the hands of a woman who knew a day's work. Although her fingernails were clean and lightly glossed with a pearly pink, they were short and blunt-cut. He thought her hands were as pretty as any he'd ever seen.

He frowned at his wayward thoughts, pulled his hand from hers and focused once again on the meeting. It was obvious that what Katie had told him about the mayor having delusions of grandeur for their small town was correct by the agenda he was attempting to push forward.

He brought up wanting a Cotter Creek exit off the freeway, which met with mixed reaction from the audience. Most were afraid that the exit would increase unwelcomed traffic through the town.

It was also obvious that Sheila Wadsworth was on the same page as the mayor. She argued each and every point in favor of his recommendations. Zack found himself wondering if the mayor and Sheila were lovers. There was something in the way their gazes met and held that made him think something was going on between the two. Although Sheila was probably fifteen years older than Aaron, she was still an attractive, vibrant woman, if you liked flash and glitz in a female.

The fact that the mayor was supposedly a happily married man wouldn't stop Sheila, who had a reputation for going after what she wanted and damn the fallout.

Zack knew the meeting was starting to wind down when he smelled the scent of fresh-brewed coffee coming from the kitchen area of the community center. According to Katie, the ladies' auxiliary provided cookies and coffee after every meeting.

Zack had a feeling that was the time the discussions got interesting and people let down their guard. An edge of frustration gnawed at his belly.

What if he never figured out who had killed Gray? Who had tried to kill Katie? How long could he spend the night on her sofa thinking about the taste of her, the feel of her naked body against his and not lose his mind?

He'd told her he was in this for the long haul, but there was no guarantee the guilty party would ever be caught. His own mother had been murdered twenty-five years ago and her murder had never been solved.

These thoughts still worried him as the meeting broke up and people began to move around the room, heading for the refreshments and visiting with each other.

"How about we join the others?" he suggested, wanting to mingle and to see what gossip he might pick up.

"Okay." She leaned closer to him, so close he felt like his heart had jumped up into his throat. "A word of warning," she whispered. "Stay away from Millie Carter's oatmeal cookies. If you eat any you'll have indigestion for a month."

He felt as if he would have stomach problems for a month just because her warm breath tickled his ear.

There was no doubt about it, Katie Sampson bothered him in a way she had never bothered him before and he didn't like it. He needed to be done with this job, with this woman, before he lost his mind.

He and Katie made their way to the kitchen area, where they found Sheriff Ramsey with a plateful of cookies in one hand and a cup of coffee in the other.

"Zack, Kate." He greeted them with a friendly nod. "Good to see you both here this evening."

Zack gave the sheriff a curt nod, wishing the man would spend more time investigating and less time socializing. He knew he was being irrational, but his frustration level with this case grew by the second.

As Katie and the sheriff visited, Zack once again swept his gaze over the people in attendance. What worried him more than anything was that for the past couple of days he'd felt a sense of impending doom, that somehow they were about to get kicked in the teeth and he had no idea from what direction the kick might come. How could he protect Katie when he couldn't identify the source of the danger?

He felt Katie stiffen next to him as Sheila Wadsworth approached them. As usual, Sheila wore enough rhinestones to make Las Vegas look dull.

"Just the woman I wanted to talk to," Zack said in greeting.

She preened with pleasure and smiled. "And just what can I do for one of the sexiest cowboys in Cotter Creek?"

Zack flashed Katie a warning glance, knowing she would love to spout off some remark that would alienate Sheila. "I was wondering about the Wainfield property."

The flirtatious smile on Sheila's face disappeared. "What about it?"

"I heard a businessman from back east bought the place, but I noticed nobody has moved in yet," Zack said.

"I just sell property, Zack, I don't regulate when folks move in." She turned her attention to the sheriff and Katie.

Zack wasn't sure why, but something about Joe Wainfield's accident bothered him. Was he grasping at straws? Trying to make something out of nothing?

Somehow, some way, he felt as if he'd lost his objectivity and that bothered him more than anything did.

Sheriff Ramsey wandered back toward the cookies and Zack stepped closer to Katie as Sheila excused herself. For the next few minutes he watched as Katie was greeted by several of the other ranchers.

"I figured you would have sold out and disappeared from Cotter Creek by now," Raymond Harris said to Katie.

"Why would you figure that?" She looked at the older man in surprise.

He shrugged big shoulders and moved the toothpick in his mouth from one side to the other. "Just figured you weren't the type to stick it out, ranching being hard work and all."

"Hard work never scared me, Mr. Harris," she replied.

Harris looked at her dubiously. "Heard you lost a lot of your men. You need something, don't hesitate to ask. We take care of our own in this town."

"Thanks, Mr. Harris," Katie replied, her throat sounding thick with suppressed emotion.

As Harris wandered off, Zack leaned closer to Katie.

"You ready to get out of here?" he asked. He felt like he was spinning his wheels, wasting his time.

"Okay," she said, obviously surprised by his abrupt need to leave.

They were headed out the door when Sheriff Ramsey stopped them. "Katie, I just got a call from one of my deputies. He had to arrest one of your hands."

"Who?" Katie asked.

"Brett Cook." Ramsey brushed cookie crumbs from the front of his protruding stomach.

"Let me guess, drunk and disorderly," Zack said.

Ramsey nodded. "He's asking to talk to Katie."

She looked up at Zack, her brow creased with worry. "Maybe I should go over to the jail and speak with him."

He nodded. He had a feeling Brett probably thought Katie would be a softer touch than Gray and would bail him out. Zack didn't intend to let that happen. In fact, he intended to encourage Katie to fire the man.

Minutes later they were in his truck and headed for the sheriff's office down the street. "Katie, the amount of work you get out of Brett isn't worth the hassles. The man is more trouble than he's worth."

"I know." Her voice was soft and when he looked at her his heart constricted. She looked small and vulnerable. He parked in front of the sheriff's office and turned to her.

"You okay?"

She hesitated a moment, then nodded. "It's been a long week." She worried a hand through her hair and sighed. "It's been difficult running the ranch from the house. I'm used to being outside overseeing things. We're short-handed and I guess I'm feeling just a little bit overwhelmed at the moment." She chewed her bottom lip, then continued. "I feel like everyone is just waiting for me to fail. Sheila can't wait to sell the ranch and everyone else seems to believe I'm not up to running the place."

Although he had no intention of ever touching her again, without his volition, his hand crept out and covered hers. She closed her eyes, as if finding his touch almost painful. When she looked at him again, there was a faint sheen of unshed tears in the depths of her eyes.

"I'm just afraid that somehow I'm going to screw

up and lose everything Dad worked for. I'm afraid that while I'm hiding in my house, the ranch is going to fall to ruin."

"We're not going to let that happen, Katie. *I* won't let that happen." Somewhere in the back of his mind he realized he was making yet a new commitment to her.

Chapter 15

Brett Cook's drunken ravings were audible the moment Kate and Zack entered the sheriff's office. Deputy Harry Wilson stood from the receptionist desk as they entered, obvious relief lifting the scowl from his face.

"Thank goodness Sheriff Ramsey found you. Maybe if you talk to him, you can get him to calm down and sleep it off," he exclaimed.

"I'll see what I can do. What happened to bring him here?"

"I was called down to Crazy Joe's. Brett was blitzed and being obnoxious. Management complained and he got mouthy with me, so I brought him in." He opened the door that led to the cell area. "Just knock when you're finished."

Kate had never been in the jail area of the offices and after taking one step through the door that led to the cells, she decided she never wanted to be here again.

There were only three cells and Brett was the only occupant in the house, but the area smelled like sour sweat, urine and booze.

She was grateful Zack was with her, especially when Brett caught sight of her and grabbed and rattled the bars of his cell like a madman. "It's about time," he said, the words slurring together.

Zack kept a hand firmly on her shoulder, the weight reassuring as she faced Brett. "Why did you want to see me?" she asked.

"Get me out of here. Pay my bail and get me out and I promise I'll pay you back." He rattled the cell bars once again. "I can't stand being in here. Just get me out, okay?"

Zack started to speak, but Kate knew it was important she handle this herself. She stilled whatever he was about to say with a look then turned back to Brett.

"I'm sorry, Brett, I can't help you out."

He stared at her with bleary eyes. "Whadda mean?"

"I'm not going to bail you out. In fact, when you get out of here, I want you to pack your bags and get off my ranch."

"What?" He stared at her as if he was certain he'd misunderstood. "Just get me out of here."

Kate straightened her back. "No. I'm not your wife and I'm not your mama. You've got a problem, Brett, but I can't fix it and I can't make it mine. When you get out, pack your bags and go get some help."

Brett slammed a palm against the cell door, his features radiating a malevolence that stole her breath away. She backed up a step. "You bitch! Get me out of here." He grabbed hold of the bars and yanked at them like a madman.

Zack stepped in front of her, his features radiating a deadly calm. "That's enough, Cook. I'll pack your things up and have them brought here. You aren't welcome at Bent Tree Ranch."

"Miss High and Mighty, you're just like your bastard father, never give a man a break." He rattled the bars again.

Zack put his arm around Kate. "Come on," he said. "Let's get out of here."

"Come back here, you bitch." Brett's voice followed them from the cell area.

Minutes later they were back in the truck. Kate felt sick to her stomach as she thought of the venom that had spewed from Brett's eyes. She'd seen him surly and hung-over, lazy and sullen, but never had she suspected the hatred he'd apparently harbored in his heart for her and her father.

"He's a drunken fool," Zack said softly.

"Yes, he is…but he's so angry." She thought of what Brett had yelled and the poison that had lit his eyes. "And apparently he harbors a big grudge against my father." She looked at Zack. "Do you think it's possible he killed Dad?"

Zack didn't answer right away. He released a deep sigh, then replied, "Anything is possible. It makes sense that Brett might have met Gray on the trail that morning and maybe Gray fired him again. Brett lost it and killed him."

"But that doesn't explain why Brett would try to kill me," she said, playing devil's advocate. "He and I hadn't fought. I hadn't fired him until tonight."

"But his rage might have been so big, killing your dad wasn't enough."

"If that's all true, will we ever be able to prove any of it?" she asked, even though she knew the probable answer.

Again he sighed and she noted that he looked tired. The lines around his eyes appeared deeper than usual. She realized that while she slept peacefully in her bed each night feeling safe and secure because of his very presence in the house, he probably tossed and turned and enjoyed little sleep while on duty twenty-four hours a day.

"All I know is that when we get to the ranch I'm going to pack up Brett's things and take them back to the jail. We'll tell all the men he isn't welcome on the property and if he's spotted hanging around they are to call the sheriff and have him arrested for trespassing."

The fact that he hadn't directly answered her question about proving Brett's guilt indicated to her that he didn't believe it would be done.

If he was the guilty party, then at least now she knew from what direction danger might come. But there was still the disturbing possibility that he was guilty only of being a mean, hateful drunk.

It was just after ten when they arrived at the ranch. "Lock yourself in and it will take me about an hour to get Brett's things delivered to the jail," Zack said as he parked his truck.

"I'll come with you to get his things and deliver them." She still felt vulnerable. It wasn't so much her physical well-being that worried her, but rather the fact that she didn't want to be alone, didn't want to have time to think.

Old feelings of inadequacy had plagued her throughout the evening. She had come away from the town meeting with the impression that all the other ranchers in the area expected her to fail, anticipated that she didn't have what it took to keep the place going.

If she'd been a son, nobody would have doubted that Gray's heir would keep the place running smoothly. She got out of the truck with Zack, refusing to dwell on these painfully familiar thoughts.

"It's still early enough, most of the men will be in town," Zack said as they walked toward the bunkhouse. "I imagine the only person we'll find is George."

Sure enough when they entered the bunkhouse the only person inside was George, who was snoring in a chair in front of the television.

He snorted and sat up as they entered, blinking his eyes in an effort to claim full consciousness. As he saw Kate, he quickly jumped out of his chair. "Is there a problem, Ms. Sampson?"

"You're fine, George. Just sit and relax," she replied.

"Brett is in jail on drunk and disorderly charges," Zack explained. "Kate has fired him and we're going to pack up his things and take them to the jail. He's not welcome here anymore."

George sat and shook his head. "Just a matter of time. That man was born mean and drunk."

"Even though we're short-handed, it was past time I fired him," Kate said.

"We'll manage," George said. "If some of us got to put in a few extra hours then we will."

Kate smiled at the older man gratefully. She didn't know all the details of his problems in the past, but over the years he'd proven himself to be a law-abiding hard worker.

She watched as Zack went to one of the cabinets and

grabbed a large black plastic garbage bag. He moved to Brett's footlocker and opened the lid.

The first items he pulled out were wrinkled clothing and a handful of balled socks. A pitiful collection of toiletries followed. Two bottles of gin appeared in Zack's hands. "I'm tempted to throw these away, but knowing Brett, he'd raise a stink about destruction of his property."

She knew he was right so said nothing as he added the bottles to the garbage bag. He picked up another armful of clothing, then stood in surprise, his gaze focused intently on the remaining contents of the foot locker.

"What?" she asked. She stepped closer so she could see into the foot locker. Her heart jumped at the sight of the last two items that remained…her father's gun and a bull horn.

George joined them and looked into the locker. "I'll be a son of a gun," he exclaimed. "I would have never guessed Brett could pull it together enough to be responsible for everything."

"We need to call Sheriff Ramsey," Zack said. "It looks like we've found our evidence."

The rest of the night went by in a blur for Kate.

Sheriff Ramsey collected Brett's personal items, including the gun and bull horn, then went back to the jail to question Brett. She and Zack returned to the jail with him and watched the interview.

Brett drunkenly denied knowing anything about the gun or the bull horn and declared his innocence in Gray's death and any of the attacks on Katie.

His denials fell on Kate's deaf ears. The way she figured it was that her father had fired Brett once again and this time Brett's pleas for another chance had fallen on deaf ears. Brett's rage had not only been directed at Gray, but also the daughter Gray had loved.

The moment she had seen that bull horn she'd felt vindicated. She hadn't been a hysterical female imagining things in a thunderstorm. That bull horn had been blown to stampede her cattle, for the sole purpose of her death.

It was almost midnight when they got back into Zack's truck to return to the ranch. She should be feeling ecstatic. The bad guy was behind bars and Sheriff Ramsey assured them Brett would be facing additional serious charges in the morning.

But as they pulled up in front of the house, although she felt relief, she didn't feel joy. It was done. Over. Her father's murderer had been caught and the danger to her was over, as well.

Her life was once again her own. She no longer had to be a prisoner in her house. She no longer needed Zack's services.

But I need him. The thought filled her with a new despair. She didn't want him to go. She didn't want this to be the end of their relationship.

He parked the truck in front of the house and turned to her. "Well, it's done." His features were shrouded in the night's darkness.

"So it seems," she said, grateful that her voice betrayed none of the tumultuous emotions racing through her.

"If you don't mind, I'll just bunk on your sofa for the rest of the night then pack up and get out of here in the morning."

"That's fine," she agreed, and opened the truck door. She just wanted to get inside and get to the privacy of her bedroom.

"Katie." She turned back to him, his features now lit by the interior truck light. "You don't have to be afraid anymore."

"I'm not. I'm just exhausted," she replied, and got out of the truck.

She went directly inside and to her bedroom. She didn't want to talk about the evening, didn't want to spend another moment with Zack, who would be gone in the morning, who probably couldn't wait to get back to his own life.

Once she was in her room she quickly undressed and pulled on her nightshirt. She turned off the light and walked over to the window, where silvery light spilled down from a full moon.

As she stood there in the darkness, in the silence of her room, she could hear Zack preparing the sofa for the night. She closed her eyes, surprised to find the sting of tears pressing hot and painful.

She'd once worried that Zack was trying to steal her father's heart away and while she wasn't looking it had been her heart he'd stolen.

He awakened before dawn, a sound in the house rousing him from sleep. Zack sat up and frowned, seeing a light shining from Gray's bedroom. He pulled on his jeans and checked his watch—4:00 a.m. What was Katie doing up at this hour?

He padded down the hall and stopped in the doorway to Gray's bedroom. Katie was there folding clothes from Gray's closet and placing them in a cardboard box. She was clad only in an oversize T-shirt, her hair in disarray, as if she'd spent the few hours in bed tossing and turning.

"Katie, what are you doing?"

"I need to pack up these things." She didn't look at him.

"At four in the morning?"

"I couldn't sleep." She turned and pulled a sweater from the closet. "Most of these clothes are in excellent shape, I'm sure one of the churches in town can make good use of them."

He moved to the foot of the bed and sat and watched her silently, wondering what was going on in her head. She moved with a manic energy and tension rolled off her in waves.

He wanted to take her in his arms, to calm her with backrubs and soft kisses, but he recognized the foolishness of such a thing. He knew his weakness. If he touched her in any way, he'd want her again. If he kissed her, he knew they'd end up in bed, and that's the last thing he needed at the moment.

He intended to walk away clean in the morning, no regrets, no baggage. He needed to get away from her because she scared him just a little bit. He had to admit, he'd gotten too close. It was time to walk away and not look back.

Hell, he didn't even know what he was going to do with his life. He didn't want to go back to the family business, but he didn't know anything else.

"Go back to sleep, Zack," she said, breaking into his thoughts. Her voice was cool and brittle, so unlike what he'd come to expect from her.

"I'm awake now. I'll keep you company."

For the first time since he'd entered the room she looked at him and in her eyes he saw raw grief and something else...the glitter of what appeared to be anger. "I don't want your company."

He stared at her for a long moment, noting the stress lines around her mouth, the circles beneath her eyes. But it was more than fatigue, he thought. "What's wrong?" he asked. He rose from the bed, forgetting his own determination not to touch her. He walked over to where she stood, the sweater still clutched in her hands, her gaze on the floor in front of her.

Placing his hands on her shoulders, he willed her to look at him. "Katie," he said softly. "Talk to me. Something is wrong. Tell me what's going on."

She jerked away from him, her eyes flashing angrily. "It's Kate, Zack. My name is Kate. I've told you that before."

He dropped his arms to his sides. "Okay," he replied slowly.

"And I'll tell you what's wrong." She folded the sweater and dropped it in the box. When she looked at him again her eyes were haunted. "My father is dead. I'm never going to have any more time with him and I wish I had all the hours back with him that you stole."

He frowned in surprise. "What?" Of all the things he'd expected her to say, this wasn't one of them. "What are you talking about?"

"I'm talking about all those hours you spent here with my father, all that time that I could have spent with him." She whirled around and grabbed another sweater off a hanger, her body vibrating with the intensity of her emotions.

"Katie—Kate, that was years ago. We were both just

kids," he said. "I was a mixed-up teenager and your dad helped me through some rough times."

"He should have been helping me. He should have spent that time sitting with me on the porch, talking to me. Now he can't and I wish I had those nights back. I wish you would have never come around."

For the first time since he'd entered the room, a stir of anger filled his gut. "Kate, I know you're grieving, but there's no reason to take it out on me." He had the distinct impression she was looking to pick a fight, but he didn't know why and he hadn't realized she still harbored a spoiled child's resentment toward him.

Her eyes narrowed and she threw the sweater into the box. "You had a huge family of your own, your father and Smokey and four brothers and a sister, but that wasn't enough for you. You had to come around here and try to destroy my relationship with my dad."

"If you had a bad relationship with your dad, it had nothing to do with me," he exclaimed, his anger reaching the boiling point. "You were spoiled and willful and difficult. I'd thought you'd grown up, but obviously I was wrong."

She sucked in a deep breath, her bottom lip trembling. "Get out, Zack. Go home. You did what I asked you to do and for that I'm grateful, but there's no more danger now and I don't want you here."

"Fine." He turned to leave the room, but paused and turned back to look at her. "I'm not making any excuses or apologies for spending time with Gray. At the time I was coming here, I felt invisible at home. I was miserable and on a path to destruction. Your father's friendship saved me. How dare you begrudge me that time, and more importantly, how dare you begrudge your father my companionship."

He knew he should just leave, but he couldn't, not yet, not until he said everything that burned inside him. "Your dad spent his life worrying about you, making sacrifices for you and loving you. He spent his time reading fashion magazines so he'd know what was important to a girl. He baked cookies and cupcakes for every party you ever had in school. He loved you, Kate. And nobody and nothing could steal that away from you. But you're so selfish you begrudge him my friendship. You begrudge me his. If you have regrets where your dad is concerned, then you might look inside yourself instead of blaming me."

She vibrated with anger, her eyes too shiny and her mouth trembling. "Get out. I want you out of here now."

"No problem." He spun on his heels and left the bedroom. It took him only minutes to pack his things and storm out of the house.

Once in his truck he grabbed hold of the steering wheel and leaned his head back against the headrest. What had just happened in there? How had things spun so crazy out of control?

Years ago he'd known she'd hated it when he'd come over to visit with Gray, that she'd spent that time trying in every way possible to disrupt their time together, to gain her father's attention. But her actions had been those of a spoiled little girl who he'd thought had grown up.

He started the truck and pulled away from the house, recognizing that it wasn't just anger she'd stirred in him, but a deep, abiding disappointment.

He'd thought she'd put her childish temper tantrums

and resentments behind her, that she'd grown into a different kind of woman, a woman who had come perilously close to owning his heart. Apparently he'd been wrong about her and he knew he should be grateful he'd found out now.

As he drove through the gates of Bent Tree Ranch, he refused to look back. It was time he figure out what he intended to do for the rest of his life.

Chapter 16

She'd done it again.

It was just after seven and Kate sat at her kitchen table drinking a cup of coffee and replaying the events of the past couple of hours in her head.

She'd allowed hurt and sorrow to take hold of her and had responded to the pain with anger. It had been easier to attack Zack and send him away than to confess her love for him and see him turn away. It didn't make her hurt any less intense, it only assured her that she would be alone with her pain.

She'd fallen into bed the night before knowing that it was time to release Zack from his commitment to her, knowing that it was time to tell him goodbye. She'd prayed for blessed sleep to overtake her so she wouldn't think about life without him, but sleep had been elusive.

After tossing and turning for several hours, she'd finally gotten up with the driving need to do something, anything, to keep her thoughts away from Zack.

She'd decided to pack up her dad's clothing, but the moment she'd begun the job she'd been swept back in time, back to old insecurities and resentments.

She sipped her coffee and tried not to think about what Zack had said to her. She didn't want to examine the past. She should be grateful that she'd managed to get rid of Zack without baring her heart, without embarrassing herself with declarations of love for him.

A knock on the front door pulled her from her thoughts. She got up from the table and went to answer. Sonny stood on the porch, his dusty cowboy hat in hand.

She opened the door and started to invite him in as had become the habit. Then she remembered Brett was in jail, the danger had passed, and she stepped outside. She didn't have to be a prisoner in her own home anymore.

"Good morning, Sonny," she greeted.

"Morning," he replied.

"I've got some bad news for you," she said. "We're two men down today. Brett is in jail and not welcome on the ranch anymore and Zack has gone back to his place and won't be working for us anymore."

Sonny frowned. "Even though it's late in the season, you're going to have to hire on some new hands."

"I know. I'll put out the word around town and put an ad in the paper," she replied, grateful he hadn't asked any questions about either man who was no longer working for her.

"Anything else I need to know?" he asked.

She frowned thoughtfully. "Not that I can think of. You might have somebody cut away some of the weeds around the root cellar door this morning. I think I'll do some cleaning out down there today."

He nodded. "I'll take care of it myself right now."

"Thanks, Sonny. Other than that, just chores as usual."

He nodded once more, then plopped his hat on his head and took off walking around the side of the house where the root cellar was located.

Kate remained on the porch, taking in the sweet morning-scented air, trying desperately not to think of Zack. She hadn't wanted to fall in love with him, but he'd made it impossible for her not to.

It wasn't enough that she loved his dark, ruggedly handsome features. It wasn't just that his broad shoulders stirred her, his kisses electrified her and a single heated gaze from him could create a throbbing warmth at the very center of her.

As important as her physical attraction was to him, there was so much more to her love for him. She loved the way he touched her hand when he knew she was worried or upset. She loved the fact that she beat him consistently at gin rummy and he didn't whine.

She loved his gentleness, his sense of humor, but more importantly she'd grown to love his heart. She took another deep breath and fought the tears that once again pressed hot, the pain that crushed in her chest.

Activity. That's what she needed. Hard work would keep thoughts of him at bay. She went back into the house and after a hot shower dressed in worn jeans and a T-shirt.

She pulled on a pair of boots, grabbed a flashlight and a garbage bag, then left the house and headed for the root cellar. Many nights her father had talked about needing to clean out the small, shelf-lined dungeon.

Kate had only been down in the cellar one time before, when she was about twelve and a particularly vicious storm had blown up. She and her father had stood on the front porch and watched the twisting, boiling black clouds grow closer and closer. The storm was perilously close when a spiraling tail appeared, dipping toward the ground.

"Come on, Katie girl, looks like it's going to be a bad one." Together they'd run for the cellar, just getting inside when hail began to pound the metal door.

At that time Kate hadn't been sure what frightened her more, the storm outside or the darkness of the cellar. But her dad had held her close and had soothed her with murmured words and soft assurances. The storm had passed without damage.

The sun was bright and hot as Kate walked toward the cellar. True to his word, Sonny had cut away the weeds that had nearly choked the immediate area. The big, heavy door opened with a groan, exposing seven wooden steps almost straight down.

She clicked on the flashlight, knowing that even with the door open, the sunlight wouldn't illuminate all the areas of the tiny subterranean room.

The smell of onions and potatoes mingled with earth and clay, creating an alien, but not unpleasant, odor. She descended the stairs and shone the light in front of her.

Bunches of onions hung in the corner and a nearly empty bin of potatoes was directly in front of her. The metal shelves along one wall held an array of canning jars.

Canned tomatoes and green beans, jellies and fruit lined the shelves, all bearing handwritten labels written by Kate's mother when she'd been a young bride.

Had the lack of a mother in her life caused her to be too possessive, too selfish, where her father was concerned? She had to concede that it had.

She couldn't see what was on the top shelf. Spying a metal bucket, she overturned it and used it to stand on to discover a stack of old newspapers and empty jars.

She stepped down and sat on the bucket, her thoughts drifting to her fight with Zack. She'd acted like a child, throwing accusations at him to still her own pain.

Closing her eyes, she thought of those times when Zack had sat on the porch with Gray. "Look at me, Daddy," she'd say as she'd pull some crazy stunt to get his attention.

"Look at me, Zack," she now whispered. Her eyelids popped open and she stifled a burst of laughter that quickly transformed into a moan of pain.

Had she been trying to get her father's attention, or had it been Zack all along?

From the moment he'd first appeared on her porch she'd suffered a childhood crush on the handsome teenage cowboy. Although she was realistic enough to recognize that life probably would have been easier for Gray had she been a son, if she looked deep in her heart she realized she'd always been certain and secure in her father's love for her.

It had been Zack's attention she'd wanted, craved. She'd wanted him to see her as bright and brave, as a peer deserving his respect and admiration. It had never been about her dad. It had always been about Zack.

Dear God, she had been in love with Zack before she'd been old enough to know what love was. She hadn't resented his relationship with her father, she'd resented the fact that he wanted no relationship with her.

She stood from the bucket, for a moment over-whelmed with the need to run to the West ranch, to find Zack and tell him everything she'd discovered about herself, about the past.

But what good would come of it? a little voice whispered. Zack hadn't told her he loved her, he hadn't hesitated packing his bags and leaving. She sank down onto the overturned bucket. It was obvious he didn't feel the same way about her. So what was the point of her telling him how she felt?

A shadow passed in front of the light spilling down the stairs from the open door. She looked up in time to see something fly through the air and land on the ground near where she sat.

"Hey, I'm down here," she yelled toward the door at the same time she clicked on the flashlight to see what had been flung down the stairs.

Her light shown on a burlap bag near where she sat. The bag undulated with movement. What the heck? She froze as several snakes tumbled from the bag. A rattling noise filled the cellar.

Snakes.

Rattles.

With a sharp cry, she jumped up to stand on the bucket as half a dozen agitated rattlesnakes left the burlap bag.

The cellar door slammed shut.

Zack tried to tell himself it was the fight with Katie that caused the heaviness in his chest and the feeling of impending doom that tensed his muscles.

He'd arrived at his place before five and had spent the next two hours trying to put Katie Sampson back in his past, where she'd been before contacting him from the hospital.

By seven o'clock he was sick of his thoughts and his own company and had headed for the main house to have coffee with his dad and Smokey.

Red was out for a morning horseback ride, but Smokey was in the kitchen clearing away the breakfast dishes. "You're a surprise," Smokey said in greeting as Zack entered the back door. "I thought you were staying close to the Sampson place."

"Problem solved. I'm officially unemployed once again." Zack poured himself a cup of coffee and sat at the large wooden table.

Smokey poured himself a cup and joined Zack. "Problem solved?"

Zack quickly explained to him about Brett's arrest and finding Gray's gun and the air horn in his footlocker. As he spoke, he steadfastly shoved away the disquiet he'd felt since driving away from Bent Tree Ranch.

When he finished, Smokey shot him a sly glance. "When I saw you and Kate together at the town meeting, I thought maybe there was something else other than employment going on."

To Zack's surprise he felt his cheeks burn and he gazed down into his coffee cup. "There was a little something going on," he conceded.

Once again heavy disappointment filled his heart. How could he explain to Smokey that he'd fallen in love with a woman who apparently didn't exist? The disappointment was tempered by a shot of surprise.

Love. He'd fallen in love with Katie Sampson. He hadn't intended to, hell…he hadn't wanted to, but he had. But she'd come at him with selfish childhood resentiments that had stunned him and made him question just what kind of woman she really was.

"So what are your plans now?" Smokey asked.

"I don't know. I'm not inclined to go back to work for Wild West." He frowned thoughtfully. "For the last ten years I've drifted in and out of people's lives as a bodyguard and haven't built much of a life of my own."

"You'll do well whatever you decide to do," Smokey observed. "There was a time when I wasn't sure you'd survive to see twenty." Smokey laughed and shook his head. "You and Kate always struck me as two peas in a pod."

Zack scowled. "I'm nothing like Katie," he protested.

"Maybe not now, but when you were younger you and Katie had a lot in common. You both fought tooth-and-nail to get the attention of the people you loved and both of you chose some fairly negative ways to do it."

Reluctantly, Zack had to concede Smokey's point. "There was a time I thought I was pretty invisible to this family," he said.

Smokey nodded. "That's one of the side effects being part of a big family. Somebody is always getting lost in the shuffle. But, as mad as you'd get at everyone, you always knew your brothers and sister and your dad and me were there for you."

It was true. No matter where Zack had traveled, no matter how mad or upset he'd gotten, he'd always known deep in his heart that he had a strong, loyal family to support him. And Katie had only had her father and her own insecurities.

His heart softened toward her, but he knew this new understanding changed nothing. She'd told him that as far as she was concerned he wasn't Prince Charming material and she certainly hadn't hesitated to kick him to the curb when the danger had passed.

Time to move on, his head told him, although his heart mourned the thought of never holding her again, never tasting the sweetness of her lips. His heart ached with the knowledge that he'd never share her laughter or see the sleepy sexiness of her first thing in the morning.

Maybe Jake would move into his place. Maybe the handsome blond cowboy was more Prince Charming material than Zack could ever be to her. A weight of depression settled on his shoulders but even that couldn't still the vague sense of uneasiness that rippled deep inside him.

"Hell of a thing," Smokey said, breaking into Zack's thoughts. "Who would have thought a drunk like Brett could have pulled off such a thing."

"In the end, he didn't pull it off," Zack replied. He finished his coffee and carried his cup to the sink. "Guess I'll head on back to my place."

"Meredith should be coming back in town sometime later today. I'm cooking fried chicken for dinner in case you're interested."

Fried chicken was Zack's sister's favorite meal. "Sounds good, I just might show up at dinnertime," he said.

Moments later he stepped out the back door and headed for his own place down the lane. As he walked, he realized he felt the same way now that he had as he'd driven away from Melissa's house. His instincts screamed out that something wasn't right.

He'd ignored his instincts then and he tried to ignore them now. It wasn't the same, he tried to tell himself.

Whatever he felt now surely had to do with the fact that he'd come too close to loving Katie. It wasn't his instincts screaming. It was sadness and grief over what might have been.

With each step he took, he replayed the events of the night before, remembering Brett's bewilderment when Sheriff Ramsey had shown him the air horn and the gun, remembering Brett's drunken outrage when Sheriff Ramsey had accused him of murdering Gray.

The man could barely get through a day without getting drunk. He could barely function in an ordinary way. Was this a man who could pull off a murder, plan a stampede and start a fire?

No.

The word thundered through him. How long had it been since Brett had looked in the bottom of his footlocker? How easy would it have been for somebody to place those items there, set up the drunk who had a reputation for trouble?

Too easy. Too damned easy.

The wrong man is in jail. The knowledge ripped through him and on some level he recognized that this had been the source of his uneasiness since the moment he'd left Katie's ranch.

He'd needed to escape her and so he'd made himself believe that the guilty party was behind bars and there was no more danger to Katie.

Danger screamed in his head. If Brett wasn't the guilty one, then a murderer was still loose and Katie was on her own. He began to run toward his house and with each and every footstep a horrifying fear gripped him.

He crashed through the front door of his house and

grabbed his keys and his gun from the table. Within minutes he was in his truck and driving toward Bent Tree Ranch.

Maybe Brett was guilty, he thought as he tromped on the gas pedal. Maybe with Brett in jail there was no danger to Katie. But what if they had all been wrong?

In his line of work, Zack had known fear before, but he'd never experienced the kind of terror that gripped him now. His knuckles turned white as he squeezed the steering wheel, praying that he wasn't already too late, that he'd find Katie still mad at him and packing up Gray's clothes.

Gratefulness swept through him as he pulled in and saw Katie's car parked where it had been the night before.

As he took the stairs of the porch to the front door, he saw Sonny in the distance. The man was heading away from the house and seemed to be in a hurry.

Zack banged on the front door, impatient as he waited for a reply. Maybe she was still so mad at him she wouldn't open the door. He didn't wait any longer. He pulled his keys from his pocket and used the key that he'd forgotten to give back to her before he'd left this morning.

The security system blinked at him as he entered the entryway and he quickly punched in the code that would shut it off. "Katie!" he called as he left the entry and headed down the hallway to the room where he'd last seen her.

She wasn't in any of the bedrooms and he hurried down the hallway toward the kitchen, his blood pounding audibly in his head.

Let her be okay. Let her be safe. The two sentences

were a mantra in his head, repeating itself again and again. *Just please, let her be all right.*

It took him only minutes to realize she wasn't anywhere in the house. He stepped out onto the porch and looked around. She had to be someplace on the property. He refused to consider any other alternative.

He stood on the porch, trying to figure in which direction to begin searching. Odd, that Sonny had appeared to be hurrying away from the side of the house. Even more odd that he'd been on foot. He was usually on horseback.

Heart bumping, adrenaline flooding, he stepped off the porch and headed around the house. Nothing appeared to be amiss as he walked to the back.

The back door was locked tight, all the windows seemed to be fine. Everything looked perfectly normal, but his anxiety level was off the charts.

As he rounded the last corner of the house he saw the root cellar door. Somebody had recently cut the weeds away from the metal door that led into the ground. But that wasn't the sight that chilled his blood. On top of the door lay a dozen concrete blocks…blocks that hadn't been there the last time he'd walked by it.

Why would somebody go to the trouble of putting so many of the heavy concrete blocks on the door? Surely they hadn't been placed there to keep somebody out. The only reason for them to be there was to shut somebody in.

Zack scrambled to remove the blocks, throwing them off the door helter-skelter, his heart once again crashing with an unsteady rhythm.

When he had the blocks removed, he opened the door. "Katie?" he called.

"Don't come down here." Her voice was low and held an unsteady intensity.

He leaned down and peered down the stairs and the sight that greeted him shot ice through his veins. Katie stood on an overturned bucket frozen like a statue. Rattlesnakes writhed around the bucket. Their tails rattling to warn of imminent and deadly strikes.

Chapter 17

The moment the door opened overhead and she heard Zack's voice, Kate had wanted to scream with joy, but she knew any sudden movement, any loud noise, could mean her death.

She'd feared she'd die down here among her mother's jars of canned goods and ancient newspapers. She had no idea how long she'd been frozen in place, silently weeping as she faced her own death and a million regrets.

Zack came down the first two steps and crouched there, the look in his eyes emphasizing the seriousness of her situation. "Are you okay?" he asked.

"As okay as I can be," she replied.

"We need to get you out of here."

A bubble of hysterical laughter threatened to erupt. "Trust me, there's nothing I'd like better than to get out of here. But how?" The laughter disappeared as despair took hold. "If I step down, I'll be bitten. They're agitated." As if to punctuate her sentence several of the snakes coiled and rattled.

He frowned. "I can't shoot them down here. The noise alone would make the others strike."

"Somebody threw them down here," she said, horror filling her for the hundredth time since that burlap bag had been tossed down the stairs. "Somebody knew I was down here and threw them, then shut the door." She paused. "It wasn't Brett, was it? We made a mistake."

"It seems we did." His jaw clenched tight. "Katie, you can jump to me."

She stared at him in horror and new tears sprang to her eyes. "No! No, I can't. It's too far." The thought of even attempting such a jump filled her with fear. If she didn't make the distance the snakes would kill her with their deadly venom and she would die before help could arrive.

"Katie, honey, listen to me." Zack's voice was as smooth and calm as she'd ever heard it. "I've seen you jump from the tallest branches of a tree down to the ground. You used to leap from one porch railing to the other trying to get your dad's attention when I'd come to visit. You can do this."

"It wasn't about me wanting my dad's attention." It was suddenly vitally important that he know what she had discovered about herself, about him, during the course of the morning. "It was about me wanting your attention, Zack. I was nothing but a kid in your eyes, but even then I wanted to be so much more. I love you, Zack. I've been in love with you since I was a kid."

Her words had stunned him. She could tell by the expression on his face. "It's okay, you don't have to love me back," she continued. "I just needed to tell you, I wanted to tell you in case I die."

"Katie, honey, can we talk about this after we get you out of here?"

"Zack…I can't jump that far." Again, fear trembled through her, making her legs feel like jelly.

"Yes, you can. I know you can and if you get to the stairs I'll grab you. Dammit, Katie, you can do this."

"I'm afraid."

"Katie Sampson afraid? I never thought the day would come that a little jump would freeze you with fear. Now come on. Jump to me, Katie. Jump into my arms." He held his arms out toward her.

Oh, to be in his arms again, she thought wistfully. Although she wanted to escape the snakes, she wanted more to be pulled against his chest, to feel his heart-beat against her own.

If she thought about what she was about to do she knew she'd freeze up or stumble over her own feet. Instead she focused only on Zack, telling herself she wasn't jumping over or away from anything but rather leaping into his arms.

Summoning her strength and her will to survive, she leaped…and gasped as she connected solidly with him. He wrapped his arms around her and pulled her up the stairs, away from the deadly rattlers.

"Are you all right?" He placed his hands on either side of her face. "No bites?" She shook her head, too weak with relief to respond. "Go to the house and lock yourself in. Call Sheriff Ramsey and get him out here. I know who did this."

"Who?" She managed to squeak the words.

"I'll tell you later." He kissed her then, a hard crush

of lips that stole what little breath she had left. "Go," he ordered, and pointed to the house.

Although she wanted to ask him why he'd kissed her, wanted to know why he'd called her honey, she was smart enough to recognize she needed to do as he'd said.

As she hurried toward the front door she saw him walking away, a determined strength in his shoulders, his gun held firm in his hand.

It wasn't until she was safely inside the house and had made the call to the sheriff's office that the trauma she'd just endured struck her. She sank to the sofa and wept tears of relief. The tears lasted only a moment as questions filled her head.

She got up and went to the front window and peered outside, thinking of the evil mind, the hatred it took to lock her in the cellar with a half dozen poisonous snakes. It was the same kind of devious mind that had tied her into her bedroom then set it on fire.

Who? Who would have done such a thing and why? There was only one person who had known that she was going to be in the root cellar that day. Sonny.

Sonny had been absent the night of the fire. He'd been Johnny on the spot right after the stampede. And, it was in the direction of Sonny's small cabin that Zack had stalked with gun in hand.

Her heart pounded with anxiety. Sonny wasn't a drunk, nor was he a young greenhorn. He knew how to handle a gun and was as strong as a moose. She hoped the sheriff arrived soon. She needed Zack to be safe…so he could tell her why he'd kissed her with such fervor.

Zack knew he had to get a handle on the fury that gripped him as he walked toward the small cabin Sonny called home. Seeing Katie surrounded by those snakes, hearing the trembling fear in her voice, had filled him with a killing rage of his own. Somebody was going to pay for Katie's terrified tears. Somebody was definitely going to pay.

He approached the cabin cautiously, using the woods surrounding the place as cover. He had no idea what Sonny's motive might be for wanting to hurt either Gray or Katie, but Zack knew in his gut the man was responsible for the snakes in the root cellar.

His suspicion was confirmed as the door to the small cabin swung open and Sonny hurried out, carrying two suitcases in his hands. He threw the suitcases into the back of his truck then disappeared into the cabin once again. Looked as though he was packing up to leave town. Only the guilty ran like a cockroach in the morning light.

Zack moved closer, crouching by the side of the truck opposite the front door. It was several minutes before he heard the screen door slam and knew Sonny had exited the house once again.

He clicked the safety off his gun and stood. "Going somewhere, Sonny?" He held the gun steady in front of him, pointed directly at the man he believed responsible for the misery in Katie's life.

"Zack! Since when do you greet me with a gun in your hand?"

"Since you chose to attack what's mine."

"I don't know what you're talking about." Sonny was bluffing.

The man's hand moved toward his holstered gun.

"I wouldn't do that if I were you," Zack warned. "I'm just itching to blow a hole through your hide. Just tell me why, Sonny? Why would you want to hurt Gray? Hurt Katie? You were like family to them."

Sonny snorted in derision. "Don't be stupid. I wasn't like family. I was the hired help, busting my butt year after year, knowing that I was never going to get ahead."

"So, you killed Gray?" Zack looked at him with disdain.

"I'm not about to admit to anything," Sonny replied, but the look on his face told Zack his answer. Sonny had been responsible for it all.

"What did Katie ever do to you?" Zack wanted to punch the man in the face as he thought of the terror that Katie had endured.

"Nothing. And Gray never did anything to me. It wasn't personal, Zack." His eyes gleamed with secrets. "It was strictly business and it's bigger than Gray and Katie and that's all I'm going to say."

That's all he had an opportunity to say for at that moment the sound of a siren split the air and within minutes Jim Ramsey had pulled his patrol car in front of the cabin.

"Zack," he said as he sized up the situation. "Kate filled me in a bit on what's going on. Sonny, you got anything to say?"

"I got nothing to say to nobody."

"Okay, then." Sheriff Ramsey handcuffed Sonny and placed him in the back of the patrol car. "You and Kate need to come down to the station and make statements. I have a feeling it's going to take a while to sort this all out."

As the sheriff drove off with Sonny in the back of his car, Zack trekked back to the house to Katie. She must have been watching for him because before he hit the porch she opened the door.

"Thank God, you're all right," she said.

"Ramsey arrested Sonny. We need to go down to the sheriff's office and make statements."

She nodded. "Just let me get my purse."

She disappeared into the house while Zack remained on the porch, his thoughts spinning in a thousand different directions.

Although Sonny had clammed up the minute the sheriff had arrived, what little he'd said before Jim had arrested him merely confused the whole situation.

Bigger than Gray and Katie. Katie had told him she loved him. Nothing personal…she'd loved him for years. Strictly business. This job had become so much more than strictly business.

He couldn't think about his relationship with Katie until things with Sonny were taken care of. He turned as she came out of the house.

Moments later they were in his truck and he was telling her what Sonny had said to him. When he finished, she frowned. "What did he mean, Zack, that it was bigger than me and my father?"

"I don't know," he admitted. "Maybe by the time we get to the office Jim will have some answers for us. All I know for certain is that Sonny is responsible for your dad's death as well as the attacks on you. He must have placed the gun and the air horn in Brett's footlocker to point suspicion in another direction."

"I thought I was going to die in that cellar." Her voice held a faint tremor. "I thought nobody would ever find me and eventually I'd grow tired and fall off the bucket." He felt her gaze on him. "What made you come back?"

"It didn't feel right. All my instincts told me we had the wrong man in jail. All my instincts told me Brett wasn't smart enough to pull off something like this."

"I'm glad you came back. I'm sorry. All the things I said to you this morning, I was upset and I didn't mean them."

"It's all right. We'll talk about it later. Right now we need to make sure we give Sheriff Ramsey enough information to keep Sonny in jail for a very long time to come."

By the time they arrived at the sheriff's office Jim had already dispatched several officers to the cabin with a search warrant and had received a phone call from one of the officers calling in what they'd found.

"A couple of things of interest," he said to Zack and Katie as the two sat with him in his office. "They found an aquarium that was used to keep snakes. They also found the same kind of rope that was used to tie your door shut on the night of the fire."

"Has Sonny said anything else?" Katie asked. "Has he said why he did all this?"

"He's refusing to say anything," Jim replied. "My men also found a savings account book in his bedroom. It shows a deposit of one hundred thousand dollars on the afternoon of your father's death."

Zack narrowed his eyes in thought. "So, he wasn't acting alone."

"I'm going to get to the bottom of this, Kate," Jim said. "We'll chase down the source of that money and figure out what in the hell is going on. I swear to you both, we're going to stay on top of this."

Zack believed Jim meant what he said, but he intended to see to it that Wild West Protective Services used every resource in its power to investigate, as well.

Bigger than Gray and Katie. "You might want to re-open the investigation into Joe Wainfield's death," Zack said, once again functioning on instinct.

Jim Ramsey's raised a grizzled eyebrow. "You think there's a connection?"

"I think anything is possible. Sonny said it was bigger than just what was happening at Bent Tree Ranch. Maybe you need to see what's happening on the other ranches around the area."

Ramsey nodded. "Looks like I've got all I need from you two. I'll stay in touch and let you know anything that turns up."

As they left the office Zack wondered if Katie's words to him while she'd been in the cellar had been the truth or simply the hysterical muttering of a woman afraid of death.

Facing Sonny had been nothing compared to the nervous tension that now rolled in his stomach as he waited to see what Katie might say.

It was almost four by the time they arrived back at the ranch. The drive home had been filled with meaningless small talk, all the while Kate had wondered what Zack was thinking, if he remembered at all the heartfelt confession she'd spilled while standing on the bucket contemplating her possible death.

They got out of the truck but instead of going inside she dropped into one of the two chairs on the porch. He eased down into the other chair.

"It seems like it's been forever since I've sat here," she said.

"I think any immediate danger to you has passed. Whatever was going on, whoever was ultimately responsible, with Sonny in jail they must realize their days are numbered."

"It will be nice to have my normal life back." Would anything ever feel normal again? she wondered. Her heart was so filled with Zack she wasn't sure how life would be without him. She only knew it would be lonely and desolate.

She expected him at any moment to get up and leave, to tell her a final goodbye and not look back. But he seemed to be in no hurry to go.

When she'd bared her soul to him, telling him that she loved him, that she thought she'd always loved him, he'd told her they would talk about it later. She couldn't bring it up now, her pride wouldn't allow it. The ball was in his court and it was up to him.

Minutes ticked by as they sat silently. Each minute was torture for her. Why didn't he say something? And if he wasn't going to say anything, then why didn't he just go?

Before she broke down. Before she cried.

"You know I have no idea what I'm going to do with my life." He finally broke the silence. "I know I don't want to work for the family business unless it involves something here in town. I might run for sheriff when the time comes, but that's not a guarantee." He didn't look at her, but rather stared off into the distance. "But I'm a good ranch hand and rumor has it you're in the market for a new ranch manager."

She was in love with him and he was talking to her about job opportunities. She tried to imagine seeing him every day, having him work with her around the ranch. She wanted him as a partner, a soul mate, not simply as a ranch manager.

"I can't do that, Zack. I can't work with you every day knowing that come night you'll go back to your own house."

"Then maybe I shouldn't go home nights."

He looked at her then, holding her half-breathless with an intense gaze. "Maybe I should stick around until we know who was the mastermind behind your dad's murder and everything that has happened here on the ranch."

There was something in his gaze that gave her hope. "Who knows how long that could take," she said, her voice unsteady. "I mean, it could be months…maybe even years before we know the truth."

He nodded. "I promised you before that I was in this until the end." He stood and held out his hand toward her. She didn't hesitate, she rose and grabbed his hand, her heart thudding furiously.

"I'm not always an easy man, Katie. I'm stubborn and can be difficult." A smile curved one corner of his mouth. "In other words, I'm not exactly Prince Charming material."

She squeezed his hand. "That's a relief, because I'm not exactly Sleeping Beauty material."

He pulled her up against him, his mouth mere inches from hers as his arms enfolded her. "I didn't expect to fall in love with anyone, especially you. But you've turned my world upside down and the only way to make it right is to spend the rest of my life with you."

"Oh, Zack, you turned my world upside down the moment I first saw you sitting here with my dad. I didn't know then what to do with the crazy feelings I had."

"Katie, your father loved you very much. He was so proud of you."

"I know. While I was standing on that bucket contemplating my death, I had time to think about my relationship with Dad. I know he loved me."

"And he was proud of you. Many a night he sat next to me and talked about you, about how strong you were, about how capable you were of anything you wanted to do." Zack framed her face with his hands. "He thought you hung the moon and stars…and so do I."

Her heart couldn't be any more full. His lips met hers in a kiss that brought tears to her eyes, happy tears. The kiss was filled with love, with tenderness and sweet, hot passion.

He pulled his lips from hers and gazed at her with those beautiful green eyes she'd loved almost all her lifetime. "So what happens when a not-exactly Prince Charming falls in love with a not-exactly Sleeping Beauty?"

She smiled up at him. "They live happily ever after."

"I was hoping you'd say that," he murmured before he captured her lips once again in a kiss that promised a modern fairy-tale kind of love.

* * * * *

THE RANCHER BODYGUARD

Chapter 1

As he approached the barn, Charlie Black saw the sleek, scarlet convertible pulling into his driveway, and wondered when exactly, while he'd slept the night before, hell had frozen over. Because the last time he'd seen Grace Covington, that's what she'd told him would have to happen before she'd ever talk to or even look at him again.

He patted the neck of his stallion and reined in at the corral. As he dismounted and pulled off his dusty black hat, he tried to ignore the faint thrum of electricity that zinged through him as she got out of her car.

Her long blond hair sparkled in the late afternoon sun, but he was still too far away to see the expression on her lovely features.

It had been a year and a half since he'd seen her, even though for the past six months they'd resided in the same small town of Cotter Creek, Oklahoma.

The last time he'd encountered her had been in his upscale apartment in Oklahoma City. He'd been wearing a pair of sports socks and an electric blue condom. Not one of his finer moments, but it had been the culminating incident in a year of not-so-fine moments.

Too much money, too many successes and far too much booze had transformed his life into a nightmare of bad moments, the last resulting in him losing the only thing worth having.

Surely she hadn't waited all this time to come out to the family ranch—his ranch now—to finally put a bullet in what she'd described as his cold, black heart. Grace had never been the type of woman to put off till today what she could have done yesterday.

Besides, she hadn't needed a gun on that terrible Friday night when she'd arrived unannounced at his apartment. As he'd stared at her in a drunken haze, she'd given it to him with both barrels, calling him every vile name under the sun before she slammed out of his door and out of his life.

So, what was she doing here now? He slapped his horse on the rump, then motioned to a nearby ranch hand to take care of the animal. He closed the gate and approached where she hadn't moved away from the driver's side of her car.

Her hair had grown much longer since he'd last seen her. Although most of it was clasped at the back of her neck, several long wisps had escaped the confines. The beige suit she wore complemented her blond coloring and the icy blue of her eyes.

She might look cool and untouchable, like the perfect lady, but he knew what those eyes looked like flared with desire. He knew how she moaned with wild abandon when making love, and he hated the fact that just the unexpected sight of her brought back all the memories he'd worked so long and hard to forget.

"Hello, Grace," he said, as he got close enough to speak without competing with the warm April breeze. "I have to admit I'm surprised to see you. As I remember, the last time we saw each other, you indicated that hell would freeze over before you'd ever speak to me again."

Her blue eyes flashed with more than a touch of annoyance—a flash followed swiftly by a look of desperation.

"Charlie, I need you." Her low voice trembled slightly, and only then did he notice that her eyes were red-rimmed, as if she'd been weeping. In all the time they'd dated—even during the ugly scene that had ended *them*—he'd never seen her shed a single tear. "Have you heard the news?" she asked.

"What news?"

"Early this afternoon my stepfather was found stabbed to death in bed." She paused for a moment and bit her full lower lip as her eyes grew shiny with suppressed tears. "I think Hope is in trouble, Charlie. I think she's really in bad trouble."

"What?" Shock stabbed through him. Hope was Grace's fifteen-year-old sister. He'd met her a couple of times. She'd seemed like a nice kid, not as pretty as her older sister, but a cutie nevertheless.

"Maybe you should come on inside," he said, and gestured toward the house. She stared at the attractive ranch house as if he'd just invited her into the chambers of hell. "There's nobody inside, Grace. The only woman who ever comes in is Rosa Caltano. She does the cooking and cleaning for me, and she's already left for the day."

Grace gave a curt nod and moved away from the car. She followed him to the house and up the wooden stairs to the wraparound porch.

The entry hall was just as it had been when Charlie's mother and father had been alive, with a gleaming wood floor and a dried flower wreath on the wall.

He led her to the living room. Charlie had removed much of the old furniture that he'd grown up with and replaced it with contemporary pieces in earth tones. He motioned Grace to the sofa, where she sat on the very edge as if ready to bolt at any moment. He took the chair across from her and gazed at her expectantly.

"Why do you think Hope is in trouble?"

She drew in a deep breath, obviously fighting for control. "From what I've been told, Lana, the housekeeper, found William dead in his bed. Today is her day off, but she left a sweater there last night and went back to get it. It was late enough in the day that William should have been up, so she checked on him. She immediately called Zack West, and he and some of his deputies responded. They found Hope passed out on her bed. Apparently she was the only one home at the time of the murder."

Charlie frowned, his mind reeling. Before he'd moved back here to try his hand at ranching, Charlie had been a successful, high-profile defense attorney in Oklahoma City.

It was that terrible moment in time with Grace followed by the unexpected death of his father that had made him take a good, hard look at his life and realize how unhappy he'd been for a very long time.

Still, it was as a defense attorney that he frowned at her thoughtfully. "What do you mean she was passed out? Was she asleep? Drunk?"

Those icy blue eyes of hers darkened. "Apparently she was drugged. She was taken to the hospital and is still there. They pumped her stomach and are keeping her for observation." Grace leaned forward. "Please, Charlie. Please help her. Something isn't right. First of all, Hope would never, ever take drugs, and she certainly isn't capable of something like this. She would *never* have hurt William."

Spoken like a true sister, Charlie thought. How many times had he heard family members and friends proclaim that a defendant couldn't be guilty of the crime they had been charged with, only to discover that they were wrong?

"Grace, I don't know if you've heard, but I'm a rancher now." He wasn't at all sure he wanted to get involved with any of this. It had disaster written all over it. "I've retired as a criminal defense attorney."

"I heard through the grapevine that besides being a rancher, you're working part-time with West Protective Services," she said.

"That's right," he agreed. "They approached me about a month ago and asked if I could use a little side work. It sounded intriguing, so I took them up on it, but so far I haven't done any work for them."

"Then let me hire you as Hope's bodyguard, and if you do a little criminal defense work in the process I'll pay you extra." She leaned forward, her eyes begging for his help.

Bad idea, a little voice whispered in the back of his brain. She already hated his guts, and this portended a very bad ending. He knew how much she loved her sister; he assumed that for the last couple of years she'd been more mother than sibling to the young girl. He'd be a fool to involve himself in the whole mess.

"Has Hope been questioned by anyone?" he heard himself ask. He knew he was going to get involved whether he wanted to or not, because it was Grace, because she needed him.

"I don't think so. When I left the hospital a little while ago, she was still unconscious. Dr. Dell promised me he wouldn't let anyone in to see her until I returned."

"Good." There was nothing worse than a suspect running off at the mouth with a seemingly friendly officer. Often the damage was so great there was nothing a defense attorney could do to mitigate it.

"Does that mean you'll take Hope's case?" she asked.

"Whoa," he said, and held up both his hands. "Before I agree to anything, I need to make a couple of phone calls, find out exactly what's going on and where the official investigation is headed. It's possible you don't need me, that Hope isn't in any real danger of being arrested."

"Then what happens now?"

"Why don't I plan on meeting you at the hospital in about an hour and a half? By then I'll know more of what's going on, and I'd like to be present while anybody questions Hope. If anyone asks before I get there, you tell them you're waiting for legal counsel."

She nodded and rose. She'd been lovely a year and a half ago when he'd last seen her, but she was even lovelier now.

She was five years younger than his thirty-five but had always carried herself with the confidence of an older woman. That was part of what had initially drawn him to her, that cool shell of assurance encased in a slamming hot body with the face of an angel.

"How's business at the dress shop?" he asked, trying to distract her from her troubles as he walked her back to her car. She owned a shop called Sophisticated Lady that sold designer items at discount prices. She often traveled the two-hour drive into Oklahoma City on buying trips. That was where she and Charlie had started their relationship.

They'd met in the coffee shop in the hotel where she'd been staying. Charlie had popped in to drop off some paperwork to a client and had decided to grab a cup of coffee before heading back to his office. She'd been sitting alone next to a window. The sun had sparked on her hair. Charlie had taken one look and was smitten.

"Business is fine," she said, but it was obvious his distraction wasn't successful.

"I'm sorry about William, but Zack West is a good man, a good sheriff. He'll get to the bottom of things."

Once again she nodded and opened her car door. "Then I'll see you in the hospital in an hour and a half," she said.

"Grace?" He stopped her before she got into the seat. "Given our history, why would you come to me with this?" he asked.

Her gaze met his with a touch of frost. "Because I think Hope is in trouble and she needs a sneaky devil to make sure she isn't charged with a murder I know she didn't commit. And you, Charlie Black, are as close to the devil as I could get."

She didn't wait for his reply. She got into her car, started the engine with a roar and left him standing to eat her dust as she peeled out and back down the driveway.

* * *

Grace drove until she was out of sight of Charlie's ranch and then pulled to the side of the road. She leaned her head down on the steering wheel and fought back the tears that burned her eyes.

A nightmare. She felt as if she'd been mysteriously plunged into a nightmare and couldn't wake up to escape, didn't know how to get out.

She'd barely had time to mourn her stepfather, the man who had married her mother when she'd been sixteen and Hope had been a baby.

William Covington had not only married their mother, Elizabeth, but had also taken on her two children as if they were his own. Grace's father had died of a heart attack and William had adopted the two fatherless girls.

He'd guided Grace through the tumultuous teen years with patience and humor. He'd been their rock when their mother had simply vanished two years ago, taking with her two suitcases full of clothing and her daughters' broken hearts.

Grace raised her head from the steering wheel and pulled back on the road. She couldn't think about her mother right now. That was an old pain. She had new pains to worry about and a little sister to try to save.

No way, she thought as she headed toward the hospital. No way was Hope capable of such a heinous crime. And Hope had always been the first one to declare that she thought drugs were stupid. She couldn't be taking drugs.

But how do you know for sure? a little voice in her head whispered. She'd been so busy the last couple of years, working at the shop and flying off for buying trips. Since the disappearance of her mother and her subsequent breakup with Charlie, Grace had engaged in a frenzy of work, exhausting herself each day to keep the anger and the heartache of both her mother's and Charlie's betrayals at bay.

Sure, lately, when she'd spent time with Hope, the young girl had voiced the usual teenage complaints about William. He was too strict and old-fashioned. He gave her too little freedom and too many lectures. He hated her friends.

But those were the complaints of almost every teenager on the face of the earth, and Grace couldn't believe they had meant that Hope harbored a killing rage against William.

She turned into the hospital parking lot and slid into an empty parking space, then turned off the engine. She stared at the small structure that comprised the Cotter Creek hospital, her thoughts filled with Charlie Black.

Six months ago, everyone in town had been buzzing with the gossip that Charlie Black had finally come home. She knew his father had died from an unexpected heart attack and had left Charlie the family ranch, but she'd assumed he'd sell it and continue his self-destructive path in the fast lane. She'd been stunned to hear that he'd closed up his practice in Oklahoma City and taken over the ranch.

She'd met Charlie two months after her mother's disappearance. She hadn't told him about her mother, rather she'd used her time with him as an escape from the pain, from the utter heart break of her mother's abandonment.

With Charlie she'd been able to pretend it hadn't happened. With Charlie, for a blessed time, she'd shoved the pain deep inside her.

She'd refused to tell him because she hadn't wanted to see pity in his eyes. She'd needed him to be her safe place away from all the madness, and for a while that's what he'd been.

As soon as she'd heard about William's murder and Hope's possible involvement, Charlie's name was the first one that had popped into her head. All the qualities she'd hated in him as a man were desirable qualities in a defense attorney.

His arrogance, his need to be right, his stubbornness and his emotional detachment made him a good defense attorney and would make him a terrific professional bodyguard, but he was definitely a poor bet for a personal relationship, as she'd discovered.

That was in the past. She didn't want anything from Charlie Black except his ability to make sure that Hope was safe.

As she got out of her car, she recognized that she was in a mild state of shock. The events of the past three hours hadn't fully caught up with her yet.

She'd been at the shop when she'd gotten the call from Deputy Ben Taylor, indicating that William was dead and Hope had been transferred to the hospital. He'd given her just enough information to both horrify and terrify her.

Her legs trembled as she made her way through the emergency room entrance. She hadn't been able to see Hope when she'd been here before, as Hope had been undergoing the stomach pumping. Surely they would let Grace see her now.

She told the nurse on duty who she was, then sat in one of the chairs in the waiting room. She was the only person there. She clasped her hands together in her lap in an attempt to stop their shaking.

Was Hope okay? Who had really killed William? He'd been a kind, gentle man. Who would want to hurt him?

She blinked back her tears and straightened her shoulders. She couldn't fall apart now. She had to be strong because she knew this was only the beginning of the nightmare.

"Grace."

She looked up to see Dr. Ralph Dell standing in the doorway. She started to stand but he motioned her back into her chair as he sat next to her. "She's stable," he said. "We pumped her stomach, but whatever she took either wasn't in pill form or had enough time to be digested. I've ordered a full toxicology screen."

"Is she conscious?" Grace asked.

"Drifting in and out. She'll be here until the effects have worn off." Dr. Dell eyed her soberly. "The sheriff is going to want to talk to her, and even with her condition I can keep him away only so long."

"I know. Charlie Black is supposed to meet me here in the next hour or so."

"Good. Deputy Taylor has been here since she was brought in."

Grace frowned. "Has he talked to her?"

Dr. Dell shook his head. "Up until now Hope hasn't been in any condition to talk to anyone. And I promised you I wouldn't let anyone in to see her while you were gone. I'm a man of my word."

"Thank you." Grace raised a trembling hand to her temple, where a headache had begun to pound with fierce intensity.

"How are you doing?" Dr. Dell reached out and took her hand in his. He'd been both Hope's and Grace's doctor since they'd been small girls. "You need anything, you let me know."

She realized he wasn't just holding her hand, but rather was taking her pulse at the same time. She forced a smile. "I'm okay." She withdrew her hand from his. "Really. Can I see Hope?"

He nodded his head and stood. "However, I caution you about asking her too many questions. Right now what she needs is your love and support. There will be plenty of time for answers when she's feeling more alert."

Grace heartily agreed. The last thing she wanted right now was to grill Hope about whatever might have happened at the Covington mansion that morning. All she wanted—all she *needed*—was to make sure that the sister she loved was physically all right. She'd worry about the rest later.

"I've got her in a private room," Dr. Dell said, as he led Grace down a quiet corridor.

She saw the deputy first. Ben Taylor sat in a chair in the hallway, a magazine open in his lap. He looked up as they approached, his thin face expressing no emotion as he greeted her.

"Grace." He nodded to her and shifted in his seat as if he found the whole situation awkward.

She knew Ben because his wife worked part-time for her at the dress shop. "Hi, Ben," she replied, appalled by the shakiness of her voice.

"Bad day, huh?" He averted his gaze from hers.

"That's an understatement." There were a hundred questions she wanted to ask him, but she wasn't sure she was ready for any of the answers. Charlie would be here soon and would find out what she needed to know.

She pushed open the door of the hospital room and

her heart squeezed painfully tight in her chest as she saw her sister. Hope was asleep, her petite face stark white and her blond hair a tangled mess.

Grace wanted to bundle her up in the sheet, pick her up and run out the door. Nobody could ever make her believe that Hope had anything to do with William's murder.

Pulling up a chair next to Hope's bed, Grace fought against a tremendous amount of guilt. In the past couple of months had she been too absent from Hope's life? Had there been things she wasn't aware of, things that had led to this terrible crime?

Stop it, she commanded herself. She was thinking as if Hope was guilty, and she wasn't. She wasn't! As soon as Charlie arrived, everything would be okay.

A knot of simmering anger twisted in her stomach. She shouldn't be alone here, waiting for Hope to wake up. Their mother should be with her, but she'd run from her responsibility and her family and disappeared like a puff of smoke on a windy day. Hope had been far too young to lose her mother. *Damn you, Mom,* Grace thought.

Hope stirred and her eyes opened. She frowned and looked at Grace in obvious confusion. "Sis?" Her voice was a painful croak.

Grace leaned forward and grabbed Hope's hand. "I'm here, honey. It's all right. You're going to be all right now."

Hope looked around wildly, as if unsure where she was. Her gaze locked with Grace's once again, and in the depths of Hope's eyes Grace saw a whisper of terror. "What happened?"

"You got your stomach pumped. Did you take something, Hope? Some kind of drug?"

Hope's eyes flashed with annoyance and she rose to a half-sitting position. "I don't do drugs. Drugs are for losers." She fell back against the bed and closed her eyes, as if the brief conversation had completely exhausted her.

Grace remained seated next to her, clasping her hand even after she realized Hope had fallen back asleep. If Hope hadn't taken any drugs, then why had the authorities found her unconscious on her bed when they'd arrived?

Had she been hit over the head? Knocked unconscious by whoever had committed the murder? Surely if she'd had a head injury Dr. Dell would have found it.

Hope slept the sleep of the drugged, not awakening even when a nurse came in to take her vital signs. The nurse didn't speak to Grace. She simply did her job with stern lips pressed tightly together.

Minutes ticked by with nauseating slowness. Grace checked her watch over and over again, wondering when Charlie would arrive. Hopefully he'd have some answers that would unravel the knot of dread tied tight in her stomach.

She leaned her head back against the chair and thought of Charlie. The moment she'd seen him again, an electric charge had sizzled through her. It had surprised her.

He was as handsome now as he'd been when they'd dated, his dark hair rich and full and his features aristocratically elegant, holding just a hint of danger. She knew those slate-gray eyes of his could narrow with cold intent or stoke a fire so hot a woman felt as if she might combust.

She'd been more than half in love with him when they'd broken up. She'd thought he felt the same way about her, but the redhead in his bed that night had told her different.

On that night she'd hated him more than she'd loved him, and in the past eighteen months her feelings hadn't changed. She rubbed her fingers across her forehead, thoughts of Charlie Black only increasing her headache.

Maybe he'd come in and tell her that Hope wasn't in any trouble, didn't need the expertise of a criminal defense lawyer or a bodyguard. Then she'd go back to the mess that had suddenly become her life and never see Charlie again.

She glanced at her watch and frowned. He was late. He was always late. That was something else she'd always found irritating about him—his inability to be on time for anything.

She didn't know why she was thinking about him anyway, except that it was far easier to think about Charlie than what had happened.

Somebody murdered William. Somebody murdered William. The words thundered through her brain in perfect rhythm with her pounding headache.

Who would want him dead? He'd been a wealthy man, a generous benefactor to numerous charities. He'd been well liked in the community and loved and respected by the two stepdaughters he'd claimed as his own.

Although he was the CEO of several industrial companies, he'd stopped working full-time a year ago and went in only occasionally for meetings.

He was kind and gentle, and his heart had been broken when Hope and Grace's mother had left him, left *them*. Tears burned her eyes again and she struggled to hold them back as she realized she'd never again see his gentle smile, never again feel the touch of his hand on her shoulder.

It was just after seven when the hospital door creaked open and Charlie motioned her out of the room. She got up from the chair and joined him in the hallway, where he took her by the arm and led her away from Ben Taylor.

"We've got a problem," he said when they were far enough down the hallway that Ben couldn't hear their conversation. His gray eyes were like granite slabs, revealing nothing of his thoughts.

"What?" she asked.

"I have every reason to believe that as soon as Hope is well enough to be released by the doctor, she's going to be arrested for the murder of your stepfather."

Grace gasped. "But why? How could anyone think she's responsible?"

He shifted his gaze and stared at some point just over her head. "Hope wasn't just found passed out on her bed. Her room had been trashed as if she'd been in a fit of rage."

"But that doesn't make her a murderer," Grace exclaimed. Although it *was* definitely out of character for Hope to do something like that. Hope had always been a neatnik who loved her room neat and tidy.

Charlie sighed and focused his gaze back on her. The darkness she saw there terrified her. "The real problem is that Hope was found covered in William's blood—and she had a knife in her hand. It was the murder weapon."

Chapter 2

Charlie watched as the color left Grace's cheeks and she swayed on her feet. His first impulse was to reach out to her, but before he could follow through, she stiffened and took a step back from him.

She'd never been a needy woman—that was one of the things he'd always admired about her and ultimately one of the things he'd come to hate. That she wasn't needy—that she had never really needed him.

"So, what do we do now?" Her strong voice gave away nothing of the emotional turmoil she must be feeling.

"Zack West wants to question her tonight. I just saw him in the lobby and he's chomping at the bit to get to her. Give me a dollar."

"Excuse me?" She looked at him blankly.

"Give me a dollar as a retainer. That will make it

official that at least for now, I'm Hope's legal counsel. She's a minor. She can't be questioned without me, and we can argue that as her legal guardian you have the right to be present, too."

She opened her purse and withdrew a crisp dollar bill. He took it from her and shoved it into his back pocket. "I'll go find Zack and we'll get this over with."

As he walked away, her scent lingered in his head. She'd always smelled like jasmine and the faintest hint of vanilla, and today was no different.

It was a scent that had stayed with him for months after she'd left him, a fragrance that had once smelled like desire and had wound up smelling like regret.

This was a fool's job, and he was all kinds of fool for getting involved. From what little he'd already learned, it didn't look good for the young girl.

If he got involved and ended up defending Hope, then failed, Grace would have yet another reason to hate his guts. Even if he defended Hope successfully, that wasn't a ticket to the land of forgiveness where Grace was concerned.

Still, Charlie knew that in all probability Hope was going to need a damn good lawyer on her side, and he was just arrogant enough to believe that he was the best in the four-state area.

Besides, he owed it to Grace. Although at the time of their breakup they'd been not only on different pages but in completely different books, he'd never forgotten the rich, raw pain on her face when she'd been confronted by the knowledge that he hadn't been monogamous.

Maybe fate had given him this opportunity to right

the wrong, to heal some wounds and assuage the guilt he'd felt ever since.

He found Zack in the waiting room. The handsome sheriff was pacing the floor and frowning. He stopped in his tracks as Charlie approached him. "If you want to question Hope, then Grace and I intend to be present," Charlie said.

Zack raised a dark eyebrow. "Are you here as Hope's lawyer?"

"Maybe." Charlie replied.

Zack sighed. "You going to make this difficult for me?"

"Probably," Charlie replied dryly. "You can't really believe that Hope killed William."

"Right now, I'm just in the information-gathering mode. After I have all the information I need, *then* I can decide if I have a viable suspect or not."

Zack had only been sheriff for less than a year, but Charlie knew he was a truth seeker and not a town pleaser. He would look for justice, not make a fast arrest in order to waylay the fears of the people in Cotter Creek. But if all the evidence pointed to Hope, Zack would have no choice but to arrest her.

"I heard you were working for Dalton," Zack said.

Dalton was Zack's brother and ran the family business, West Protective Services, an agency that provided bodyguard services around the country.

"I told him I'd be interested in helping out whenever he needed me," Charlie replied. "But I need to get this situation under control before I do anything else."

"Then let's do it," Zack said. He headed down the hallway toward Hope's room and Charlie followed close behind.

Dr. Dell met them at her door, his arms crossed over his chest like a mythical guardian of a magical jewel. "I know you have a job to do here, Sheriff, but so do I. She's still very weak, so I want this interview to be short and sweet."

Zack nodded, and the doctor stepped away. Grace's eyes narrowed slightly as Zack and Charlie entered the room. She sat next to the bed, where Hope was awake.

The kid looked sick and terrified as her gaze swept from Charlie to Zack. "Hope, you remember Zack West, the sheriff," Grace said. "And Charlie is here as your lawyer."

Hope's eyes widened, and Charlie had a feeling she hadn't realized just what kind of trouble she was in until this moment. Tears filled her eyes and she reached for her sister's hand.

"I want to ask you some questions," Zack said. He pulled a small tape recorder from his pocket and set it on the nightstand next to the bed. "You mind if I turn this on?"

Hope looked wildly at Charlie, who nodded his assent. Charlie stood next to Grace, trying to ignore the way her evocative scent made him remember the pleasure of making love with her and how crazy he'd been about her.

He couldn't think about that now—he knew he shouldn't think about that ever again. He couldn't go back and change the past and that terrible mistake he'd made. All he could do was step up right now and hopefully redeem himself just a little bit.

"I told her about William," Grace said to Zack, her chin lifted in a gesture of defiance. "She knows he was murdered but insists she had nothing to do with it."

A knot of tension formed in Zack's jaw. "I need to hear from her what happened today," he said, and focused his gaze on Hope. "What's the first thing you remember from this morning?"

Hope raised a trembling hand to her head and rubbed her temples. "I woke up around nine and went downstairs to get some breakfast. Nobody was around. It was Lana's day off, and I figured William was still in bed. Lately he'd been sleeping in longer than usual."

She stopped talking as tears once again filled her blue eyes. "I can't believe he's gone. I just don't understand any of this. Why would somebody do this to him? What happened to me?"

"So, you made yourself breakfast, then what did you do?" Zack asked, seemingly unmoved by her tears.

Grace's lips were a thin slash, and her pretty features were taut with tension. Several more strands of her shiny blond hair had escaped her barrette and framed her face.

Charlie was surprised to realize he wanted to do something, anything to erase that apprehensive look on her face, to alleviate the tortured shadows in her eyes.

"After I ate breakfast, I was still tired, so I went back to bed," Hope replied. "And I woke up here." Her features crumbled. "I don't know what happened to William. I don't know what happened to me." She began to cry in earnest, deep, wrenching sobs.

Grace got up from her chair and put her arms around Hope's slender shoulders and glared at Zack as if he were personally responsible for all the unhappiness on the entire planet.

"Isn't this enough?" she asked, those blue eyes of

hers filled with anger. "Can't you see what this is doing to her?"

Unfortunately, Charlie knew that Zack was just getting started. "Grace, let's just get this over with," he said. "Zack has to question her sooner or later. We might as well get it finished now. We'll give her a minute to pull herself together."

Zack waited until Hope calmed down a bit before asking about any tensions between her and William and probing her about any fights her stepfather might have had with anyone else.

Charlie protested only a couple of times when he thought the questions Zack asked might incriminate Hope if she answered.

Despite Charlie's efforts to protect Hope, what little information Zack got from the girl offered no alternative suspect and merely added to the mystery of what exactly happened in the Covington mansion that morning.

After an hour and a half of questioning, it was Grace who finally called a halt to the interrogation. "That's enough for tonight, Zack," she said firmly, as she rose from her chair. "Hope is exhausted. She isn't going anywhere. If you have more questions for her, you can ask them another time."

Zack nodded and reached over and turned off the tape recorder, then slipped the small device into his pocket. "I'll be in touch. I guess I don't have to tell you and Hope not to leave town."

"Innocent people don't leave town," she replied vehemently.

Zack left the room and Grace leaned over her sister. "We're going to go now, honey. We need to take care of some things. Nobody will bother you for the rest of the night. Just get some sleep and try not to worry. Charlie is going to fix all this, so there's nothing to worry about."

Charlie nearly groaned out loud. Sure, that was easy for her to say. But he was a defense attorney turned rancher, not a miracle worker.

They left the room together, and once out in the hallway Grace slumped against the polished wall. For the first time since arriving at his ranch, she looked lost and achingly fragile.

His need to touch her—to somehow chase away that vulnerable look in her eyes—was incredibly strong. "Do you need a hug?" The ridiculous words were out of his mouth before he'd realized he was going to say them.

She released a bitter laugh and shoved off the wall. "I'd rather hug a rattlesnake," she said thinly.

If he had any question about the depth of her dislike for him, her curt reply certainly answered it.

"It doesn't look good, does it?" she asked.

"It doesn't look great," he replied.

"So what happens now?" she inquired, as they continued down the hallway to the hospital's front doors.

"Nothing for now. Questioning Hope is only the beginning. We really won't know how much trouble she's in until Zack's completed his investigation into the murder."

They stepped out into the unusually warm spring night air, and again he caught a whiff of her sweet floral scent. He wanted to ask her if she was dating anyone, if she'd found love with somebody else in the eighteen months since they'd been together.

He reminded himself he had no right to know anything about her personal life, that he'd given up any such right the night he'd gotten drunk and fallen into bed with a woman whose name he couldn't even remember.

"I don't want to wait for Zack," she said. "I want us to investigate this murder just as vigorously as he will."

Charlie looked at her in surprise. "That's a crazy idea!" he exclaimed.

"Why is it crazy? You told me once that you worked as an investigator before you became a lawyer."

"That was a long time ago," he reminded her.

She crossed her arms, a mutinous expression on her face. "Fine, then I'll investigate it on my own." She turned on her heels and walked off.

Charlie sighed in frustration. "Grace, wait," he called after her. "I can't let you muck around in this alone. You could potentially do more damage than good for Hope."

"Then help me," she said, her voice low with desperation. "I'm all that Hope has. The only way to make sure she isn't railroaded for a crime she didn't commit is for me to find the guilty person, and that's exactly what I intend to do—with or without your help." She paused, her eyes glittering darkly. "So, are you going to help me or not?"

He shoved his hands in his jeans pockets and shook his head. "I'd forgotten just how stubborn you could be."

"I don't think you want to start pointing out character flaws in other people," she said pointedly.

To Charlie's surprise, he felt the warmth of a flush heat his cheeks. "Touché," he said. "All right, we'll do a little digging of our own. The first thing you should do is make a list of William's friends and business associates. We need to pick his life apart if we hope to find some answers."

"I can have a list for you by tomorrow. Why don't you meet me at my shop around noon, and we can decide exactly where to go from there."

"You're going into work?" he asked in surprise.

"I'd rather meet you at the shop than at my place," she replied.

"All right, then, tomorrow at noon," he agreed reluctantly. Charlie had worked extremely hard over the last six months to gain control and now felt his life was suddenly whirling back out of control.

She nodded. "Charlie, you should know that just because I came to you for help—just because I need you right now—doesn't mean I like you. When this is all over, I don't want to see you again." She turned and left without waiting for a response.

Jeez, he seemed to be watching her walking away from him a lot, especially after throwing a bomb at him. Still, he couldn't help but notice the sexy sway of those hips beneath the suit skirt and the length of her shapely legs. A surge of familiar regret welled up inside him.

He was a man who made few excuses or apologies for the choices he made, but the mistake of throwing Grace away would haunt him until the day he died.

The morning sun was shining brightly as Grace parked in front of her dress shop on Main Street. She turned off the engine but remained seated in the car, her thoughts still on the visit she'd just had with Hope.

Hope had been no less confused about the events of the day before and didn't seem to understand that at the moment she was the best suspect they had.

Fortunately, Dr. Dell wanted to keep her under observation for another twenty-four hours, and that was fine with Grace. The tox screen had come back showing a cocktail of drugs in Hope's system but Hope was still vehemently denying taking anything. At the hospital, Hope was safe and getting the best care.

Grace wearily rubbed a hand across her forehead. The day was just beginning, and she was already exhausted. Her sleep had been a continuous reel of nightmares.

She'd been haunted by visions of Hope stabbing William and then taking the drugs that knocked her unconscious. And if that hadn't been bad enough, images of Charlie also filled her dreams.

Charlie. She got out of the car and slammed the door harder than necessary, as if doing so could cast out all thoughts of the man.

She focused her attention on the shop before her. Sophisticated Lady had been a dream of hers from the time she was small. She'd always loved fashion and design, and five years ago for her twenty-fifth birthday, William had loaned her the money to open the shop.

Grace had worked her tail off to stock the store with fine clothing at discount prices, and within two years she'd managed to pay back the loan and expand into accessories and shoes.

Now all she could think about was whether she'd sacrificed her sister's well-being for making her shop a success. She'd spent long hours here at the store, and when she wasn't here she was away on buying trips or at Charlie's place for the weekend.

As much as she hated to admit it, she didn't know what had been going on in Hope's life lately, but she intended to find out.

She entered the shop, turned on the lights and went

directly to the back office, where she made a pot of coffee. With a cup of fresh brew in hand, she returned to the sales floor and sat on the stool behind the counter that held the register.

Much of her time the night before had been spent thinking about William, grieving for him while at the same time trying to figure out who might want him dead. The list of potential suspects she had to give to Charlie was frighteningly short.

The morning was unusually quiet. No customers had entered when Dana Taylor came through the door at eleven-thirty. "Hey, Grace," she said, her tone unusually somber. "How are you holding up?"

"As well as can be expected," Grace replied. "Right now I'm having trouble wrapping my mind around it all."

"I'm so sorry," Dana replied sympathetically.

"I was wondering if maybe you'd be available to take some extra hours for a while. I'm going to be busy with other things."

"Not a problem," Dana replied, as she stowed her purse under the counter. "When Ben got home from the hospital last night, he told me not to expect to see a lot of him for the next week or two." She didn't quite meet Grace's eyes.

"There's a new shipment of handbags in the back. If you have time this afternoon, could you unpack them and get them on display?" Grace asked, desperate to get over the awkwardness of the moment.

"Sure," Dana agreed. "Any business this morning?"

"Nothing. It's been quiet." Grace turned toward the door as it opened to admit Charlie.

An intense burst of electricity shot through her at

the sight of him, and instantly every defense she possessed went up.

"Morning, ladies," he said as he ambled toward the counter. Clad in a pair of snug jeans and a short-sleeved white shirt, he looked half rancher, half businessman and all handsome male.

His square jaw indicated a hint of stubbornness and his eyes were fringed with long, dark lashes. His nose was straight, his lips full enough to give women fantasies of kissing them. In short, Charlie was one hot hunk.

His energy filled the air, and despite her wishes to the contrary, Grace felt a crazy surge of warmth as she gazed at him.

"Good morning, Charlie," Dana replied. "How are things out at the ranch?"

"Not bad. The cattle are getting fat, and I've got a garden full of tomato and pepper plants that are going to yield blue-ribbon-quality product."

Pride rang in his voice, a pride that surprised Grace. Two years ago, the only things that put that kind of emotion in his voice were his fancy surround-sound system, his state-of-the-art television and the new Italian shoes that cost what most people earned in a month.

He turned his gaze to Grace. "We need to talk," he said. His smile was gone, and the enigmatic look in his gray eyes created a knot in Grace's stomach.

"Okay. Come on back to my office," she said.

He followed her to the back room, where she turned and looked at him. "Something else has happened?"

"No, I just have some new information."

"What kind of information?" She leaned against the desk, needing the support because she knew with certainty whatever he was about to tell her wasn't good.

"Did you know that Hope has a boyfriend?" he asked.

She frowned. "Hope is only fifteen. Their relationship can't be anything serious."

One of his dark eyebrows quirked upward. "When you're fifteen, everything is serious. His name is Justin Walker. Do you know him?"

Grace shook her head, and a new shaft of guilt pierced through her. She should have known her sister's boyfriend. What other things didn't she know? "So, who is he?"

"He's a seventeen-year-old high school dropout with a bad reputation," Charlie replied. "And there's more. Apparently Justin was a bone of contention between William and Hope. William thought he was too old and was bad news and had forbidden Hope from seeing him."

Grace sat on the edge of her desk. "How did you find out all of this?"

"I had a brief conversation with Zack this morning. I wanted to be up-to-date on where the investigation was going before meeting you today. And there's more."

She eyed him narrowly. "I'm really beginning to hate those words."

"Then you're really going to hate this," he said. "On the night before the murder, Hope and William went out to dinner at the café. An employee told Zack that while there, they had a public argument ending with Hope screaming that she wished he were dead."

Grace's heart plummeted to her feet, and she wished she didn't hate Charlie, because at the moment she wanted nothing more than his big strong arms around her.

Chapter 3

Justin Walker lived with a buddy in the Majestic Apartments complex on the outskirts of town. The illustrious
name of the apartments had to have been somebody's
idea of a very bad joke.

The small complex had faded from yellow to a
weathered gray from the Oklahoma sun and sported
several broken windows. The vehicles in the parking
lot ran the gamut from souped-up hot rods to a rusty
pickup truck missing two tires.

"You sure you want to do this?" Charlie asked dubiously, as he parked in front of the building and cut
his engine.

Grace stared at the building in obvious dismay. "Not
really, but it has to be done. I want to know exactly what
his relationship with Hope was…is. I want to hear it
from him, and then I want to hear it from my sister."
She turned to look at Charlie. "Does he work?"

"He's a mechanic down at the garage, but he called in sick this morning."

"You managed to learn a lot between last night and now," she observed.

He shrugged and pulled his keys from the ignition. "It just took a phone call to find out if he was at the garage today. Somehow I knew you'd want to talk to him." He directed his gaze back at the building. "But, just because he isn't at work doesn't mean he's here."

"There's only one way to find out." She opened her car door and stepped out.

Charlie joined her on the cracked sidewalk and tried not to notice how pretty she looked in the yellow skirt that showcased her shapely legs and the yellow-flowered blouse that hugged her slender curves.

This whole thing would have been so much easier if during the time they'd been apart she sprouted some facial hair or maybe grown a wart on the end of her nose.

"Which unit is it?" she asked.

"Unit four." He pointed to the corner apartment, one that sported a broken window. Grace grimaced but marched with determined strides toward the door, on which she knocked in a rapid staccato fashion.

Charlie stepped in between her and the front door, protective instincts coming into play. He had no idea if Justin was just a loser boyfriend or an active participant in William's murder.

The door opened and a tall young man gazed at them with a wealth of belligerence. He looked like he wasn't having a good day. "Are you more cops?" he asked, his dark eyes wary and guarded.

Grace moved closer to the door. "No. I'm Grace Covington, Hope's sister, and this is her lawyer, Charlie Black. Are you Justin?"

He hesitated a moment, as if considering whether or not to tell the truth, then gave a curt nod of his head, his dark hair flopping carelessly onto his forehead. "Yeah, I'm Justin. What do you want?"

"Sheriff West has already talked to you?" Charlie asked.

Justin's eyes darkened. "He was here half the night asking me questions."

"May we come in?" Grace asked.

Justin's eyes swept the length of her and he scowled. "You don't want to come in here. The place is a dump." He stepped outside and closed the door behind him.

"You were dating my sister?" Grace asked.

Justin barked a dry laugh. "I wouldn't exactly call it dating. She's not allowed to date until she turns sixteen. We hung out, that's all. When she'd show up down at the garage after school, I'd take a break and we'd just talk. It was no big deal."

There was hostility in his voice, as if he expected them to take issue with him. "Were you sleeping with her?" Grace asked. Charlie wasn't sure who was more surprised by the question, himself or Justin.

Justin gave her a mocking smile. "Don't worry, big sister. As far as I know your baby sister is still as pure as the driven snow."

"Where were you yesterday morning?" Charlie asked. "Your boss told me you weren't at work." He felt Grace stiffen next to him.

"Funny, the sheriff asked me the same thing." Justin clutched his stomach. "I've been fighting off this flu bug. Yesterday I was here in bed, and if you don't believe me, my roommate will vouch for me. I didn't leave here all day."

"And your roommate's name?" Charlie asked.

Justin stepped back toward his apartment door. "Sam Young, and now I'm done answering your questions." He stepped back inside and shut the door firmly in their faces.

"Do you believe him?" Grace asked when they were back in Charlie's car and headed for the hospital.

He cast her a wry glance. "In the words of a famous television personality, I wouldn't believe him if his tongue came notarized."

Her burst of laughter was short-lived, but the sound of it momentarily warmed his heart. Charlie always loved to hear her laugh, and there had been a time when he'd been good at making her do so.

"After we speak with Hope, I need to find out if I can go to the house and get some of her things," Grace said. "Dr. Dell thought he would release her at some point this evening or first thing in the morning, and we'll need to get some of her clothes and things to take to my place."

"When we get to the hospital, I'll call Zack and see what can be arranged."

"I'd like to talk to Hope alone. I don't think she'll be open about her relationship with Justin if you're there, too."

"Okay," he replied. He glanced at her and caught her rubbing her temple. "Headache?"

She nodded and dropped her hand back into her lap. "I think it's a guilt thing."

"Guilt? What do you have to feel guilty about?" he asked in surprise.

A tiny frown danced across her forehead, doing nothing to detract from her attractiveness. "I should have been paying more attention to what was going on in her life. I should have been putting in less hours at the store and spending more time with her."

"Regrets are funny things, Grace. They rip your heart out, but they don't really change anything," he replied. He was an old hand at entertaining regrets.

"You're right." She reached up, massaged her temple once again and then shot him a pointed look. "You're absolutely right. The past is over and nothing can change the damage done. What's important is to learn from the mistakes made in the past and never forget the lesson."

Charlie frowned, knowing her words were barbs flung at him and had nothing to do with the situation at hand. They spoke no more until they arrived at the hospital.

As she disappeared into Hope's hospital room, he called Zack West to find out what was going on at the Covington mansion. Zack informed him that the evidence gathering was finished and said Grace was free to get whatever she needed for Hope.

When Charlie asked him for an update, he merely replied that it was an ongoing investigation and there was nothing new to report.

As he waited for Grace, he sat in one of the plastic chairs in the waiting room. Charlie had a theory that murder happened for one of three reasons. He called it his "three *R*" theory. Rage, revenge and reward were the motives that drove most murderers.

At the moment, the officials were leaning toward rage—a young girl's rage at being stymied in a love relationship by an overbearing father figure.

The news was certainly filled with stories of young people going on killing rampages against authority figures. Had Hope snapped that morning and stabbed William while he slept and then, filled with remorse, taken drugs in a suicide attempt?

Hopefully they would be successful in coming up with an alternative theory that would explain both William's death and Hope's drugged state.

He looked up as Grace entered the room. She sat next to him as if too exhausted to stand. "What did she have to say about Justin?" he asked.

"She told me she's crazy in love with him, and she thinks they belong together forever, but she hasn't gotten physical with him yet."

"That's different from Justin's story. He made it sound like she was no big deal to him," Charlie observed.

"Maybe he doesn't feel the same way she does. Maybe he was afraid to tell us how he really feels about Hope," she replied.

"Maybe," Charlie agreed.

Grace reached up and tucked a strand of her shiny hair behind her ear. "She's not being released today. She's running a fever and Dr. Dell wants to get to the bottom of it."

"You still want to go by the house?" She sat so close to him he could feel the heat from her body. He used to tease her about how she was better than a hot water bottle at keeping him warm on cold wintry nights. He wished he could tell her how he'd been cold ever since he'd lost her.

She nodded. "Whether she's here or at my place, I'm sure she'd be more comfortable with some of her own things. Besides, I'd like to talk to Lana, William's housekeeper. She'd know better than anyone what was going on between William and Hope, and if anyone else was having a problem with William."

Grace jumped up from the chair, newfound energy vibrating from her. "We need to find something, Charlie, something that will point the finger of guilt away from Hope. I can't lose her. She's all I have left."

She looked half frantic, and again a soft vulnerability sagged her shoulders and haunted her eyes. This time Charlie didn't fight his impulse—his need to touch her. He reached out for her hand and took it in his. Hers was icy, as if the heat of her body was unable to warm her small, trembling hand.

"We'll figure it out," he said. "I promise you that we'll get to the bottom of this. I won't let Hope be convicted of a crime she didn't commit."

What he didn't say was that if Hope was guilty, not even the great Charlie Black would be able to save her.

The Covington estate was located on the northern edge of town, a huge two-story structure with manicured grounds, several outbuildings and a small cottage in the back, where Lana Racine and her husband, Leroy, lived.

As Charlie pulled into the circular drive and parked in front, Grace stared at the big house and felt the burgeoning grief welling up inside her.

The sight of the bright yellow crime-scene tape across the front door nearly made her lose control, but she didn't. She couldn't.

She'd spent her life being the strong one—the child her mother could depend on, the teenager who often took responsibility for her baby sister and the woman who'd held it together when her mother deserted them.

Charlie didn't know about her mother. When they'd been dating, she told him only that her mother had moved away, not that she'd just packed her bags and disappeared from their lives.

Without an explanation.

Without a word since.

Was she sunning on a beach in Florida? Eating crab cakes and lobster in Maine? Or was she out of the country? She'd always talked about wanting to go to France.

Grace welcomed the raw anger that took the place of her grief—it sustained her, kept her strong.

She glanced back at Charlie, wondering if she should tell him about what had been going on in her life when she'd met him. She dismissed the idea. She couldn't stand the idea of seeing pity in his eyes, and after all this time, what difference did it make?

"Are you sure you're ready to go in there?" Charlie asked.

She focused back on the house and nodded. "I'll just get some of Hope's things, then we can go talk with Lana and Leroy."

She almost wished Charlie weren't here with her. He'd stirred old feelings in her, made her remember how much she'd once cared about him. She'd thought her hatred of him would protect her from those old feelings—that it would vaccinate her against the "wanting Charlie" emotion. She'd been wrong.

All day she'd been plagued by memories of the taste of his lips on hers, the feel of his hands stroking the length of her. Their physical relationship had been nothing short of magic. He'd been an amazing lover, at times playful and at other times intense and demanding.

But it wasn't just those kinds of memories that bothered her. Remembering how often they had laughed together and how much they'd enjoyed each other's company had proved equally troubling.

Amnesia would have been welcome. She would have loved to permanently forget the six months with Charlie, but spending time with him now unlocked the mental box in which she'd placed those memories the night she'd walked away from him.

Focus on the reason he's in your life, she told herself. Hope. She had to stay focused on Hope and finding something, anything, that would reveal the young girl's innocence.

She got out of the car, grateful to escape the small confines that smelled of him—a wonderful blend of clean male and expensive, slightly spicy cologne. It was the same scent he'd worn when they'd been dating, and it only helped stir memories she would prefer to forget.

Charlie pulled away the crime-scene tape, and Grace used her key to open the front door. They walked into the massive entry with its marble floor and an ornate gilded mirror hanging on the wall.

"Wow," Charlie said, obviously impressed. "I'd heard this place was a showcase, but I had no idea."

"William was an extremely successful man," she replied. "He liked to surround himself with beautiful things."

"I know you said your mother married him when you were sixteen. What happened to your father?"

"He died of a heart attack when mom was pregnant with Hope. We were left with no insurance and no money in the bank." Grace paused a moment, thinking about those days just after her father's death. There'd been a wealth of grief and fear about what would happen to them now the breadwinner was gone.

She walked from the entry to the sweeping staircase that led to the second floor. Placing a hand on the polished wood banister, she continued, "William was like a knight in shining armor. He and Mom met at the grocery store, and he swooped into our lives like a savior. He was crazy, not just about Mom, but also about me and Hope."

"He didn't have children of his own?" Charlie asked.

"No. He'd been married years before, but it ended in divorce and there had been no children. We were all the family he had."

"Who is his beneficiary?"

Grace looked at him in surprise. "I have no idea. I hadn't even thought about it."

"Maybe your mother?" he asked.

"Maybe," Grace agreed, although she wasn't so sure. Grace's mother had ripped the very heart out of William when she'd disappeared. William had been a good man, generous to a fault, but he hadn't been a foolish man, especially when it came to money.

"Let's get Hope's things and get out of here," she said, her heart heavy as she climbed the stairs.

Charlie followed just behind her as she topped the stairs and walked down the long hallway toward Hope's room. The door was closed and she hesitated, unsure she was ready for whatever was inside.

Hope had been found covered in blood, clutching the knife in her hands, her room trashed. Grace grabbed the doorknob and still couldn't force herself to open the door.

Charlie placed a hand on her shoulder. "We don't have to do this. We can buy Hope whatever she needs for the time being."

How could a man who had been incredibly insensitive eighteen months ago, a man who had been so thick he hadn't recognized the depths of her feelings for him, be so in tune to what she was feeling now?

She didn't have the answer but was grateful that he seemed to understand the turmoil inside her as she contemplated going into Hope's room. Deep within, she knew she was grateful that he was here with her.

"It's all right. I can do this," she said, as much to herself as to him.

She straightened her shoulders and opened the door. A gasp escaped her as she saw the utter mess inside. She took several steps into the room and stared around in horror.

Ripped clothes were everywhere. The French provincial bookshelf had been turned over, spilling its contents onto the floor. A hole was punched in the Sheetrock wall, as if it had been angrily kicked.

The bed had been stripped. She imagined that the investigators had taken away the bedclothes. "Definitely looks like somebody had a temper fit in here," Charlie said from behind her.

Grace's mind whirled with sick suppositions. Was it possible that a rage had been festering in Hope for some time? Their mother's defection had been difficult on Grace, but it had been devastating for Hope. Grace had been twenty-eight years old when their mother had left, but Hope had been a thirteen-year-old who desperately needed her mom.

"I'll just grab some clothes," Grace said. She'd taken only two steps toward the closet when her foot crunched on something.

She looked down and saw the arm of a porcelain doll. She knew that arm. She knew that doll. It had been Hope's prized possession, given to her on the birthday before their mother had disappeared.

Crouching down, she found the rest of the doll among the mess of clothes and books and miscellaneous items that had fallen from the bookcase.

The porcelain arms and legs had been pulled from the cloth body. The head was smashed beyond repair, and the body had been slashed open.

Rage. There was no doubt that rage had destroyed the doll. The rage of a daughter whose mother had left her with a man who hadn't been able to understand her needs, her wants?

Hope's rage?

The breakdown that began in Grace started with a trembling that seemed to possess her entire body. Her vision blurred with the hot press of tears, and for the first time she wondered if her sister had committed the crime, if it was possible that Hope was guilty.

Chapter 4

Charlie saw it coming: the crack in her strength, the loss of her control. Until this moment Grace had shown an incredible amount of poise in dealing with the mess that had become her life.

Now she looked up at him with tear-filled eyes and lips that trembled uncontrollably, and he knew she'd reached the end of that strength.

"Grace." He said her name softly.

"She couldn't have done this, Charlie? Surely she didn't do this?" They weren't statements of fact but questions of uncertainty, and he knew the agony the doubts must be causing her.

Again the crazy, overwhelming need to hold her, to be her soft place to fall, swept over him. He touched her shoulder, then placed his hand beneath her arm to help her to her feet.

The tears in her eyes streamed down her cheeks, and when Charlie wrapped his arms around her, she didn't fight the embrace—she fell into it.

Her body fit perfectly against his, molding to him with sweet familiarity. A rush of emotions filled him—compassion because of the ordeal she was going through, fear for what she might have to face, and finally a desire for her that he couldn't deny.

The vanilla scent of her hair coupled with that familiar jasmine fragrance filled his head, making him half dizzy.

The embrace was over soon after it began. Grace jumped back as if stung by the physical contact. "I'm okay," she exclaimed as a stain of color spread across her cheeks.

"I never thought otherwise," he replied dryly. He'd be a fool to think that it had been *his* arms she'd needed around her, *his* comfort she'd sought. She'd just needed a little steadying, and if it hadn't been him, it would have been anyone.

She didn't need steadying anymore. Her shoulders were once again rigid as she went around the room, gathering clothes in her arms. After he took the clothes from her, she went into the adjoining bathroom and returned a moment later with a small overnight bag he assumed held toiletries.

"That should do it," she said. Any hint of tears was gone from her eyes, and they once again shone with the steely strength they'd always possessed.

They left the bedroom and went back down the stairs. She relocked the front door, then they stowed Hope's things in the car and headed back to the caretaker cottage where Lana and Leroy Racine lived.

If Charlie was going to mount a credible defense for Hope, he knew that to create reasonable doubt he had to identify another potential suspect with a motive for murder.

He'd never met the Racines, and as he and Grace walked across the lush grass to the cottage in the distance, he asked her some questions about the couple.

"How long have Lana and Leroy worked for William?"

"Lana was William's housekeeper when my mother married him. She married Leroy about ten years ago and soon after had their son, Lincoln."

"Leroy works the grounds?" he asked.

She nodded. "William hired him when he and Lana got married. As you can see, he does a great job."

"Theirs is a happy marriage?"

She shrugged. "I assume so. I'm not exactly privy to their personal life, but they seem very happy. They're both crazy about Lincoln."

They fell silent as they reached the house. It was an attractive place, painted pristine white with black shutters. The porch held two rocking chairs and several pots of brilliant flowers.

Grace knocked on the door, and an attractive redhaired woman who looked to be in her forties answered. She took one look at Grace and broke into torrential sobs.

Grace's eyes misted once again, and she quickly embraced the woman in a hug. "I can't believe it," Lana cried. "I just can't believe he's gone."

"I know. I feel the same way," Grace replied.

Lana stepped away from her and dabbed at her eyes with a tissue from her pocket. "Come in, please." She ushered them into a small but neat and tidy living room, where Grace introduced Charlie.

"Would you like something? Maybe something to drink?" Lana asked as she motioned for them to sit in the two chairs across from the sofa.

"No, thanks. We're fine. I wanted to ask you some questions," Grace said. "Is Leroy here?"

"He just left to pick up Lincoln from school." Lana looked at Charlie. "Lincoln goes to the Raymond Academy in Linden."

Charlie had heard of the exclusive private school located in a small town just north of Cotter Creek. Tuition was expensive, especially for parents working as a housekeeper and a gardener.

On the end table next to him, he noticed the picture of a young boy. He picked it up and looked at it. The dark-haired boy looked nothing like his red-haired mother. "Nice-looking boy," he commented, and put the picture back where it belonged.

"He's a good boy," Lana said, pride shining in her brown eyes. "He's smart as a whip and never gives us a minute of trouble."

"Must be tough paying to send him to the Raymond Academy," Charlie observed.

"It is, but Leroy and I agreed early on that we'd make whatever sacrifices necessary to see that he gets the best education possible." She twisted the tissue in her lap. "Although with William gone, it looks like both of us are going to be without jobs, so I don't know how we'll manage Lincoln's school costs."

"I'd like to talk to you about William and Hope," Grace said. "You know Hope is in the hospital—that the sheriff believes she killed William and then took some sort of drug to knock herself unconscious?"

"That's nonsense. I spoke to Zack West and told him it was ridiculous to think that Hope would do such a thing. She's a sweet child and couldn't possibly do something like this. Did Hope and William argue? Absolutely. She's a teenager and that's what they do, but there's no way anyone will make me believe she killed him."

"Then that makes two of us," Grace said with fervor. It was obvious that Lana's words completely banished whatever momentary doubt had gripped her while in Hope's bedroom.

"Do you know of anyone William was having problems with?" Charlie asked. "A neighbor? A business associate? Anyone?"

Lana shook her head. "Believe me, I've racked my brain ever since I found him dead in his bed." Again a veil of tears misted her eyes.

"I can't think of anyone. He was a wonderful and gentle man. He was so good to me. One time, before I was married to Leroy, I wasn't feeling very well. I called William and told him I thought I had the flu and shouldn't come cook dinner for him. He showed up on my doorstep thirty minutes later with a pot of chicken soup he'd bought at the café. That's the kind of man he was. Who would want to kill a man like that?"

"That's what we're going to try to find out," Charlie said. He stood and pulled a business card from his back pocket. "If you think of anything that might help our defense of Hope, would you please give me a call?" He handed the card to Lana.

At that moment the front door opened, and Leroy and

Lincoln came in. After Lana made the introductions, she told Lincoln to go to his room and do his homework.

As the well-mannered young boy disappeared into the back of the house, Charlie felt the chime of a biological clock he didn't know men possessed.

Since moving back to the family ranch in Cotter Creek, he'd been thinking about kids and recognizing that if he intended to start a family, it should be soon. He wasn't getting any younger.

Charlie sat down and turned his attention to Leroy. He was a big, burly man with a sun-darkened face and arms. His face seemed better suited for prize fighting, but at the moment his rough-hewn features held nothing but concern for his wife.

Leroy sat next to her and put an arm around her shoulder, as if to shield her from any unpleasantness.

Charlie asked Leroy the same questions he'd asked Lana and got no different answers. Leroy talked about what a wonderful man William had been and how he'd even helped pay for their wedding.

"I wish to God I knew who was responsible for this," Leroy said, his blunt features twisted with pain. "But, like we told the sheriff, we don't have a clue."

"We appreciate your time," Charlie said, recognizing that nothing more could be learned here. Once again he stood, and Grace followed suit.

"Grace?" Lana looked decidedly uncomfortable. "I know this probably isn't the time or the place, but Leroy and I don't know what we're supposed to do. Should we move out of here?"

Grace frowned thoughtfully. "I wouldn't do anything right now. We'll see what's going to happen with the estate. I'll check into it and let you know what's going on. Although I think Leroy should keep up the grounds, I'd prefer you stay out of the house for the time being." She took Lana's hand and smiled. "Consider yourself on paid vacation at the moment."

They all said their goodbyes, then Charlie and Grace left. "They must be terrified, not knowing what will happen to them now that William is gone," Grace said, as they walked back to the car.

"You should probably talk to William's attorney and find out about his will. Maybe he made some kind of provisions for them in the event of his death."

"His attorney is in Oklahoma City. I wonder if anyone has told him William is dead."

"I'll check with Zack," Charlie said. "And you might think about making funeral plans."

He could tell by the look on her face that she hadn't thought of that. "Oh, God. I've been so overwhelmed. Of course I need to take care of it." She looked stricken by the fact that she hadn't thought about it. "I'll speak with Mr. Burkwell tomorrow to find out what needs to be done." Jonathon Burkwell owned the Burkwell Funeral Home, the only such establishment in the town of Cotter Creek.

When they got to the car, Grace slid into the passenger seat and Charlie got behind the wheel. He started the engine, but then turned to look at her. "Have you called your mother, Grace? Maybe she should come help you take care of things."

Before replying, she averted her gaze and stared out the window. "No, there's no point in contacting her. She's out of the country, and there's really nothing she can do here. I'll be fine without her. Hope and I will be fine."

He studied her pretty profile. As a criminal defense attorney, Charlie was accustomed to people deceiving him, and he knew all the subtle signs of a liar. Right now he had the distinct feeling that Grace was lying to him about her mother.

It had been a day from hell. Grace sat at her desk in the back of the dress shop finishing up the payroll checks. The store had closed at seven, but on the night before payday she always stayed late in case any employees wanted to pick up their checks early.

She didn't mind staying. She was reluctant to go home and face the emptiness of her house and the tumultuous emotions that had been boiling inside her all day.

She'd spoken with William's attorney first thing that morning. He hadn't heard about the murder and was shocked. He, in turn, surprised Grace—she and Hope were the sole beneficiaries to William's fortune. Grace only hoped that fact didn't add to the body of evidence building against her sister.

The rest of the morning was spent making the necessary arrangements at Burkwell's funeral home. It was one of the most difficult things she'd ever done.

At noon, she and Charlie had taken the clothes and personal items to Hope. Grace visited with her sister while Charlie went to the cafeteria for a cup of coffee.

After the hospital visit, they'd gone back to the Covington mansion, where she went through William's desk, seeking something that might tell them who would have wanted him dead.

She still hadn't made herself open the door to William's room—the place where he had died—although she knew eventually she'd want to search it for anything that might help build a defense case for Hope.

She'd returned to the store at three-thirty, and now it was almost eight. She was exhausted but made no move to head home.

She'd just finished writing the last check when she heard the faint whoosh of the store door opening. "Grace?" a familiar voice called.

Grace jumped up from the desk and hurried out of her office. Standing just inside the door, with an eight-month-old baby boy on her hip, was Rachel Prescott, Grace's best friend.

"Oh honey, I just heard the news." Rachel approached her with a wrinkle of concern dancing across her forehead. "Jim had a three-day conference in Dallas, and I decided to go with him. We just got home a little while ago. How are you doing?"

"I'm okay. At least I'm trying to be okay." Grace smiled at the baby boy, who gave her a sleepy smile in return, then leaned his head against his mother's chest. "How's my Bobby?" She reached out and stroked his silky dark hair.

"He's pooped. He didn't have his nap today. So, tell me, what's this I hear about Hope being a suspect?"

"The medical examiner determined that William was killed between six and ten in the morning. Hope was the only one home. There were no signs of forced entry, and the murder weapon was found in Hope's hand." As Grace ticked off the pertinent points, a wave of discouragement swept over her.

Rachel laid a gentle hand on Grace's shoulder. "Sounds bad, but we both know Hope isn't capable of killing anybody." Grace smiled gratefully.

"I also heard you've hooked up with Charlie Black again," Rachel added, a hint of disapproval in her voice.

"Not hooked up as in 'hooked up,' I've just hired him to investigate the murder, and if the world goes crazy and Hope is arrested, I want him to defend her."

Rachel raised an eyebrow. "And who is defending you from Charlie?"

Rachel was the only person who knew the truth about how Charlie had broken Grace's heart, and she'd proclaimed him the most black-hearted, vile man on the face of the planet. At the time, Grace had relished her friend's anger on her behalf.

"Don't worry, I have no intention of making the same mistakes where Charlie is concerned. I just need him right now. He's good at what he does, but that doesn't mean I want him in my life on a personal level. I haven't forgotten, and I certainly haven't forgiven him."

Unfortunately, that didn't mean she didn't want him on some insane level. Over the last couple of days, she'd realized there was a part of her that had never really gotten over him.

"I just don't want to see you hurt again," Rachel said. "It's bad enough that you haven't dated since the breakup."

"That has nothing to do with him," Grace protested. "You know how busy I've been here at the shop."

"I know this place has become the perfect excuse for you," Rachel replied dryly.

Grace didn't respond. She couldn't exactly argue the point because she knew there was more than a kernel of truth to Rachel's words.

"Take that baby home and put him to bed," she finally said.

"Is there anything I can do? Any way I can help?" Rachel asked.

"Just pray they find the guilty party and that they don't arrest my sister," Grace replied. At that moment, the door to the shop opened once again, and one of her young, part-time employees came in to get her paycheck.

When Rachel and Bobby left, Grace gave the high school girl her check and then returned to her desk in the back room. She'd give it another half an hour or so before locking up the store and going home.

She kicked off her shoes beneath the desk and reached for the mug that held the last of the lukewarm coffee she'd been drinking all evening.

Charlie. Drat the man for being as attractive as he'd been eighteen months ago. From all indications, he appeared to have settled into ranching and small-town life with his usual aplomb.

The hard edge he'd possessed before seemed to be missing. He was still strong and self-assured, but he somehow seemed a bit more sensitive than he'd been during their six months together.

Not that it mattered. The familiar saying flitted through her mind: *Screw me once, shame on you. Screw me twice, shame on me.* She would be a fool to allow Charlie back into her heart in any way, shape or form. Charlie had proven himself unable to keep his pants on around other women.

Her present attraction to him was surely just due to her belief that he could save her sister and somehow make sense of the senseless.

She closed her business checkbook and locked it in

the bottom desk drawer. Time to go home. Maybe tonight she would sleep without nightmares.

Maybe tonight visions of a blood-covered, knife-wielding Hope wouldn't haunt her. Maybe images of a dead William wouldn't visit her dreams.

Once again she heard the *whoosh* of the shop door opening. She quickly unlocked the desk drawer, pulled out the checkbook and then walked in her stocking feet from the office into the other room.

"Hello?" She frowned as she looked around the room. It was dimly lit with only a few security lights on, and she didn't see anyone inside.

Odd, she could have sworn she'd heard the front door open. Maybe she'd just imagined it. She glanced around one last time, then returned to her office, sat back in her chair, put the checkbook away and locked the drawer.

She moved her feet beneath the desk, seeking the shoes she'd kicked off minutes before. Suddenly Grace was eager to get home to the two-bedroom house she rented. She'd lived there for the past five years, long enough to fill it with her favorite colors and fabrics and make it a home where she enjoyed spending time.

Successful in finding her shoes, she stood and stretched with arms overhead, grateful that this trying day was finally at an end. Maybe tomorrow won't be so difficult. One could hope, she thought.

She grabbed her purse, turned off the office light and stepped out. Just as she was about to head for the front door, she felt a stir in the air and saw in her peripheral vision a ruffling of the dresses hanging on the rack.

"Hello? Is somebody here?" Her heartbeat quickened, and she gripped her purse handle. "Who's there?"

A dark shadow with a bat or length of pipe raised

over his head exploded out of the clothes rack. He didn't make a sound, and the scream that rose up in the back of Grace's throat refused to release itself as she threw her purse at him and turned to run back to the office.

A lock. There was a lock on the office door. The words thundered through her brain as her heart threatened to burst out of her chest.

She had no idea who he was or what he wanted, but she didn't intend to stick around and ask questions. She ran past a mannequin and knocked it over, hoping to block his attack and gain an extra second or two to reach the office.

The mannequin banged to the floor, and she heard a hissed curse. Deep. Male. Oh, God, what was he doing in here? What did he want?

She gasped as she reached the office door, but before she could grab the knob and turn it, something hard crashed into the back of her head. She crumpled to her knees as shooting stars went off in her brain.

The intruder kicked her twice in the ribs and frantic thoughts raced through her scrambled brain as she struggled to regain her breath. She knew if she didn't do something he was going to kill her.

"Grace?" The familiar female voice came from the front door, although to Grace it sounded as if it came from miles away. "Grace, are you here?"

It was only then that the scream that had been trapped inside her released itself. The attacker froze, then raced for the back door of the store. As he went through it, the alarm began to ring. The loud, buzzing noise was the last sound Grace heard as she gave in to the shooting stars and lost consciousness.

Chapter 5

Charlie stepped on the gas, breaking every speed limit in the state of Oklahoma as he raced toward the hospital. His heart beat so hard he felt nauseous and every nerve ending he possessed screamed in alarm.

He'd called Grace at home to make arrangements for meeting the next day, and when he didn't get her there, he'd tried Sophisticated Lady to see if she was working late. Deputy Ben Taylor answered and told him there'd been an attempted robbery at the store and that Grace had been transported to the hospital. He had no information on her condition, and Charlie jumped into his car almost before he could hang up the phone.

Now he squealed into the hospital lot and parked, his heart still pounding the rhythm of alarm. How badly had she been hurt? Had they caught the person who had broken in?

He raced into the ER and nearly ran into Zack coming out. He grabbed the man by his broad shoulders. "What happened? Where's Grace? Is she all right?"

Zack held up his hands. "Calm down, Charlie. She's going to be fine. She's got some bruised ribs and a possible concussion."

Charlie's heart dropped to his toes as he released his hold on Zack. "And you call that fine? Ben Taylor said something about a robbery at the store."

"We think that's what it was, but he was interrupted by Ben's wife showing up to get her paycheck. I've got to get back to the store, but if you want to see Grace, she's in examination room two."

Charlie hurried down the hallway, his hands clenching and unclenching. Bruised ribs? A possible concussion?

A simmering rage began to burn in his stomach as he thought of somebody hurting Grace. He hoped to hell Zack would find out who was responsible.

Charlie wasn't a violent man. He was accustomed to using his brain and mouth to solve fights, but at the moment, he wanted nothing more than to find the person who hurt Grace and beat the holy hell out of him.

The door to the examination room was closed. Charlie gave a soft knock but didn't wait for an answer before opening the door.

Clad in a worn, pale-blue-flowered hospital gown, Grace sat on the edge of the examining-room table, her arms around her waist as the doctor sat in the chair before her.

Her eyes widened slightly at the sight of Charlie, and she winced as she shifted positions. "You didn't have to come here." Her normally strong voice was weak, reedy. The sound of it squeezed his heart.

"Of course I had to come here," he replied. "How is she?" He looked at the doctor, who wore a name tag that proclaimed him to be Dr. Devore.

"I have sore ribs and a headache. Other than that I'm fine," she answered. "In fact the doctor was just releasing me."

"Against my better judgment," Dr. Devore muttered beneath his breath. "She has quite a goose egg on the back of her head."

Charlie shot a look at Grace. She sighed and raised a trembling hand to her head. "He's worried that I might have a concussion and thinks I should spend the night."

"Then you should stay," Charlie said.

"I don't want to," she said crossly and dropped her hand from her head. "I'm a grown woman, Charlie. I know what's best for me, and I just need to go to bed. I'll be fine after a good night's sleep."

"If she goes home, somebody should stay with her throughout the night," Dr. Devore said, as he stood. "And if she suffers any nausea, vomiting or blurred vision, she needs to come right back in. I'll write you a pain prescription for your ribs, and the nurse will complete your discharge papers. Then I guess you can go."

"You aren't going home alone," Charlie said the moment the doctor left the room. "You have two choices, Grace. You can either have me as a houseguest for the night or you can come back to the ranch with me."

He saw the mutinous glare in her eyes and quickly continued, "Be reasonable, Grace. You shouldn't be alone. What if you get dizzy in the middle of the night and fall? What if you start throwing up and can't stop? Somebody needs to be with you."

"I don't want you in my house," she said hesitantly.

"Then come to mine," he replied. "I have a comfortable guest room, and if you're worried about being alone with me, don't be. Rosa will be there."

Once again she raised a hand to her head and winced. "Okay, I'll go to your place."

Her relatively easy capitulation surprised him and made him wonder just what had happened tonight in the shop and what was going on in her head. He intended to find out before the night was over.

"Can you take me by my house to get a few things?" she asked.

"Absolutely."

The nurse came in with her prescription and discharge papers. She reminded them of all the signs to watch for and to return to the emergency room should Grace experience anything unusual.

Charlie stepped out of the room so Grace could get dressed, and while he waited for her he called Rosa to make sure she had the guest room ready.

When Grace opened the door of the examining room and stepped out, Charlie wanted to wrap her in his arms, hold her tight and make sure that nobody else ever hurt her again.

She was in obvious pain as they walked to his car, and once again rage coupled with fierce protectiveness filled him.

Their first stop was at the pharmacy, where they filled the prescription for her pain pills. He wanted her to wait in the car while he ran in, but she insisted on going in.

From the drugstore, he drove to her house. He'd never been inside it before. Their dates had usually taken place in Oklahoma City when she was there on business.

They'd had two dates here in Cotter Creek when he'd come back to visit his father, and it had been on those dates he'd met Hope, but he'd never been invited into her personal space.

As he stepped into her living room, two things struck him: the lime and lavender color scheme that was both soothing and sensual, and the magnificent scent of jasmine and vanilla that lingered in the air.

When Grace disappeared down the hallway to her bedroom, he walked around the living room, taking in the furnishings and knickknacks that showed the nuances of her personality.

The sofa looked elegant yet comfortable, and the bookshelf held an array of paperback books and framed photos of both Hope and William. What was curiously missing were any photos of her mother. Again Charlie wondered about the whereabouts of the elusive Elizabeth Covington and the relationship she had with her daughters.

Right now, what he really wanted to know was what Grace's bedroom looked like. Was her bed covered with luxurious silk sheets that smelled like her? Did she still own that sexy little red nightgown that hugged her curves and exposed just enough skin to make his mind go blank?

He sat on the sofa and mentally chastised himself. He had to stop thinking about things like that—had to stop torturing himself with memories of how her long hair had felt splayed across his bare chest and how she loved to cuddle and run her finger through his thatch of chest hair.

He remembered the two of them running naked into his kitchen to bake a frozen pizza after a bout of hot, wild sex, slow-dancing on his balcony and the philosophical debates that usually ended in laughter.

She was smart and sexy—everything he'd wanted in a woman—but he'd thought she was playing for fun and hadn't realized she was playing for keeps. She'd breezed into his life every weekend or so. She hadn't been inclined to share much information about her personal life. Instead they had spent their time together living in the moment.

Now, as he sat on the sofa with those old regrets weighing heavy, he realized that despite their intense relationship there were many things he didn't know about her, many things they hadn't shared.

He stood up when she returned to the living room with a small, flowery overnight bag in her hand. He took the bag from her, and moments later they were in his car, headed toward his ranch.

"You want to tell me exactly what happened tonight?" he asked.

"I figured you already knew. Somebody tried to rob the store."

He glanced at her. She was ghostly pale in the light from the dashboard. "That's the short version. I want all the details," he said gently.

She leaned her head back against the seat, winced slightly and closed her eyes. "I was in the back in the office and went out to greet whoever had come in, but I didn't see anyone so I went back to the office to lock up my desk and get ready to leave. I was halfway to the front door when he came out of the rack of clothes."

Charlie's hands tightened around the steering wheel as he heard the slight tremor in her voice and felt her fear grow palpable in the car.

"And then what?" he asked.

"He had a bat or something like that in his hands. I ran back toward the office. I knew if I could get inside I could lock the door and call for help." She drew a tremulous breath. "I almost made it." She opened her eyes and gave him a wry smile. "I guess I shouldn't have stopped to admire that cute blouse on the mannequin."

Her smile began to tremble and fell away as tears filled her eyes. "I'd just reached the office door when he hit me in the back of the head. I fell to my knees and he started to kick me." A small sob escaped her, but she quickly sucked in a breath to stop her tears. "If Dana hadn't come in for her paycheck, I don't know what would have happened."

"You didn't see who it was? You couldn't make an identification?"

"No. All I saw was a big, dark shadow." She sucked in another breath and wiped her eyes before the tears could fall. "I guess I should be grateful that he didn't get the money in the cash register." Once again she leaned her head back and closed her eyes.

Charlie said nothing, but his blood ran cold. What kind of a robber would walk right past the cash register and hide in a rack of clothes? If he'd truly been after quick cash, why not take the money from the register and escape out the front door?

His hands clenched tighter on the steering wheel as alarms rang in his head. What she'd just described didn't sound like an attempted robbery. It sounded like attempted murder.

* * *

Under any other circumstances, Grace would have never agreed to go to Charlie's for the night, but the truth was that she was afraid to be alone. The attack had shaken her up more than she wanted to admit, and even now as she closed her eyes, all she could see was a vision of the big shadow leaping out at her.

Almost as upsetting as the attack itself was the fact that she couldn't think of a single friend who would welcome her into their home. Over the last couple of years she'd been so focused on the store, she hadn't taken the time to nurture friendships. Her relationship with Rachel was the only one she'd managed to maintain, and she was reluctant to barge into Rachel's happy home, where she lived with her adoring husband and baby boy.

With William gone and Hope in the hospital, she really had no place else to turn but to Charlie. At least Rosa would be there.

A surge of anger swelled up inside Grace. Her mother should be here. Her mother should be the person calming her fears, offering her support and comfort. The anger was short-lived. She was unable to sustain it as her head pounded and her ribs ached.

She was grateful when Charlie pulled up to the ranch. Lights blazed from almost every window. All she wanted was a pain pill and a bed where she'd feel safe for the remainder of the night.

Rosa greeted them at the front door, fussing like a mother hen as she led Grace to the airy, open kitchen. "I'm going to make you a nice hot cup of tea, then it's bed for you, you poor thing."

As Grace eased down into a chair at the table and Charlie sat across from her, Rosa bustled around, preparing the tea. Despite the pounding of her head, Grace found the hominess of the room comforting. Maybe a cup of tea would banish the icy knot inside her chest.

It smelled like apple pie spices, and a vase of fresh-cut daisies sat in the center of the round oak table. The yellow gingham curtains added a dash of cheer.

"Tell me again what happened," Charlie said.

"She will not," Rosa said, her plump face wrinkling in disapproval as she shot a stern look at him. "There will be time for you to talk tomorrow. Right now what she needs is to drink that tea and get into bed. Haven't you noticed that she's pale as a ghost and in obvious pain?"

Grace looked at Charlie, and in the depths of his gray eyes, she saw compassion and caring and a flicker of something else, something deeper that both scared her and sent a rumbling shock wave through her.

She quickly broke eye contact with him and stared into her cup. Coming here had been a mistake. She didn't want to see Charlie here in his home environment, one so different from his apartment in Oklahoma City.

"You want one of those pills?" Charlie asked.

She nodded. "I'd like a handful, but I'll settle for one."

"Your head still hurt?" he asked, as he got the bottle and shook out one of the pills.

"The only thing that takes my mind off how bad my head hurts is the pain in my ribs." She forced a small smile that turned into a wince.

"I'm just going to go turn down your bed and fluff your pillows," Rosa said, and left the kitchen.

Grace took the pill and sipped her tea, the warmth

working its way into icy territory. She'd been cold since the moment the attacker had leapt out of the clothes rack. She would have given him any money she had if he'd demanded it. He hadn't needed to hit her over the head and kick her.

She was aware of Charlie's gaze on her, intent and somber. "What?" she finally asked. "What are you thinking, Charlie?"

"I'm thinking maybe we have a lot to talk about tomorrow."

Instinctively she knew he was talking about more than William's murder case, about more than the attack on her tonight. She frowned.

"Charlie, if you think I'm going to talk about anything that happened before three days ago, then you're wrong. I have no desire to go back and hash out our past. I told you what I want from you. I want you to keep Hope out of jail. I appreciate what you're doing for me tonight, but don't mistake my need for your abilities as an attorney and investigator for a need for anything else. Don't mistake my gratitude for anything other than that."

Her speech exhausted her. Thankfully at that moment Rosa returned to the kitchen and Grace stood, a bit unsteady on her feet.

Charlie was at her side in an instant, his arm under hers for support. "Let's get you into bed," he said.

She was already feeling the initial effect of the pain medication, a floating sensation that took the edge off and made her legs a bit wobbly. She rarely took any kind of pain meds. She hated the feeling of being even slightly out of control.

Charlie led her down the hallway, and for a single,

crazy moment, she wished he were going to crawl into bed with her. Not for sex—although sex with Charlie had always been amazing.

No, what she yearned for was his big, strong arms around her. He'd always been a great cuddle partner, and she'd never felt as loved, as safe, as when she'd been snuggled against him with his arms wrapped around her.

"You should be okay in here," he said as they stepped into the room.

The guest room was large and decorated in various shades of blue. The bed was king-sized, the bedspread turned down to reveal crisp, white sheets.

"Do you want me to send in Rosa to help you get into your nightclothes?" he asked.

"No, I'll be fine," she replied. Her voice seemed to come from someplace far away. She looked up at him, his face slightly blurry, and again she was struck by a desire to fall into his arms—to burrow her head against his strong chest and let him hold her through the night.

"You need to go now, Charlie," she said, and pushed him away.

He stepped back toward the door. "You'll let me know if you need anything?"

"You'll be the first to know."

He turned to leave but then faced her once again. "Grace? I could kill the man who did this to you." His deep voice rumbled and his eyes flashed darkly.

She sat on the edge of the bed. "I appreciate the sentiment," she said. "Good night, Charlie."

"'Night, Grace." He closed the door, and she was alone in the room.

It took what seemed like forever to get out of her

clothes and into her nightgown. She went into the ad-joining bathroom and brushed her teeth, then returned to the bedroom, where she turned out the bedside lamp and fell into bed.

It was only when she was finally alone that she began to cry. She didn't know if her tears were for William, for Hope, for her mother or for herself.

And she feared they just might be tears because, in the past, Charlie Black hadn't been the man she'd thought he was, the man she'd wanted him to be.

Chapter 6

It was just after two in the morning, and Charlie sat in the recliner chair by the window in the living room, staring out at the moonlit night.

He'd grown up on the ranch, and some of his happiest memories were of things that occurred here. He'd loved the feel of a horse beneath him and the smell of the rich earth, but in college, his head had gotten twisted, and suddenly the ranch hadn't seemed good enough for him.

He'd been a fool. A shallow, stupid fool.

A year ago he would have never dreamed that he'd be back here on the ranch. He'd been living in the fast lane, making more money than he'd ever dreamed possible and enjoying a lifestyle of excess.

Meeting Grace had been the icing on the cake. He'd eagerly looked forward to the two weekends a month she came into town and stayed with him. Although he would have liked more from her, he got the feeling from her that he was an indulgence, like eating ice cream twice a month. But nobody really wanted a steady diet of ice cream.

He'd thought he was her boy toy. They'd never spoken about their relationship, never laid down ground rules or speculated on where it was going. They'd just enjoyed it.

Until that night. That crazy Friday night when things—when *he*—had spiraled out of control.

He shoved these thoughts from his mind and closed his eyes and drew a weary breath. He was tired, but sleep remained elusive. The attack on her earlier tonight worried him because it didn't make sense.

If the goal of the person in the store had been to rob it, then why carry in a bat, why not a gun? Why leave the cash register untouched and go after Grace? Had he thought that her cash might be locked away in the office? Possibly.

He sat up straighter in his chair as he sensed movement in the hallway. He reached over and turned on the small lamp on the table next to his chair.

Grace appeared in the doorway. She was wearing a short, pink silk robe tied around her slender waist, and her hair was tousled from sleep. She didn't appear to be surprised that he was still awake.

"Can't sleep?" he asked.

"I had a bad dream. I tried to go back to sleep, but decided maybe it was time for another pain pill." She walked across the room to the sofa and curled up with her bare legs beneath her. "What's your excuse for being up this time of the night?"

"No bad dreams, just confusing thoughts."

"What kind of confusing thoughts?" she asked, and then held up a hand. "Wait, I don't want to know, at least not tonight." She reached up and smoothed a strand of her golden hair away from her face. "Talk to me about pleasant things, Charlie. I feel like the last couple of days have been nothing but bad things. Tell me about your life here at the ranch. What made you decide to move back here?"

"You heard about Dad's heart attack?"

She nodded. "And I'm sorry."

"Initially I was just going to come back here to deal with whatever needed to be taken care of to get the place on the market and sold, but something happened in those days right after I buried Dad."

He paused a moment and stared back out the window, but it was impossible to see anything but his own reflection. In truth, his life had begun a transformation on the night that Grace left him, but he knew she wouldn't want to hear that, probably wouldn't believe him, anyway.

He looked back at her. "I realized that I hated my life, that I missed waking up in the mornings and hearing the cows lowing in the pasture, that I missed the feel of a horse beneath me and the warm sun on my back. I realized it was time to come home to Cotter Creek."

She leaned her head back against the cushions. "When I was planning to open a dress shop, William told me I could use the money he loaned me to open one anywhere in the country, but it never entered my mind to be anywhere but here," she said. "Cotter Creek is and always will be home. I love it here, the small-town feel, the people, everything. Has the transition been tough for you?"

"Learning the ins and outs of ranching has been challenging," he admitted. "Even though I grew up here I never paid much attention to the day-to-day details. I already had my sights set on something different than the ranch. My ranch hands have had a fine time tormenting the city boy in me. The first thing they told me was that cow manure was a natural cleaner for Italian leather shoes."

She laughed and that's exactly what he'd wanted, to hear that rich, melodic sound coming from her. She was a woman made for laughter, and for the next few minutes he continued to tell her about the silly things that had happened when he'd first taken over the ranch.

He embellished each story as necessary to get the best entertainment value—needing, wanting, to keep her laughing so the dark shadows of fear and worry wouldn't claim her eyes again.

"Stop," she finally said, her arms wrapped around her ribs.

"You need that pain pill now?" he asked.

"No, I don't think so. To be honest, what I'd like is something to eat. Maybe I could just fix a quick sandwich or something. I didn't eat dinner last night," she said with a touch of apology.

"I'll bet there's some leftover roast beef from Rosa's dinner in the fridge. Want to come into the kitchen, or do you want me to fix you a plate and bring it to you?"

She unfolded those long, shapely legs of hers. "I'll come to the kitchen." She stood and frowned. "We won't wake up Rosa, will we?"

"Nah. First of all she sleeps like the dead, and secondly her room is on the other side of the house." Charlie got up and followed her into the kitchen, trying not to notice how the silky robe clung to her lush curves.

He flipped on the kitchen light, and as she slid into a chair at the table, he walked over to the refrigerator, then turned back to look at her. "If you'd rather not have leftover roast, I could whip up an omelet with toast."

She looked at him in surprise. "You never used to cook."

He knew she was remembering that when they had been seeing each other he'd always taken his meals out, keeping only prepared food in his apartment that required nothing more than opening a lid or popping it into the microwave.

"When I came back here to the ranch, I learned survival cooking skills. Rosa takes three days off a week to stay with her son and his family, and during those days I'm on my own. So, cooking became a necessity, and to my surprise I rather like it."

"The roast beef is fine," she replied.

He felt her gaze lingering on him as he got out the leftover meat and potatoes and arranged them on a plate, then ladled gravy over everything and popped it into the microwave.

Was she remembering those midnight raids they'd made on his refrigerator after making love? When they'd eat cold chicken with their fingers or eat ice cream out of the carton?

Did she remember anything good about their time together, or had his betrayal left only the bad times in her head?

"Are you dating, Grace? Got a special fella in your life?" he asked.

She raised a perfectly arched blond eyebrow. "If I

had somebody special in my life, I wouldn't be sitting here now," she replied, confirming what he'd already assumed. "I've been too busy at the shop to date, besides the fact that I'm just not interested in a relationship."

The microwave dinged and Charlie turned around to retrieve the food. He wanted to ask her if he was responsible for the fact that she didn't want a relationship, if he'd left such a bad mark on her heart that she wasn't interested in ever pursuing a relationship again. If that was the case, it would be tragic.

He placed the steaming plate before her, got her a glass of milk and sat across from her as she began to eat.

"What about you?" she asked between bites. "Are you dating somebody here in town? I'm sure there were plenty of fluttering hearts when the news got out that you had moved back."

"I would venture a guess that yours wasn't one of those that fluttered?"

She raised that dainty eyebrow again. "That would be a good guess," she replied.

He leaned back in his chair and shook his head. "I'm not seeing anyone, haven't for quite some time. Apparently Dad hadn't been feeling well for a while before his death, and the ranch had kind of gotten away from him. I've been incredibly busy since I moved back. I haven't had the time or the inclination to date."

"Charlie Black too busy for fun? Hold the presses!" she exclaimed.

He gazed at her for a long moment. "You've got to stop that, Grace," he finally said. "If you want my continued help, you need to stop with the not-so-subtle digs. I understand how you feel about me. You don't have to remind me with sarcastic cuts."

She held his gaze as a tinge of pink filled her cheeks. "You're right, I'm sorry." She turned her attention to her plate and set her fork down. "I'm just so filled with anger right now and you're an easy target."

He leaned forward and covered her hand with his, surprised when she didn't pull away from him. "We'll sort this all out, Grace. I promise you."

She surprised him further by turning her hand over and entwining her fingers with his. "I hope so. Right now everything just seems like such a mess."

"It is a mess," he agreed. "But messes can be cleaned up." Except the one he'd made with her, he reminded himself.

She let go of his hand and picked up her fork once again. As she continued to eat, Charlie once again spoke of ranch life, trying to keep the conversation light and easy.

When she was finished eating, she started to get up to take her plate to the sink, but he stopped her and instead grabbed the dish himself.

"I'm not used to somebody waiting on me," she said.

"You never struck me as a woman who wanted or needed anyone to wait on you," he replied, as he rinsed the dishes and stuck them in the dishwasher. "One of your strengths is that you're self-reliant and independent. And one of your weaknesses is that you're self-reliant and independent." He smiled and pointed a finger at her. "And no, that doesn't open the door for you to point out all my weaknesses."

She laughed, then reached up and touched her temple. "Now I think I'm ready for a pain pill and some more sleep."

When she got up from the table, Charlie tried unsuccessfully not to notice that her robe had come untied. As she stood, he caught a glimpse of the curve of her creamy breast just above the neckline of the pink nightgown she wore beneath.

Desire jolted through him, stunning him with the force of it. Maybe this was his penance, he thought, as he followed her out of the kitchen. Fate had forced them together, and his punishment was to want her forever and never have the satisfaction of possessing her again.

As they passed through the living room, he turned out the lamp, knowing that if he didn't get some sleep tonight he wouldn't be worth a plugged nickel the next day.

When they reached the door to her room, she turned and looked at him. Her gaze seemed softer than it had since the moment she'd pulled up in her convertible and demanded his help.

"Thank you, Charlie, for feeding me and letting me stay here tonight. I really appreciate everything." She reached up and placed her palm on the side of his cheek, and he fought the impulse to turn his face into her touch. "Part of you is such a good man."

She dropped her hand to her side. "I just wish I could forgive and forget the parts of you that aren't such a good man."

She turned and went into the bedroom, closing the door firmly in his face.

Grace woke with the sun slashing through the gauzy curtains and the sound of horse hooves someplace in the distance. She remained in bed, thinking about her life, about what lay ahead and, finally, about Charlie.

Funny that the man who had hurt her more than any

man in her life was also the one who made her feel the most safe. She'd slept without worry, comforted by the fact that Charlie was in the room across the hall.

Surely it was just because of all that had happened, that she'd so easily let him back in her life.

She was off-kilter, careening around in a landscape that was utterly foreign to her. Was it any wonder she'd cling to the one person she'd thought she'd known better than anyone else in the world?

With a low moan, she finally pulled herself to a sitting position on the side of the bed. She'd felt awful the night before, and although her head had stopped pounding, her body felt as if it had been contorted in positions previously unknown to the human body.

Her ribs were sore, but not intolerably so. No more pain pills, she told herself, as she headed for the bathroom. What she needed was a hot shower to loosen her muscles and clear her head. Then she needed to get Charlie to take her home.

Before falling asleep last night, she'd come to the conclusion that the attack in the shop had been an attempted robbery. It was the only thing that made sense.

The robber had obviously thought there was nothing in the register and probably assumed she had a safe or a cash box in the office. He probably wouldn't have attacked her at all if she'd gone directly to the front door and left instead of noticing the sway of the clothes on the rack in front of his hiding place. She went to the bathroom and turned on the shower.

She'd never felt such terror as when he'd jumped out of the clothes rack and raced toward her, the long object held over his head. If he'd hit her just a little harder, he could have bashed her skull in and killed her.

Shivering, she quickly stepped beneath the hot spray of water, needing the warmth to cast away the chill her thought evoked.

The shower did help, although her ribs still ached when she drew a deep breath or moved too fast. She dressed in the jeans and blouse she'd packed in her overnight bag, then left the bedroom in search of Charlie.

She found Rosa in the kitchen by herself. The plump woman sat at the table with a cup of coffee in front of her. When she saw Grace, she jumped to her feet with surprising agility.

"Sit," Grace exclaimed. "Just point me to the cabinet with the cups. I can get my own coffee."

"What about breakfast?" Rosa asked, as she pointed a finger to the cabinet next to the sink. "You should eat something."

"Nothing for me. I'm fine. I had some of your roast beef at about three this morning. It was delicious, by the way." Grace poured herself a cup of the coffee and joined the housekeeper at the table. "Where's Charlie?"

"Out riding the ranch. He should be back in a little while. How are you feeling this morning?"

"Sore, but better than last night." Grace took a sip of the coffee.

"Charlie was worried about you. I could see it in his eyes. He used to get that look when his mama was having bad days. She had cancer, you know. She was diagnosed when he was ten and didn't pass away until he was fourteen. Those four years were tough on him, but I'm sure you knew all that."

"Actually, I didn't," Grace replied. She'd known that Charlie's mother had passed away when he was a teenager, but that was all she'd known.

At that moment, the back door opened and he walked in, bringing with him that restless energy he possessed and the scent of sunshine and horseflesh. The smile he offered her shot a starburst of warmth through her.

"Grace, how are you feeling?" He shrugged out of a navy jacket and hung it on a hook near the backdoor, then walked to the cabinet and grabbed a cup.

"Better. A little sore, but I think I'm going to live." She didn't want to notice how utterly masculine he looked in his worn jeans and the white T-shirt that pulled taut across his broad shoulders. With his lean hips and muscled chest and arms, he definitely turned women's heads.

She'd always thought he was born to wear a suit—that elegant dress slacks and button-down shirts were made for him. But she'd been mistaken. He looked equally hot in his casual wear.

"I'm glad you're feeling better," he said, as he joined them at the table. "Did you get breakfast?"

"Said she didn't want any," Rosa replied.

"And I don't. What I'd like is for you to take me home now." She looked at Charlie expectantly.

He frowned and Rosa stood, looking from one to the other. "I'm going to go take care of some laundry," she said, and left the two of them alone at the table.

Charlie took a sip of his coffee, eyeing her over the rim of the mug. "I wish you'd consider staying here for a couple more days," he said.

"There's no reason to do that. I'm feeling much better." She wrapped her fingers around her cup as his frown deepened.

"You might be feeling better, but I'm not. I don't like what happened to you last night, Grace."

She laughed. "I wasn't too excited about it, either, but it was an attempted robbery. It could have happened to anyone."

"But it didn't happen to anyone. It happened to you." His gaze held hers intently. "And given what happened to William, it just makes me nervous. It makes me damned nervous."

She leaned back in her chair and looked at him in surprise. "Surely you can't think that one thing had anything to do with the other?" she exclaimed. "You're overreacting, Charlie."

"Maybe," he agreed, and took another sip of his coffee.

"How can you possibly connect what happened to William to the attack on me at the store last night?"

"I can't right now." His lips were thin with tension. "But, I'd prefer we be too cautious than not cautious enough."

"Then I'll do things differently at the store. I realize now how incredibly stupid it was of me to leave the shop door unlocked when I was in the back room. Maybe whoever came in knew that it was payday and hoped I'd have some of the payroll in cash. I just can't believe it was anything other than that, and there's no reason for me to stay here another night."

She wasn't going to let him talk her into staying. Last night after he'd fixed her the meal and walked her back to the bedroom, she'd almost kissed him. When she'd placed her palm on the side of his face, she'd wanted to lean in and take his mouth with hers.

It had been an insane impulse, one that she was grateful she hadn't followed through on, but she felt the need to gain some distance from him.

There was no way she wanted to stay here another night with him. She was more than a little weak where he was concerned.

"I suppose you're going to be stubborn about this," he said.

"I suppose so," she agreed.

He drained his coffee cup and got up from the table. "Just let me take a quick shower and I'll take you home."

"Actually you can just drop me at the shop."

"You're actually planning to work today?" He raised an eyebrow in disapproval. "Don't you think it would be wise to give yourself a day of rest?" He carried his coffee cup to the sink.

"Actually, I think you're right. While you're showering, I'll make arrangements for somebody else to work both today and this evening. My ribs are still pretty sore, and I didn't get a lot of sleep last night. A day of lazing around sounds pretty good."

He nodded, as if satisfied with her answer. "Give me fifteen, twenty minutes, then I'll be ready to take you to get your car."

As he left the kitchen, Grace sipped her coffee. Although she didn't want to admit it, there was a part of her that dreaded going back into the store, where last night she'd thought she was going to die.

She heard a phone ring someplace in the back of the house. It rang only once and then apparently was answered. It reminded her that she needed to make some calls.

She dug her cell phone out of her purse, grateful that Rosa had left it on the kitchen table, where she would find it easily this morning. She made the calls to arrange for the shop to run smoothly without her today.

Thankfully she had dependable and trustworthy employees to take over for her. She also needed to check on the final funeral arrangements for William.

When the calls were finished, she got up from the table and carried her cup to the sink, then went back to the bedroom to retrieve her overnight bag.

She could hear running water and knew Charlie was in the shower. She sat on the edge of the bed as memories swept over her—memories of hot, steaming water and Charlie gliding a bar of soap over her shoulders and down her back, of the feel of his soapy hands cupping her breasts, of his slick body pressed against her. More than once they'd left the shower stall, covered with suds and fallen into Charlie's king-sized bed to finish what they'd started.

She shook her head to dislodge the old images. Rising from the bed, she grabbed her bag, then went back into the kitchen to wait for Charlie.

Grace pulled out her cell phone and called the hospital. "Hi, honey," she said when Hope's voice filled the line.

"Grace!" Hope instantly began to cry.

"Hope, what's wrong?" Grace squeezed the phone more tightly against her ear. "Honey, why are you crying? Has something happened?"

"I heard from a nurse this morning that something bad happened to you last night, that you were attacked. I thought I'd never see you again, that it would be just like Mom and you'd be gone forever."

Grace wished she could reach through the line and hug her sister. "I'm not going anywhere, Hope. You can always depend on me," she said fervently.

Again she mentally cursed her mother for abandoning them, for going away and leaving behind so many questions and so much pain.

"It was a robbery attempt, Hope, but I'm okay. I promise and we're going to be okay. You and I together, we're going to be just fine. We're going to get through all of this." She glanced up as Charlie entered the room, bringing with him the scent of minty soap and shaving cream. "I'll be in to see you sometime this morning, okay? You just hang in there. You have to be strong."

She hung up and stood to face Charlie. "I'm ready," she said.

"You'd better sit back down."

It was only then that she saw the darkness in his eyes, the muscle working in his jaw. A screaming alarm went off inside her.

"Why? What's going on?" Her heart began to beat a frantic rhythm and her legs threatened to buckle as she sat once again.

"I got a call from Zack." He frowned, as if searching for words, which was ridiculous because Charlie was never at a loss for them. "Hope is being arrested this morning. She's going to be charged with first-degree murder."

Grace grabbed hold of the top of the table, her fingertips biting into the wood as his words reverberated through her head.

Chapter 7

If there was any chance of Charlie becoming a drinking man again, the events of the past three days certainly would have driven him to the bottle.

Hope had been arraigned on Tuesday morning in front of the toughest judge Charlie had ever butted heads against. The prosecuting attorney, up for reelection in the fall, had come with both barrels loaded. He'd suggested the judge send a message to the youth around the country, that no matter what the age or the circumstances, murder was never acceptable.

He'd requested no bail be set, and although Charlie had argued vigorously, nearly garnering himself a contempt charge, the judge had agreed with the prosecutor.

Hope would await trial at the Beacon Juvenile Detention Center in Oklahoma City. A plea deal had been offered to her. The authorities believed it was probable she hadn't acted alone, that it was her boyfriend, Justin, who actually killed William.

Hope refused to accept the deal, sticking to her story that she had no idea what had happened that morning at the house.

William's attorney had traveled to Cotter Creek and sat down with Charlie and Grace to go over the will. The estate had been left to Grace and Hope, with Grace as executor. He'd left some of his money to local charities and a generous amount to Lana for her years of service. He'd also left a small amount of money to Grace's mother.

After the meeting with the lawyer, they had visited with the Racines. Grace assured Lana and Leroy that she had no intention of selling the house anytime soon and would continue to pay their salaries if they wanted to stay on doing their usual duties. She also told them about the money William had left to Lana.

Hope's incarceration at the detention center was difficult for Grace, although as usual she kept a stiff upper lip and didn't display the emotions Charlie knew had to be boiling inside her.

Charlie now checked his watch with a frown. Time to leave. He was picking Grace up at ten for William's funeral. After the ceremony was over, they were driving into Oklahoma City to visit Hope. It was going to be a grim, long day.

He left the ranch and headed toward Grace's place. Charlie felt that tingle of excitement, a crazy swell of emotion in his chest—the same feeling he'd always gotten when he knew she was coming into Oklahoma City for the weekend. He would spend the entire week before filled with eager anticipation, half sick by wanting the days of the week to fly by quickly. By Saturday night, he'd be sick again, dreading the coming of Sunday when she'd return to Cotter Creek. He'd never asked her for more than what she gave him, was afraid that in asking he'd only push her away from him.

He shoved these thoughts out of his head as he pulled up in front of her house. She was waiting for him on the porch, a solitary woman in an elegant black dress. He got out of the car as she approached, and his heart squeezed at the dark, deep sadness in her eyes.

"Good morning," he said, as he opened the car door to let her in. "Are you ready for this?"

"I don't think you're ever ready for something like this," she replied.

He closed the door, went back around to the driver's seat and got in. "You look tired," he said, as he headed toward the cemetery. The wake had been the night before and was followed by an open house at Grace's place.

"After everyone left last night, I had trouble going to sleep," she said. "I'm sure I'll sleep better once the funeral is over and I get a chance to see that Hope's okay."

He nodded. "Zack turned over copies of William's financial records to me. I spent last night going through them looking for any anomalies that might raise a flag."

"Let me guess, you didn't find anything."

"Nothing that looked at all suspicious." He felt the weight of her gaze on him.

"We aren't doing very well at coming up with an alternate suspect," she observed.

"Unfortunately it isn't as easy as just pulling a name out of a hat. I intend to make a case that Justin is responsible."

"Then why hasn't he been arrested?" she asked. "Zack has made it pretty clear he thinks Justin was involved."

"Thinking and proving are two different things. Unfortunately Justin's roommate has provided him with an alibi for the time of the murder." His roommate, Sam Young, certainly was no paragon of virtue. Sam worked in a tattoo parlor and had a reputation for being a tough guy.

They fell silent for the rest of the drive to the cemetery. When they arrived, the parking lot was already filled with cars, indicating that there was a huge turnout of people to say goodbye to William Covington.

The Cotter Creek Cemetery was a pretty place, with plenty of old shade trees. Wilbur Cummins, the caretaker, took particular pride not only in maintaining the grounds but also in making sure that all the headstones were in good shape. A plethora of flowers filled the area.

As they waited for the ceremony to begin, people walked over to give their regards to Grace.

"I'm so sorry for your loss," Savannah West said, as she reached for Grace's hand. Savannah worked for the Cotter Creek newspaper and was married to one of the brothers who ran West Protective Services.

"Thanks." Grace turned and looked at Charlie. "Savannah is one of my best customers at the shop."

Savannah shoved a strand of wild red hair away from her face. "Still no arrest in the attempted robbery and assault?"

Grace shook her head. "I wasn't able to give Zack any kind of a description, so I'm not expecting any arrest."

"The criminals are running amuck in Cotter Creek. Zack is just sick about it and about what's happening with Hope," Savannah said.

Charlie felt the wave of Grace's despair as she nodded stiffly and her eyes grew glassy with tears. Savannah grabbed Grace's hand once again. "Zack was against making the arrest, but that ass of a prosecutor Alan Connor insisted."

"It doesn't matter," Charlie said. "Hope is innocent, and we'll prove it where it counts, in a court of law."

Grace placed a hand on his arm and smiled gratefully. Then it was time for the service to begin. As the preacher gave the eulogy, Charlie scanned the crowd.

Grace was right. Other than Justin, they hadn't managed to come up with a single lead that would point them away from Hope.

It was an eclectic crowd. Ranchers uncomfortable in their Sunday suits stood beside men Charlie didn't know, men who wore their expensive power suits with casual elegance. He assumed these were business associates of William's, and he noticed Zack West had those men in his sights as well.

Was it possible that William had been working on a business deal nobody knew about? Something that might have stirred up a motive for murder? At this point, he was willing to grasp at any alternative theory to Hope being a murderer.

Lana and Leroy Racine stood side by side, Leroy's big arm around his wife's shoulders as she wept uncontrollably. Certainly they had nothing to gain by William's death; rather, it was just the opposite. They stood to lose both their jobs and their home.

The only people who had a lot to gain by William's

death were Grace and Hope, both of whom Charlie would have staked his life were innocent. But how had Hope gotten drugged? Who had managed to get into the house without breaking a window or a door? Who had killed William?

What he hoped was that Zack was doing his job and would give him a heads-up if he discovered any leads. Right now, coming up with a reasonable defense for Hope seemed impossible.

Grace remained stoic throughout the funeral, standing rigidly beside him. An island of strength, that was how he'd always thought of her. An island of a woman who took care of herself and her own needs, a woman who had never really needed him. And he was a man who needed to be needed.

When the ceremony was finally over and the final well-wishing had been given, most of the crowd headed for their cars, and Charlie gently took hold of Grace's arm.

"You ready to go?"

She nodded wearily. "I loved him, you know. He was as loving and kind a father as I could have ever asked for." She leaned into Charlie.

They were halfway to the car when a tall, gray-haired man who greeted Grace with a friendly smile stopped them. She introduced him as Hank Weatherford, William's closest neighbor.

"I was wondering if we could sit down together when you get a chance," Hank said. Grace looked at him with curiosity. He continued, "I've been trying to talk William into selling me the five acres of land between his place and mine. It's got nothing on it but weeds and an old shed. Now that he's gone I thought maybe you'd be agreeable to the idea."

Charlie narrowed his eyes as he stared at the older man. Interesting. A land dispute over five acres hardly seemed like a motive for murder, but Charlie smelled a contentious relationship between Hank Weatherford and William.

"Mr. Weatherford, I'll have to get back to you. I haven't decided yet what I'm going to do with the estate," Grace said.

He nodded. "Just keep in mind that I'd like to sit down and talk with you about those five acres."

"I'll keep it in mind," Grace agreed.

"That was interesting," Charlie said once he and Grace were in his car. "What's the deal with these five acres?"

"William always talked about having it cleaned up and maybe putting in a pool or a tennis court, but he never got around to it. I imagine Hank is tired of looking at the mess." She shot him a sharp glance. "Surely you don't think Hank had anything to do with William's death."

"Take nothing for granted, Grace. You'd be amazed at why people commit murder."

From the cemetery they went to her place, where they both changed clothes for the drive to Oklahoma City. Charlie had brought with him a pair of jeans and a short-sleeved light blue dress shirt, and he changed in her guest room.

She changed from her somber dress into a pair of jeans and a peach-colored blouse that enhanced the blue of her eyes and her blond coloring.

By one o'clock they were on the road. They hoped

to get to the detention center by three, which would let them visit with Hope for an hour.

Grace seemed a million miles away as they drove. She stared out the window, not speaking, and she had a lost, uncertain look that was so unlike her, and it broke Charlie's heart just a little bit more.

She was still in his heart, as deeply and profoundly as she had been when they'd been seeing each other. He didn't want to love her anymore and knew that she certainly didn't love him, but he didn't know how to stop loving her. Over the past week it had become the thing that he did better than anything else.

He'd known when he'd gotten involved in this case that it was going to end badly. He could live with a broken heart, but if he didn't figure out how to save Hope, he knew he'd break Grace's heart once again. Charlie wasn't sure he could live with that.

As Grace stared out at the passing scenery, she was surprised to realize she was thinking of her mother. There were times when she glanced at herself in the mirror and saw a glimpse of the woman who had deserted them.

How could a woman who'd been a loving mother and good wife just pack her bags and leave without a backward glance?

And how long did it take before thoughts of her didn't hurt anymore?

She hadn't told anyone about Elizabeth, although she was sure most people in town knew about the vanishing act. Now she wanted to talk about it, especially to Charlie. She turned to look at him.

He looked so amazingly handsome, so cool and in

control. She knew it was a façade, that he was worried about Hope, about her.

"You've asked me several times over the last couple of days about my mother." She tried to ignore the coil of tension that knotted tight in her stomach.

He shot her a quick glance. "You said she was out of the country."

She twisted her fingers together in her lap, fighting both the anger and despair the conversation worked up inside her. "The truth is I don't have any idea where she is."

He said nothing, obviously waiting for her to explain.

She sighed and stared out the window for a long moment, then looked at him once again. "Two years ago while William was at a meeting and Hope was at school, my mother apparently packed a couple of suitcases and left."

Charlie frowned. "And you don't know where she went?"

"Don't have a clue." Grace tried to force a light tone but couldn't. She heard the weight of her pain hanging in her words. "I don't know where she went or why she left us without an explanation."

"And you haven't heard from her since?"

"Not a letter, not a postcard, nothing." She twisted her fingers more tightly together. "I don't mind so much for me. I mean, I'm a grown woman, but how could she walk out on Hope?"

"What did William have to say about it?" he asked.

"He said they'd had a fight the night before. At first he thought she'd just gone to a friend's house to cool off and would be back before nightfall. But she didn't come home that day, or the next, or the next. He was utterly heartbroken."

"Did you go to the sheriff?"

"Yeah, but a lot of good it did us. Jim Ramsey was the sheriff at the time. Did you know him?"

He nodded. "I know there was a big scandal about his involvement in a murder and that Zack stepped into his shoes."

"William went to file a missing persons report, but Ramsey insisted there wasn't much he could do. Mom was of legal age. She'd taken her clothes and things with her, and if she didn't want to be a wife and mother anymore that was her right."

She'd had no right, Grace thought. She'd left behind three broken hearts that would never heal. "William hired a private investigator to search for her, but he never had anything to report, he never had a lead to follow."

Charlie was quiet for a long moment. "Why didn't you tell me this when we were seeing each other? It must have happened right before we met."

"Oh Charlie, there were a lot of important things we didn't talk about when we were together. We talked about whether we wanted to go out to dinner or stay in. You talked about your work and I talked about mine, but we didn't talk about what was going on with our lives when we were apart."

"You're right," he said flatly. "And it was one of the biggest mistakes we made. We should have talked about the important things."

Too late now. Grace looked out the window once again while a plethora of thoughts whirled through her head. It seemed as if the last two years of her life had been nothing more than a continuous journey of loss. First her mother, then Charlie, then William. And if something didn't break the case against her sister wide open, then Hope would be another loss.

A black, yawning despair rose up inside her. She'd been strong through it all, focused on getting from one day to the next without allowing herself any weakness.

At this moment, sitting next to the man who'd betrayed her trust, with thoughts of her mother and Hope heavy in her heart, she felt more alone than ever before.

"If I lose Hope, I won't have anything else to hang onto," she said. "My entire family has been ripped away from me, and I don't understand any of it."

"I'm going to see what I can do to find your mother," Charlie said.

She looked at him in surprise. "How are you going to do that?"

"I doubt if Jim Ramsey ever did anything to find her. It's tough for somebody to just disappear. She had a driver's license and tax records. With her Social Security number, we can start a search."

Grace frowned thoughtfully. "At this point, I'm not sure I care about finding her. Betrayal is a tough thing to get past."

He flashed her a quick glance. "Forgiveness is the first step on a path to healing."

"Forgiveness is for fools," she exclaimed with a touch of bitterness.

They didn't speak again for the remainder of the drive. The Beacon Juvenile Detention Center was on the south side of Oklahoma City. Set on twenty acres of hard, red clay, the building was a low, flat structure surrounded by high fences and security cameras. The place had a cold, institutional look that Grace found horrifying.

As Charlie parked in the lot designated for visitors, a lump formed in Grace's throat as she thought of her sister inside.

Hope had never been anywhere but in the loving environment of William's home. How could she possibly cope with being locked up in this place with its barbed wire and truly bad kids?

"She doesn't belong here, Charlie," she said, as the two of them walked toward the entrance. "She isn't like the other kids in this place."

"I know, but right now there's nothing we can do about it." He reached for her hand, and again she was struck by how he seemed to know exactly what she needed and when.

She clung tightly to his hand, feeling as if it were an anchor to keep her from going adrift. The afternoon heat radiated up from the concrete walk, and Grace kept her gaze focused on the door.

Once inside, Charlie identified himself as Hope's lawyer and Grace as her sister. They were told to lock up their personal items, including Charlie's belt, and then were led to a small interview room with security cameras in all four corners and a guard in a khaki uniform outside the door.

Grace sat at the table with Charlie at her side and waited for her sister to be escorted inside. "We need to go back to the house, Charlie. We need to tear apart both William's and Hope's rooms to see if we can come up with something that will exonerate Hope."

"The sheriff and his men have already been through everything at the house," he said.

"Maybe they missed something." She heard the despair in her own voice. Being in this place made her feel desperate, for herself and for her sister. "You've got to do something, Charlie. I can't lose Hope."

"Grace, look at me." His eyes were dark, his gaze intense. "Right now we can't do anything to get Hope out of here. What I have to do is be prepared for when her trial comes up and make sure I do my job then. You told me when you came to me that it was because you needed a sneaky devil, and I was as close to the devil as you could find. You have to be patient now and trust that when the time is right, this sneaky devil will do his job."

Grace drew a tremulous sigh, the hysteria that had momentarily gripped her assuaged by the confidence she saw shining in Charlie's eyes.

At that moment the door opened and Hope walked in.

Charlie could tell the hour had passed too quickly for the two sisters, but at least Grace was leaving with the knowledge Hope was physically all right, although she was frightened and depressed.

It twisted his heart seeing the two of them together, how they'd clung to each other. Grace had remained calm and confident in front of Hope, assuring her that everything was going to be all right. It was only as they left the place that she seemed to wilt beneath the pressure and remained unusually silent.

They stopped on the way home for dinner at a little café that advertised itself as having the best barbecue in the state. The boast was vastly exaggerated. It was a quiet ride back, and Charlie could tell Grace's thoughts were on the sister she'd left behind. The sun was sinking low in the sky as they reached the edge of Cotter Creek.

He'd been stunned by what she'd told him about her mother. Charlie knew about grieving for a mother. He'd been devastated by the loss of his mother, and he'd had four years of preparing himself for her death. The death of a woman with cancer was understandable. The disappearance of a mother was not.

Hope was all she had left, and if he didn't manage to somehow come up with a defense for the young girl, then Grace would be truly alone and would probably hate him all over again.

He couldn't let that happen. As they drove down Main Street, he finally broke the silence that had grown to mammoth proportions. "We'll go back to the house tomorrow. I'm not sure we'll find anything helpful, but we'll search those rooms and see if anything turns up. I'll call Zack tomorrow and see if he's come up with anything new. We'll talk to Justin's roommate again and try to find a crack in the alibi."

He pulled up in her driveway and turned to look at her, wanting to take away the unusual slump of her shoulders and the dark look of defeat radiating from her eyes. He would prefer them filled with icy disdain.

"I swear to God, I'll make this right," he exclaimed. "I'll do everything in my power to make it right."

She broke eye contact with him and unfastened her seat belt. When she looked back at him, her eyes were filled with warmth, and she leaned across the seat and placed her lips on his.

Swift hunger came alive in him as he tasted those lips he'd dreamed about for so long. When she opened her mouth to him, he wanted to get her out of the car, take her into his arms and feel the press of her body against his, tangle his hands in her lush, silky hair.

The scent of her filled his head, dizzying him as the kiss continued. Charlie had always loved to kiss Grace. Her soft, full lips were made for kissing.

She broke the kiss long before he wanted her to and then opened her car door. "Don't bother walking me in," she said, as if to let him know the kiss had been the beginning and end of anything physical between them.

"Are you confusing me on purpose?" he asked, his voice thick and husky with the desire that still coursed hot and thick through his blood.

"I just figure if I'm confused you should be, too," she said, only adding to his bewilderment. "Call me in the morning to set up a time to go to the house." She slid out of the car and straightened up.

From the corner of his eye, Charlie saw a figure step around the side of her house. Everything seemed to happen in slow motion. He saw the figure raise an arm, heard the report of the gun and at the same time screamed Grace's name.

Chapter 8

Grace leapt back into the car just as she heard a metallic ping above her head.

"Stay down," Charlie cried, as he threw the car into reverse and burned rubber out of her driveway. She screamed and hunkered down in the seat as the passenger window exploded, sending glass showering over her back.

Her heart pounded so hard that she felt sick as Charlie steered the car like a guided missile. Her mind stuttered, trying to understand what just happened.

Somebody had shot at her. A bullet had narrowly missed her head. The words screamed through her head but didn't make sense.

As she started to sit up, Charlie pressed on the back of her head to keep her contorted in the seat, and below the window level.

"Stay down. Are you all right? Did he hit you?" The urgency in his voice made every muscle in her body begin to tremble as the reality of what had just happened set in.

"No, I'm all right. I'm okay." Her voice was two octaves higher than normal, and she felt a hysterical burst of laughter welling up inside her. "If somebody is going to try to kill you, it's great when he's not a good shot."

Her laughter turned into a sob. "My God, somebody just tried to kill me, Charlie. What's going on with my life?"

"I don't know." His hand on the back of her head became a caress. "You can get up now. I don't think anyone is following us."

Tentatively she straightened to a sitting position, but she couldn't control the quivering of her body. "Did you see who he was?"

"No, he was in the shadows of the house and everything happened too damned fast. I'm taking you to my place tonight."

"If you think I'm going to argue with you, you're mistaken." She wrapped her arms around herself, attempting to warm the icy chill that possessed her insides.

"First we're going to take a couple of detours to make sure we're not being followed." As if to prove the point, he turned off Main, careened down a tree-lined street and then turned again onto another street.

"Charlie, why would somebody want to kill me?"

"I don't know, Grace. The first thing we're going to do when we get to my place is call Zack West. We need to report what happened."

He cursed beneath his breath. "I didn't see this

coming. Jesus, if you hadn't jumped when you did, he would've nailed you."

Her trembling grew more intense. "Don't remind me." She brushed away the pieces of glass that clung to her. Her head pounded where she'd been hit before and she felt like she might throw up. "You're going to need a new window."

"That's the least of our problems right now," he replied, his voice still tense as his gaze continually darted to his rearview mirror.

They didn't speak again until they reached Charlie's ranch. He parked in front of the porch, got out of the car and came around to help her out.

It was only after she collapsed on his sofa that the shivering began to ease. As he got on the phone to call Zack, she stared out the window and replayed that moment when she'd seen the dark figure just out of the shadows, sensed imminent danger and dove back into the car.

What if she'd waited a second longer? What if he'd pulled the trigger a second sooner? The trembling she thought she had under control began again, and tears pressed hot in her eyes.

Somebody had tried to kill her. Why? *Why?* When Charlie hung up the phone, she looked at him, and he pulled her up into his arms.

"It's okay now. You're safe here," he said, as he held her tight. She burrowed her head into the crook of his neck, breathing in the familiar scent of him as her heartbeat crashed out of control with the residual fear.

He ran his hands up and down her back as he whispered in her ear words meant to soothe. Her trembling finally stopped, but still she remained in his embrace, unwilling to let go of him until the cold knot in her stomach had completely warmed.

There was a feeling of safety in Charlie's strong arms, and she needed that sense of security after what had just happened.

Finally she stepped back from him and sank to the sofa. "I can't believe this," she said, as Charlie began to pace back and forth in front of her. "How could this be happening to me?"

He went to the window and looked out, then began to pace once again, his lean body radiating with energy. "In light of what just happened, there's no way I think that the attack in the store was an attempted robbery," he said.

The cold chunk in her stomach re-formed as she stared at him in horror. "You think it was the same man as tonight? That he wanted to kill me that night in the store?"

"That would be a reasonable assumption. Give me a dollar."

"What?" She stared at him blankly as he held out his hand.

"Give me a dollar," he repeated.

She grabbed her purse from the sofa and pulled one out and handed it to him. "What's that for?"

He shoved the bill into his pocket. "You just hired me to be your professional bodyguard." His eyes were dark and simmered with a banked flame. "From now on you won't go anywhere, do anything, without me at your side. Until we know what's going on and who wants you dead, it isn't safe for you to be anywhere alone."

Grace leaned back against the sofa. Her life was spinning out of control and she didn't know why. Somebody wanted her dead, but she didn't know who. "Where's Rosa?" she asked, surprised that the housekeeper hadn't made an appearance yet.

"Today is her day off. She won't be back here until sometime tomorrow afternoon." Charlie once again moved to the window and peered outside, his back rigid with tension.

"Do you think whoever it was might come here?" she asked, fear leaping back into her voice. "If he recognized you, then what's to stop him from coming here and trying to get me again?"

Charlie turned away from the window and looked at her. "I won't let that happen." He walked over to the wooden desk in one corner of the room and opened the bottom drawer. "From now on anywhere we go there will be four of us. You and me and Smith & Wesson." He pulled out an automatic, checked the clip, then stuck the gun in his waistband at his back.

"I'm a hell of a shot and won't hesitate to pull the trigger if I think it's necessary," he added.

The sound of car tires crunching the gravel of the driveway drifted inside, and he turned back to the window. "It's Zack."

He opened the door to admit the lawman, and for the next twenty minutes Grace and Charlie explained to Zack what happened at her house and how it had been too dark for either of them to identify the man.

"You should be able to find a couple of slugs in my car," Charlie said. "One went into the passenger side and the other one shot out the window."

Zack nodded and looked at Grace. "And you don't have any idea who this person might be? No spurned boyfriends, no business problems of any kind?"

Grace shook her head. "I can't imagine who might want to hurt me. Do you think this has something to do with William's murder?"

Zack frowned. "I don't know what to think. I'll collect what evidence I can from Charlie's car and send some of my deputies over to your house to check for further evidence."

"There's something else I'd like for you to do," Charlie said. "Two years ago Grace's mother, Elizabeth, disappeared. I intend to do an internet search to see if I can find out anything about where she might be right now, but you have better access to government records and can go places I can't. Would you check it out and see if you can find where she might be living now?"

"You think she might have something to do with all this?" Zack asked.

"No, that's impossible," Grace exclaimed. Her mother might have deserted them, but she'd never have anything to do with the terrible things happening now.

Charlie and Zack exchanged a look that let Grace know they weren't as sure about her mother's innocence. "I'll check it all out and get back to you sometime tomorrow," Zack said. "I'm assuming that you'll be here?"

Grace nodded. "I don't want to go home right now."

Zack nodded with understanding. "That's a good idea. I recommend you don't go anywhere alone unless absolutely necessary and then take precautions for your own safety."

He got up from the chair where he'd been sitting, a weary frown on his face. "I don't know what in the hell is going on around here, but I'd sure like to get to the bottom of it."

"This has to put a new light on Hope's case," Grace said.

"We don't know that this incident is tied to William's murder," Zack replied. "And if it is, it doesn't necessarily do anything positive for Hope's case. The argument could be made that with you dead, Hope is the sole beneficiary of William's fortune."

Grace gasped. "That's a ridiculous argument," she exclaimed.

"I assume you'll be checking out Justin Walker's whereabouts for this evening," Charlie said.

"He's top on my list," Zack replied.

"You might also check out Hank Weatherford," Grace said. "Apparently there was some tension between him and William about some land William owns that butts up next to Hank's place."

Zack nodded. "Anything else you think of, no matter how small, call me."

"I'll walk you out," Charlie said, and the two men left the house.

Grace stared blankly at the front door, her mind reeling with everything that had happened—with all the possibilities of who might be responsible.

Did Hank want that five acres badly enough to kill for it? It seemed ridiculous to even consider such a thing, but thinking that Hope had somehow masterminded William's murder—and the attempted murder of Grace herself—in order to get all his money seemed equally ridiculous.

The other possibility—her mother—flirted at the edges of her mind, and although she wanted to dismiss it completely out of hand, she couldn't.

Pain blossomed in Grace's chest. Thoughts of Elizabeth always brought enormous grief, but this was different—more raw.

Maybe her mother had found another man and didn't know that William had changed his will so she was no longer the sole beneficiary. Perhaps she and her new man had decided to take out everyone who stood in the way of her getting that money.

It sounded crazy and sick, but Grace had seen enough to know that money could twist people into ugly semblances of themselves.

Or maybe what happened tonight had nothing to do with William's murder. *Somebody tried to kill me.* The words whirled around in her head, and again the cold knot retied itself in her chest.

She needed to think of something else, anything else. What she needed to do was make arrangements yet again for somebody else to open the store in the morning. She wasn't sure she'd be in at all.

Grace picked up Charlie's phone and dialed Dana's cell phone number. She answered on the second ring. "Dana, I hate to bother you, but could you open the store in the morning and work until Stacy comes in for her evening shift at four?"

"You know it's no problem," Dana replied. "I love working at the store. I'm just waiting for the time that you start sending me on buying trips, and I can take on more responsibility."

"What would that handsome husband of yours do without you if I sent you out of town?"

Dana laughed. "That handsome husband of mine would just have to cope, wouldn't he? Everything all right, Grace?"

"No, not really, but I appreciate your help with the

store. I'll be in touch sometime tomorrow," she said, as Charlie came back through the door.

She hung up the phone. "That was Dana. I called her so she could open the store in the morning. She's a real jewel. Sometimes I don't know what I'd without her." She was rambling, embracing thoughts of the store to keep away other, more troubling ideas.

"She wants to start going on buying trips for me. She has great taste. I probably should let her go." Charlie's face blurred as tears filled her eyes. "She would do a good job."

"Grace," he said gently. "Why don't we get you settled in bed? Things won't look so grim in the morning." He held out his hand to her.

She took his hand and stood with a small laugh. "Somehow I don't think sunshine is going to fix any of this."

"Who knows? Maybe tomorrow Zack will find something that will identify your attacker."

She used her free hand to wipe at her tear-filled eyes. "I didn't know you were such an optimist, Charlie," she said, as they walked down the hallway toward the guest room she'd stayed in before.

"What are we going to do?" she asked when they reached the doorway. "How are you going to be my bodyguard, prepare a defense case for Hope and investigate all this? You aren't Superman."

He reached up and touched her cheek with a gentle smile. "Let me worry about it. You'd be surprised at what I'm capable of when I put my mind to it."

"Are you capable of getting me something to sleep in? I don't have anything."

He nodded. "How about one of my T-shirts?"

"Perfect," she agreed.

He dropped his hand from her face. "I'll be right back." He disappeared into the room at the far end of the hallway and returned a moment later with both a T-shirt and a toothbrush still in the package. "Try to get some sleep. We'll figure it all out in the morning," he said, handing her the items.

She nodded. "I'll see you in the morning." As he murmured a good-night, she closed the door between them and prayed that sleep would claim her quickly and banish all the horrible thoughts and images from her mind.

Rage, revenge or reward.

Charlie sat in his chair in the darkened living room and worked the motives for murder around in his head. No matter how he twisted everything, he couldn't make sense of it.

His heart accelerated in rhythm as he thought of that moment when he'd seen the figure in the shadows, watched as the figure raised his arm and knew that Grace was in danger. His heart had stopped then and hadn't resumed its regular, steady beat until they'd pulled up here at the ranch.

Moonlight filtered through the trees and into the window, making dancing patterns across the living room floor. He stared at the shifting patterns, as if in staring at them long enough something would make sense. Although he hadn't wanted to show his fear to Grace, the truth was he was afraid for her.

It was bad enough that somebody had tried twice to kill her, but almost as troubling was not having a clue as to the identity of her perpetrator.

Owning and operating a dress shop wasn't exactly a high-risk profession, and she'd insisted to Zack that there weren't any spurned lovers, no stalker boyfriends, nothing that could explain what was going on.

So what *was* going on? A dead man, a child facing trial and two attempted murders. As crazy as it sounded, Charlie's thoughts kept returning to the missing mother. She was the one piece of the puzzle that remained a complete mystery.

Why had she left? Where was she now? After Grace went to bed, Charlie had done a cursory internet search for her but found nothing.

The fact that Grace hadn't told him about her mother when they'd been dating indicated to him how little she'd thought of their relationship. He hadn't been important enough in her life to share that particular heartbreak.

He reached up and touched his bottom lip, where the feel of that brief kiss in the car lingered. Why had she kissed him? And if their relationship had meant nothing to her, then why did she hate him for how it had ended?

To say that she confused him was an understatement. What he didn't find confusing at all were his feelings for her. He loved her. It was as simple and as complicated as that. He'd never stopped loving her.

And she would never forgive him.

He released a weary sigh and glanced at the clock with the luminous dial on the desk. After two. Time to go to bed. He wasn't accomplishing anything here and needed to be fresh and alert tomorrow.

When he stood to go to his bedroom, he saw her standing in the doorway. By the light of the moon he could see her clearly—her tousled hair, the sleek length of her legs beneath the T-shirt, which fell to midthigh, and the fear that widened her eyes.

"Bad dream?" he asked, trying to ignore the white-hot fire of desire in the pit of his stomach.

"I don't need to be asleep to have bad dreams," she replied, her voice filled with stress. "I haven't been able to sleep. I've just been tossing and turning. I can't get it all out of my head—the noise of the bullet hitting the car, knowing that if I hadn't jumped into the car when I did another bullet might have hit me."

"You want something to eat? Maybe a glass of milk?" Although he tried to keep his gaze focused on her face, it slid down just low enough to see her breasts—her nipples hard against the cotton material. He quickly glanced up once again as every muscle in his body tensed. "Maybe putting something in your stomach will help."

"No, thanks. I'm not hungry." She took a step toward him, and he saw the tremble of her lower lip. "I was wondering if maybe I could sleep with you."

He knew she didn't mean sleep as a euphemism for anything else. She was afraid to be alone, and even though he knew how hard—no, how torturous it was going to be to lie next to her and not touch her, he nodded his head. "Sure, if that's what you want. My bed is big enough for the two of us."

"Thank you," she said gratefully.

He followed her down the hallway to the master bedroom and wondered how in the hell he was going to survive the night.

Chapter 9

Charlie tried to halt the rapid beating of his heart as she stood next to the bed. After he pulled down the covers, she slid in and curled up on her side facing him.

He placed his gun on the nightstand, then self-consciously unbuttoned his shirt and shrugged it off. It was silly to feel shy about undressing in front of her. She'd seen him naked more times than he could count, but that was before, in a different time under different circumstances.

Kicking off his shoes, he glanced at her to see that her eyes were closed. That made it easier for him to get out of his jeans. Normally he slept naked, but tonight he got beneath the sheet wearing his briefs, feeling as if he needed a barrier between them, even if it was just thin cotton.

"'Night, Charlie," she said softly, as he turned off the bedside lamp.

"Sleep tight, Grace," he replied. He squeezed his eyes closed, willing sleep to come fast, but how could he sleep with the scent of her eddying in the air and her body heat radiating outward to him?

He tried to count sheep, but each one of them had silky blond hair and a killer body beneath a white T-shirt. He knew she wasn't sleeping, either. He could tell by her uneven breathing that she was still awake.

They remained side by side, not touching in any way for several agonizingly long minutes. He gasped in surprise as she reached out and laid a warm hand on his chest.

"Grace," he said, her name nothing more than a strangled sigh that hissed out of him.

She scooted closer to him and trailed her fingers across the width of his upper body, tangling them in his tuft of chest hair. "What?" she whispered.

"You can't lie here next to me and touch me like that and not know that you're starting something."

"Maybe I want to start something." The words were a hot whisper against his neck. "I want you to hold me, Charlie. I want you to make love to me and take away the coldness inside me."

There was nothing he wanted more, but he didn't move. "You've had a scare, Grace. It's only natural that you'd reach out to somebody, but I don't want you to do something tonight that you'll regret in the morning."

Once again her hand swept across his chest and he held his breath. "As long as you understand that it isn't the beginning of anything, that it's just sex, then I won't regret anything in the morning," she replied.

Jeez, how many men would have loved to hear from a woman that it was just about sex and nothing else?

Still he hesitated. He didn't want to give her another reason to hate him. He told himself that one of them had to be strong.

She moved closer, molding herself against his side. "I know you still want me, Charlie. I've seen it in your eyes; I've felt it in your touch. I want you now. Not forever, but just for now."

Even though he would have preferred now and forever, he wasn't strong enough to stop himself from turning to her. Their lips met in an intense kiss that tasted of the sweet familiarity of past liaisons and of present fires.

Just that easily he was lost in her, in the taste of her, the scent of her and the heat of her body, so close to his. He cupped her face in his hands as the kiss continued, their tongues swirling together as their breaths quickened.

He pulled her into his arms, half across his body as his hands caressed her back and made their way to the bottom of the T-shirt.

He broke the kiss and plucked at the shirt. "Take it off. I want to feel your body next to mine."

She sat up and in one smooth movement pulled the shirt up and over her head. She tossed it to the floor at the end of the bed, then went into his arms once again.

Her soft, supple skin was hot against his, and he cupped her breasts, his thumbs moving over her hard nipples. The tiny gasp she emitted only served to ratchet up his desire.

He wanted her moaning like she once had beneath him, making those mewling noises that had always driven him wild.

She rolled over on her back, and he took one of her

nipples into his mouth as she tangled her fingers in his hair. He teased first one, then the other nipple, sucking then flicking his tongue to give her the most pleasure.

"Charlie," she moaned, his name a sweet plea on her lips.

His hand moved down her flat stomach and lingered at the waist of her panties. Touching her was sheer pleasure, the smoothness of her skin making his blood thicken as he grew hard.

"Take them off," she said, and lifted her buttocks from the bed so he could pull the panties down and off. With her naked, he quickly took off his briefs. Then they came together—hot flesh and hotter kisses.

Although he was hungry for her, he wanted to take his time. He wanted it slow. He wanted to pretend that they had never stopped being lovers, that there was nothing bad between them.

He re-memorized the sweet curves of her hips, the silky length of her legs. His lips found all the places he knew would stoke her pleasure higher, and the taste of her drove him half mindless.

Grace had always been an active participant in lovemaking, and this time was no different. Her mouth and hands seemed to be everywhere—behind his ear, on his chest above his crashing heartbeat, along his inner thigh.

Knowing that if he allowed her to continue with her caresses, it was going to be over before it began, Charlie pushed her onto her back once again, and his fingers found her damp heat.

She arched her hips to meet his touch as she whimpered his name. Every muscle in her body tensed, and he knew she was almost there, almost over the edge. He quickened his touch and felt the moment when her climax crashed down on her. She froze and then seemed to melt as she cried his name over and over again.

Knowing he was about to lose control, he quickly disengaged from her and fumbled in his nightstand for a condom. His hands trembled uncontrollably as he pulled on the protection and then eased into her with a hiss of pleasure.

He froze, afraid that the slightest movement would end it all. The moonlight filtered through the curtains, dappling her face with enough light that he could see the bright shine of her eyes, a pulse beating madly in the side of her neck.

She closed her eyes, and he felt her tighten her muscles around him, creating exquisite pleasure for him. Her fingers dug into his lower back, and he slowly eased his hips back, then stroked deep into her.

The rush of feelings that filled him was overwhelming, not just the physical ones, but the emotional ones as well. She was hot, sexy and felt like home. She scared him more than any potential killer they might face.

He had confidence that he could keep her safe and sound from any threat, but he didn't know how to make her forgive him. He wanted her to be his woman forever, but she'd made it clear she was his just for now.

He'd had his chance with her and blown it. Now his job was to fix her life so that she could once again move on without him.

Grace woke up with the light of dawn drifting through the window and Charlie spooned around her back. She remained still, relishing the feeling of safety his arms provided, the warmth of his body against her.

Making love with him had been as magical last night as it had been eighteen months ago when they'd been an item. Charlie was a passionate man, a thoughtful lover who never took his own pleasure before giving pleasure to her. Her body still glowed warm with the residual aftermath of the night of love.

Had last night been a mistake? Definitely.

If she allowed herself, she could be as in love with Charlie as she had been before, but she wouldn't allow it. There was still a simmering rage inside her where he was concerned, a place where forgiveness could find no purchase.

She slid out of bed, wanting to get up before he awakened. She knew how much Charlie loved morning sex, and although there was a part of her that would have welcomed another bout of lovemaking with him, she didn't want to be available for compounding her mistake.

The last thing she needed to do was think about Charlie and her confusing feelings for him. What she needed to do was figure out why somebody would want her dead.

She used the shower in the guest room, hoping to let Charlie rest for as long as he could. She'd fallen asleep before him the night before and had no idea when he'd finally drifted off.

Charlie was mistaken. Nothing seemed clearer in the light of day, she thought, as she stood beneath a hot stream of water. William was still dead. Somebody was gunning for her and Hope was facing life in prison. No amount of morning sun could put a happy spin on things.

When she was dressed, she went into the kitchen,

surprised to find Charlie making coffee. Apparently he'd been in the shower at the same time as her. His hair was damp, and he smelled of minty soap and that cologne that had always driven her half wild.

"Good morning," he said, and gave her a tentative glance.

"Don't worry, there aren't going to be any repercussions from last night," she assured him, as she sat at the table.

"That's good. I was worried that you'd accuse me of taking advantage of you," he replied, pouring them each a cup of the fresh brew.

"I think I was definitely the one taking advantage last night," she replied dryly.

He set the mugs on the table then took the seat across from her. "Grace, we need to talk. We need to talk about us."

She held up a hand and shook her head. "Please, Charlie, don't." She steeled her heart against him, against the flash of vulnerability she saw in his eyes. "There's so much going on in my life right now. I can't think about anything else except getting Hope out of that horrible place and trying to figure out why somebody tried to shoot me last night."

He held her gaze for a long minute and then nodded reluctantly. "Okay, we won't do it now," he agreed, but there was a subtle warning in his words that let her know this wasn't finished—*they* weren't finished.

But they were, she thought, and the old, familiar anger rose up inside her. His betrayal hurt just like her mother's had, and she'd never forgive her mother nor was she ever likely to forgive him. She'd be a fool to trust him with her heart again, and Grace wasn't any-body's fool.

"You need to decide if you want to stay here with me or if you want me to stay at your place with you," he said. "There's no way I want you staying anywhere all alone right now."

She wanted to protest the plan, but she knew she couldn't return to her life as if nothing had happened. She frowned thoughtfully. "I'd really prefer to stay at my own place, but don't you need to be here at the ranch?"

"I've got a good foreman who can see to things," he replied.

Wrapping her fingers around her mug, she frowned again. "I hate the idea of taking you away from your life here."

He smiled, the gesture warming the gray of his eyes. "You bought my services as a bodyguard for a dollar. Until this thing is resolved, wherever you go, I go. If you want to stay at your place, then all I need to do is pack a bag."

"If you don't mind, I'd appreciate it," she said. Maybe her world would feel more normal if she were home among her familiar things. "I'd like to go back to the house today." She took a sip of her coffee and then continued. "We should talk to Lana and Leroy again. Maybe they will have remembered something helpful."

"I think they would have called if that was the case," he said. "But, if you want to touch base with them, we can do that. Have you thought about what you intend to do with the house and the property?"

"No. I suppose eventually I'll sell. I'll never live in the house, and I don't want it sitting empty forever."

Grief for William pierced through her. He'd loved that house so much.

"The real estate market isn't great right now, but I imagine a home like that will move fairly quickly."

"I need to give Lana and Leroy a heads-up that at some point they'll need to find another place to live. At least with the money William left to Lana I know they won't be out on the street." She sipped her coffee, thinking about everything that needed to be done to settle William's estate.

Somebody tried to kill you yesterday. The words jumped unbidden into her head. She took another sip of her coffee and tried to think of a single person she'd upset or offended.

"This can't be personal," she said aloud.

"What?" Charlie looked at her in confusion.

"Whoever is trying to kill me. It has to be about something other than dislike or anger at me personally. I know it sounds conceited, but I can't think of anyone who could hate me. I run a dress shop, for God's sake. I've never had a problem with anyone in town."

"We have a missing mother, a dead stepfather, a sister who we believe has been set up to spend the rest of her life in prison, and somebody trying to kill you. It's like somebody is trying to erase the entire Covington family."

"Surely you don't think my mother's disappearance has anything to do with what's happening now," she said.

He sipped his coffee, a new frown creasing his forehead. "I don't know. Last night I did a quick search on the computer for your mother but got no results." He swept a hand through his thick, dark hair. "I keep working everything around in my head trying to make sense of it, but I can't get a handle on it. Do you have a will?"

"No, I haven't gotten around to making one yet."

"So, if something happened to you, everything you own would go to Hope as your sole living relative?"

"I guess." She narrowed her eyes. "Charlie, I don't care how bad this looks, Hope wouldn't do this. Please, don't lose faith in her innocence."

"I'm just looking at all the angles," he said, and took another drink of his coffee. "Why don't we eat some breakfast and head to your place? I'll stow my stuff there, and then we can head over to the mansion to see what we can find."

It was after nine when they left the ranch to go to Grace's house. Charlie had a small suitcase in the backseat and his automatic pistol in a holster beneath his jacket.

The knowledge that he was carrying a gun to protect her sent a new rivulet of disquiet through her. The shooting the night before and the attack at the store had had a dreamlike quality to them, but his gun made them terrifyingly real.

"I really appreciate you staying at my place," she said, as they drove down Main Street toward her street. "I have a nice guest room, where I hope you'll be comfortable." She wanted to make it clear there would be no repeat of last night, that she had no intention of him sleeping next to her in her bed.

"I'm sure I'll be fine," he replied. "You need to stop by the store for anything?"

"No. Dana will have things well under control. She should have a shop of her own. She has all the skills to run her own business."

"You've certainly made a success of it," he observed.

She frowned. "I suppose." Yes, she had made a success of her shop, but at what price? Certainly in the last two years she'd kept too busy to nurture her relationship with her sister. A hollow wind blew through her as she thought of the choices she'd made.

She had plenty of friendly customers, but few friends, and when she'd needed somebody to hold her close, to take away her fear, there had been nobody except the man she'd once dated, a man who had broken her heart. Yeah, right, some success she'd made of her life.

The wind coming in from the broken window felt good on her face. Charlie had cleaned up the glass before they'd gotten into the car. The plan was for him to hire someone to come out to Grace's house to replace the window. They'd use her car for the remainder of the day.

When they reached her place, Charlie pulled up in the driveway and cut the engine. "I'll come around for you," he said, pulling his gun from his holster. "We'll walk together to the front door with you just in front of me. I don't want a repeat of last night."

As he got out of the car, the reality of the situation slammed into her. Somebody had tried to kill her last night. Somebody had tried to put a bullet in her head.

She gazed around her yard and the house, looking for a shadow, a movement that would indicate somebody lying in wait for them. A new knot of tension twisted in the pit of her stomach.

He opened her door and pulled her out and against his chest. They walked awkwardly toward her front door, with him acting as a human shield against danger.

Grace didn't realize she'd been holding her breath

until she unlocked the door and stepped into the entry hall. It was only then that she breathed again.

"Stay right here and don't move," Charlie said. "I want to check out the house." He kept the front door open. "If somebody is in here, I'll let you know and want you to run to the car and drive to the sheriff's office." He handed her the car keys, then disappeared into the living room.

Grace's heart beat frantically with fight-or-flight adrenaline as she held the keys firmly in hand and waited for him to return. What if somebody was here—lying in wait for them? What if that somebody bashed Charlie over the head or shot him?

Once again her breath caught in her chest as she stood rigid with taut muscles—waiting...hoping that there was nobody inside.

Finally he came back, his gun back where it belonged. "It's okay," he said. A devilish gleam lit his eyes. "The purple bedroom is hot."

She laughed as the edge of tension faded. "The purple bedroom is mine. You get the one across from it. Why don't you put your things in there? I'm going to change my clothes before we leave again."

"I'll just go get my suitcase from the car," he said. As he went out the front door, Grace walked down the hallway to her bedroom.

She'd always loved the color purple in all its glorious shades. When she'd moved into the house, she'd decided to indulge herself by painting the walls of her bedroom lilac and finding a royal purple satin spread for the bed. The end result gave the aura of both relaxation and hedonistic pleasure.

Her dresser top held framed photos along with an

array of perfume bottles and lotion. She walked over to the dresser and looked at the pictures. There was one of Hope in a pair of footed Christmas pajamas, her face lit with a beautiful smile.

There was also one of William, Hope and Grace. It had been taken six months after her mother's disappearance. The three of them had been at a carnival, and although they all sported smiles on their faces, the smiles didn't quite reach their eyes.

She turned away from the bureau and unbuttoned her blouse, then walked to her closet. Maybe today they'd find something at the house that would exonerate Hope. Even though logically she knew that Zack and his men would have gone over the crime scene with a fine-tooth comb, she still clung to the belief that somehow she and Charlie would find something that the authorities had missed.

She leaned against the doorjamb for a long moment, staring at the clothes inside the closet. Grace was exhausted even though she'd slept soundly after making love with Charlie. It wasn't physical fatigue but rather a mental one.

She grabbed a short-sleeved blue blouse from a hanger, then turned around. A scream welled up inside her and exploded out as she saw a face at her window.

Chapter 10

The scream ripped through Charlie, electrifying him with terror. He pulled his gun and raced across the hallway into her room.

She stood in front of the closet, her face a pasty shade of white. "He was looking in my window," she managed to gasp.

That's all Charlie needed to hear. He tore out of her bedroom, down the hallway and out the front door. He raced around the side of her house and spied a tall, lean figure running toward the fence that surrounded her yard. It was a privacy fence, and there was no way in hell he'd be able to jump it.

"Stop, or I swear I'll shoot," Charlie yelled, as the man leapt up to grab the top of the fence.

Unsuccessful, the man fell back to the ground then turned to face Charlie. It was Justin Walker. His eyes widened to saucer size as he saw the gun Charlie held in his hand.

Instantly he raised his hands. "Hey, man, don't shoot me."

"What are you doing here?" Charlie asked, his gun not wavering from the young man's midsection. "Did you come back here today to finish what you tried to do last night?"

Justin frowned. "Last night? Dude, I don't know what you're talking about."

He looked genuinely perplexed, but Charlie wasn't taking anything for granted. "Get inside the house. I'm calling the sheriff." He gestured with his gun for Justin to move.

"Hey man, there's no need to call the fuzz. I wasn't doing anything. I just wanted to talk to Grace, that's all. I wanted to talk to her alone." As he protested his innocence, he moved toward the house where Grace stood at the back door, her eyes wide with fear.

"You have any weapons?" Charlie asked, as they reached the back porch.

"Hell no. I didn't come here looking for trouble," he exclaimed.

"Well, you found it," Charlie said. Despite Justin's protests, Charlie quickly patted him down, making sure the young man had no weapons on him.

Grace opened the backdoor. "Justin, what are you doing here?" she asked. She seemed to relax as she realized Charlie had things under control.

When they got into the kitchen, Charlie gestured for Justin to sit at the table. "I just wanted to talk to you," Justin said to Grace. "I was just going to stand at the window and try to get your attention, but then you saw me and screamed, and I freaked and ran."

"Maybe we should just call Zack and let Justin explain everything to him," Charlie said.

"No, please, don't do that." Justin slumped in the chair, an air of defeat in his posture. "He already thinks I killed Hope's stepdad. I don't need any more trouble from him."

"What do you want to talk to me about?" Grace asked. She remained standing next to the counter on the other side of the room from Justin. Charlie was standing as well, his gun still clutched in his hand.

Justin swept a hand through his dark, unruly hair. "I wanted to ask you about Hope. I just wanted to know if she was okay."

"Why do you care? According to you, the two of you were just casual friends, hang-out buddies and nothing more," Grace replied.

Justin's cheeks colored with a tinge of pink. "She was nice to me, okay? I liked her. When she turned sixteen, we were going to start officially dating. I just wanted to know if she was doing all right, that's all."

"She's fine, coping as well as can be expected," Grace said.

"Where were you last night?" Charlie asked.

"I was home, with my roommate."

Charlie narrowed his eyes. "Your roommate is a pretty handy alibi whenever you need one."

This time the flush of color in Justin's cheeks was due to anger, not embarrassment. "I can't help it if it's the truth."

"Should we call Zack?" Charlie asked.

Grace studied Justin's face for a long moment and

then shook her head. "No, just let him go. I think he's telling the truth."

"I am," Justin exclaimed.

Charlie wasn't so sure, but he complied with Grace's wishes. "Go on. Get out of here. But if I see you around Grace again, I won't wait for the sheriff to ask you questions. I'll beat your ass myself."

Justin didn't speak again. As Charlie lowered his gun, he jumped out of the kitchen chair and ran for the front door. Charlie followed, making sure he left the house.

When he returned to the kitchen, Grace still leaned against the cabinets. "You okay?" he asked.

She nodded. "Now we know there was definitely something romantic going on between Hope and Justin." She looked dispirited, as if she knew this new information would only make things worse for Hope. "It will be easy for the prosecution to make a case that Hope killed William because William wouldn't let her see Justin."

"It doesn't change anything," Charlie replied with a forced lightness. "Go change your clothes so we can get out of here."

As she left the room, Charlie tried to get the sound of her scream out of his head. His heart had stopped when he'd heard her. He hoped he never heard that particular sound from her again.

A few minutes later they were in her car and headed to the Covington mansion. "I think tomorrow I just might stay in bed all day," she said with a sigh. "At least there won't be any surprises there."

"Unless I'm there with you," Charlie said, and wiggled his eyebrows up and down in Groucho Marx fashion. He wanted to make her laugh to ease the tension that thinned her lips and darkened her eyes.

He was rewarded as a small giggle escaped her. "You're wicked, Charlie Black," she exclaimed before sobering back up. "I hope you're as good a lawyer as you were two years ago. Hope is going to need every one of your skills."

"I've already requested that Zack give me copies of all the interviews he conducted with people immediately after the murder. I plan on getting all the discovery available to start building our case. Believe it or not, Grace, I'm working on it." He tapped the side of his head. "I do my best work in my head long before I commit anything to paper. I have a theory about murder."

"And what's that?"

"I call it the three *R*s. Most murders are committed for one of three reasons: rage, revenge or reward."

"And which category do you think William's murder falls into?" she asked.

He turned down off the main road and into the long Covington driveway. "I'm still trying to figure it out. The prosecuting attorney is probably going to argue rage—Hope's rage at a figure of authority who kept her from seeing the boy that she loved. Or he could possibly argue reward—that with William out of the picture she would be a very wealthy young lady."

She sighed. "Sounds grim."

He flashed her a reassuring grin. "Grim doesn't scare me. It just gets my juices flowing." He pulled up in front of the house and cut the engine, aware of Grace's gaze lingering on him. He unbuckled his seat belt and turned to look at her. "What?"

"Do you miss it? Being a lawyer? The adrenaline rush of the courtroom and the high stakes?"

He hesitated before answering, not wanting to give

her a flippant response. "I'll tell you what I miss. I miss my father, who would have been proud of the man I've become over the last year. I regret the fact that I'm thirty-five years old and haven't gotten married and started a family of my own. To answer your question, no, there's absolutely nothing I miss about my old life." *Except you.*

The last two words jumped into his mind and for some reason irritated him. He wasn't sure if the target of his irritation was himself or Grace.

"Come on, let's get inside and see what we can find," he exclaimed.

Even though he had checked the rearview mirror constantly to make certain they hadn't been followed, he once again escorted her inside with his gun pulled and his body shielding hers.

Once they got inside, Charlie followed Grace to William's office, which was located in one of the bedrooms upstairs. As she sat at the desk and began to go through the drawers, he walked over to the window and stared out to the backyard. Grace still refused to go into the bedroom where William had been murdered, but Charlie had gone in and had found nothing to help find his killer.

He had little hope that she would find anything useful. She'd already been through the desk once before, but he knew she needed to do something to feel as if she were actively helping her sister.

Leroy had apparently been working hard. The flower beds in the backyard exploded in vivid blooms, with nary a weed in sight. The bushes were neatly trimmed and the grass was a lush green carpet.

Rage. Revenge. Reward. Somebody out there had a motive for killing William. If Justin and Hope had worked in concert to commit the murder, then why had she been passed out on the bed in an incriminating manner? Why didn't they just alibi each other?

Was it possible that the issue of those five acres had created such contention that Hank lost control and killed William? Hank was no young man, but it didn't take a lot of strength to stab a sleeping man in the back.

Charlie could smell Grace. Her dizzying scent not only fired his hormones, but also somehow touched his heart. Anger was building in him where she was concerned, an anger he didn't want to feel and certainly didn't want to acknowledge.

He knew he'd hurt her badly in the past, but he was irritated by the fact that she refused to talk about it and clung to her sense of betrayal like it was a weapon to use against him at her whim.

He realized, though, that she was fragile now, and the last thing he wanted to do was add to the burdens she was already shouldering. He had to keep his emotions in check.

Once she had searched through the desk, she returned to Hope's bedroom. He stood at the door as she pulled open drawers and picked through the mess on the floor. She'd been through it all before and found nothing. He sensed her desperation but didn't know what to do to ease it.

It was almost three o'clock when he finally called a halt to her search. "Grace, there's nothing here," he said. "If there had been something, Zack would have found it, and if he missed anything, you would have found it by now."

She sat in the middle of Hope's bedroom floor, sorting through a box of keepsake items that belonged to her younger sister.

She put the lid back on the box and sighed. "I know you're right. I just feel compelled to do something to help. It doesn't feel right for me to work at the shop and go about my usual routine while everything else is falling apart."

"I know, but a daily routine is necessary, especially the part where we eat to stay strong. My stomach has been growling for the past hour."

She rose to her feet. "Why didn't you say something?"

He smiled and fought an impulse to reach out and tuck a stray strand of hair behind her ear. "I just did. But before we leave I'd like to check out the property that Hank and William had been arguing about."

She frowned at him. "Okay, but there really isn't anything there but a bunch of weeds and trees." Grace stood up, and they went downstairs.

"You once mentioned something about an old shed," he said, when they reached the front door. "You know what's in it?"

"Probably nothing. I think at one time it used to be a gardener's shed, but it hasn't been used in years." As she locked the door, Charlie once again gripped his gun.

He looked around the immediate area, seeking any threat that might come at them, at her. She turned from the door and stood just behind him.

The Covington place was isolated enough that it would be difficult for anyone to approach without being noticed. He felt no danger, saw nothing that would give him pause. While inside he'd spent much of the time at the windows, watching the road for any cars that didn't belong and checking the grounds for anything unusual.

"Where's that property?" he asked.

"Around back, behind Leroy and Lana's place."

"I want you to walk right in front of me. I don't think there's anyone around, but I don't want to take any chances."

"I'd like to stop by Lana's and let them know that I've decided to sell this place. The new owner might want to continue their services and let them remain in the cottage, but it's also possible they need to start making other plans."

The walk to the cottage was awkward, with her walking nearly on the top of his feet. As always, her nearness raised the simmering heat inside him, and he tried to ignore it as he kept focused on their surroundings.

Lana and Leroy weren't home. Nobody answered Grace's knock and no vehicles were parked in front of the place. "Maybe they both went to pick up Lincoln from school," Grace said.

"He seems like a nice kid." They headed for the side of the cottage.

"He's certainly the apple of their eyes," she replied. "Lana was pregnant when she married Leroy, and William and I were just grateful that he stepped up and did the right thing. It seems to have worked out well."

She pointed in the distance where the manicured lawn ended and an area of trees and overgrown brush began. "That's the land Hank was talking about. It never bothered William because it's so far away from the main house, but Hank's place is just on the other side, and I can understand why he'd want to see it cleaned up. The shed is on the other side of that big oak tree."

They headed toward the area where the shed was located. Charlie didn't want to leave any stone unturned. He figured it was probably empty or full of gardening tools that had rusted and rotted over the years. When they reached the wooden structure, Charlie returned his gun to his holster and eyed the old padlock on the door.

"I can't imagine why it would be locked," Grace said. "Nobody has used it in years. I wouldn't have any clue where to begin to look for the key."

"Who needs a key?" Charlie replied. He eyed the rotten wood around the lock on the door. Tensing his muscles, he slammed his shoulder into the door and was rewarded by splintering wood.

Another three hits and the door came away from the lock, allowing him to open it.

He pulled the door open just a bit and peered inside. The first thing he noticed was the unpleasant musty odor that wafted in the air. Then he saw the two flowered suitcases that sat on the floor just inside the door.

His heart began to bang against his ribs. Then he saw the sandal—a bright red woman's sandal. Inside it was the remains of a foot.

He reeled back and slammed the door. "We need to call Zack," he said, and turned to face Grace. Dread mingled with horror as he stared at her.

"Why? What's in there?" She tried to get past him to the door, but he stood his ground.

He grabbed her by the shoulders, his heart breaking for what he had to tell her. "Grace, stop. Listen to me."

She looked at him wildly, as if she knew what he was about to say. "Tell me, Charlie. What's inside the shed?"

"I'm sorry. I'm so damned sorry." He pulled her into his arms and held her tight, knowing she was going to need his strength. "Grace, I think it's your mother. Your mother's body is in the shed."

Chapter 11

Grace sat on the sofa in William's opulent living room, numb and yet as cold as the worst Oklahoma ice storm. She had yet to cry, although she knew eventually the numbness would pass and the pain would crash in.

It was late. Darkness had fallen, and still Zack and his men were processing the scene. Charlie was out there with them, but he'd insisted Zack leave a deputy with Grace.

Ben Taylor stood at the window, staring out in the distance where a faint glow of lights shone from the area behind the cottage.

For two years Grace had hated her mother for abandoning them. For two years she had cursed the name of the woman who had given birth to her. The anger was what had sustained her. Now it was gone and she had nothing left to hang on to.

She hadn't left them.

She'd been murdered.

The words flittered through Grace's head, but she couldn't grasp the concept, didn't yet feel the reality deep inside her.

The front door opened and a moment later Zack and Charlie walked into the room. Charlie immediately came to her side and sat next to her, his hand reaching for hers.

She allowed him to hold her hand. Somewhere in the back of her mind Grace realized his skin was warm against her icy flesh, but the warmth couldn't pierce through the icy shell that encased her.

"Zack wants to ask you a few questions," Charlie said gently.

"Of course." She looked at Zack, who sat in the chair across from them, his green eyes expressing a wealth of sympathy.

"Do you know of anyone your mother was having problems with at the time of her disappearance?" Zack asked.

"No." Her voice seemed to float from very far away.

Zack frowned. "Charlie mentioned that William had told you he and your mother had a fight the night before she disappeared."

She was having trouble concentrating. She felt as if she were in some sort of strange bubble, where things were happening around her and people were talking to her, but she really wasn't involved in any of it.

"Grace?" Charlie squeezed her hand.

She looked first at Charlie, then at Zack. "Yes, William told me they had an argument, but it wasn't a big deal. They were happily married, but like all couples they occasionally had disagreements."

She stared at Zack and then turned once again to gaze at Charlie. "What's happened to my family? Everyone has disappeared and now somebody is trying to make me disappear." Her voice had a strange, sing-song quality.

"I need to get her home," Charlie said to Zack. "She's in shock."

"Yes, please take me home. I need to go to bed. I need to sleep. Things will be better in the morning, won't they, Charlie?"

He didn't answer her, but he wrapped an arm around her and pulled her against his side. "Zack, if you have any more questions for her, they can be asked tomorrow."

Zack nodded and stood at the same time Charlie helped her up from the sofa. At that moment Lana came flying into the room.

She looked around. "Is it true? Elizabeth is dead?" Zack nodded, and she began to sob.

Grace broke away from Charlie and went to her. She wrapped her arms around Lana and vaguely wondered why the housekeeper was crying for her mother and she wasn't.

"I need to ask you some questions," Zack said to Lana. "Both you and your husband."

Lana nodded and Grace stepped back from her. "Do you know who would do this? Do you know who would kill my mother and pack her suitcases and stuff her in an old shed?"

"I don't know." Lana looked around wildly. "I don't understand any of this. First William and now your mother." Lana began to weep once again as Zack led her to a chair.

Charlie grabbed Grace by the arm. "Come on, let's get you home."

Once they were in the car, Grace leaned her head back and closed her eyes. "I'm so tired."

"We'll get you home and tucked into bed," he said.

"And I'm cold. I'm so cold. I don't feel like I'll ever be warm again." She wrapped her arms around herself and fought against the shivers that tried to take control.

"You will," he replied. "Eventually you'll get warm again and you'll laugh and enjoy life. Time, Grace. Give yourself time. It's true what they say about time healing all wounds."

Once again she closed her eyes. She knew eventually the agonizing grief over losing her mother would probably ease, but how could she get over her guilt? For two years she'd hated a woman who hadn't left them but instead had been brutally murdered.

Emotion swelled in her chest and made the very act of breathing difficult. She fought against it, afraid to let it take her—afraid that once she let it loose she would lose what little control she had left.

"Somebody must have hated us," she murmured, more to herself than to Charlie. "Somebody must hate us all, but I don't know who it could be."

She sighed in relief as Charlie pulled up in her driveway. All she wanted was to sleep—hopefully without dreams. It was the easiest way to escape the confusion and pain that had become her life.

Charlie helped her out of the car, and once they were inside he led her directly to her bedroom. She sat on the edge of the bed and tried to unbutton her blouse, but her fingers were all thumbs.

"Here, let me help," Charlie said. He crouched down in front of her and unfastened the buttons. There was nothing sexual in his touch, only a gentleness she welcomed as he pulled the blouse from her arms.

He retrieved her nightgown from the hook on the back of her bedroom door and carried it to her. "Here, while you put this on, I'll turn down the bed."

Dutifully she stood and took off her bra and pulled the nightgown over her head. Then she took off her pants, and by that time the bed was ready for her to crawl into.

She got beneath the covers and shivered uncontrollably. "Charlie, could you just hold me until I get warm?"

He quickly stripped down to his briefs and then slid beneath the sheets and pulled her into his arms. She welcomed the warmth of his skin as she shivered in his arms.

He stroked her hair and kissed her temple. "It's going to be all right," he said softly. "You're strong, Grace. You're one of the strongest women I've ever known. You're going to get through this."

"You don't understand. She wasn't just my mother, she was my best friend." The words pierced through a layer of the protective bubble she'd been in since learning of her mother's death. "And I don't feel very strong right now." Tears burned her eyes as grief ripped through her.

Charlie seemed to sense the coming storm and tightened his arms around her. "Let it go, Grace," he said softly. "Just let it go."

"I never understood how she could have just walked

away from me…from us. Oh, God, Charlie, for two years I've hated a dead woman who didn't leave us by choice." She could no longer contain the sobs that ripped through her as the realization of the loss finally penetrated the veil of shock.

Charlie said nothing. He merely held tight as she cried for all she'd lost, for all she still might lose. She had always believed someplace deep in her heart that she would see her mother again, that somehow the wounds would be healed and they would love one another again.

That wasn't going to happen. Elizabeth couldn't rise up from the dead to spend even one precious instant with her children.

She cried until there was nothing left inside her and then, completely exhausted, she fell into blessed sleep.

"The initial finding is that she was probably strangled," Zack said to Charlie when he called the next morning. "Her larynx was crushed, and the coroner could find no other obvious signs of trauma. And there's no way she packed her own suitcases. The clothes inside were shoved in, not neatly folded. She was probably killed someplace else, then the suitcases were packed to make it appear that she'd left."

"And I suppose the suspect list is rather short," Charlie said dryly.

"Yeah, as in there isn't one." Zack's frustration was evident in his voice. "I've got the mayor chewing on my ass wanting answers as to what's happening in his town, and I don't have any answers to give him."

"I wish I could offer you some," Charlie replied.

"I interviewed both Lana and Leroy Racine last

night. They remembered where they were on the day Elizabeth disappeared. Lana was in Oklahoma City getting her son a checkup with his physician and Leroy spent the day fishing. Other than that, I haven't had a chance to question anyone else. Hell, to be honest, I'm not even sure where to begin. I'm still trying to break Justin Walker's alibi for William's murder."

"You really think those kids killed him?" Charlie asked.

"I don't know what to think. I just collect the evidence and let the prosecuting attorney do the thinking. How's Grace doing this morning?"

"Still sleeping." And for that Charlie was grateful. He picked up his coffee from the table and took a sip. "Got any ideas about what's going on as far as the attacks on her?" he asked.

"I was hoping maybe you had some," Zack replied.

"I don't have a clue." Charlie frowned. It wasn't even nine o'clock and already his level of frustration was through the ceiling. "I don't suppose this new development changes anything with Hope's case?"

"A slick lawyer like you can probably make an argument that it should, but I don't think it will hold much weight. How do you tie a two-year-old murder into William's?"

Charlie blew out a deep breath. "I don't know, but in my gut I feel like they're all related—Elizabeth's and William's murders, Hope's incarceration and the attacks on Grace. Somehow they're connected, but I just can't get a handle on it."

"Well, if you do, I hope I'll be one of the first people you'll tell."

"And you'll let me know if anything new pops?"

"You got it," Zack replied.

Charlie hung up and stared out the window, his thoughts on the woman sleeping in the master bedroom. He was worried sick about her. She'd sat on the sofa in William's house like a stone statue, seemingly untouched by everything going on around her.

He'd always known she was a strong woman, but he'd known it wasn't strength that was keeping her so calm, so composed. Her brain had shut down, unable to handle any more trauma.

When the grief finally hit her, it had been horrible. Her sobs echoed in Charlie's heart, pulling forth his own grief for her. The worst part was knowing that he couldn't fix this for her. There was nothing he could say or do that would make her pain go away.

When she'd finally fallen asleep, exhausted by her river of tears, Charlie remained awake, his mind working overtime in an attempt to make sense of it all.

He could protect her from a gunman and make sure nobody could get at her without coming through him. But he couldn't protect her from grief, and that broke his heart.

Glancing at the clock, he was surprised to see that it was nearing ten. Grace never slept so late. He got up from the table and walked down the hallway to her purple bedroom, wanting to make sure she was okay.

She was awake but still in bed. "Hey," he said, and walked over to sit on the edge of the mattress. "How are you feeling?"

"As well as can be expected," she said. She sat up and pulled her legs up against her chest. Her eyes were slightly puffy from the tears, but Charlie thought she'd never looked as beautiful.

He reached out and smoothed a strand of her hair away from her face. She caught his hand and pressed it against her cheek. "I don't think I'm ready to face this day yet," she said softly.

"Then don't. There's nothing you need to do. If you want to stay in bed all day, nobody is going to complain. I'll even serve you your meals in here if you want me to," he said.

She smiled and reached up and pressed her mouth against his. He realized then that she must have gotten out of bed while he was on the phone with Zack, for her mouth tasted of minty toothpaste.

He tried to steel himself from the fire of desire that instantly sprang to life inside him, but as she pulled him closer it was impossible to ignore.

A familiar ache of need began deep inside him, not just in his body but also in his heart. It was obvious what she wanted, and even though he knew he was a fool, it never entered his mind to deny her.

The kiss quickly became hot and hungry, and within seconds Charlie was naked and in bed with her. Last time, their lovemaking had been a slow renewal of old passion—a rediscovery between lovers—but now it was fast and hard and furious.

She encouraged him as he took her, her fingernails digging into his back, then into his buttocks. She cried out his name, whipping her head back and forth as she rocked beneath him.

He knew it was grief driving her to the wildness that possessed her. He held tight to her, as if to keep her from spinning off the face of the earth, and she cried out when she climaxed, a combination sob of pain and gasp of pleasure. He followed, losing it with a moan of her name.

Afterward he got up, grabbed his clothes and went into the bathroom to dress. Once again he felt a burgeoning anger swelling in his chest, and it was directed at Grace.

She had used him. He had the feeling that he could have been any man in her room just now. She'd just needed somebody and he was available.

She insisted she didn't want him and would never forgive him but pulled him into her bed and made him feel like he was the most important man in her world.

They needed to talk, but he was aware that now wasn't the time. She'd just lost her mother. She certainly wasn't in her right frame of mind, and he'd be a fool to attempt any meaningful conversation about the crazy relationship he now found himself in with her.

Just leave it alone, he told his reflection in the mirror. That's what a smart man would do. He drew a deep breath, sluiced water over his face and then did exactly what he'd told himself he wouldn't do.

"We need to talk," he said, when he returned to her bedroom.

Those beautiful blue eyes stared at him warily. "Talk about what?"

"About us, Grace. We need to talk about us." He refused to be put off by the vulnerable shine in her eyes.

She sighed, a tiny wrinkle appearing in the center of her forehead. "Do we really need to do this now?"

"We've put it off for eighteen months. I think we're past due for a conversation."

She raked a hand through her tousled hair. The sun

drifting through the window caught and sparkled off her glorious golden strands.

His love for her blossomed so big in his chest he couldn't speak. How did you get into an unforgiving heart? How could he make her understand that he wasn't the same man he'd been in the past?

"Let me shower and have some coffee, then I guess we'll talk," she finally said with obvious dread in her voice.

He nodded and left her there with her hair shining and her eyes filled with a sadness. He feared that he'd just made a huge mistake.

Grace stared at her reflection in the bathroom mirror. "What are you doing?" she asked the woman who stared back at her. "What are you doing making love with him when you hate him? Have you forgotten what he did to you?" No wonder he wanted to talk. She'd given him so many mixed signals it was ridiculous.

She whirled away from the mirror with a sigh of disgust. She'd let him get back into her heart. Somehow the drama of the past few days caused her to let down her guard.

She started the water in the shower and stepped in, hoping the stream would wash away the foolishness she'd entertained since he'd reentered her life and restore her to sanity.

When she'd come to him for help with Hope, she'd thought her anger and bitterness would shield her against any old feelings that might rear their head. But she hadn't expected his quiet support—his sensitivity to her every mood, his gentleness when she needed it most. She hadn't imagined his desire would be as fiery, as focused, as it had been before, and she certainly hadn't anticipated that he'd know when she needed a laugh.

She hadn't planned to fall in love with him all over again. She raised her face to the water, fighting against the new set of tears that burned her eyes. She couldn't go back. There was still a core of bitterness that remained inside her, an anger she refused to let go of for fear of being hurt again by him.

Stepping out of the shower, she grabbed a towel. She'd known this was coming. She'd known eventually they would talk about it. For weeks after she'd left him, he'd called, sent flowers and tried to communicate with her, but she hadn't given him a chance. The calls hadn't been answered and the flowers had gone directly into the trash.

Eventually he stopped reaching out to her, but there had never been any real closure between them. Now there would.

She dressed in a pair of bright yellow capris and a white and yellow blouse, hoping the sunny color would somehow bring warmth and comfort to her heart.

The one thing she couldn't think about was her mother. The grief would consume her. Her guilt would destroy her. It was better to stay focused on Charlie, to embrace the old rage that had once filled her where he was concerned.

She left her bedroom and found Charlie at the kitchen table. "The coffee is fresh," he said.

She nodded and poured herself a cup, then sat across from him, her fingers wrapped around the warmth of the drink. Grace was surprised to see a throbbing knot of tension in his jaw and the darkness of his charcoal eyes that looked remarkably like the first stir of anger.

"I can't imagine why you want to rake up the past," she finally said.

"Because it's there between us, because maybe if we talk about it, then you can finally let it go." He leaned back in his chair and studied her. "What I did was wrong, Grace. It was wrong on about a thousand different levels. Hell, I don't even remember that woman's name. I was drunk and she drove me home from the bar. It was a stupid thing for me to do, but I think we both need to accept some responsibility for what happened."

She sat up straighter in her chair and narrowed her eyes. "I certainly didn't encourage you to get stinking drunk and fall into bed with the first available woman." That old storm of anger whipped up inside her and the taste of betrayal filled her mouth.

"That's true and that's a mistake I'll always regret." A deep frown furrowed his forehead. "I'd won one of the biggest cases of my career that afternoon. Do you remember? I called you and wanted you to drive in, so we could celebrate, but you told me you had other plans for the weekend."

The heat of anger warmed her face. "So it's like the old song: if you can't be with the one you love, love the one you're with? If I wasn't available, it was okay for you to just find somebody else? That's not the way you have a loving, monogamous relationship."

"That was part of the problem," he exclaimed, a rising tension in his voice. "We never defined what, exactly, our relationship was. We never talked about it. We never discussed anything important."

He shoved back from the table with a force that surprised her and got up. "Hell, you didn't even tell me about your mother. You'd drive to my place twice a month for the weekend, but I didn't know what you did for the rest of the time. You never shared anything about your life here."

"And that makes it okay for you to cheat on me? Don't twist this around, Charlie. Don't make me the bad guy here." She embraced her anger, allowed it to fill her. It swept away the grief caused by her mother's death, the fear about Hope's future and the concern for her own personal safety.

He leaned a hip against the cabinets and shook his head. "I'm not trying to make you the bad guy. I'm trying to explain to you what my state of mind was that night. I was confused about you, about us."

"And while we were seeing each other how many other times were you confused?" Her voice was laced with sarcasm. "How many other women helped you clear your mind?"

"None," he said without hesitation. "You were always the one I wanted, but I never knew how you felt about me. I was afraid to tell you how I felt because I thought it would push you away." His voice was a low, husky rumble. "Tell the truth, Grace. I was just your good-time Charlie, available for a weekend of hot sex and laughs whenever you could work it into your schedule."

She stared at him in stunned surprise. "That wasn't the way it was, Charlie." Why was he twisting everything around and making it somehow feel like her fault? "Damn it, Charlie, that's not the way it was," she exclaimed.

He shoved his hands in his pockets and stared at her with dark, enigmatic eyes. "And the worst thing is we're back to where we started, only this time I'm your bad-time Charlie. Whenever you need somebody to hold you, to make love to you, you reach out to me because I'm the only man available."

She stood, her legs trembling with the force of her anger with him. She gripped the edge of the table with her hands. "You feel better, Charlie? You've managed to successfully turn your faults into mine. You've somehow absolved yourself of all guilt for cheating on me and made it all about my shortcomings. Congratulations," she added bitterly.

"I don't feel better. I feel sick inside." He reached up and swept a hand through his hair, and when he dropped his hand back to his side, his shoulders slumped in a way she'd never seen before. "I love you, Grace. I loved you then and I love you now and you've told me over and over again that you can't—or won't—forgive me. Well, I can't…. I won't make love to you again because it hurts too damn bad."

He turned on his heels and left the kitchen. A moment later she heard the sound of her guest-room door closing.

She sank back into the chair at the table, her legs no longer capable of holding her upright. This was what he did, she told herself. He twisted words and events to suit his own purposes. It was what made him a terrific defense attorney. It was why she'd contacted him to help with Hope's case.

He was an expert at making the guilty look innocent, at directing focus away from the matter at hand. He'd used those skills very well right now, but that didn't change the facts—didn't make his betrayal her fault.

Damn him. Damn him for telling her he loved her. And damn him for making her love him back. But just because she loved him didn't mean she intended to be a fool again.

He was right. She refused to forgive him, wouldn't take another chance on him. Her life was already in turmoil and that's what she had to focus on.

She had another funeral to plan. Her heart squeezed with a new pain as she thought of her mother. What she'd told Charlie about being friends with her mother was true.

They'd often met for lunch, and on most days Elizabeth would drop into the shop just to see what was new and spend some time with Grace. They'd shared the same sense of humor, the same kind of moral compass that made them easy companions.

So why had Grace been so quick to believe that her mother had done something so uncharacteristic as pack her bags and leave without a word? Instead of fostering her anger, she should have been out searching, beating every bush, overturning stones to find her mom. She should be thinking about Hope. God. She hated the fact that she was only allowed to see her at the detention center once a week. Hope was only able to call her every other day or so.

He loved her. The words jumped unbidden in her mind. Deep inside her, she'd known that he was in love with her. His feelings for her had been in his every touch, in the softness of his eyes, in the warmth of his arms whenever he'd comforted her.

And he was somewhat right about having been her good-time Charlie. When they'd met, she'd still been reeling from her mother's abandonment, and those weekends with him had been her escape from reality.

But why hadn't he seen that he'd been so much more

than that to her? Why hadn't he recognized how much she'd loved him then? Maybe because she hadn't really shown him?

He was wrong about one thing. He was wrong to believe that when she made love with him he could have been anyone, that he just happened to be the man available. She'd wanted Charlie.

Grace felt as if she was born wanting Charlie, but that didn't mean she wanted to spend her life with him. That didn't mean she intended to forgive him and let him have a do-over with her.

They couldn't go on like they were, with him in her face every minute and in her bed whenever she wanted him.

It was time to let him go. She hoped he would still act as Hope's lawyer, but he couldn't be her bodyguard any longer. She'd have to make other arrangements.

It had been difficult to tell him goodbye the first time, but then she'd had her self-righteous anger to wrap around her like a cloak of armor. Now she had nothing but the realization that sometimes love just wasn't enough.

Chapter 12

Charlie walked out of the bedroom and back into the kitchen, but Grace wasn't there. She must have disappeared into her own room. He poured himself a cup of coffee and carried it to the window, where he stared outside.

How did you make a woman believe that you weren't the man you had once been? Losing Grace had shaken him to the very core, but it took his father's death to transform him.

His father hadn't liked the man he had become— a name-dropping, money-grabbing, slick lawyer who never managed to make time for the man who raised him.

Mark, Charlie's father, had called him often, wanting him to come home and spend a little time at the ranch. Every holiday Mark had wanted Charlie home, but Charlie was always too busy. And then his dad was gone.

In the depths of his grief, Charlie came to realize his own unhappiness about the choices he'd made in his shallow life in the fast lane.

He'd recognized that what he truly wanted was to get back to the ranch, build a life of simple pleasures and hopefully share that life with a special woman.

When he fantasized about that woman, it was always Grace's face that filled his mind. He'd wanted her to be the one to share his life and give him children.

But it wasn't meant to be. There was no forgiveness in her heart, no room for him there. He turned away from the window as he heard the sound of heels on the floor.

He raised an eyebrow in surprise as he saw Grace, dressed in a cool blue power suit with white high heels and a white barrette clasped at the nape of her neck.

"I'm going into the shop for the day," she said. She walked over to where he stood and held out her hand. "Give me a dollar," she said.

He frowned. "What?"

"You heard me. Give me a dollar."

Charlie pulled his wallet from his back pocket, opened it and took one out. She took it from him and shoved it into the white purse she carried.

"I've just gotten my retainer back for your bodyguard services. I'd still like you to continue with Hope's case, but your services to me are no longer needed." Her cool blue eyes gave nothing away of her emotions.

"Are you crazy?" he exclaimed. "Have you forgotten that somebody is out to hurt you? Just because you can't trust or forgive me, isn't a good enough reason to put yourself at risk."

"I won't put myself at risk," she replied. "When I get to the shop, I'll give Dalton West a call and arrange for West Protective Services to keep an eye on me."

The idea of any other man being so intimately involved in her life definitely didn't sit well with him. Nobody would work harder than he at keeping Grace safe.

He set his cup down on the table. "Grace, for God's sake, don't let our personal issues force you to make a mistake. I can take care of you better than anyone."

She shook her head, her eyes dark with an emotion he couldn't discern. "I'm not making one. I feel like for the first time since William's murder I'm thinking clearly." She twisted the handle of her purse. "We can't go on like this, Charlie. It's too painful for both of us. I have enough things in my life to deal with right now without having to deal with you."

It surprised him that she still had the capacity to hurt him, but her words caused a dull ache to appear in the pit of his stomach.

"If you defend Hope, I'll pay you what I would pay any defense attorney," she continued. "And then we'll be square." She pulled her key ring from her purse. "I'd appreciate it if you're gone by the time I get home from the shop this evening."

"At least let me follow you to the shop," he said.

She hesitated and then nodded. "Okay."

He went back into the guest bedroom and packed what few things he'd brought with him. It wasn't until now that he realized how much he had hoped that they might be able to let go of the past and rebuild a new, better relationship.

Now, without that tenuous hope, he was empty. He carried his small bag down the hallway and found Grace waiting for him at the front door.

"Ready?" she asked. He noticed the slight tremble of her lower lip and realized this was just as difficult for her.

He nodded, and together they left the house. Charlie's car was in front of hers, the passenger window now intact. He walked her to her car door as his gaze automatically swept the area for any potential trouble.

When she was safely behind the steering wheel, he hurriedly got into his car. She pulled out of the driveway, and he followed her.

He could see her blond hair shining in the sunlight as they drove, that glorious hair that smelled vaguely of vanilla.

Again a painful ache swelled in his chest. He told himself it was good he got the opportunity to explain that terrible Friday night to her. He'd wanted her to know that he'd loved her despite what he had done.

Not that it mattered now.

He followed her down Main Street and parked in the space next to her. He was out of his car before she could get out of hers.

"I'll see you inside," he said, as he opened her car door.

He hovered at her back as she unlocked the shop and then they went in together. "I'll be fine now, Charlie," she said once she had the lights on and the Open sign in the window. "Nobody would be foolish enough to try to hurt me here during the middle of the day. People are in and out all day long."

He felt relatively confident that she was right. In the

light of day in a fairly busy store, surely she'd be safe, but that didn't mean he intended to leave her safety to chance.

"You'll see to Hope?" she asked, and again her lower lip quivered as if she were holding back tears.

He nodded, the thick lump in his throat making him unable to speak for a moment.

"Charlie, thank you for everything you've done for me. I don't know how I would have gotten through the last week without you."

"I wish things could be different," he said, a last attempt at somehow reaching into her heart. "I wish you trusted that I'm different and realized how loving you is the biggest part of me."

Her eyes misted over and she stepped back to stand behind the cash register, as if needing a barrier between the two of them.

"Just go, Charlie." Her voice was a desperate plea. "Please just get out of here."

"Goodbye, Grace," he said softly, as he walked out the door and out of her life.

She watched him leave and had a ridiculous desire to run after him and tell him she didn't want him to go. Instead, she remained rooted in place as tears slowly ran from her eyes.

Angrily she wiped them away. It was better this way. They'd had their chance to make it work almost two years before and they'd blown it. Grace just wasn't willing to risk her heart again.

Stowing her purse beneath the counter, she tried not to think about the last time she'd been here.

Instead she went to the back room and dragged out

a box of sandals that had come in so she could work on a new table display.

As she unpacked the cute, multicolored shoes, she tried to keep her mind off everything else. She needed a break. She desperately needed to not think about the murders or Hope and Charlie.

Here, in the confines of the shop, she'd always managed to clear her head by focusing on the simple pleasures of fabrics and textures. During those tough weeks after her mother disappeared, she'd found solace here. And when she and Charlie broke up, this place had been her refuge.

Today it didn't work. Nothing she did kept her mind off the very things she didn't want to think about. She had three customers in the morning and sold two pairs of the sandals she'd just put on display.

At noon she realized she hadn't made arrangements for lunch. Although the café was just up the street, she really didn't feel comfortable walking there alone. She should have packed a lunch, she thought, as she walked to the front window and peered outside.

She froze as she saw Charlie's car still parked next to hers. He was slumped down in the driver's seat but straightened up when he saw her in the window.

What did he think he was doing? They'd each said what needed to be said for closure. They'd said their goodbyes.

She opened the door, and before she could step out he scrambled from his car with the agility of a teenager. "What are you still doing here, Charlie?" she asked him, as he joined her at the door.

"It's a free country. I've got a right to sit in my car in

a parking space on Main Street for as long as I want." He raised his chin with grim determination.

She narrowed her eyes. "What are you really doing?"

"Have you called West Protective Services yet?"

"Not yet. I was going to call after lunch."

"It's entirely up to you if you want to hire somebody else, but that doesn't mean I'm going to stop watching over you. I can guard you better than anyone you can hire, Grace, because I care about you more than anyone else. Don't worry, I don't intend to be an intrusion. There's really no way you can stop me short of getting a restraining order."

He'd often accused her of being stubborn, but she saw the thrust of his chin, the fierce determination in his eyes, and she knew it would be pointless to argue with him.

"Fine," she said, a weary resignation sweeping over her. "You can go now."

"What are you doing for lunch?" he asked.

"I'm not really hungry," she lied.

"Okay, then I'll just go back to being a shadow," he replied. He left her standing at the door and went back to his car.

She returned to her position behind the cash register and sat, trying to forget that she now had a shadow she didn't want and a heartache she knew would stay with her for a very long time.

Thirty minutes later her "shadow" reappeared in the store with a foam container from the café. He set it on the counter in front of her without saying a word, then walked out the front door.

Her stomach growled as she opened the lid. A cheeseburger was inside, its aroma filling the air and making her stomach rumble. She pulled off the top bun and saw just mustard and a pickle. Onions were on the side.

He'd remembered. After all this time, he still knew exactly how she liked her burgers. And it was this fact that broke her.

Tears blurred her vision as she stared at the burger and a deep sob ripped out of her. This time she knew what her tears were for. They were for lost love…they were for Charlie.

She only managed to pull herself together when the door opened and Rachel came in. "I just heard," she exclaimed, and immediately wrapped her arms around Grace's shoulders.

For one crazy moment, Grace thought she was talking about Charlie, but then she realized Rachel must have heard about her mother, and that made her tears come faster and harder.

All the losses she'd suffered over the last week came crashing back in on her. "Come on, let's go into the back," Rachel said. Grace locked the front door and allowed Rachel to lead her to the office. Grace sat at her desk and Rachel pulled a chair around a stack of boxes to sit next to her.

Grace grabbed a handful of tissues from a nearby box and dabbed at her eyes. "I've been so angry at her. I hated her for leaving and now I learn she's been dead this whole time."

"Does the sheriff have any leads?"

Grace shook her head. "None. Charlie thinks it might all be related, Mom's murder and William's." She began to cry. "Oh Rachel, I've made a mess of things. I've fallen in love with Charlie again."

"Grace, who are you fooling? You never stopped loving him," Rachel replied. "I saw him outside sitting in his car. What's really going on between the two of you?"

"Nothing now. Nothing anymore. He's just keeping an eye on me because of the attack the other night. And I want him to defend Hope when her case comes to trial." Grace decided not to go into the whole story about the shooting and how somebody was trying to kill her. "He says he loves me, that he always has."

"What are you going to do about it?" Rachel asked.

Grace sighed. "Nothing. I do think he's changed, Rachel. I believe that he's a different man than he was before, but I still have a knot of anger that I can't seem to get past where he's concerned."

"There are other good defense attorneys, Grace. If you really want to put him in your past, if you really have no desire to have anything to do with him, then find another attorney for Hope. Get Charlie Black completely out of your life."

Those words haunted Grace long after Rachel left the store. Grace ate the cold burger and considered her alternatives. She knew she should do what Rachel suggested, but she told herself that she wasn't convinced any other lawyer would work as hard as Charlie to defend Hope.

The afternoon was busier than usual. Prom was in less than a month, and more than a few high school girls came in to try on the sparkly gowns Grace carried just for the occasion.

When there weren't any customers in the store, Grace drifted by the window, oddly comforted by the fact that Charlie remained in his car.

"It's like having my own personal stalker," she muttered with dark humor at seven o'clock, as she turned the Open sign to Closed and locked the door.

She carried the cash register drawer to the back office to close out and sank down into the chair at the desk.

She was tired but didn't want to go home. Tonight she would be alone, without Charlie. She assumed he'd probably sleep in his car in her driveway, and while the idea that he would be uncomfortable bothered her, she would not allow her emotions to manipulate her into inviting him back in.

Let him go completely. A little voice whispered inside her head. *Or grab him with both hands and hold tight.* It has to be one or the other.

Because there had been more sales than usual during the day, it took her longer than normal to close out the books. It was almost eight by the time she locked up her desk. Still she was reluctant to leave.

She stood and stretched with her arms overhead and eyed the stack of boxes next to her desk. She should spend another hour or two unpacking the new products. There was a box of swimwear and another of beach towels and matching totes.

It wouldn't be long before summer was upon them. Where would Hope be this summer? Would she still be locked up in the detention center awaiting her trial, or would some evidence be found that would bring her home before the dog days of summer?

She would need to be mother and father to Hope now. She wouldn't be able to spend long hours here. She'd need to be available for her sister, to guide and love her.

As much as she loved the store, she loved her sister more. Dana could take on more responsibility and Grace could be what Hope needed, what she wanted.

She pulled the top box off the tall stack, moved it to her desk and opened it. It would take her about an hour to tag all the swimwear, and then she'd go home.

As she worked, she kept her mind as empty of thought as possible. It was just after nine when she finished. She was just about to leave her office when she heard a knock on the back door.

Who on earth…? She walked to the door and hesitated with her hand on the lever that would disarm the security alarm. "Who is it?" she yelled through the door.

"Grace, it's me, Leroy Racine. I need to talk to you. I remembered something…something about the night before William was murdered."

Was it possible this was the break they had been looking for? Grace disarmed the door and opened it partway to look at the big man. In the dark, she could barely discern his features. "What are you talking about?"

"The night before William's murder he had a visitor, a business associate of some kind. I was outside working, but I heard them yelling at each other."

Grace's heart leapt with excitement as she opened the door to allow him inside. "Come on into my office," she said, and gestured him into the chair where Rachel had sat earlier in the day.

Leroy sank into the chair and Grace sat at her desk. "I don't know why I didn't remember this before," he said.

"So, exactly what is it that you've remembered?" Grace asked. She leaned forward, hoping, praying that whatever information Leroy had would point the finger of guilt away from Hope and to the real killer.

"It's really not what I've remembered as much as it is what I need to finish." He pulled a wicked, gleaming knife and leaned forward, so close to her that she could feel the heat of his breath on her face. "Tomorrow everyone will talk about how the robber who got away the other night came back here, only this time with tragic results. Don't scream, Grace, don't even move."

Leroy? Her mind struggled to make sense of what was happening. Grace stared into his dark eyes and knew she was in trouble, the kind of trouble people didn't survive.

Zack West's car pulled up beside Charlie's, and the lawman stepped out and walked up to his window. "Everything all right? You've been parked here for the whole day."

Charlie opened his car door and stepped out, his kinked muscles protesting the long hours in the car. "I'm just waiting for Grace to call it a day so I can follow her home." He shot a glance toward the darkened storefront. "I think she's working late on purpose just to aggravate me." He leaned against the side of his car and frowned. "Why are women so damned complicated?"

Zack laughed. "I don't know. I certainly don't always understand Kate, and we've been married for a while now." Zack headed back to his car. "I just wanted to make sure everything was all right here."

"Everything is fine," Charlie assured him. "I'm hoping she's going to call it a night pretty quickly, so I can get her home safe and sound."

Zack nodded, then got back into his car and pulled away. Charlie folded his arms and gazed at the shop.

How much longer was she going to be? He wouldn't put it past her to be cooling her heels intentionally, knowing he was sitting out here waiting for her.

Charlie had already made arrangements with Dalton West to help him keep an eye on her. Once Grace was back in her house, Dalton would take over surveillance on her place while Charlie went home and grabbed a shower and a couple of hours of sleep.

By the time Grace woke up the next morning, Charlie would once again be on duty for the day. He didn't care what she said. He wasn't going to leave her unprotected until they figured out exactly what in the hell was going on.

Eventually he'd need to figure out a way to cast her not only out of his thoughts, but out of his heart as well.

He checked his watch, then got back into his car and leaned his head back, waiting for her to call it a night.

Chapter 13

"Leroy, what are you doing?" Grace's voice was laced with the terror that coursed through her. She stared at him, trying to make sense of what was going on.

"What am I doing?" He smiled then, a proud, boastful smile. "I'm completing a plan that's been ten years in the making."

"What does that mean?" Grace slid her eyes toward the top of her desk, looking for something she could use as a weapon. Inside the drawer was a box cutter and a pair of scissors, but on top there was nothing more lethal than a ballpoint pen.

Leroy's eyes glittered darkly and he leaned forward, as if eager to share with her whatever was going on in his head. "It started when I met Lana and found out she was carrying William Covington's baby."

Grace gasped and stared at him incomprehensively.

"What are you talking about? Lincoln is only ten years old. William and my mother were married at the time he was conceived. William wouldn't have cheated on my mother."

Leroy laughed, but there was nothing pleasant in the sound. "Ah, but he did. Your mother had flown to Las Vegas to help out one of her friends who was having a difficult pregnancy. Remember? She was gone for two weeks, and on one of those nights William and my lovely wife crossed the line. It only happened once, but that was enough for her to wind up pregnant."

She reeled with the information. Lana and William? What Leroy said might be true, but it still didn't illuminate everything that had happened over the last week and a half.

The fact that he hadn't lowered the knife and still held it tightly in his hand as if ready to thrust it into her at any moment kept a lump of fear firmly lodged in her throat.

If she screamed, he could gut her before anyone would hear her cry for help. She thought of Charlie in his car out front and wanted to weep because she had no way of letting him know she was in danger.

"What do you want, Leroy? Money? I have my cash drawer in the desk. Just let me unlock it and I'll give you everything I have."

"Oh, Grace, I definitely want money, but I'm not interested in whatever you have in that drawer," he replied. "I've been a very patient man and soon my patience is all going to pay off." He must have seen the look of confusion on her face for he laughed once again. "William's money, Grace. That's what I'm after. Lincoln is a Covington heir—and why should he share an inheritance when he can have it all."

Grace had been afraid before, but as the realization of his words penetrated her frightened fog, a new sense of terror gripped her. "You killed William? It was you? And you set up Hope to take the fall."

Again a proud grin lifted the corner of Leroy's mouth. "It was genius. Your sister, she's a creature of habit. Every morning she makes herself breakfast and drinks about a half a gallon of orange juice. That girl loves her juice."

"You drugged it," Grace exclaimed.

"It was brilliant. She went back to bed and passed out. I killed William, trashed her room, smeared her with blood and put the knife in her hand. And before she goes to trial I'll make sure the prosecutor has all the evidence he needs to send her away for the rest of her life."

"I don't understand any of this," Grace cried, tears misting her vision as she tried to buy time. "Did you kill my mother, too?"

Leroy leaned back in the chair, but the knife never wavered. "Apparently William decided to come clean to your mother about that night with Lana. The next morning your mother came to the cottage wanting to talk to Lana, but she'd taken Lincoln into Oklahoma City for a doctor's appointment. You see, for me to make sure my stepson inherited all of William's money, I needed to make sure nobody else was going to inherit it. Your mother was the first obstacle in the way. I strangled her, and since nobody was home at the mansion, I packed a couple of her suitcases to make it look like she took off."

Grace closed her eyes as grief battled with terror

inside her. Reward. Charlie had been trying to figure out the true motive of William's murder and now she knew. Money. William's money. Leroy wanted it all not for Lincoln, but for himself. With Lincoln being underage, Leroy and Lana would be in charge of the fortune.

What did Lana know? Was she a part of this? God, it would be the final betrayal to learn that the loving housekeeper had helped plot all these murders.

Grace opened her eyes and realized she was going to die here now if she didn't do something.

"I had to bide my time after your mother died. I knew I couldn't take out William too quickly or people would be suspicious," he said.

"People *are* suspicious," she said, barely able to hear her own voice over the pounding of her heartbeat. "You'll never get away with this, Leroy. When you try to collect William's money, the suspicions will only get bigger."

"Suspecting and proving are two different things. William's murder is going to be pinned on Hope. Your mother's murder happened two years ago, and by the time I plant bugs in some people's ears it will all make perfect sense."

His dark eyes gleamed bright. "You see, the way the story will go is that your mother found out about William's night with Lana and was going to leave him. They fought and things got out of control and he killed her. Two years later, Hope began to suspect what had happened and believing that William was responsible for your mother's death, she killed him. And you, you're just the tragic victim of a store robbery. Nobody can tie up all the pieces so they point in my direction. You'll all be gone and a DNA test will prove Lincoln to be a rightful heir."

Grace knew she was running out of time. She had to do something to escape or at least to draw attention. Once again her gaze shot around, looking for anything that might help her.

The stacked boxes next to where he sat caught her eye. She tensed all her muscles, knowing it was very possible she'd die trying to escape him, but she would certainly be killed if she did nothing.

Now or never, she told herself as Leroy continued bragging about how smart he'd been to pull off everything. *Now or never,* the words screamed through her head.

She exploded from the chair and knocked down the stack of boxes. They toppled on top of Leroy as she ran for the door of the office, sobs of terror ripping out of her.

The sales floor was dark, lit only by the faint security lights and the dim illumination coming through the front window. She focused on the door. If she could just get out, Charlie would be there and everything would be all right.

She made it as far as the table display of sandals before she was tackled from behind. They both tumbled to the floor. Shoes fell on top of them as they bumped against the table.

Leroy cursed and momentarily let go of her. Frantically Grace crawled on her hands and knees into the middle of a circular rack of blouses, swallowing her sobs in an effort to hide from him.

If she screamed for Charlie, she would pinpoint her location to Leroy, who apparently hadn't seen exactly where she had gone. Even if Charlie heard her scream, she was afraid he wouldn't be able to get inside before Leroy killed her.

She could smell the man, the sour scent of sweat. She could hear him moving around the store, hunting her like a predator stalking prey.

Her body began a tremble she feared would move the blouses. Drawing deep, silent breaths, she tried to control the fear that threatened to erupt. She tensed as she heard Leroy's footsteps getting closer…closer still.

"Grace, you're just prolonging the inevitable," he said softly. The rack of blouses shook and despite her desire to stay silent, a slight whimper escaped her as she realized he knew where she was hiding.

She had to scream and she had to move. It was the only way Charlie might hear her and get out of his car to check it out.

At that moment, the knife slashed through the rack of blouses and a scream ripped out of her.

Charlie drummed his fingers on the steering wheel in time to the beat of the music from his radio. He was beginning to wonder if Grace was going to spend the entire night in the store.

Main Street had emptied of cars long ago, and most of the townspeople were now in their homes, watching television or getting ready for bed.

Charlie would love to be getting ready for bed, especially if Grace was waiting in it. He couldn't help but think of the last two times they made love and how he would happily spend the rest of his life loving her and only her.

What was keeping her from him? There had been

moments over the past week when he hadn't felt the burden of their past between them and thought she'd gotten past her bitterness. He'd felt her love for him and entertained a tiny flicker of hope that there might be a future for them together.

He rubbed a hand across his forehead, weary with the inactivity of the day and thoughts of Grace. It was done. There was no point in trying to figure out what went wrong this time. Apparently she'd never really gotten over their past and refused to even consider any future with him.

He frowned as he saw a shadow move across the plate glass window in front of the shop. Sitting up straighter, he breathed a grateful sigh. Good, maybe she was getting ready to go home.

He got back out of the car and stretched with his arms overhead, then shoved his hands in his pockets and waited for her to walk out the front door.

Again he saw shadowy movement inside the store and heard a noise—a scream. Alarm rang in his head as he yanked his hands from his pockets and ran to the front door. Locked.

"Grace?" he yelled and banged on the door with his fists. Wild with fear as he saw not one figure, but two, he looked around frantically, needing something he could use to break the door down.

He spied a heavy flowerpot in front of the store-front next door. As soon as he grabbed it, he threw it at the window.

The pot went through with a crash and the entire window cracked and shattered. Before the glass had cleared enough for him to get inside, Grace opened the front door.

She was sobbing and held an arm that was bleeding. "It's Leroy," she cried. "Leroy Racine. He ran out the back door. Charlie, he killed them. He killed them all and he tried to kill me."

"Get in my car and lock the doors," he said, refusing to look at her bloody arm. He was filled with an all-consuming rage. "Call Zack. My cell phone is on the passenger seat."

He pulled his gun and took off around the side of the building, knowing Leroy had to be using the alley for his escape. Leroy? As Charlie ran, a million questions raced through his head.

Leroy was a big man, not as fast on his feet as Charlie, and on the next block from Grace's shop he spied the man rounding a corner.

Charlie had never wanted to catch a man more in his life. As he raced, his head filled with visions of Grace being hit over the head with an object, of her being kicked in the ribs. The rage that ripped through him knew no bounds. He wanted to kill Leroy Racine, but first he wanted to beat the hell out of him.

"Stop or I'll shot," Charlie yelled, as he saw Leroy just ahead of him. "I swear to God, Racine, I'll shoot you in the back and not blink an eye."

Leroy must have recognized the promise in Charlie's voice, for he stopped running and turned toward him, a frantic defeat spread across his face.

At that moment the whine of a siren sounded in the distance, and Charlie knew Zack or one of his deputies was responding to Grace's call.

"Get down on the ground," Charlie commanded. "Facedown on the ground with your hands up over your head."

Leroy hesitated but must have seen something in Charlie's eyes that frightened him, for he complied. Charlie kicked the knife Leroy held in one hand and sent it spinning several feet away. He leaned over him and pressed the barrel of his gun into the back of Leroy's head.

"Don't try anything," he warned the big man. "Don't even blink too hard. One way or the other you're going away for a very long time. It's either going to be jail or hell."

At that moment Zack ran toward them, his gun drawn and his eyes wide as he saw Charlie. "He killed Elizabeth and William, set up Hope to go to prison and tried to kill Grace." Charlie's voice grew hoarse with anger. "His knife is over there."

"Charlie, you can step away from him," Zack said, his voice deceptively calm. "I've got him now."

Reluctantly, Charlie pulled his gun from the back of Leroy's head and straightened. Before anyone could stop him, he drew back his boot and delivered a swift kick to Leroy's ribs.

Leroy yelped and raised his head to look at Zack. "Did you see that? I want him arrested for assault."

Charlie looked at Zack, who shrugged. "I didn't see anything," Zack replied.

"I've got to check on Grace. She was hurt," Charlie said, as Zack pulled Leroy to his feet and cuffed him.

Charlie took off running in the direction he'd come from. He still didn't have any real answers, couldn't figure out why Leroy had done what he'd done, but at the moment answers didn't matter—only Grace did.

She saw him coming and got out of his car. In the light from the nearby street lamp, he could see that her cheeks were shiny with tears, and she held her arm against her side, one hand pressed against the opposite upper arm.

"Charlie," she cried, as he neared. "Thank God you're okay."

He reached her and pulled her gently into his arms, careful not to hurt her.

As he smelled the familiar scent of vanilla in her hair and felt the warmth of her body against his, Charlie did something he couldn't remember doing since he was a young boy and his mother had died—he wept.

It was nearing dawn when Charlie followed Grace home. The night had been endless for Grace. At the hospital, she'd received eight stitches in her arm and then spent most of the rest of the night with Zack, telling him everything Leroy had told her.

She was beyond exhaustion yet elated. Zack promised her that first thing in the morning he'd get the wheels of justice turning to release Hope.

Hope was coming home, and it was time to tell Charlie a final goodbye. When they reached her house, she pulled into the driveway and parked. Charlie pulled in just behind her.

She didn't have to be afraid anymore. She could get out of her car without waiting for Charlie and his gun to protect her. She no longer needed him as a private investigator, a criminal defense attorney or a bodyguard. It was time for them to move on with their lives.

She got out of the car with weariness weighing on her shoulders and the whisper of something deeper, something that felt remarkably like new heartbreak.

Charlie joined her on the sidewalk and silently

walked with her to her front door. "You're going to be all right now, Grace," he said.

She unlocked the door and then turned back to face him. His features looked haggard in the dawn light, and she fought her impulse to reach up and lay her palm against his cheek. "Yes, I'm going to be all right," she replied softly.

"Hope should be released sometime tomorrow, and the two of you can begin rebuilding your lives." He reached a hand up, as if to tuck a strand of her hair behind her ear, but instead he quickly dropped his hand back to his side. "You don't have any reason to be afraid anymore. It's finally over."

She nodded, surprised by the rise of a lump in her throat. He stared at her, and in the depths of his beautiful gray eyes, she saw his want, his need of her and she steeled herself against it, against him.

"Then I guess this is goodbye," he said, although it was more a question, a plea than a statement.

Her chest felt tight, constricted by her aching heart. "Goodbye, Charlie." She said the words quickly, then escaped into the house and closed the door behind her. She leaned against the door and felt the hot press of tears at her eyes.

She should have been happy. The bad times were behind her, so why was she crying? Why did she feel as if she'd just made the biggest mistake of her life?

Chapter 14

"It's just a movie, Grace," Hope said plaintively. "We'll go straight to the theater, and when the movie is over, we'll come right back here."

Grace took a sip of her coffee and frowned at her sister. It had been a week since Hope had gotten out of the detention center and moved into Grace's house.

The spare bedroom was now filled with all things teenage. Grace welcomed the chaos, the laughter and the drama that had filled the last seven days of her life.

Hope's release wasn't the only positive thing that happened over the last week. Although Lana had been devastated to learn that the man she'd married had done so only for the sake of Lincoln's inheritance, the knowledge that he'd murdered William and Elizabeth had nearly destroyed her.

She'd come to Grace begging for forgiveness, both

for the horrific things her husband had done and for her own mistake in sleeping with William on that single night.

She'd explained that William had been missing Elizabeth desperately and invited her to have a drink with him. One drink led to half a dozen and suddenly they were both making the biggest mistake of their lives.

She hadn't told William that she'd gotten pregnant. She met Leroy a month later, and when she gave birth William assumed, like everyone else, that Lincoln was Leroy's child.

Grace assured her there was nothing to forgive and made Lana promise that she would allow Grace and Hope to get to know Lincoln, who would share in the inheritance that William had left behind.

"Earth to Grace." Hope's voice penetrated Grace's thoughts. "So can I go to a movie with Justin or not?"

Grace sighed, wishing this parenting stuff was easier. "I don't know, Hope."

Hope reached across the table and took Grace's hand in hers. "Grace, I know Justin has made some stupid mistakes in his past, like dropping out of high school, but he's really a nice guy. He deserves another chance."

"You'll go right to the theater and come right back here?" Grace asked.

"Pinky swear," Hope replied, lacing her pinky finger with Grace's.

"Okay. We'll consider this a test run."

"Cool." Hope was out of the chair almost before the words had left Grace's mouth. "I've got to call him and tell him I can go."

As she ran for her bedroom, Grace leaned back in

her chair and sighed. This would be the first time Hope would be out of her sight since coming home.

Maybe part of her reluctance in letting Hope go was because Grace didn't want to spend the evening alone. Being alone always brought thoughts of Charlie and a sadness that felt never ending.

She hadn't seen him in the past week, but every time she got beneath the sheets on her bed she saw him in her mind, felt him in her heart.

Forgetting Charlie was proving more difficult than she'd thought. She got up from the table and carried her coffee cup to the sink, then stood by the window and stared out into the backyard.

He'd accused her of holding back, of confusing him when they'd been dating. She remembered the night he'd called her, so excited by his big win in court that day, asking her—no, begging her—to drive in to celebrate with him.

The sheer force of her desire to be with him had frightened her, and she'd told him she couldn't make it. Hours later she'd changed her mind and decided to surprise him. Unfortunately she was the one who had gotten the biggest surprise.

Hope walked back into the kitchen. "It's all set. Justin will pick me up at seven."

Grace turned from the window and forced a smile. "And you told him you needed to be home right after?"

"Yeah, but I was thinking maybe after the movie Justin could come in and we could bake a frozen pizza or something. I think if you talk to him for a while, you know, get to really know him, then you'll like him."

"That sounds like a nice idea," Grace replied.

Hope walked over to stand next to Grace and looked

out the window. "When Mom left, I thought nobody else would ever care about me," Hope said softly. "I figured if my own mother didn't like me enough to stick around, why would anyone else like me?"

Grace put her arm around Hope's slender shoulders. "I know. I felt the same way."

"But, then I met Justin and even though he had a reputation as a tough guy, he made me feel better. He told me I was pretty and nice and that it was Mom's problem, not me, that drove her away."

"And now we know that she didn't leave us at all," Grace replied.

They were silent for a few minutes, and Grace knew they were both thinking of the mother they had buried two days before.

Hope finally looked at her. "It's important to me that you give Justin a chance, Grace. You don't have to worry about him taking advantage of me, or anything like that. Justin knows I want to stay a virgin for a long time and he's cool with that."

"I promise I'll give him a chance," Grace replied.

Hope reached up and kissed Grace on the cheek. "I'm going to go take a shower and get ready. Seven o'clock will be here before I know it."

Once again she left the kitchen and Grace turned her gaze back out the window. She could definitely relate to those feelings Hope described, of believing that if her mother didn't love her enough to stick around that nobody else would really love her.

She'd carried that emotion into her relationship with Charlie, and despite her deep feelings for him, she'd kept a big part of herself walled off from him, certain that eventually he'd leave her, too. She had to be un-worthy of love because her mother had found her so.

Charlie told her she needed to accept partial respon-sibility for the demise of their relationship, and he was right.

She had treated him like a good-time Charlie, flying into his life for fun and laughs but never sharing with him any piece of herself, of her life here in Cotter Creek.

No wonder he hadn't seen their relationship in the same way she had. She'd given him so many mixed signals.

And now it was too late for her, for them.

Charlie sat on the back of his favorite stallion and gazed at the fencing he'd spent the last week repairing. It had been grueling physical work, but he'd welcomed it because it kept his mind off Grace.

He hadn't even gone into town during the past week. When he needed supplies, he sent one of his ranch hands in to get them. Charlie hadn't wanted to run into Grace or even see her storefront.

He wondered if everyone had that one love who stayed with you until the day you died and haunted you with a bittersweet wistfulness.

Leaning down, he patted his horse's neck, then grabbed the reins and turned around to head back to the house. It was too bad there wasn't a pill he could take that would banish all thoughts of Grace Coving-ton from his mind. He was just going to have to live with his regrets and the overwhelming ache of what might have been.

Just then, as he approached the corral, Charlie saw

the car pull into his driveway. Her car. His heart leapt, then calmed as he cautioned himself with wariness.

Maybe something else had happened—a legal issue she wanted help with or a question that needed to be answered. As he dismounted from the horse, she stepped out of her car, the fading sunlight sparking on her glorious hair and tightening the lump that rose up in his chest.

She looked lovely in a turquoise-and-white sundress, with turquoise sandals on her feet and a matching purse slung over her shoulder.

She couldn't keep doing this, he thought, as he walked slowly toward where she stood. She had to stop using him as her go-to man.

"Grace, what's up?" he asked, his tone curt.

She leaned against her car door. "Hope just left to go to a movie with Justin."

He frowned. "And you drove all the way out here to tell me that? Gee, thanks for the info, but I'm not sure why I need to know that." He stuffed his hands in his pockets, afraid that if he allowed them to wander free he'd reach out and run a finger across her full lower lip.

"Earlier this evening Hope and I had a chat about our mother and how she felt when we thought she'd abandoned us. She told me she thought nobody would ever love her again, and I realized that's exactly how I'd felt."

She pushed off from the door, her eyes dark and so sad that Charlie felt her sadness resonating in his own heart. "I hope both of you feel better about things now that you know the truth," he said.

"I don't feel better," she exclaimed and her eyes grew shiny with tears. "Oh, Charlie, you were right about me. I did use you, but somewhere along the line I fell in love with you."

"And then I got drunk and stupid and screwed it all up," he replied, as a hollow wind blew through him. "We've been through all this, Grace."

He sighed with a weariness that etched deep into his soul. "I can keep Hope out of jail for a crime she didn't commit and I can probably keep you safe from some crazy stalker, but I don't know how to get you to trust me again."

She took several steps closer to him and that amazing scent of hers stirred the desire he would always feel for her. Still he kept his hands firmly tucked into his pockets, not wanting a moment of weakness to allow him to touch her in any way.

"I swore I didn't believe in second chances, that only a fool would give a man her heart again after he'd broken it once." Again her eyes took on the sheen of barely suppressed tears. "And then I realized I'd never really given you my heart for safekeeping the first time. How could you know you were breaking it when you didn't realize it was yours?"

Charlie stared at her, afraid to believe what he thought her words might mean. "Why are you here, Grace?"

"I'm here because I realize I'm a different person now than I was when we were dating. And if I can believe that I'm a different person, then why can't I believe that you are? I'm here because for the first time in a year and a half I don't have my anger at you to fill me up, to protect me. And without that anger all I'm left with is my love for you."

Tears fell from her eyes and splashed onto her cheeks. "I'm here to find out if it's too late for me…for us."

Charlie's heart swelled so big in his chest he couldn't speak. He yanked his hands out of his pockets and opened his arms to her.

She fell into his embrace and he held her tight, feeling as if he were complete for the very first time. The scent of vanilla and jasmine smelled like home. Grace smelled like home.

"Charlie?" She raised her face to look at him. "It's not just me anymore. I'm a package deal. Hope is and will always be a part of my life."

"I always wanted a sister-in-law," he replied.

"Sister-in-law?" Grace stared at him, and that sweet lower lip of hers trembled. "Is that some kind of a crazy proposal, Charlie?"

He dropped his hands to his sides and smiled at her. "Give me a dollar."

"What?"

"You heard me, give me one." He held out his hand.

She opened her purse and pulled out a dollar bill. He took it from her and shoved it into his back pocket. "You've now retained the lifelong services of a criminal defense attorney and bodyguard." He pulled her into his arms, his gaze warm and soft, relaxed. "Better yet, you've got my love through eternity."

She returned to his embrace. "All that for a dollar? You're cheap, Charlie."

He grinned at her. "Only for the woman I love." His smile faded and he gazed at her intently. "Marry me, Grace. Marry me and be my wife. Share my life with me."

Charlie's words filled Grace with a kind of happiness that she'd never before experienced. This was right, she thought. This was the first right thing that had happened in a very long time, and she had no doubt that it would last forever.

"Yes, Charlie, I want to marry you. I want you to be my good-time Charlie, my bad-time Charlie, my forever Charlie."

He kissed her then, a hungry yet tender kiss that held both the regrets of the past and the promise of the future. He wasn't the only one with regrets. Grace knew that their future together might have begun sooner if she'd been less afraid of putting her heart on the line when they'd been dating.

"Better late than never," she murmured, as their kiss finally ended.

"Second chances, Grace. Sometimes that's all we need." His eyes glowed with a light that always weakened her knees and curled her toes. "How long does that movie last?"

She grinned. "Long enough," she exclaimed, and grabbed his hand. Together they ran for the ranch house, where his bed and their future awaited.

* * * * *

We hope you enjoyed reading this special collection from Harlequin® books.

If you liked reading these stories, then you will love **Harlequin® Romantic Suspense** books!

You want sparks to fly! **Harlequin Romantic Suspense** stories deliver strong and adventurous women, brave and powerful men and the life-and-death situations that bring them together.

Enjoy four *new* stories from **Harlequin Romantic Suspense** every month!

Available wherever books and ebooks are sold.

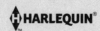

ROMANTIC suspense
Heart-racing romance, high-stakes suspense!

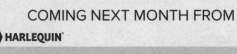

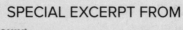
Tonight, Rachel would tell him the truth. If he couldn't
forgive her or trust her after that, well then, that was the
end of the time she'd spend with him. She swallowed hard
on the lump forming in her throat. She hoped and prayed
it wouldn't come to that. In the meantime, she would look
her best to deliver her confession.

In her bathroom, she touched up the curls in her hair
with a curling iron, applied a light dusting of blush to her
cheeks to mask their paleness and added a little gloss to
her lips.

Dressing for her confession was more difficult. What
did one wear to a declaration of wrongdoing? She pulled
a pretty yellow sundress out of the closet, held it up to her
body and tossed it aside. Too cheerful.

A red dress was too flamboyant and jeans were too
casual. She finally settled on a short black dress with thin
straps. Though it could be construed as what she'd wear
to her own funeral, it hugged her figure to perfection and
made her feel a little more confident.

As she held the dress up to her body, a knock sounded
on the door.

"Just a minute!" she called out. Grabbing the dress, she unzipped the back and stepped into the garment. "I'm coming," she said, hurrying toward the door as she zipped the dress up.

She opened the door and her breath caught.

Noah's broad shoulders filled the doorway. Wearing crisp blue jeans and a soft blue polo shirt that matched his eyes and complemented his sandy-blond hair, he made her heart slam hard against her chest and then beat so fast she thought she might pass out. "I'm sorry. I was just getting dressed and I haven't started the grill…"

He stepped through the door and closed it behind him. "My fault. I finished my errands earlier than I expected. I could have waited at a park or stopped for coffee, but…I wanted to see you."

"Hey, yourself. I'm glad you came early." And she was. The right clothes, food and shoes didn't mean anything when he was standing in front of her, looking so handsome.

He leaned forward, his head dropping low, his lips hovering over hers. For a moment, she thought he was going to kiss her…

If you loved this excerpt, read more novels from
THE ADAIR AFFAIRS series:

CARRYING HIS SECRET by Marie Ferrarella
THE MARINE'S TEMPTATION by Jennifer Morey
SECRET AGENT BOYFRIEND by Addison Fox

Available now from Harlequin® Romantic Suspense!

*And don't miss a brand-new **THE COLTONS OF OKLAHOMA** book
by* New York Times *bestselling author Elle James,
available September 2015 wherever
Harlequin® Romantic Suspense books and ebooks are sold.*

www.Harlequin.com